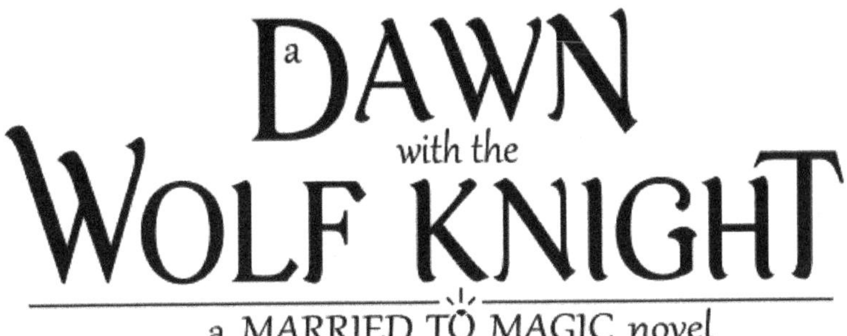

ELISE KOVA

Silver Wing Press

a DAWN with the WOLF KNIGHT

a MARRIED TO MAGIC novel

ELISE KOVA

This book is a work of fiction. The names, characters and events in this book are the products of the author's imagination or are used fictitiously. Any similarity to real persons living or dead is coincidental and not intended by the author.

Published by Silver Wing Press

Cover Artwork by Erion Makuo
Developmental Editing by Rebecca Faith Editorial
Line Editing by Melissa Frain
Proofreading by Kate Anderson

ISBN (paperback): 978-1-949694-63-5
ISBN (hardcover): 978-1-949694-62-8
eISBN: 978-1-949694-59-8

Also by Elise Kova

Married to Magic

A Deal with the Elf King
A Dance with the Fae Prince
A Duel with the Vampire Lord
A Duet with the Siren Duke
A Dawn with the Wolf Knight

Arcana Academy

Arcana Academy

Air Awakens Universe

AIR AWAKENS SERIES
Air Awakens
Fire Falling
Earth's End
Water's Wrath
Crystal Crowned

VORTEX CHRONICLES
Vortex Visions
Chosen Champion
Failed Future
Sovereign Sacrifice
Crystal Caged

A TRIAL OF SORCERERS
A Trial of Sorcerers
A Hunt of Shadows
A Tournament of Crowns
An Heir of Frost
A Queen of Ice

Loom Saga

The Alchemists of Loom
The Dragons of Nova
The Rebels of Gold

See all books and learn more at:
http://www.EliseKova.com

for everyone who isn't afraid
to give their whole heart

Table of Contents

Abyss
Eversea
Lifetree
Lake of Anointing
Evalon
Fae Wilds
Dreamsong
The High Court
The Bleeding Woods
Carron
Westwatch
Elf Kingdo
N

The Grove
Den
Gualla
Lykin Plains
ake Calduwyn
Hollast
Vampir Mountains
Tempost
Castle Tempost
Sea Gate
Midscape
Quinnar

one

To enter the woods as a human is death. The lykin have roamed the tree-covered, fog-blanketed edge of our world for generations uncounted, feasting on all creatures within. The packs of man-beasts have their forests, and the humans have their towns.

Then…there's me. She who maintains the protective charms that keep one from the other and preserve the fragile peace of both.

I have no place with the lykin. I cannot shed my flesh for fur and run with the spirits of the ancient wood. But I have no place with the humans, either. When they look at me, they see an other. A kindly outsider. Someone who has their features, but does not share in their ways or struggles. I belong to neither.

I'm the witch in the cottage.

I adjust the pin at my throat that holds my velvet cloak shut. Labradorite, to protect me from the knowing of the elves. Dangling from my ears are tiny chandeliers, crafted by the finest glassworkers down the rivers and across the distant seas. A suitable gift for negotiating with any clever fae who might cross my path. There is always fresh blood in my veins for a rogue vampir, should such an offering be needed… The sirens I need not fear in the woods, and the roar of dragons has not been heard in the eternal mist that clouds the lands to the north for more than a thousand years. A long enough time that stories of them have been almost entirely forgotten by the people who once feared them.

But more precious than all of these tokens, rare as many are, is the cloak around my shoulders. Sewn nearly three hundred years ago, every weaver witch of my family has worn and added to it in tiny thread, hand spun and dyed. Our power—what precious little we have clung to—stitched and bound to us.

The cloak will keep me safe tonight. My hand rests on the satchel at my hip. Keep *us* safe.

"One last time into the wood, Grandma," I say, reassuring. Alone, I go where no other human will tread. Past the crimson ribbons tied around the small trees that act as a barrier between the lands of men and lykin.

It's not my first time here. I began coming to collect herbs and stones following my mother's death when I was fourteen. Grandma was too old by then, her feet too tired, to make the hike. Especially in the dark nights of the new moon.

I rest my hand on one of the large sentries that stand among the outer rung. In my other hand, I gather my cloak, searching for a specific stitching of two eyes, completely blackened with heavy thread. I close my eyes and the darkness behind my lids is barely more complete than the night itself. Even the stars can't penetrate the heavy boughs of the trees, and there is no moon. I would be a fool to come here when the lykin's magic is strongest.

I state my intention clearly for all those of this world, and of the other, who might hear. "Spirits of the old wood, guardians of nature's order, I come to your doorstep as a humble guest. I seek passage through your domain and will take nothing that is not freely given."

A soft breeze picks up behind me, landing like a gentle touch between my shoulder blades. It's little more than a whisper and is gone as soon as I feel it.

"Thank you." When I open my eyes, my vision can pierce the night. At least enough for me to see the path ahead. I start forward.

When I was a girl, Grandma would tell me tales of the forest in her time. The raw and wild magic that flowed through the veins of the earth itself, making it come alive. She said that when her great, great, great grandmother walked these woods, the magic was so powerful that the spirits took human shapes, strolling alongside our ancestors.

Even in my lifetime, the woods have grown quiet and still by comparison to when I was a girl. Perhaps my early memories are colored by the whims of childlike wonder—a proclivity for the fantastical. But I don't believe so.

In my heart of hearts, I can feel the magic retreating from our world. A wellspring exhausted, or a weary giver with now-empty palms, I can't know which. If I could, I would fix it. Every tree I touch hums only softly beneath my fingers. The rocks that my ancestors long ago set out as markers have gone cold and silent.

It is a bad omen, when even the rocks cannot keep magic in their stony grip.

It takes nearly an hour to navigate the old trail into the deepest part of the forest that we have ever dared to go. Eventually, the narrow path between the trees begins to open. The thin soles of my shoes meet soft moss and tiny grasses, rather than lumpy roots, packed earth, and rock. I emerge into a clearing and inhale the fresh air deeply; the density of the forest and all its magics—even depleted as they are—weighs on my chest.

The clearing is lined by a nearly perfect circle of pine. No mortal hands tend this place, and yet nothing dares to grow and encroach on the space of the giant redwood at the center. It is the oldest tree in the woods and was said to have been planted by the hands of a long-ago human queen who married the king of the elves in exchange for all our lives and safety. No one alive is quite sure any longer if it was meant to be a gift to the lykin, or a boon to the dwindling bloodline of witches. So it has become a neutral territory for both our kinds. A place where human and beast are safe and welcome to dwell under its boughs.

It has become the graveyard of witches.

I clasp my hands before me, bow my head, and whisper, "Thank you, spirits, for allowing me passage. I come before you to return my grandmother to the land from whence she came."

Every step up to the base of the ancient redwood is harder than the last. I had thought I said my goodbyes when I held her hand as the life left her body. I had thought there were no tears left to cry when enough spilled from my lids to douse the funeral pyre that I had to build alone. But I was wrong.

The lump in the back of my throat is thick. My eyes burn and my heart is heavy as I reach into my satchel and retrieve a simple, wooden jar. The last thing made by her hands. Kneeling, I lean the jar against the trunk of the tree as I sink my fingers into the wet, mossy earth and begin to dig.

The land receives me. Opening for the woman who loved and served it with all her days. The hole doesn't need to be deep, so it only takes a few minutes to make.

But…the jar quivers in my hands.

"Death is not something to fear, or lament. It is a gift, as much as life," I say aloud—her words. She told me them often in her final days. Grandma knew the time was near for her. Up until the end, she looked after me, giving me comfort. I force a smile as a few lonely tears spill down my cheeks and into the hole I settle the jar within. They water the moss I pile atop. Settling her ashes into their final resting place. "I know," I say on a ragged breath, "I know that you would not want me to go into this next chapter with fear. But, Grandma, I am afraid. What am I to do without you?"

I have no friends, only cordial acquaintances in town. The only person I was ever truly close to, the only one to truly know me, was the huntsman's son…and he betrayed and abandoned me the night I had been ready to give him everything.

Heavy tears slowly fall. Each one reminds me of every day I've spent since her death. I give in to this final moment of mourning. My last goodbye. And then I lean back on my heels and stare up at the branches above, swaying with soft breezes and blotting out alternating stars.

"Look after her," I whisper. "Gods of the Great Beyond, care for her soul as she leaves this mortal coil. I return her to you." My fingertips press into the soil once more, as if I am trying to hold myself—ground myself in the here and now. "Spirits of this earth…we have always served you dutifully. But our magic is waning. Soon, my family will no longer be able to defend you as we always have. I am weak, and alone. Please, do not abandon me."

In the silence that follows my words, I listen to the rustle of trees and the hum of crickets for any sign of answer. And, then…

A howl.

Wolf? I rise to my feet, looking in the direction of the sound. Another howl. No…worse… I know the sounds of these woods—was taught them with every breath.

That is no wolf.

But it can't be. The lykin bed down on the new moon. They draw their strength from the cycles in the sky. Now is their weakest time. Especially since it is the first new moon following the Blood Moon. They should be weary from their revelries. In all my twenty-two years, I have never heard the howl of a lykin on the new moon.

I'm ready to make a hasty departure, but I am halted. This strange night is not yet done with me.

A young woman bursts through the tree-line opposite me.

She is barefoot, with mud staining her ghostly pale skin up to the hem of her white, sleeveless, linen dress. Her hair is bright silver and hangs nearly down to her waist, streaking behind her as she sprints, like a falling star. I have never seen another human in the forest, save for my family. Another witch, perhaps? If so, something has gone terribly wrong for her to traverse these woods of magic and beasts without protection of any kind. There's no stitching on her dress.

The woman doesn't seem to notice me. She keeps looking behind and then up at the branches of the tree. It is because of the latter that she doesn't notice the thick roots that spill around the redwood. Her toes catch, ankle crunches, and she lets out a cry as she falls.

A third howl rings out in reply, jolting me to my senses.

I rush toward her but she ignores me, murmuring to herself through the pain. She clutches something to her chest that she then places on the root. It's a simple, silver ring adorned by a giant moonstone nestled between two, crescent arcs facing in opposite directions. The woman rummages around root and moss, ultimately grabbing a rock.

"Are you all right?" I ask.

She doesn't seem to notice me until I'm kneeling at her side.

"You can't stop me!" She pushes me, possessing more force than I previously thought her form capable of.

I fall back. "I'm not trying to—"

I'm reaching out to her as she brings the rock down on the stone, shouting words that I do not recognize and cannot understand. They're almost like a song—a haunted and angry melody. The rock smashes into the ring, shattering it.

We are both thrown. It feels as if someone has punched me in the center of my chest, compressing my ribs and knocking all the wind from between them. I gasp, wheezing a few times before I can get a few breaths and the pain fades.

"No…no, no…I shouldn't…" The woman pats herself over her chest and legs as she kneels. "What went wrong? What did I do wrong?" Tears stream down her face.

She doesn't have the pointed ears of a fae or elf, nor the fangs of a vampir. Lykin? Perhaps…but if she were, she would likely have taken her wolf shape when she'd been injured. I sense no ill intent from her, and she has yet to harm me.

Another howl; her head whips around. It's closer this time. I know fear when I see it in her wide eyes as they spin to me. Her lips part. I feel as if for the first time she's acknowledging my presence.

"You… I'm so sorry." She shakes her head slowly. "I am so sorry for pulling you into this."

I move to her side once more. It's easier than I expected. All the pain has vanished from my body following whatever ritual she performed.

"It's all right," I tell her. Her face is twisted in pain as though she has endured wounds far, far worse than the ankle and tumble.

"Please…help," she says between her pants and whimpers. "Help me. Don't let them take me back." Whoever—or whatever—she is no longer matters when she asks like that.

"Yes, of course." I look back in the direction she came from. There's an ominous aura permitting the air. Birds take flight in the distance, rising from the treetops like a beacon of war. "Who's chasing you?"

"The wolf king." She hangs her head, silver strands slipping over her trembling shoulders. Her words are as bitter as poison. "He claims to own me."

My blood goes cold. The king of the wolves. The alpha of all packs. But stronger than my fear is disgust. *Owns her?* Bile tickles the back of my throat and I swallow it down.

"I know somewhere safe, somewhere not even the king of the wolves can go." So long as my barriers hold…

"What?" She looks back to me with what I dare say is hope illuminating her dark eyes.

"Are you lykin?" The barriers won't let her out if she is.

"No." Her lips twist.

A witch, then. Like me. I can't stop a smile. Even in this desperate moment, it's as if the world is giving me what I asked for: a companion. Perhaps she is alone, too, and the ancient spirits of this wood have brought us together.

"Let's get you out of here."

"Where?" she asks.

"My cottage is not far." I dare to touch her. She's like ice. I need to get her somewhere warm, quickly. Even in summer, our fields this far north have a chill and the woods are always wet and cold.

She sways as she tries to stand. Her ankle barely holds her weight.

I quickly shift my thinking upon seeing the state she's in. "Instead, let's stay here. This is a sacred place—one of peace. Underneath the boughs of the redwood we should be safe. Perhaps we could parley—"

"He cares not for redwoods or pacts. We must go. *Now.*" She grabs my arm tightly.

Another howl rips through the woods, this one closer than the last. The hairs on my arms and neck stand on end, my skin puckering to gooseflesh. It is the sound of a raw predator. The sound that fuels nightmares.

I don't dare to argue with her sentiment. Everything in me tells me to run. Even the mosses under our feet seem to ripple away from the noise.

"He'll have to find us to catch us." I unfasten the pin at my neck and pull my arms from the slit of my cloak. Then, I place it over the woman's shoulders, fastening it at her neck instead of mine. I have other protections in the jewelry I wear; blessings are woven into the ties that hold the thick braid of my dark, rusty hair. But she, so far as I can tell, has nothing. I turn and kneel. "On my back. You can't run with your ankle like that."

She doesn't fight me, reaching around my shoulders and locking her arms around my neck as I slide my hands under her clammy thighs.

We stand together and I shift, adjusting the cloak so it falls over my shoulders as well—it should offer some protection from their magical senses. She's lighter than I expected, but her height makes her a bit awkward to hold.

More howls, even closer. I can hear the ripping of leaves and breaking of limbs.

Run.

The instinct is raw. Primal. Every fiber of my being realizes that she spoke the truth: we are not safe here. Before the wolves can howl again, I'm off.

I can't outrun them. But I can try to outmaneuver them. I can leverage every scrap of magic I have.

The lykin are certainly following their noses, hot on her tail. I deviate from the main path, venturing down through a field of lavender and rosemary that grows not far from the main trail. Perhaps it will be enough to mask our scent and confuse them, if only to buy us a few extra minutes.

There's another howl behind us—louder than all the others, more like a roar. The forest goes quiet and still. The hymns of the night insects halt. Animals quiver in their dens.

I run even faster, rejoining the main trail where my feet can be surer. Still, I can't move fast enough. They're going to catch up, I know it. The hike into the woods that took nearly an hour, I try to run in half that time. But I only go as fast as I can be certain I won't stumble. If I were to trip and fall…that would be the end of this chase.

"Please," I beg the woods. "Please help us."

Miraculously, the trees heed my words. They come alive, branches that might have snagged on the flapping cloak moving away with creaks and groans. Their roots flatten slightly.

"Thank you!" I pant. I have never seen the woods come so alive, so ready to heed my requests. I take it as a good omen.

Yet, the moment I have a sign of hope, it's tempered with the sounds of snapping limbs and branches close behind. Of growls and snarls. They're close.

But so is the entrance to the woods and the line of ribbon-wrapped trees that crafts a barrier to this place.

I sprint out, racing across the border that keeps the land of the humans from that of the lykin. The woman has grown heavy on my back. Her clammy skin sticks to mine with the cold sheen of sweat that coats my neck and face. Her head hangs limp on my shoulder, her grip slack—consciousness has left her.

It isn't until I've gone a safe distance that I slow my pace. A roar that transitions into a shrill howl that makes even the stars tremble has me turning. Behind me, right at the edge of the trees, are three massive wolves. No…not wolves. Lykin.

They are larger than the wolves that prowl the less magical woods to the southeast of town. The smallest is nearly the size of a pony and has easily three times the muscle under all its fur. But it is the eyes of the largest that meet mine. They shine ominously as the beast dips its muzzle slightly. His attention darts from the woman to me and back, ultimately fixating on me. His lips curl back, baring his teeth with a low growl.

I grip the woman even tighter, the instinct to keep her safe greater than at any other point. She wasn't lying. The lykin are hunting her. But the why remains a mystery.

The largest wolf stomps both of his paws into the ground at the barrier of the trees. He lets out another roar of frustration. But he doesn't—can't—leave the wood. Only witches can go through the barrier. I wonder if this mighty beast is the wolf king himself, come to settle whatever score he might have with the mysterious stranger limp on my back.

With a grunt and a huff, he shakes his steely head and turns back into the woods. The other two follow and disappear under the dark canopy of the trees. I nearly collapse then and there as the terror crashes upon my shoulders with the realization that the fragile peace I always took for granted might have only ever been an illusion.

two

My cottage is not far, but the walk down the hills feels like it takes three times as long as normal. When I see that familiar thatched roof, the wattle and daub walls that were freshly patched last summer, I let out a heavy sigh of relief. We made it.

I open the latch with my elbow and enter the almost completely dark, one-room cottage. Behind me, I pull a crimson, silken rope over the door latch, draping it haphazardly. The silver bell at the end chimes softly—the sound of old, protective spells engaging once more, and a mechanical warning should anyone force entry.

My only light is the angry embers that still smolder in the hearth, waiting for me to return and stoke them into a flame. I settle my new companion on Grandma's old bed—mine is in the loft—and leave her there, heading to the fire. The first order of business is to get heat. She's not going to warm up if we're nearly able to see our breath, even indoors.

Crouching by the fire, I rest a palm on the mantle. "Folost?"

The flames perk up in response. They almost take the shape of a face, white-gold eyes shining at me before they flicker away.

"We have a guest." I tilt my head toward the bed.

One tongue of flame rises, swiveling over toward the bed. It seems to lean out from the hearth, as if trying to get a better look. The small lash of fire vibrates with excitement, or agitation… Grandma was always better at reading the moods of the little fire spirit than I was. Excitement was the correct assumption, it'd seem, as the embers spark to a roaring flame, enough that I rear back as the wave of heat that radiates out from it smacks me across the face.

"Glad you're excited for company." It's a bear when Folost is feeling moody. The whole cottage is freezing until he can be convinced to come around again. It made mourning Grandma's loss all the harder when the house was frigid each lonely night.

As I move away from the hearth, I swear I nearly hear a response: *Special company, indeed.* I halt, glancing back at the tiny spirit. Everything seems normal.

Shaking my head, I head to the wash basin in the opposite corner of the room, at the foot of Grandma's bed. I hear that many houses in town have a science called plumbing these days—running water on command. A novelty that seems almost as magical as living among the spirits of the woods. As for me, my mornings are spent gathering water from the well. Luckily, I didn't go through it all and don't have to venture outside. I'd rather not disturb my protective wards tonight.

My hands pause in the water, a cloth gripped tightly. The eyes of the lykin still bore into me. A chill drags its finger down my spine and I fight a shiver, looking to the door. The rope and bell are still in place. Undisturbed. If the lykin were able to find a weakness or break in my barrier, they would've by now.

I wring out the washcloth and return to the bedside. My fears are confirmed. My guest has gone from frozen to burning up.

"Folost, that's enough," I whisper with a glance to the hearth. Nothing can heat the cottage like Folost when he's determined.

Two golden eyes appear in the roaring flame, narrowing at me slightly. I narrow my eyes in return. The fire dims, but only slightly.

"It's all right," the woman says with a soft sigh. "I'll grow accustomed soon enough."

"Don't exert yourself. Rest." I finish dotting her brow with the cloth, removing the thin sheen of sweat from her cheeks and neck. The movement is all too familiar. It was only a week ago that Grandmother died. "You're safe here. The lykin didn't follow us from the woods."

"Safe." She says the word with disbelief as her eyes scan the cottage. They land on the chime slung over the door handle. On Folost with a warm little smile. "So it would seem."

"Are you…" I struggle to find the words. In my small area, everyone knows of me. And they're kind enough. But those from distant towns—even from the city—are wary of witches. Or even disbelieving of them entirely. The ancient magics are long forgotten from this land and those who keep their ways alive are growing more and more cloistered out of fear of misunderstanding. But she was in the woods, a place where regular humans shouldn't be able to venture. The wolf king was hunting her. She can clearly see the markers of a witch. It would be nice to not be so alone… "Are you a witch, too?" I ask, before fantasies of a companion can overtake me.

She brings her attention back to me. Those all-black eyes of hers are like hollow pits. Deep enough to swallow me whole.

"I am not."

"Then how were you in the woods?" If there is a weak point of the barrier somewhere, I should know and fix it quickly, before the wolf king can exploit it. Humans should grow more and more discomforted the closer they get to the woods—driven to turning around before they can enter.

"I am of a magical sort, though not a witch," she says softly.

"What?" She now has my sole focus. "Fae? Elf?" Perhaps the stories of their pointed ears were wrong.

She shakes her head.

"Vampir?"

More shaking.

"You said you were not a lykin," I remember.

"I am not." That rejection is firmer than all the others.

"Then…"

"My name is Aurora." She pats my hand gently, as if that is enough for me to know for now.

"Lovely to meet you, Aurora. I'm Faelyn," I say, though my mind is still trying to come up with what kind of creature she might be, if not a fae, elf, witch, vampir, or lykin. Surely not a siren…I thought they were confined to their seas.

"Faelyn," she repeats. "A good old name originating from the first tongue of your ancestors. Loved by magic, it means, I believe."

"Loved by the elves, I was always told." I am caught off guard by how seemingly normal this interaction is. As if we are just two friends chatting. As though she's not a magical stranger I found in the woods.

"Elves, magic, synonymous to early humans." She shrugs.

"Aurora…are you a spirit?" I whisper, fear and fascination fighting, suppressed by the improbability of the question. But my gut keeps pulling me toward that conclusion. However impossible. I can't let it go.

She brings her eyes back to mine. A slight, tired smile. "I am."

"How?" I shift to face her better, trying to see her in a new light. Her hair is a silver so pure it's platinum. Her eyes are darker than pitch. And her skin is nearly unnaturally pale… She is human at a glance, but the longer I inspect her, the more unsettling her appearance becomes. She's like a too-perfect version of human—an artist's representation, close, but not quite real. "All the spirits I've ever known keep the forms they represent." Like Folost in his hearth, or Mary in her pot on the windowsill. And, while they can communicate in their ways, they cannot speak the common tongue.

But the stories of ancient spirits did say they could take humanlike forms… Perhaps she is one of the last of that long-ago time? The mere notion of it has me in awe.

Aurora looks out the window, turning her gaze from everything within. When she speaks, the words are heavy, a little sad, and filled with so much longing it is a wonder that we don't both drown in it. "I made a request of an old god, long, long ago, for the body of a human… and my wish was granted."

I know better than to ask more, even though I'm burning with curiosity. It's not my place and there are things in my past that I would never want anyone to dredge forward again. Whatever history is wrapped up in Aurora's story, it clearly brings her great pain to even think about. Why a spirit would want to have the body of a human when their natural forms are nothing but power and the raw essence of nature itself is beyond me. But, for now, I leave it be.

"And you were being hunted by the wolf king?"

"He sees me as something to be possessed. I am little more than a token for him to bind himself with to validate his throne. So I fled. I was trying to free myself and, in the process, bound myself to you, instead." Her words are heavy with guilt, but all I feel is a rush of excitement.

All the spirits in the house were bonded to my grandma. She had told me of the processes involved, and the methods of doing so. But I have never found a spirit with which to bind myself.

Spirit binding is one of the oldest magics. One that Grandma always said was mostly forgotten by the other lingering witches of our age. When they lost their abilities to bind with spirits, they ultimately lost their magic. Which was another reason why she bound Folost and Mary to me just before her death. She'd tell me stories of long ago when our family had dozens of spirits who lived alongside us. But now, there are only two. And they are small and frail compared to the magics of old… not that I'd ever let either hear me say as much.

Binding a spirit allows a mortal to call upon them, trading his or her magic for a favor from the spirit. Like seeing in the dark, or forging a fire. Sometimes, the spirits decide to make their homes alongside the witches, forging a truly symbiotic relationship where power and safety are shared. A single spirit cannot be bound to more than one individual, so it's little wonder the king of the wolves abandoned his hunt when he laid eyes on us.

I wonder both what magics she will render me capable of and what I will be able to do for her in return.

"It is my honor to be bound with you." I rest my hand gently on the back of hers. "May I ask what you are the spirit of?"

She levels her gaze with mine. Her stare carries the weight of the coldest winter's night. My breath catches in my throat.

"No," she finally whispers.

I give a slight nod. There's the same sensation as when she mentioned the deal made to give her this human form. I can feel in my bones that it is not my place to ask, nor my need to know. At least…not yet.

So it shall be left at that.

"Aurora, may I ask one more thing?"

"You may certainly ask, but I might not feel inclined to answer," she says with a tired smile.

"Do you want to be bound to me?" For all my excitement over finally bringing a new spirit under my roof, of my own accord, the binding hardly went as Grandma said they would. And she speaks of being bound to the wolf king with such disdain.

"No." The word isn't cruel. A simple fact. "I was trying to find freedom. But fate seemed to have other plans."

"Then we shall undo this binding between us."

Her eyes shine with amusement and, dare I say, fondness. She does not appear as young as I first thought her in this light. If anything, she regards me with the same wisdom Grandma always did.

"I fear it might not be so simple as unraveling your binding with the other spirits, little weaver witch. The ring I destroyed held a part of my power. I had hoped to absorb it into myself. But, instead, it went into you." Aurora rests her hand on the center of my chest. "Separating my power from me was not an act done by mortal hands, but by the old gods far, far from here. I had been trying to call upon them at the foot of the redwood, but it seems I must stand before them once more at their great tree to have them pull it from you and properly return it to me."

"Then we shall go to them," I declare, taking her hand in both of mine.

"Faelyn?" Her pale brows furrow in confusion.

"If I do not have the power to free you, we shall go together to find the person—old god who does." I smile through the brief twinge of disappointment I feel at losing the first spirit I'm bound to. It is the right decision. I merely wish the circumstances were different. "I will not keep you and use your strength against your will. So, together we shall find the freedom you seek."

"The journey will be long, and difficult, if it can be done at all," she says softly.

"Then I will get supplies in the morning and we will ready ourselves to leave in the coming days."

"You have no idea what this journey would entail."

"I don't need to." I squeeze her fingers. "It is the right thing to do."

"You…would truly free me?" Her eyes are shining. "Even though you hardly know me? Even though I can grant you immense power should you choose to take it?"

Immense power…no wonder the forest seemed to heed me more than it ever had before… "'Immense power' is worth little if taken by force. I only want what is freely offered, and won't have it any other way."

"Thank you, Faelyn." She squeezes my fingers and brings her

forehead to my knuckles, drawing a shuddering breath. I rest my other hand on her quivering shoulders.

"Do you need to eat?" I ask, shifting the topic for her. Aurora has endured a great deal already tonight; we don't need to linger on subjects that give her turmoil.

She nods. "While I might be a spirit in essence, this form that I am trapped within is mortal enough that it requires sustenance to thrive."

"Can this physical form be—"

She doesn't allow me to finish the question. Though it was a macabre one anyway.

"Killed? Yes. No," she answers enigmatically. "My immortality as a spirit did not entirely leave me, even though I took this form. This body cannot be killed by natural means—aging, starvation, cold, illness. Though I still know the pain of those things."

Something about the way she says those words, her bitter, tired, and grim expression that accompanies them, causes my heart to ache for all this woman has endured—all I barely understand.

"To kill me," she continues grimly, as if forcing the words, "it would take intent by a mortal hand in a magical act. Hunger cannot kill me, but a charmed stake driven through my heart could."

"Let's not linger on driving anything through your heart." I stand and cross back to my hutch, looking through the various baskets and jars, ready to leave the topic behind. I am going to keep her safe. "When I go to the market tomorrow, I will get enough supplies for both of us on the journey, then. I don't have enough food here for two people."

"I hope I will not be too much of an imposition." She sounds genuinely guilty. Looks it, too, with the way she picks at her nails.

"No, no!" I say hastily. "Not in the slightest. It's my *honor* that you're here. But the last time I went to market I was shopping for only one person." For the first time in my life, I shopped only for one. The memory sobers me. Of assessing how much less food I needed when it was only me to feed, even though Grandma ate like a bird those final months. *You're all right, Faelyn,* I tell myself, *the pain fades a little more each day*. Eventually there will come a day where the mere passing thought of her doesn't debilitate me.

Having the distraction—and a journey away from this place—might be just the balm I needed. Like always, the woods provided.

"Is there anything that you don't eat? Or any foods you particularly enjoy, should I be able to find them?" It occurs to me that if she is the spirit of some kind of animal or plant, she might have strong feelings about certain foods.

Aurora shakes her head. "Any food is fine with me." A pause, then, "Actually, were I to be honest, I would prefer vegetables over meat. And meat cooked well through, were we to eat it."

"Vegetables are a preference we share." I close the hutch with a smile. It will be easier to keep vegetables fresh on the road. Meat wouldn't last long and I don't have time to dry any. "Then we shall wake with the dawn to head to market."

She doesn't bother to even try to hide her cringe.

"What is it?"

A coy little smile slinks across her lips. "I am more of a night person than a daytime one. Dawn is when I might bed down and usually do not wake until dusk. Rarely, I'll be up in the afternoon…depending on the season, weather, and my moods."

I laugh. She has timeless eyes, but many mannerisms of a youthful woman. There was a time I, too, lamented early rising. "All right. I can go alone. And, before you can worry, know it'll be no trouble."

"Thank you."

"My pleasure and my honor." I cross the room to the loft ladder that's on the far wall from her bed—the opposite side of Folost's hearth. On the way, I grab a satchel off the wall, different from the leather one I took into the woods. "I sleep up in the loft, so if you need anything, you can shout and I'll hear without trouble. There are wards on this house and I've confirmed them to be in place, so you'll be safe." My hand pauses on a middle rung. "Oh, one more thing…our other house guests are Folost and Mary. Mary is the marigold in the small pot on the kitchen window. Folost is in his hearth.

"I don't know if you have a better way to communicate with them than I. But even if you don't, Folost can take direction in the common tongue. If he chooses to listen," I add with a pointed glare to the hearth. One golden eye swings my way and there's a huff as a log collapses. I roll my eyes. "So if you're too warm in the night, just let him know to relax a little."

She turns to the fire with a knowing glint in her eyes. Aurora tilts her head slightly and I swear I see a tongue of flame mirror the gesture as I climb up to the loft.

Before I sleep, I retrieve a small sewing kit from what was Grandma's satchel. Running my fingers over the rainbow of threads, I select one as pale as her hair, another as black as her eyes. With them, I stitch the shape of a ring with a pale moonstone flanked by crescents into the red cloak to commemorate our meeting.

The night passes without issue, despite my waking up twice to make sure Aurora is still there—that I didn't dream the night's surreal events. In the morning I wake when the stars are still burning the sky. I know every creaky board and slick rung of the ladder, so I'm able to descend and quietly gather my things without Aurora so much as stirring.

I take my leather satchel off its peg, adjusting it around the pin of my cloak. Opening the hutch, I relieve its shelf of bundles of sticks, dried flowers, herbs, and fruits, carefully placing them into the satchel. Then I take the silver chime in hand and slowly remove the silken cord off the door latch.

The sun has not yet crested the horizon and I am off to market.

The closest township is almost a two-hour walk away. The market is held each morning on the town green and goes until all the goods are sold. So departing early is crucial if I don't want to be left with table scraps and empty pots for dinner. If I can, I like to make it right when the stalls are opening and the farmers and tradespeople are setting out their wares. All the choices I could want are mine and I'm not bothered too much… It doesn't matter that I've lived here my entire life; being the town witch tends to attract stares.

I savor the slowly lifting fog off the tall grasses and give thanks to the last of the crickets and owls that are tucking in for the day. Perhaps that is what Aurora is: the spirit of an owl. She is quite noble like one. I imagine her natural form is that of a snowy, feathered creature. Regal and stoic.

Do wolves hunt owls? I suppose they could. Or perhaps there's a rivalry beyond their animal forms.

What if she is the ancient spirit of the wolf that first gave lykin their powers? The thought nearly has me tripping over my feet. No…such a creature wouldn't be at odds with the lykin, would they? I continue musing throughout my walk. Every theory seems as plausible and unlikely as the last.

The sun greets me as I arrive in town, shining off the roofs still glossy with dew. The market folk know me well and are surprised to see me again so soon. I usually make this walk only once every month. I give them enigmatic, half explanations about "needing more supplies," and "not having enough essential material." They are not lies. Nor is it my fault that the townsfolk presume me to be doing something more with the sweet corn and beans than putting them in a pot.

I do not pay with silver or gold. Money is a tricky thing—ill will clings to it more than the dirt in the stamped grooves of the coin. Instead, I pay in the bundles I've prepared. Most know already to hang the strung bunch of sticks and flowers over their door and burn it with the next full moon. Even though everyone saw me so recently, they're all eager to receive the little blessings of protection that will ward off the evils of the world—lykin included. For when the bundles burn every new moon, the smoke rises from their chimneys and sweeps across the hills to the forests. The ash sinks into the ground, and the barriers I maintain on this land are renewed once more.

Knowing I'll be gone for a bit longer than normal, I tell them how to make their blessings last longer. Hopefully the townsfolk will listen and will keep safe without me for a few weeks. One or two ask for an extra blessing—a small embroidery on the baker's favorite apron and the cobbler's shoe. It's a good thing I brought my weaver kit so I can accommodate, since I get quite good gifts for these. Aurora will need a decent pair of boots for our journey.

It's late afternoon when I finally begin to make my way back. I hum to myself, delighting in the warmer summer weather. I nearly have crested one of the last hills before home when the smell of smoke fills my nose.

It is a distinct aroma—woodsmoke, clear and pure. But there's something else in it. A stinging that makes my eyes water.

For a moment, I am back before my grandma's pyre. A fire so bright it nearly steals all the light from the sky. There's a sharp buzzing in the air that is magic escaping its worldly tethers.

Dread fills me. I know in my gut with horrible, sinking certainty what has transpired. Yet, I begin to run, as if I can somehow outpace this fate. It cannot be real. I refuse to hold this truth in my mind alone. My eyes must share the burden.

I crest the top of the hill, breezing past the thin, lonely trees that extend out from the dark forest of the lykin. There, in the distance, is my home—the home of my ancestors, the home I was born in, grew up in, and inherited. The only home I have ever known.

And it is ablaze.

three

I STARE IN SHOCK FOR A SINGLE BREATH. My soul leaves my body. The sounds of the world vanish and there's nothing but the sharp inhale of air through my nose.

Suppressing the scream, I begin running down the hill. The boots I bartered for from the cobbler are rolling alongside my frantic feet. I am nearly at the house when the walls give in with a series of cracks and a resounding snap that feels as if my spine itself has broken in two. The roof collapses, tumbling down. A wave of heat staggers me.

"Aurora? Aurora!" I scream, wondering if I am now beholding a second funeral pyre. She said she was immortal, didn't she? So she should have been able to get out, right? How did this even happen? Folost should have— "Folost!"

I round the crumpled building, calling out to the spirits that are, were, *are* bound to me. The entities I was responsible for. Who were entrusted to me to keep them safe.

"Mary, Folost, Aurora…" I stagger and half collapse at the edge of the burning remnants of my home. It feels as if I am the one who is ablaze; my skin is poked through and consumed by fire. The magic that was built into the very foundation of our home evaporates into the late afternoon air with a sigh. My lineage and legacy—what Grandma entrusted to me—all in flames. "Grandma…" I choke out. "Grandma!"

Burying my face into my hands, I weep. The well out back is too small. The stream is too far. And even if they were not, what could be done? The house is little more than cinders and, with it, so is everything I had once held dear.

Were I an older witch, a stronger one in a different time, I would've been able to summon the water to me. Or perhaps I would've had a spirit of winds or rain bound to me that could bring a storm. But I have none of these things.

Still, I lift my hands and hold my palm to the fire; the other grabs for a stitched shape of a flame on my cloak. "Folost, please, lend me your strength." I will the blaze to heed my commands.

But no magic comes. Even with a small spirit of flame and whatever power of Aurora's that's within me to magnify, I can't command the blaze. So all I can do is try to quench the fire with my angry tears.

It is dusk when the fire finally begins to exhaust itself. The ground was too wet for the flames to jump to the grasses. The trees were too far. All that remains is a smoldering square of blackened earth. Tiny flames still greedily consuming the last remnants. One flame rises higher than the rest, like a last gasp, mocking me.

But then it does it again. The same way and in the same spot.

I rub my eyes to make sure I didn't imagine it. Nothing. Then, a third ribbon of orange-red. Flickering. Fading. I did not imagine the two gold eyes that swung my way.

"Folost?" I scramble to the edge of the embers. There are circles of fire dotting the remains. The nearest is within arm's reach, where a withered marigold has spilled out of a fallen clay pot.

I inhale sharply and rush to the well, immediately drawing a bucket and returning as quickly as I can without spilling. Slowly, I tip the bucket, quenching the earth with a hiss, cooling down a path safe enough for me to tread to where Folost burns—careful not to get him wet in the process.

The ground in Folost's ring is singed…but it is not as burnt as the rest. Flooring I recognize is covered in blackened soot. The little fire spirit wasn't strong enough to save the house, but he protected what he could.

"Folost, you're incredible." I crouch down, wiping my face with the heels of my hands. The grief is passing, taken over by motivation.

Mary's pot has been cracked and is hot to the touch. She's limp. Shriveled by the heat and losing petals. But I can still feel her presence.

"Hang in there. Both of you." I carefully collect Marigold from the hot dirt, leaving the pot, for now. I rush her away from the smoldering ruin and settle her in the cool, damp earth. "I know you need water, but if I doused you now, it'd be a shock. Just wait a moment to cool some first," I tell her before going back to Folost. "Thank you for saving her. Are you all right?"

Two eyes appear, then disappear, then appear. A blink, as I understand it. One blink means yes. I can almost feel the word echoing within me with pride.

"Thank you for doing what you could." Even though my cheeks are still streaked with tears for all I've lost, I won't lose sight of what I have. I thought everything was gone. But what was truly important was spared—my friends, the cape around my shoulders, the sewing satchel safely tucked underneath it against my hip. "This is a debt of gratitude I'll never be able to repay, Folost."

He burns a little brighter and higher, like a child puffing out his chest.

"Did Aurora get out?"

Yes.

I heave a sigh of relief at the blink of his eyes. "Where did she go?"

Tongues of fire point to the woods, as if blown in that direction by an unfelt breeze.

"Did she…start the fire?"

A blink. Another. *No.*

Another monumental sigh of relief. I was afraid that somehow she didn't believe or trust me. That she thought I might try to keep her as trapped as the wolf king.

"She really is a spirit, too, right?"

One blink. *Yes.*

"I didn't think she was lying, for the record," I say with a side-eye to Folost that threatens to turn into a scolding if he ever told Aurora about my even asking. "How did the fire start?"

The little flames go rigid, the wobbling and variance small and tight. Four narrow pillars extend up, fanning out. At first, I think Folost is making trees. Something about the woods? *No.* The truth becomes as clear as daylight when another bit of flame extends from rear haunches. A column stretches to a snout and pointed ears.

Wolf.

Confusion is smothered by a rage unlike any I've ever known. For centuries, my family honored the treaty made with the ancient lykin. We preserved their lands, as agreed, performed the rites and kept well the spirits as best we could. We allowed the lykin to hunt in the woods to their stomachs' content, free of human meddling.

Even last night, when the wolf king had us in his sights, he could not cross the barriers. Or, perhaps he could, but he chose not to. He wanted me to think the barriers stood and to feel safe. This act was one of spite—meant to threaten and scare me into quiet submission.

The wolf king toyed with us then destroyed my home and stole Aurora.

I dig my hands into the ash and soot. The wet, burnt wood, brittle from the flames and my dousing. My anger shifts, narrowing on the forest.

"I am going to get her back. I won't let them have her." Aurora's haunted eyes still fill my vision. I can't abandon her to them. Not when her magic is still within me. I made a promise to her, one I intend to keep.

The wolf king wanted to subdue me. To have me cowering in fear. All he's done is removed all reason for me to stay. If the barriers cannot hold them back, there's little point in maintaining them. If the lykin care not for our treaties and the goodwill of our ancestors, then neither will I. I have nothing to lose and everything to gain by going after him and Aurora.

Folost sways eagerly at my proclamation.

"You want to come?"

More swaying.

Behind me is the bright aroma of a marigold in full bloom. Mary has rooted herself into the earth, no doubt drawing on its moisture. Her petals are outstretched as far as they can reach. The missing ones have regrown.

"You, too?" I ask her.

She goes stick-straight.

"All right, then." I lightly touch Mary's small, clay pot. It's almost cool enough to handle. "Folost, we're getting you ready to go first."

He flickers out of existence, reappearing in the remnants of the hearth.

The majority of the embers are still too hot to walk over without making trips back to the well to douse my path. But that's a good thing right now—I'm counting on the heat.

I carry one last bucket to the remnants of the hearth. One brick is different from the rest—handmade and fired from the same river clay as Mary's pot. It also bears Grandma's thumbprint in its center.

"Folost, go burn somewhere else for a minute. I'll be quick," I command. He hesitates, staying in the hearth near his brick. "I promise, it'll be all right." I hope.

Putting his faith in me, the little fire spirit flickers to life elsewhere in the remnants of the home. Taking a breath, I dump the bucket of water on top of the still scorching bricks of the hearth.

The second the cool water meets the hot brick, it lets out an almost screeching hiss. Cracking and snapping sounds fill the air. I return to the well, and repeat the process once to ensure that the cracks run good and deep and the pieces are now cool enough to handle. I sift through them, finding one small shard that has the edge of Grandma's thumbprint.

The sliver of brick in hand, I race back through the pathway of mud and ash, to the firmer ground, and up the hill. Along the way I collect Aurora's boots that had fallen, re-slinging them over the strap of my satchel. I hastily rummage around the base of the nearest tree, looking for the sturdiest stick I can find that's slightly larger than the shard of brick. On my return to the burnt patch, I retrieve my knife from my bag and notch a spot for the piece to wedge within.

Kneeling once more, I coat the top of the stick in wet mud. Ideally, I'd have some other clay. But Folost is mindful of where he burns; he shouldn't jump to the wood.

"All right, come along." I hold out the stick to a still flickering ember.

Folost jumps from burning patch to burning patch with sparks trailing behind him. He's all too eager to return to the little token that helps ground him in this world. The small crackling seems to whisper, *Thank you.*

"You're welcome," I reply. Then, my focus shifts. "Right, Mary, your turn." I cross back to her, sticking Folost's little torch into the ground near her. Then I retrieve her pot, now cooled. I safely replant her and then, using some plain twine from the sewing satchel, I affix it to the heavy belt at my hips, making sure she won't easily fall.

My friends situated, I allow myself to catch my breath, taking stock of what I have. If the house was going to burn down, this was the time for it to happen. I emptied the hutch of bundles this morning. Because I'd gone into market, I had my cape and both my satchels. One of which is still laden with supplies for the road.

The empty boots at my side are a reminder of who's still missing.

"Right." I scoop up the tiny torch that gives off all the light of a candle. But Folost has never looked mightier to me. I focus on the tiny flame. "You've done so much, friend, but can you sense where Aurora is?"

A pause. A shift as the flame circles the sliver of brick. Then two eyes. A single blink. *Yes*.

"Can you lead the way?"

Yes.

"Mary, tell me if we are walking into danger." I trust the small plant to commune with her larger counterparts as we ascend the hillside.

There's a burst of floral aroma that smells like affirmation. I wonder if I'm having an easier time communing with both thanks to Aurora's magic. It might not have been enough to save my home, but it will be enough to save her.

I start up the usual path, but a streak of compressed grasses distracts me. Diverting course, I head for the track, kneeling beside it. Sure enough, it has the markers of large and heavy feet—eight of them. Two lykin. I follow the trail up to the edge of the woods.

Branches are broken. Split and dangling at uncomfortable angles. Folost illuminates the singes that blacken the trees where woven ribbons should have proudly fluttered in the breeze, and the claw marks that dig trenches into the earth. But the most stomach-churning thing that Folost's light lands on is the drops of blood.

One of the lykin, or Aurora's?

I fear I already know the answer. But for the lykin's sakes…I hope I'm wrong.

four

The woods I once knew like a friend have now become an enemy. A sinister aura hangs from every branch and lurks behind every tree trunk. It's all made worse by the iron scent of blood.

Folost swivels around the top of my makeshift torch. I do not question and simply follow wherever he points, trusting him to lead me to Aurora.

Would I know if it was Aurora whose blood was spilled? I had not been able to sense Folost and Mary in the flames. But they are much smaller spirits than Aurora. Weaker. Not that I'd say as much to them.

I would know if she were hurt, I insist to myself. She was the first spirit I ever bound on my own and she only asked one thing of me—to keep her safe. And what did I do? I failed.

The memory of the silver charm, dangling harmlessly by the handle as I left, is so sharp that I nearly stumble. It is as though my own mind has punched me in the stomach with a vision so clear, so brutal…

The barriers on the house weren't fully in place.

Had I woken her and asked her to replace it, then maybe they wouldn't have been able to sense her. Maybe, in my time of mourning, I had neglected the barriers on the woods enough that the ribbons burned and frayed easier than they should have. It's because of me that they could get her.

I must rescue her at all costs.

It isn't long before Folost guides me off the main path that leads to the great redwood and I am instead trudging through brush and bramble in a section of the woods I've never been before. Mary does a good job of helping keep the thorniest bits of foliage away from me by communing with the other flora around us.

Her words, as I presume them to be, are more like a soft humming that pulses across my senses. Her magic is as gentle as a nighttime breeze. And, in response, the small branches bend as they're able before rustling softly back into place.

I've never sensed her so keenly before. Part of me wonders if I simply hadn't paid her enough attention, but I don't think that's the case. I have always attended her and Folost with the most care I can give. These heightened senses must be from Aurora's magic.

Should I feel guilty for leveraging powers she never intended to give? Aurora made it clear that she did not want to be used by others… I run a hand over my stomach, trying to quell its uneasiness. If I am to use her power, then getting her back and keeping her safe would be what she'd want me to use it for, I think. I hope. Still, it'll be something I ask her forgiveness for later.

We make our way through the dense woods for what feels like hours. How much time has actually passed? I could not say.

Without warning, Folost goes dim and the brush ahead of me thickens unnaturally—like a barrier forming to block my path. Instinctively, I crouch down, keeping myself low to the ground and drawing my cloak tighter around me. If we are actually close to the lykin, I'll need all the protection I can get from their keen senses. Folost is nothing more than a little ember smoldering atop the fragment of brick from his hearth. But the tiny blue-white flames ripple in the direction of the thicker brush.

I glance between the two of them.

Mary understands my unspoken question and tiny marigold blossoms pop up from the mossy, wet earth despite it being nowhere near close to their season. They dot the moss ahead of me, stretching underneath the thickened brush. *Ahead, but slowly*, is the message I get from them both and the living woods around me.

I dig the bottom of my makeshift torch into the soil between two roots and rest the torch itself against a nearby tree, trusting my little fiery friend not to singe the bark. Folost pulls himself forward to the front of the stone. Flickering and barely visible. I set Mary next to him.

"I'll come back for you both," I mouth more than whisper.

Two golden eyes meet mine. A single blink, even though it was not a yes or no question. He understands and believes what I say. Mary sags and straightens, almost like a bow. The two spirits know I will not abandon them, which means they also believe I can accomplish what must be done. Their confidence is the reassurance I need.

With it tucked against my heart, I continue on through the thicket.

I'm on my stomach, moving with the grace of an inchworm. Even though she is not with me, Mary continues to guide my path with tiny red blossoms blooming before me. Almost through the thick brush, I see a flicker of orange light.

I move even slower, pressing myself as flat as possible. I take mud and moss, smearing it on my face—pressing it into my nose. My cloak might protect me from the lykin's magical senses but they still have keen smell and hearing. The last thing I want is for them to pick up the smell of my nervous sweat.

Finally, I reach the edge of the brush and get my first glimpse of Aurora's captors.

My suspicions were right: two lykin. They take the form of men at present. One of them is wiry, all lean muscle and scars that line his exposed arms and run underneath his hair-covered chest. I presume there to be some on his face, as well, but I can't see them through the thick, copper beard that covers his features from his ears down. He has a head of extremely short-cropped, rusty hair—not unlike mine—however his is dusted with silver.

The other man is younger than the first, roughly the same as my twenty-two years, if I had to guess. He is thick with muscles; biceps bulge and dip, angles as sharp as the grooves carved into his stomach that disappear into a pair of tight black trousers. The only other clothing he wears are a pair of worn, black boots and a thick leather band on his right wrist. The muscles in his back fan out like tucked wings when he puts his hands on his hips. He looks like he could snap me in two with little effort. An assessment that is further emphasized by his dark, furrowed brows and the way strands of black hair fall into his face, shadowing his glower.

Even though he is the younger of the two, something about him feels distinctly more…kingly to me. If I was forced to guess which of these men was the larger of the three wolves I saw last night, it would be the younger. But that does beg the question, what happened to the third wolf?

Aurora is bound and seated by the fire. Her hands are affixed behind her back and I see a line of rope tying her to a nearby tree so she can't run. A trail of red runs down her face from a wound at her hairline, dripping into her lap. Other cuts and bruises dot her arms. My realization from last night returns—it is an unimaginably cruel fate to be immortal, but able to feel pain as if you were not.

"You were too rough with her," the younger man snarls at his counterpart. He speaks with the deepest resonance I've ever heard.

"You should listen to Evander," Aurora says to the older man. "Conri's going to be cross with you when he finds out how you've treated me."

"Conri won't find out." The wiry man stomps to loom over Aurora. There's the air of violence around him that makes even me shiver. "I've seen how quickly you can mend. You'll be as pure as starlight by the time we get you back to your king. Won't you?"

Aurora purses her lips and narrows her eyes, saying nothing.

"I asked you a question, spirit." The smaller man grabs Aurora's face, jerking it in his direction, extending her neck painfully.

I bite my cheeks to keep from shouting out. My nails dig into my palms, knuckles white. I can't help Aurora if I'm caught as well or, worse, killed. The best thing I can do is bide my time and help her escape the first moment I can.

Aurora still says nothing.

"Now tell us where the ring is," he demands.

"I told you, I don't have it anymore." Aurora stares up at him with the slightest bit of smugness. "And you'll never find it, either. A wolf king will never again hold my power."

"How dare—Your absence has almost caused the loss of a generation of pups and a new age of bloodshed, yet you sit there with your obnoxious little smile, as if you're all too pleased for it—as if you can abandon your duty. You serve us."

"Were I a servant, I might at least be offered a modicum of respect. No, your wicked kings have made me a slave," Aurora says with more venom and hate and pain than I had thought possible from her. A deep sorrow courses through me. "But I will be free. One way or another. Damn the lykin."

The man raises his other hand as a fist. "How dare you—"

"Enough, Bardulf." The younger man, Evander, catches the older's wrist. I see Bardulf straining against him, but he's not nearly strong enough to shake Evander's grip.

"You want to tussle again?"

Evander ignores the challenge. "Go for a run and sweat out your rage. She's riling you up so you can't think clearly."

Bardulf wrests his hand free with a grunt and stomps off in the direction opposite of me—thank the old gods. He murmurs the entire time, all hateful things about Aurora.

Neither of the two moves for a long minute.

Finally, Aurora speaks. "What was the point?" The question is pain and anger.

"I don't know what you're talking about." Evander shifts his stance, looking down at Aurora.

"Were you just toying with me?" She glares up at him. "Some kind of sick thrill to go on the hunt?"

Evander says nothing. He won't even look at her. Aurora spits at his feet.

"You're just like the rest of his pack, twisted and disgusting. You're nothing more than a pup with a tail between your legs the moment it gets tough."

"Take caution not to speak to a knight of the king with such disdain," he says coolly. "When we return to Midscape and are around Conri again, I won't be able to allow it to slide."

It's become clear to me that neither Evander nor Bardulf is the wolf king. The man named Conri seems to be. I breathe a little easier given the way they speak of him. It doesn't sound like he's close by.

"No? Your rebellious streak ended with me?"

"Aurora—" He sighs heavily. "You know what happens when we cross him."

"I do not care about the king. He is not my king—need I remind you, he is not yours, either, Evander. He killed—"

"Watch your tongue."

"Or what? You'll strike me like Bardulf?" The words are almost a challenge. One I'm pleased to see that Evander doesn't rise to.

"No matter how we feel, we are forever bound to him by our oaths."

"Do not speak to me of deals and promises and oaths." Aurora is on her feet. She strains against the rope holding her to the tree. Evander continues to linger, just beyond her reach, as her eyes dig daggers into him. "I have kept oaths from long before your parents were even pups, suckling at their mothers' teats. So I will not be reminded by a man-child of what oaths I must and must not keep." Her voice is as cold as the darkest winter's night.

Evander continues to stand as tall and strong as a stone wall against her. But eventually he walks away without another word, sitting on the opposite side of the fire. As he approaches, I see his cheek by his eye is bruised and I hope Aurora put up a fight when they tried to take her.

With his back to me, I now can see massive scars that run between Evander's shoulder blades, as though a wolf took its two front paws and dragged its claws across him. They're deep grooves with raised sides. Gnarled. Painful to even look at. Whatever, or whoever, did that to him was vicious, indeed.

"We should get rest while we can," he murmurs. Aurora doesn't even bother to look at him. Evander nestles himself into the moss and, soon, his breathing slows into a steady cadence.

I take my opportunity but I don't rush. Haste will make noise and there's still Bardulf out there. With any luck, however, Evander will fall into a deep sleep and Bardulf will spend the night chasing the growing moon in the opposite direction from me.

Folost and Mary are waiting where I left them and I quickly collect both.

"I need you to burn through a rope," I whisper to Folost. It'd take me far too long to cut through it with my knife. But Folost can get through it in a few seconds if he's determined enough.

A blink in the tiny flame.

"Thank you." We're off through the woods, moving in a wide arc around the clearing with Aurora. Every step is agonizingly slow. But I persist at my steady pace. When Folost makes a sudden deviation on his stone, I turn sharply and push past a low bush to find myself at the edge of the clearing behind Aurora.

Her back is now to me, so I can't see if she's awake or if she took Evander's advice and tried to sleep. I guess it's the former, just from her resistance to them so far. I grab the rope affixed to the tree and give a light tug.

Aurora's head whips around. Her brow instantly relaxes upon seeing me at the edge of the trees. Her lips part slightly and then ease into a relieved smile.

I give her a nod and move the torch to the rope. Folost wastes no time, making a ring of fire around the thick cord. He burns white hot, but small. All the while I keep my eyes on Evander. It's hard to make out his features between the night and the stark brightness of the flames. But if he had woken, I think he would've made a motion for me. There's no way he wouldn't be able to see me. Just once, I think I see him twist. But he shifts and settles again.

Just a little bit more… I will Folost to move faster. The rope is fraying; he's down to its core. Then…

Snap. The rope sags. Aurora is free.

She spares one look at Evander before slinking back toward me. I move backward, giving her space. As she plunges into the shadows, she gives me a nod. One I return.

We don't even waste time on the bindings around her wrists, we're off.

I trust Folost to guide us back to the main path without need of instruction. He's a clever little spirit and I'm sure he knows where we need to go. Once we get back to—

The thought causes me to stumble, nearly toppling over. Aurora pushes her shoulder into me, steadying me. She glances my way. I shake my head and carry on.

The house is gone. Where will we go? Where is safe, if the lykin are willing to leave the woods?

We'll go southwest. Far from the Lykin Woods. We'll travel as far as we need to find a safe place to rest. Then we'll keep moving until we can find a way to return Aurora's power to her. After that, when the time is right, we'll rebuild.

A house is just timber and clay, even one as magical as mine was… I have my life, and my spirits. So long as that is true, we'll be all right.

The main path is nearly in view when a rustle of leaves at our left alerts me to the presence of another. I barely have time to look in that direction before a massive, copper wolf lunges at me through the darkness.

five

A scream escapes me as claws sink into my shoulders and I am crushed into the ground. Folost flies away, knocked from my grip by force and surprise. I try to twist, landing as best I can so Mary isn't crushed. The lykin lands atop me and I am gouged further by back paws on my thighs. Hot breath glazes over my cheeks with a snarl as a maw of sharp teeth shine in Folost's tiny light.

"Get off of her!" Aurora shouts, kicking at the wolf's side. It does little good.

The wolf swings his head, snapping at Aurora with his deadly maw. She snarls back, baring her teeth. I'm helpless to do anything other than be pinned under the wolf's weight, feeling every claw sink deeper and deeper into my muscle. Waves of pain leave me gasping.

There's another rustling of leaves. A second wolf emerges, but it takes me a second to see from where. This beast is as black as midnight and seems to absorb what little light there is.

The second beast shakes his coat, as if emerging from water. In the process, the fur ripples away like mist and shadow. Paw turns to boot in a single step. Black fur becomes black trousers, fitted to the waist. Evander straightens, as though he was just crawling on all fours. A man in place of where a wolf once was.

"We're not here to hunt humans," he cautions Bardulf. "She is not our concern."

Another snap from the wolf atop me. Bardulf glares up at Evander and they lock eyes. Possibly speaking with senses alone.

"I said, get off!" Aurora kicks Bardulf again, this time in the side of his face, breaking the silent communication between the two wolf knights.

I need to get up. But all I can see is stars dotting the heavy canopy above, floating through my vision, my temples splitting. Hot blood seeps and pools around me, steaming against the cool night air. My body is going numb. Shock, likely. That's probably what's happening… I'm going into shock. If I understand what I'm feeling, then I can push through it.

"Enough of this!" Evander grabs Bardulf by the back of his neck, like a mother wolf grabbing her cub, and throws him away. Bardulf changes his shape midair, a string of curses erupting from him as he lands heavily.

"You think you can manhandle me, you packless orphan?" Bardulf recovers and thrusts his chest out, almost meeting Evander's.

Evander says nothing to him and turns away, focusing instead on Aurora and me. "You convinced a human to help you and now she'll pay the price for it." His eyes shift to meet mine and there's a brief pause. His lips part slightly and then twist into a harder line. As if he is disgusted by the mere sight of me. "You shouldn't be here, witch. You have already lost your home tonight. Go before you lose your life, too."

It's these men's fault I nearly lost everything dear to me. Hatred has me pushing off the ground. "I'm not leaving without Aurora."

"Faelyn, don't," Aurora cautions.

"She's bonded with me, and me alone. Your king can't have her power any longer," I declare. "So let us leave. And when you both return to him, tell him to stop hunting us. It's over."

The words seem to echo through the woods. The two lykin go perfectly still. Like statues cast in an artist's rendering of pure shock.

"You…cannot bind yourself with any but the wolf king," Bardulf stammers at Aurora. "It's impossible."

"I assure you, it's not." Aurora doesn't sound nearly as pleased as I would've thought. Is this not her opportunity to finally rid herself of those who would be her captors? Shouldn't she delight in telling them she can no longer be used?

"Where is the ring? Take us to it. Now!" Spittle flies from Bardulf's mouth as he stomps toward her.

"I already told you, I don't have it." Aurora is perfectly calm in the face of his rage.

Bardulf moves faster than I'm able to process. He's behind me, an arm around my neck. Hooked tightly. I wheeze. My shoulders hurt too much to put up much of a fight. With every movement I make, more blood leaves me.

"Don't!" Aurora shouts.

"Let her go." Evander steps forward. "She's not our concern." He grinds out every word.

"She made her our concern when she stole the ring." Bardulf squeezes even tighter. I gasp like a fish on land. "Where is it?" he snarls in my ear.

I can't answer.

"She doesn't have it! I destroyed it!" Aurora says quickly. "When the ring broke, my power went into her. Not me. She's the one who has the other half of my essence now. She… *She is the ring.*"

Both of them go still for a second time. The words and their meaning dawn on them as it does on me. Her power is within me, the power the wolf king coveted, and hunted. Aurora told me that he would be after her now…but I didn't take the danger seriously enough. I couldn't comprehend it. Nor did I think hard enough on what this power could've meant.

Why did I think some barriers would keep the wolf king himself from getting what he wanted? We should have left last night. Why didn't I press her harder for the truth, details, something?

Shock slackens Bardulf's arm around my throat. He releases me and I collapse, wheezing.

"Undo it," Bardulf says quickly. He looks genuinely panicked.

I look to Aurora, but she's focused on the men. She said she was sworn to be bonded to the wolf king…but instead, she and I are. And I know as well as I presume Bardulf does that…

"The power cannot be properly transferred by mortal hands," Aurora says solemnly. "To remove it from her, we would have to stand before the old gods in the siren's Eversea and beseech them for aid, as I did ages ago. Take me there and perhaps—"

"You really think we will take you to the old gods? Where you can just ask to be restored to your original form and leave the lykin forever?" Bardulf scoffs. There's a crazed, panicked look in his eyes. He takes another step back toward me. "I say we just kill her. Put the power back that way."

Evander stops him with an arm. "Didn't you hear Aurora? We can't."

"Exactly. If you kill her, who knows what will happen," Aurora cautions solemnly. "The magic already didn't act as I thought it would—seeking out another, more temporary physical form, rather than my own. If you kill her, maybe it'll transfer again, maybe not. Do you really want to risk half my essence being lost, forever, to all of us?"

Bardulf seems to really consider this. "But we can't… We…" He looks to Evander. "What do we do?"

"We take them both to Conri," Evander declares. "It will be up to the king of the wolves, alpha of all packs, to decide what is to be done. He will want to meet the human that stole the spirit of the moon."

six

Spirit of the moon… Ancient. Primordial. One of the oldest and most powerful spirits in legend. And, if the stories are to be believed, the spirit that fuels the powers of both the lykin and the vampir with her shifting shape and constant pull.

I look to Aurora in shock, and awe. Her eyes are drawn to mine as if she senses my attention.

"Sorry I didn't have a moment to tell you yet," she says softly. There's genuine apology in her voice. "At first I wasn't sure about…" *You.* The word is left hanging as pain and guilt flash through her eyes. "I vowed I was going to tell you everything while you were gone."

"There wasn't time," I say, mostly in a daze still. I've hardly known her for a day. I can't rightly be cross.

"Sorry, again, that I wrapped you into my mess."

"It's all right," I murmur. Shock compounds in me. The spirit of the moon… I should have known that with the wolf king hunting her, she was someone incredibly important. I suppose I did…I just didn't care. It didn't matter. Aurora needed help and help was something I could give. It was a reason to keep moving, a good one—she was wronged by a man who should have handled their relationship with care. I know that hurt all too well.

"Let's move." Bardulf pushes the middle of my back and I stumble forward. I let out a soft cry at the pain in my thighs and shoulders, my whole body nearly giving out from the agony.

Evander seizes my elbow and pulls, keeping me upright. I clench my jaw and suppress a pained whimper. I've little doubt my agony would be triumph for these men. As if to test me, his grip tightens further as our gazes collide. Noses nearly touching.

Silver eyes. Razor-edged. They gleam as brilliantly as the moonlight the lykin swear themselves to. For a moment that stretches on and on, I find myself ensnared by an almost hypnotic allure of them. The crushing grip of his fist is a mere shadow compared to the intensity by which his gaze threatens to devour me.

"We should bind her." Bardulf's words break our focus on each other.

"She's a human. What can she do? Run? Let her try and see how well that works out." Evander releases me with a slight push, as if he's suddenly disgusted he touched me at all. As if that moment—whatever it was—hadn't happened. "We're faster and stronger. If she tries to run, *then* we kill her." He glances over his shoulder as he walks away from me. A shudder runs down my spine. He has the eyes of a predator and they are focused on me, and me alone. "And if we do hunt her down, her end will not be merciful."

"I understand," I say. But even as my insides are turning to jelly, I'm already trying to plan Aurora's and my escape. I am not allowing her to go back with these men.

"Good, let's carry on, then." Evander starts onward.

I don't move. "If you're not binding me, then Aurora shouldn't be either."

"You dare to—" Bardulf begins.

"If you can hunt me down with such ease then you can track and stop her without issue, too," I interrupt. "And we're both equally valuable, each with half her power, aren't we?"

The veins in Bardulf's neck bulge, a flush creeping up toward his cheeks.

But, before he says anything, Evander interjects with a heavy sigh. "Just do it so we can be gone. The night is wearing thin."

Grumbling, Bardulf unknots Aurora's wrists as I collect the boots that fell from my person when he tackled me.

"Here." I hold them out to her. "I noticed you were barefoot and I thought that…" I trail off, not wanting to mention our plans of the journey. "That you might need them. The cobbler in town is excellent, so they're of good make—I've had mine for years." I stick out my foot for emphasis.

Aurora's expression crumples a bit at the mention of our grand plan to escape, but she recovers quickly. She accepts the boots with both hands, as if they're a precious token and not leather bound and stitched. "Thank you, Faelyn. That is deeply thoughtful of you."

As Aurora pulls on the boots, I go and collect my torch. Fortunately, Folost is resilient—he still sparks at the top of it. Mary wasn't utterly crushed by Bardulf, either.

"What's that?" Bardulf narrows his focus on Folost. "Think you can fight us with that puny little fire spirit at your side?"

"His name is Folost," I correct, and start to walk, ignoring the pain in my shoulders and thighs. I'll have to tend to my wounds, but I don't think they're going to take kindly to me asking for a reprieve and I'm determined to stay on their good side. Or, at least have them continue to see me as a pathetic human. The more they underestimate me, the better my chances are for getting away with Aurora. "And, unfortunately, I do not possess eyes with as keen of sight as yours. I need a way to light my path, or I'm going to slow you down further."

My submissiveness works perfectly. Bardulf snorts and nods approvingly. Evander doesn't even look my way; he's already charging ahead into the underbrush.

"I'm sorry I got you both into this mess," I say under my breath for Mary and Folost alone.

The marigold shudders, as if swept by a chill.

Folost blinks twice. What he says is, *No*. But what I understand it to mean is, *Don't blame yourself.*

I smile at both of them as we begin to walk, Aurora at my side. My little family.

"If anyone is to blame, it's me." Aurora massages her wrists. The lykin can probably hear us, but for once they don't interrupt. Perhaps they want to overhear whatever our conversation is to see if there's any information to glean from it. "I was the one who—"

"It's all right." I touch her elbow lightly. There's so much guilt in her voice. So much pain. I've only begun to gather enough information to spin together an idea of her story. But what I've heard, seen, and surmised is more than enough to weave a picture of a desperate woman—spirit—who was trying to do anything to secure her freedom. "I'm not upset. You had your reasons and my involvement wasn't intentional on your part by any measure. Magic can be unpredictable at times, that's just the way of it."

Aurora's eyes meet mine and they hold so many unsaid words it's amazing they don't overflow as tears. I wish I could offer her reassurance. Even though I don't think I have nearly as much experience with love, and men, and romance as an immortal spirit does. Still, what little experience I do have, was one of the most painful times of my life.

"Yes, but—" She stops short. "You're bleeding a lot."

"I'm all right. It looks worse than it is," I lie.

"No, you need to stop. We must attend these."

I grab Aurora's elbow, giving it a reassuring squeeze. "I said, it looks worse than it is, I'm all right."

"We should—"

I shake my head firmly and give her a pointed look. Aurora purses her lips and turns back to the lykin. I can almost feel her holding herself back from calling out on my behalf. It's as if Evander senses it.

He glances over his shoulder. "Is there a problem?"

"None," I say for us both.

"Good."

And that is where the conversation dies.

We trudge through the forest in painful silence. Painful because it is awkward and tense being around these men. And painful because the blood has seeped down to my socks. I hold Folost tighter, ignoring the ache it causes in my shoulder. It'd be easier if I set him down, but that's the furthest thing from my mind as an option right now.

At long last, when the moon hangs low in the heavens, we arrive at a barrier forged of undulating darkness. It writhes and pulses, infused with otherworldly magics. Contorting incessantly, its form refuses to remain constant even for a second, as though it is living, breathing.

"Is this…" I gasp.

"The Fade," Aurora finishes for me.

I knew it. The Fade is a magical barrier between our world and the world of magic—Midscape. My grandmother told me stories of this protective barrier, the only thing keeping our world and nonmagical humans from being overrun by those with powers beyond our comprehension. She always said the line between worlds was closer than we thought—close enough that the roots of the great redwood tree could stretch across the barrier, enough for our spirits, and us in turn, to leech magic.

But I never really thought it was *this* close. Close enough for me to walk to it in a single night. For me to touch it.

"Rhave," Evander calls at the edge of the magical black mist. Nothing happens. He sighs and presses his fingers into the black leather band on his wrist. "Rhave." A little more annoyed and impatient this time.

From the corners of my eyes, I see Aurora quirk her lips into the slightest little smirk.

"Would you like me to give it a try, Sir Evander?" she says sweetly.

He shoots her a glare and tries again. "Rhave, you are commanded by a knight of the wolf king to grant us passage."

"Ooh…'a knight of the wolf king,' he says. Best not keep the honorable knight waiting," a voice whispers, as soft as the rustling trees. It comes distinctly from the wall of fog ahead of us, but from no particular spot. Rather, it is as if the shadow itself speaks. This is the second talking spirit I have met in two days and, despite my current predicament, I cannot believe my luck. Perhaps, magic isn't as dead and gone as we once feared. Rhave's tone shifts, becoming heavy with concern. "Aurora? I did not expect to see you again so soon."

"I hoped to never see you again," she remarks dryly. "No offense, Rhave."

"None taken." There is a camaraderie among spirits, it'd seem. A fact that draws a smile to my face. No wonder Folost took so quickly to Aurora last night. "Should I not let them through?"

Aurora seems to consider it.

"What are you going on about?" Bardulf demands to know. I tilt my head at him, confused. The words have been clear enough to me. "If the Fade doesn't open, we'll kill the girl." He thrusts a finger in my direction.

"I take offense to being called girl," I say. "I'm twenty-two years grown." Not that I expect him to listen at all.

Bardulf snorts and proves himself to be the example of my expectations.

"Need I remind you the risks of killing her?" Aurora folds her arms.

"Risks be damned. If I can't get what I need with words, I'll get it with blood." Bardulf walks toward me. Aurora half steps in front of him.

"Let us pass, Rhave. Conri would come anyway to force your hand if we delayed enough. And I'll have no more blood on my account." The way Aurora speaks leaves me to wonder if she has seen blood spilled for her before. Was it in her name? Or because of her? Either way, she doesn't strike me as a woman who relishes violence.

The shadows ahead condense into the vague figure of a man. It's a hazy outline. I blink and I can't be sure I saw it at all. From moment to moment, the man becomes a deer, then a wolf, then back again.

"If only I could swallow these noble knights whole…" The way Rhave speaks it makes it clear that he does not find the knights noble at all. A sentiment I'm inclined to agree with given what limited knowledge I have of them.

I glance at the two men. They don't react to Rhave's comments, despite my thinking they would. Evander stares off at nothing. Bardulf paces restlessly.

"Ah," Aurora hums softly, drawing my attention. "They can't understand us."

"What? But…"

"The tongue of spirits. With a part of my magic, you can understand them now," she explains.

"I can't understand Folost and Mary."

"Well, that's because—"

"Stop stalling." Bardulf stops his pacing and returns to exhausting his energy on us. "Open the Fade, now, or I'll be led to believe that you're conspiring against us."

If only he knew…

"Rhave, if you please." Aurora's shoulders slump slightly with the weight of resignation.

"I'd rather not, but if you insist." Rhave moves to the side, absorbing back into the living shadow that is the wall of the Fade. I'm not sure if he is some kind of spirit of safe passage, or of shadow. Either seems a safe bet. Were I a more powerful witch, I would probably be able to tell at a glance. Grandma told me stories of how her mother's mother could sense a spirit's presence without even having to see them.

A narrow tunnel splits the Fade, the swirling mist pushing to the sides enough to give passage. It is still a world of complete darkness, the grasses blackened, shadowed trees punching through the walls of the tunnel.

Evander starts in first, leading the charge. He motions to Aurora, who follows a step behind. Bardulf thrusts his finger toward me and then the tunnel, as though I might have somehow been confused as to what was expected of me.

Refraining from giving him a smart remark, I step forward. Though, I pause at the entrance of the Fade. I can feel Mary quivering at my hip. Folost smolders, hanging on the side of the stone closest to me. I hold him a little lower, wishing I could wrap an arm around him to help him feel safer.

"Go," Bardulf barks.

I ignore him, instead staring into the shadow and stating my intention. "Thank you, Rhave, for this passage you've offered us. I will accept your graciousness with gratitude. I will not take anything from your domain which is not offered nor leave my mark upon it."

There is no response. I wait, worried that somehow Aurora is misinformed and I do not actually speak his language.

"Enough mumbling. Go!" Bardulf pushes me between my shoulders again, causing me to stumble. Pain shoots down to my ankles, causing my knees to buckle.

I tip forward, trying to catch my balance. But the ground of the Fade doesn't feel quite solid under my feet. I clutch Folost, trying to hold him aloft. I twist my body, reaching out on instinct to stabilize myself so I don't land on Mary. My fingers close around something warm and solid and I'm able to quickly right myself.

The shadows slowly pull away from me. I release what I held onto and meet the eyes that carve hollows into the Fade. Rhave hovers there and, for a second, neither of us moves.

"Look after her, please," he whispers.

"I will," I vow with ease.

"Enough talking." A hand closes around the back of my neck, shoving me forward again.

I stumble, but am able to keep myself mostly upright this time. "You don't have to manhandle me."

Bardulf leans in and snarls. "I can do to you whatever I please."

A shiver runs down my spine, and not from the chill that lives in this strange barrier between worlds. He means it. And there is so much left unspoken around those words.

"Bardulf, Faelyn, enough delay," Evander barks. "We need to keep moving; the wolf king is expecting us to return with haste, and you know he does not take kindly to being kept waiting."

There's enough ominous undertones to those words as well that I only feel colder.

What will this "wolf king" be like?

I have to get Aurora and myself back across the Fade as soon as I can. But, to get home, we must venture farther past this unnatural barrier and into the magical world beyond: Midscape.

We traverse the void that is the Fade along the pathway made for us by Rhave. Within it, I see the shadows of beasts and creatures just beyond my scope of comprehension. They pass alongside us. There one moment and gone the next. They leap across our path as wisps of smoke, gaining form once they're back in the safe embrace of the magic that they were born into.

Briefly, a shadowy wolf walks alongside me, more solid than the rest. One of his ears is hooked unnaturally, as if a chunk is missing. With a flash of gold eyes, he's gone.

The Fade is a wondrous place…and a cold one. I find myself shivering more and more with every step. My feet feel heavy and my vision grows as tunneled as the path ahead. The streak of white that is Aurora's hair and the broad, scarred swath of Evander's back are my targets, the only things keeping me going on the right path.

We trudge through shadowed forest and thick marsh, across rocky bluff and into smooth grassland before pale moonlight can be seen once more in the distance. The far opening of the tunnel is like a beacon, shining from a lighthouse on a distant shore.

As easily as we entered the Fade, we leave it. No sooner have I stepped foot into the land of Midscape, than the pot containing Mary at my hip explodes, sending shards of clay into my flesh and dirt showering everywhere. The torch in my hand bursts into flame, and, for a moment, I am blinded by light.

seven

I let out a yelp of surprise and drop the torch before the fire can reach my hand and singe my flesh. Like balls of yarn let loose, viny tendrils unfurl from my hip at the same time as the flame's explosion. The foliage weaves together, forming a torso, two legs, and two arms. There is a head of tightly woven stems, two massive leaves for ears. A halo of marigolds like hair sprouts all around the green head.

The wood of my makeshift torch is instantly turned to ash. But the shard of brick is enveloped in a hovering orb of flame. Instead of legs, the fire flickers down to a point. Two tongues of flame become arms. Then, a head, with two glowing, golden eyes.

"Mary? Folost?" I stammer, looking between the two.

"Just so, Faelyn." Folost raises a fiery arm to his torso, where the brick is—where a heart would otherwise be.

"What in the—" Bardulf leaps to action, as if wanting to protect Aurora and myself.

"They're harmless," Aurora says dully. "Calm yourself."

I give Aurora a thankful look and turn back to my spirit friends. "You both can speak?"

"In this world where magic is still strong, we can…to those who are capable of understanding. Our powers were diminished with time in the Natural World," Mary says. Where Folost's voice crackles like the roar of a fire, Mary's is sweet and light, like the buzz of pollinators drifting on meadow breezes.

"We need to carry on," Bardulf gruffly reminds us. I shoot

him a glare that hits about as well as a sharpened stick against plate armor.

"Bardulf, my simple-minded friend." Evander tsks with a shake of his head.

"How dare you," Bardulf snarls.

"Can you not see the benefit we bring to Conri?" Evander motions to me.

"I see Aurora's power split and half of it is in a thing that thinks and walks rather than a ring to be worn." Bardulf begins to pace again. He is more shark than wolf, circling in the waters around us.

"Conri has not only the moon spirit, and her power, but the power of a weaver witch with spirits in tow." Evander gestures as though this should have been an obvious assumption.

These men are in competition for which I hate more, being called a "thing," or having my abilities coveted as though they are something to be possessed and used. But I keep my discomfort concealed. After all, Evander seems to have Bardulf no longer circling. And Evander's plans of offering my skills to Conri is something to worry over in the future.

"Folost, Mary, now that you've been successfully returned to Midscape, you should go and commune with the old gods to fully restore your strength," Aurora says gently. "There are precious little of us left."

I'm completely pulled from worrying about the men, and I focus back between the woman and my bonded spirits—my friends. I knew that, under no circumstances, would I ever leave them behind. But the idea that they might leave me never once crossed my mind and I suddenly feel so selfish for it.

"Do you need to regain your strength? Are you both unwell?" It's a silly question, given what I just saw. If they had been well, then they wouldn't have been relegated to such weakened forms for decades. Was this somehow my fault? Did I keep them at my side well past when I should have set them free? "I hadn't known that you were suffering… I am so sorry."

"You need not apologize," Folost says warmly.

Mary lifts a pointed arm and a small vine unfurls, a marigold at its end, that wraps around my wrist. "Fear not; we shall not abandon you, Faelyn."

"I…" I can't say it wasn't a fear of mine. They know me too well. Have seen every moment of my life where someone I love left. Be it my mother going into the woods and never returning. The boy I loved abandoning me with nothing but a broken heart to remember him by. Or clutching my grandmother's hand every hour until the magic uncoiled from her body. But I must be strong for my friends now. It doesn't matter what happened to me in the past, I won't hold them back. "I know you wouldn't abandon me. But looking after yourself and your well-being isn't abandoning. I love you both, and want you both well, foremost."

"You don't have to tell us. We know. You never failed to ensure Folost had enough charcoal, or that my soil was properly watered." The vines shift into what I think is a smile. "You might not see us often in these forms, here, as they take great effort for us to maintain. But we will be with you. You know how to call upon us, whenever you need."

A vine reaches out to the ground, selecting a small shard of clay from the pot that shattered at my hip. Mary lifts it, holding it before me. I accept the token with both hands. Grandma's thumbprint dents its surface. Folost does a similar motion, passing the shard of brick from within him into my hands. It's burning hot, but only for a fleeting moment. Somehow, I don't seem to really feel the singe at all.

"We are honored to be bound to a witch such as you. Never hesitate to call upon us whenever you need." With those last words, Folost's flames wrap in on himself and sputter out of existence with a puff of smoke.

Mary's vines return to the earth, withering and becoming soil for the worms to feed on right before my eyes. She leaves behind a trail of marigold petals that catch a breeze that smells of woodsmoke. Of home.

As the wind picks up…they're gone.

My hands are still before me, clutching the tokens that are the last remaining tethers I have to my friends. I had thought that I would keep them with me, always—keep them safe. When, really, I was taking them home. They might still be bound to me, but they are not slaves. They are free to go and, honestly, I wish it for them. Even if it makes my heart ache and eyes sting at the mere idea of all I've lost and let go of in such a short period of time—enough to make the cold that's wrapped over my shoulders heavier than my ruby cape sink deeper into my marrow—I love my spirit friends enough to want to see them well. With me, or without.

Aurora's eyes are glassy also as she stares at the spots where the two spirits were. I wonder what is going through her mind. From all I've heard, I can only imagine that she, too, is yearning for freedom. For the ability to wander as far as she pleases. For a form that will enable her to return to the origins of her essence. But unlike Folost and Mary, Aurora is trapped in her mortal body. She is hunted by the wolf king.

"This way," Evander says, matter-of-fact, starting down a beaten path between two rolling hills. Completely oblivious that I just lost two of my dearest friends.

Bardulf lingers, arms folded, staring me down. Somehow, even at half of Evander's weight, he manages to be more imposing.

"We should rest here," Aurora calls after Evander, ignoring the obvious and unspoken command from Bardulf to move.

"No. We'll rest at camp." Evander doesn't even look back before responding. He's already halfway down the hill.

"Evander, she needs rest now."

Evander pauses, looking back to me. His silvery eyes are as cold as the sliver of moon above. "Is this true? Do you need us to go easier on you, human?"

"I can persist just fine." I am amazed my words are even as I fight chattering teeth. The night is colder in Midscape, I think. Vaguely, a part of my mind wonders what else is different in this world. But I can't summon the energy to be as enthusiastic about discovering such things as I know I should be.

"Good. We should get across the narrow strait while Gruvun still waits." Evander continues forward.

Aurora gives me a worried look but I offer a nod of assurance. She begrudgingly follows behind Evander, in front of me. Bardulf continues to loom over my shoulder. I make it a point to slowly place my friend's tokens in my pocket before starting onward.

The hills slope into a coastline of pale sand. Little more than a strip of white, shining in the moonlight against a calm strait of water the same color as the night sky. I have never seen the sea before, though I have heard its stories from the traders that used to come through town, hawking goods from all the way to the west. The stories were enough to make me regard this body of water with some apprehension. Especially when Evander climbs into a small rowboat that has been beached upon the shore, frothy waves lapping around its far-too-thin-looking hull.

Aurora is next. I force myself over the side. Then Bardulf. The moon spirit and I sit in the middle, with Evander at the bow and Bardulf at the stern.

"Gruvun, take us back," Evander says to the ocean. The tide sweeps in, but only around our little vessel, lifting us and carrying us into the open water.

Immediately, I sense a surge of magic with the tides. I've never seen someone other than a witch summon a spirit. But the lykin have their own ways of channeling magic.

We are practically untouched by the waves, speeding across the dark sea with ease. I glance over the side of the vessel; there's nothing but ripples and sea foam. It's astounding that Aurora made this journey alone…and in the state she was in. No wonder she collapsed from exhaustion shortly after we met.

"Gruvun, were you able to deliver my message?" Aurora asks the water on the opposite side of the rowboat.

"I was," the water laps against the hull in reply. Nothing fundamentally changed about the movement of the boat, but somehow the waves sound different. The urge to stand and peer over is nearly overwhelming, but I refrain. I do not want to be cast overboard. "She is ready to receive you."

"And she thinks she will have the power to fix me?"

"She has taken her form. It will not be an issue… She is more mobile than the last, but she will not be able to come to you. She is still entrapped."

Aurora shifts, staring at her joined hands between her knees. Entrapped. That one word seems to haunt her.

"'She' is the old god you wished to see?" I ask, hoping that Evander and Bardulf can't understand me. Evander's eyes flick my way, but then he turns back to the distant shore. I can't tell if it was a look of comprehension or not. Since Aurora doesn't correct me, I assume I've done well enough to speak in the language of spirits.

"Goddess, yes." Aurora continues to stare into the damp hull of the boat. "There have been some…complications surrounding her…"

"But she is still your best chance?"

Aurora nods.

"Then we will continue our quest." My voice drops to a whisper, even though it's clear Evander and Bardulf can't really understand me.

Aurora lifts her chin and looks to me. Her lips curve into a smile, the thin lines around her eyes and mouth revealing the edge of the weariness she works so hard to keep hidden. It is an expression of resignation. But still having just enough hope that she doesn't refuse me outright.

"Who is this?" Gruvun asks. A wave crests a little higher on my side of the boat. I swear I see foamy eyes that make my heart both light and as heavy as lead simultaneously.

"I'm Faelyn," I introduce myself.

"A weaver witch? In these parts? How odd."

"A friend," Aurora corrects.

I share a smile with her.

"Look after her, 'friend.'" Gruvun has the last word, as the distant shore has neared.

A flickering light that was little more than a speck on the horizon has transformed into a bonfire. The land is flat, almost completely level with the sea. Defiant blades of grass poke through the thin strip of sand, almost at the water's edge. The boat crunches up against the sand of the bone-white shore.

Evander and Bardulf jump from the vessel. Aurora follows much more slowly, and with significantly more grace. I move as well, my hands quivering as I grip the wood and pull myself over slowly. Pins tingle down my legs from the awkward way I was sitting and the blistering wind as we sped across the sea.

"Thank you, Gruvun," I say to the small waves that lap against the shore, well behind where the boat was deposited.

The water rushes up, farther than the last, to soak my feet. I can hardly feel the chill, even though the leather of my boots is thin. It is not a good sign.

There's a small camp erected in the sand around the bonfire. Three simple wedge tents are set up at cardinal points, each a fair distance from the other on the empty beach. On the side of each of the tents, three vertical bars have been painted in red. The symbol's meaning is one I do not know.

"She will share my tent," Aurora declares, much to my relief.

But Evander has other intentions. "She is with me."

"Excuse me?" I blink, startled.

"Come," he snaps, and starts off toward the tent, farthest to the right.

"I am not comfortable with this." I don't move, instead widening my stance as though I'm bracing myself.

Pivoting on his heel, Evander storms back in my direction and halts just short of our chests touching. This close, I can see every shade of silver in his mercury eyes. He fixes me with a penetrating glare—the look of a predator, as unyielding as his corded muscle. Yet, despite oozing intensity, there's an absence of malice around him. Oddly…I don't feel threatened. If anything, this all feels performative. Yet, I do not know who the performance is for.

"You will not be comfortable with much of anything if your wounds aren't attended to," he says in one of the lowest voices I've ever heard. Words reserved only for me.

"I'm fine," I insist.

"Don't lie to me." He leans forward, inhaling deeply. "I can smell how much blood you lost; you're beginning to stink a lot like death."

"Telling a lady she stinks. You really know all the right things to say, don't you?" I fold my arms, ignoring the pain in my shoulders and just how right he is.

"Sarcastic remarks aren't going to mend your injuries."

"I can look after myself."

"Ah, yes, because a witch from the Natural World knows *so much* about Midscape." His tone grows thin with annoyance.

"I'm quite resourceful."

"I'm sure you are." Oddly, the agreement sounds sincere. "But you will find no horsetail or rose here to stave the bleeding. No willow, elm, or chamomile." He leans slightly more forward. "You might be able to summon your marigold spirit, but will that be enough?" Before I can answer, his eyes flick over to Aurora and then back to me with a knowing glint. "And think of what you're risking on her behalf by allowing your strength to be sapped like this—you could be making her more vulnerable to illness, or death, even."

My hands ball fists of my cloak. I am a witch of the wood. I am powerful and can see to my own wounds without help from this manipulative cur.

But, sometimes, true power is knowing when to accept help, Grandma's voice reminds me from the Beyond.

I hold in a sigh and relax my fingers. I could take care of myself. I know I could. But it would take longer and be less effective than any care he can give, more time than what I suspect I have. Moreover, if I show them too much of what I'm capable of, they might begin to watch me closer, realizing I'm a threat.

Lie low. Wait. Bide my time.

There's no way I will be able to escape with Aurora tonight if I am exhausted from blood loss. The cold driving me to shivers and numbness isn't just from the weather and shock of all I've been through tonight. I know it's not. Just as I know that these men would force treatment upon me, after a time. Not for my sake, but Aurora's. I am their prisoner, now, as much as she is. And we are both seen as possessions of the wolf king.

Gather my strength. Then escape.

"All right," I relent. "I would appreciate your assistance."

"Good." Evander leans away with a smug smirk. The man thinks he's beaten me. He's probably imagining that I'll fall right into line. He has another thing coming.

Evander starts for his tent and I am right behind him. Ignoring the pain and keeping my head tall as I willingly walk into the wolf's den.

eight

THE INSIDE OF THE TENT IS AS SPARSE AS I EXPECTED. There's a bedroll off to one side, a decently sized rucksack settled on some canvas and leathers at its foot. It's clearly a traveler's tent, designed for packing light and moving fast.

"Sit." Evander crouches over the pack and begins to rummage through it.

I oblige him, sitting off to the side by the entrance. I can see, through the flaps, Aurora and Bardulf exchanging some tense words, but I can't make out what those are from here. The way they're speaking, though, has my hair standing on end. There's something about that man that I just don't trust. Even more so than Evander. I suspect the reason is because Aurora always speaks to Evander with annoyance, agitation, disheartenment… but never with true animosity or hostility. Not with fear. Bardulf is a different story.

"Here." Evander retrieves a small bottle, following some rummaging around in his bag. He pulls out the stopper and hands it to me. "Drink this."

"What is it?" I sniff, trying to discern the ingredients in the tonic.

"Not poison. I'm not going to kill you when you have Aurora's magic within you." He's back to rummaging.

"The paragon of kindness, aren't you? Saving me, healing me, only so that your wolf king can do as he likes with me and Aurora once you deliver us to him." I give the liquid a swirl, peering into the bottle. It doesn't seem out of the ordinary, so far as I can tell. "I am nothing more than a prisoner to you."

"I could show you how we lykin treat our prisoners, if you'd like. Though I will assure you, it is far more unkind than the decency humans usually give." He shoots me a glare. "At least, this way, you will be of sound mind and body to beg for the wolf king's mercy."

"I do not beg."

"That's what they all say before they are under his claws." Evander's gaze drifts back to the bag, though his hands don't move. His shoulders hunch slightly and I see the top edges of his scars over one shoulder. Were they given to him by the wolf king himself? The way Evander speaks has me suspecting it.

"What will he do to me when we get to him?" I dare to ask, my voice little more than a soft whisper as I take a small, tentative sip of the concoction he gave me. The medicinal herbs—and possibly anything unsavory—are buried underneath a strong minty taste. Overall, not unpleasant, but I wish I could pick out the individual ingredients. It'd certainly make me feel more reassured.

But my throat doesn't burn, I don't grow dizzy. It seems he's spoken the truth, and I take another drink, deeper this time, and allow a warming sensation to seep into my bones. I feel stronger by the second—a powerful brew, indeed.

Evander settles away from his pack, sitting on his bedroll. A small, wooden canister rests within his slack grasp, yet his focus is elsewhere—on me. In the dimly lit tent, his eyes pierce the shadows that cling to him. They burn with countless, unsaid emotions, too complex for me to decipher.

It has been years since a man—since any soul—has regarded me so intently. Such fervor. Even though it ignites discomfort within me to feel so bored into, I cannot tear my gaze away. There's an unspoken invitation, a silent plea for understanding. It's as if he's waiting, or perhaps anticipating my next move…or waiting for me to come to my own conclusion about my question. I find I can think of little beyond how thick my breath feels.

"A witch of your age should know what the moon spirit means to the lykin," he says, finally.

"The moon spirit gives the lykin powers, enhancing them, allowing lykin to take their shapes at any point in her cycle, so long as her light is in the sky. That is to say, save for the new moon." It strikes me that these men, and their wolfish forms that I've seen, are currently at their weakest. What will they be capable of when the full moon comes?

"That and more." Evander bends his legs, his black trousers stretching as he tucks his knees against his elbows. Even though the stance has him pulling in his legs, he somehow seems to take up more space. There's an ominous aura that surrounds him, filling the tent. "Long ago, our ancestors made a blood pact with the great wolf spirit of the sacred woods of Den. With this power flowing through our veins, we could take on the shapes of his kin. But the transformation was hard on our bodies and could only be done when the moon was full and our magics were at their strongest.

"The alpha of a pack—a man who came to be known to all lykin as Bewulf the Uniter—decided to solve this problem for all our brethren. He went on a great journey and sought out the spirit of the moon to make a pact with her. That was all he'd intended." Evander's voice softens and his eyes drift to the narrow slit between the flaps of the tent's opening. Aurora and Bardulf are both gone—retreated into their individual abodes, I hope. Evander's attention focuses on the middle tent of the three, barely visible from where he sits. "Aurora and Bewulf fell in love. Aurora gave everything to be with the man who had won her heart. To live as close to a mortal life as she could with him. She asked the old gods for this boon and they granted it by way of splitting her power, rendering her mortal—more or less. The rest of her power was placed in a ring, one that she presented to her lover. So deep were her affections that she put her life in his hands."

I stare into the narrow opening of the bottle I still hold, peering into the depths of the reddish liquid within. It's a small amount of tonic… but it feels deep enough to swallow me whole. To drown in. I hear Aurora's story, but the visions in my mind's eye are not of her.

They're of me, years ago…

I'm sixteen and in my loft. I gather a stretch of red thread I carefully dyed myself, a white and red candle, a few other ritual items. Heart fluttering with excitement and anticipation. Tonight is the night I'm supposed to swear myself to another before the old gods. My feet don't make a sound, as silent as the door behind me. I am a night lark that soars across the grasses and into the forest, to the great redwood tree.

I had been ready to give myself wholly that night. Everything I had. Everything I would be…for a child's love. Nothing real, in the grand scheme of things. Probably for the best it didn't work out. I can see that now. Yet, the pain is real. The pain I felt then and have tried to ignore ever since.

Liam never showing that night is the hardest blessing that I was ever given.

"Aurora lived with the first wolf king until the end of his mortal days," Evander continues, oblivious to my pain. "After he died, she was going to take the ring and make the journey to return to the old gods that live among the primordial waters of the siren. She'd ask them to restore her power, granting her freedom from her human body to return to her place as a spirit. But she was not allowed to leave."

"Your people trapped her." Even though I knew this truth already, it is no easier to hear. Especially given the scale of time of which Evander is speaking. The first wolf king would've been thousands of years ago…

Evander nods. His expression is hard and grim. He seems to gain no pleasure from these dark truths of his people's history. Perhaps he has more of a heart than I first suspected.

"The next alpha decreed that Aurora would never set foot anywhere beyond the Lykin Plains on Midscape so that she 'could not abandon her oath to our people.' As long as she is on our land, she is bound to the vows she made to Bewulf. She tried to run for our borders, many times, but there have always been too many patrols for her to make it out of the wolf king's magical reach and to the siren," he continues.

So she came to the Natural World, instead, I realize. She fled to the one place that they probably did not have patrols. The one place that a magical spirit would never be expected to go: a land void of inherent magic.

"All this began a push and pull of power among the lykin. Aurora has been traded from king to king with a ring for thousands of years. Sometimes willingly, sometimes not. To have the ring of the moon spirit is to be considered ordained as our natural leader. To hold the ring is to hold the power."

"She is not something to be traded and used," I object, louder than

I intended, but my emotions are running hot on her behalf. I clutch the little bottle with white knuckles. "She's a noble spirit, one of the most ancient to walk among us."

"Are we to let her go and give up the power she offers our kind? Even now, without the ring in the possession of a lykin, our powers are beginning to wane to what they once were."

"That is your natural state!"

"Is it? For our ability to take our wolf forms only came about when we swore a blood bond to the ancient wolf spirit." He arches his brows. "Or should we revoke that, too? Truly return to what is 'natural?'"

"That depends, are you holding that wolf spirit captive for the sake of your transformations?"

"It is free to come and go," he reluctantly admits.

"As it should be." There is nothing but bitterness in my words. "The brutality you show spirits is truly breathtaking."

"I—" Evander stops his objection with a shake of his head. When he returns his attention to me, a thin, crescent smile arcs across his lips. His words are pure malice and the jar quivers in his hands from his grip. "You're right. We are a brutal people. Aurora's suffering is but one page in a long tome of my kind's viciousness. Alphas of packs have unflinchingly killed boys and girls that might have been a challenge to them. Our grasses are watered with the blood of those who lost age-old battles for supremacy. Entire packs were wiped out by men and women in search of one thing—the only thing that will give you the respect and authority over every lykin that breathes: Aurora's bond."

I look out to her tent, too disgusted to settle my eyes upon Evander for a moment longer. I was convinced well before this that I had to do all I could for Aurora. But that dedication has been hammered upon my heart.

"Well, there is no ring anymore. So your kind will have to figure out what to do without it."

He chuckles so deeply his voice cracks slightly. His words are gravel when he says, "There is no ring, but her power still lives."

"I don't know how to give it up, and even if I did, I wouldn't."

"What makes you think you're going to have a choice?" He arches his brows. "All King Conri wants is to control Aurora's power and have her at his side to show off his legitimacy to any who would doubt him. He won't care about you, just the power within you."

Warmth had just been returning to my body when a fresh chill runs through my veins. I look back to Evander's shadowed face. He's dipped his chin slightly, his hair falling into his eyes.

"What is he going to do to me?" I return to my earlier question with new understanding.

"I cannot say. The alpha of the great pack can be an…unpredictable man." Evander contradicts his words by glancing away. It's only a flick of his eyes to the corner of the tent and back. But it's a tell I've seen in others before. He's lying.

"Guess what he'll do."

"You'll be able to ask him yourself, tomorrow." Evander hands me the cannister of salve. "Rub this on your wounds."

"What?" I take the small jar numbly. I hardly register the instruction.

"He waits for our return in a town not far from here. Pray that he is in a decent mood."

I stare at the jar, not moving. *Tomorrow.* Aurora and I must leave tonight if we want to have any chance of escaping. How do I get to her?

"My wounds are on my thighs," I say. "I would have to disrobe to apply this salve. I'm going to Aurora's tent to—" I've barely moved to leave when Evander catches my wrist.

"You think I'm going to let you go so you can try to escape with her?" He arches his brows. He's seen right through me. Not that my plan was particularly unpredictable. But I'd hoped…

"I wouldn't."

"Spare me." He rolls his eyes and pulls me toward him. I am between his knees. His legs are like a cage on either side of me. Evander's breath his hot on my neck as he growls. "You and Aurora are two pieces to the puzzle. She can't leave without you…nor you without her. If you were to try, he would hunt you down, relentlessly. And I can't return to the wolf king without you both in hand if I want to keep my flesh on my bones."

My hands quiver, betraying my inner turmoil. Evander's fingers glide over mine, rough and warm. Finding comfort in their steadiness feels like a betrayal. His fingertips are thick with calluses, rough, and as much a testament to a harsh life as the scars on his back.

This close, I'm drawn to the binding encircling his wrist. The ornament captivates me. Strips of black leather have been wrapped around an under band. Intricate black stitching is nearly lost amid all the shadows. The pattern, though hardly perceptible in the dim light, almost looks like the stitching of a weaver witch.

"Now, Faelyn, you will apply the salve"—his hands move mine, pulling off the wooden lid to the jar—"and then we will go to sleep."

Evander gently relinquishes my hands, only to find placement on either side of my ribs. I cannot help a soft yelp of surprise. With tender care I didn't suspect him to possess, he maneuvers me toward the back of the tent and then moves behind me, turning to face the entrance.

He's offering me privacy, I realize with surprise. I'd been expecting that his hands would follow mine as they slipped under the waistband of my trousers, then beneath my shirt. Seeking to exploit the movements. To show me just how vulnerable I was to him in my current predicament.

But he refrained. While I'm grateful for it, I'm not about to laud him for exhibiting the bare minimum of decency. Especially not when doing so has helped keep his groin from being crushed under my elbow or heel. If he thinks I won't fight through fear then he's in for a rude awakening.

Even with our backs to each other, my heart races, pounding against my ribs as I place my satchels in the corner and slowly undo the ties at the top of my trousers. Evander remains as still as a statue. Yet, without looking, without him moving, I can feel him there. The only other time I have been so acutely aware of a man's breathing was moments before Liam's lips first met mine.

I scoop the salve and slip my hand under the band of my trousers, reaching for the torn flesh of my thighs. There must have been something in the tonic to numb the pain, because pressing the salve into the ravaged skin isn't nearly as agonizing as it should have been. I finish one thigh, then move on to the next.

"I'm not going to hurt you." Evander says it so softly that I think I imagine it.

"What?" I ask, hoping I did.

"I can hear how fast your heart is beating… Faelyn, I won't hurt you."

"What makes you think I will ever be able to trust you?" My hands move to the wounds on my shoulders, exposing my stomach and lower chest in the process.

"Nothing." He chuckles softly. The sound lacks all joy; it's fueled by bitterness. "Nor should you."

"Contradicting yourself isn't exactly inspiring confidence." I finish up, wiping the remaining salve on my trousers before lacing them back up. "I'm done."

"It isn't?" Evander turns at the same time as I do, our eyes meeting once more. "Are you certain? Because your heart slowed."

"It slowed because my pants were done up again. Don't flatter yourself."

"Are you saying taking off your pants around me makes your heart race?" There's the bare minimum of a smirk.

I hand him the salve with a slight narrowing of my eyes, not dignifying that with a response. "I should rest."

"You should." He returns the jar to his pack and then moves to the side of the tent without the bedroll at the same time as me. We nearly bump into each other. "Take the bedroll," he says as I glare up at him. We're so close that the wavy strands of his hair nearly brush against my forehead.

"I'm going to sleep with Aurora."

"What part of 'I'm not letting you out of my sight' did you not understand?" Evander tilts his head to the side. His hair does touch me with the motion and it's so brief that I fight a shiver.

"You can't honestly expect me to sleep here."

"Take the bedroll," he repeats. "I'll take the ground."

"How kind," I sneer.

"I try, just for you." He mocks me with a smile.

I roll my eyes and shift to the bedroll. I do need to keep my strength, and arguing isn't going to get us anywhere.

"You're not going to lull me into a false sense of security," I caution. "You told me what your people are capable of."

"Good that you remember. It'd be even more dangerous if you forgot. Your caution might be the only thing that keeps you alive here in Midscape." He settles on the ground next to the bedroll. I hope it's full of spiky shells and rocks. I hope the sand chafes and grinds and gets in his ears. "Other than me."

"You're keeping me alive?" I snort softly in disbelief as I lay down. The moment I'm horizontal, exhaustion hits me all at once. My lids are immediately heavy.

"Yes, Faelyn, I am," he insists softly.

"For your king." As I tuck farther into the bedroll, I'm enveloped by his scent—a blend of salt, musk, and windswept meadows that is somehow both achingly familiar and, yet, like nothing I have ever smelled before.

Evander whispers something else, but I don't hear it. Sleep is already too heavy upon me. The edges of dreams of a dark wolf bounding gracefully through open fields, unbridled and free, begin to fill my mind. The vivid image stirs within me a vague sense of longing for something long, long gone. Despite myself, I can't help but wonder what to make of the man who is both captor and, if he is to be believed, an unlikely ally.

nine

My stomach is trying to eat itself. It growls louder than a lykin and I wake in a ball. As I open my eyes, I meet another set that I have only just begun to familiarize myself with.

Evander has a slight smirk on his face. His attention darts to my stomach. I sit quickly and narrow my eyes at him.

"Hungry?" He stretches languidly.

"Obviously."

Evander sniffs. "It smells like Aurora or Bardulf has already begun taking care of the matter."

I mirror his action. There's a faint aroma of charred fish on the air.

"Let's hope it's Aurora." I retrieve my satchels from the corner of the tent, glancing into the bags to make sure all my rations are there.

"I didn't steal from you while you slept." Evander props his head on his knuckles, lounging.

"For your sake I hope not." I give him a sidelong glance.

"So feisty, even first thing in the morning. Where do you find the energy?" Evander snorts. "And you shouldn't hope it's Aurora. For being mortal—more or less—for thousands of years, you'd think she would've learned how to cook."

I slowly slide one strap over my shoulder, then the other. The way Evander speaks about her is almost fond…friendly. It's juxtaposed uncomfortably with the image I first had of him, jeering at a tied-up Aurora.

"What is your relationship with Aurora?" I dare to ask, trying to sound as nonchalant as possible.

"She's the moon spirit, I'm a knight of the wolf king, I keep her safe," he says simply, placidly. The answer sounds practiced and void of sincerity. "I don't covet her, if that's what you're getting at."

"No? You wouldn't want to claim her and be king?" The words are as bitter as ash in my mouth.

"I assure you, I've little interest in being the wolf king. It's not a role with longevity."

I turn to study him. I can't shake the feeling there's more that he's not saying. But I'm not going to pry. *Yet.*

Evander doesn't stop me as I leave the tent. But his eyes do follow me as I maneuver around him. He lies back, allowing me to half crawl over him to depart.

The moment I'm free of him, I fill my lungs to the brim, exhale tension from my shoulders, and cross to the bonfire. It burns as brightly as it did last night, which is even more impressive when I realize that there is no fuel for the fire—no wood or coal. It blazes in a divot of sand. I must've been in quite the state, indeed, to have missed the impressive aura of magic that surrounds the flame. Spirit magic, no doubt.

"Good morning, Faelyn." Aurora rounds the flame, handing me a fish on a skewer. "I asked Gruvun if he was willing to bring us some food and he obliged. If my stomach was growling, I knew yours would be, too."

"Thank you." I take the skewer. Evander was right, Aurora seems to use "burnt" as seasoning. But it's sustenance and allows the rations in my bag to last a little longer untouched. Giving us more supplies for when we do run. I tear into the crispy flesh of the fish to the white meat below, taking care to pick any larger bones out with my teeth, tongue, and fingers. "Bardulf?"

"Still sleeping, I believe." Aurora takes a bite of her fish as well. "Evander?"

"Awake, but apparently he likes to lounge." I glance over my shoulder and back at the tent. There's no sign of the man. "I thought you weren't an early riser?"

"I am when I want to have a word." Aurora's voice drops to a hush. "Was it all right last night?"

I'm returned to my exchange with Evander—the revelations of the first wolf king and Aurora. Her fate being intertwined in such a cruel way with the lykin originating from a good and pure emotion. The feeling of Evander pulling me to him whispers across my skin. His scorching heat. The overwhelming nature of his presence enveloping me, his rough hands cradling mine as he growled his words into my ear.

"He's a brute," I say quickly, before my face heats. "But he didn't do anything untoward." Not really? I'm still fighting shivers of the memory of him at my back. It's been far too long since I was last touched. There's no shame in admitting that it felt good, is there?

"Good." Aurora breathes a sigh of relief.

"He did tell me some of the lykin's history," I admit. "And yours."

She chews a moment, longer than necessary for fish. "Can't really have their history without mine, can you?"

"I admit to asking questions. My curiosity got the better of me... I'm sorry for prying into your past without you there. But..." I squeeze her shoulder and meet Aurora's dark eyes. "I would like to hear your story from you, whenever, if ever, you're willing to share with me. I am sure what you have to say is much more the truth of the matter than anything Evander would tell me."

"I will tell you whatever you desire to know." Even though she says that, her weighted tone and adverted eyes say otherwise.

"When you're ready," I reiterate. Aurora shrugs, as if that is a small matter. It is not, and I would have her know it. "You have endured too much and have had too much forced upon you. I will not be another person making demands for things that you're not ready to share, or do not wish to give."

She simply stares out across the strait. There's a numbness to her gaze, an unfocused quality of her eyes. Aurora steps away and takes another bite of her fish, saying nothing. I worry I've upset her. But even if I have...I've said nothing I don't believe to be true.

"Aurora."

She finally brings her attention back to me.

"I mean it," I say, as gently as possible. "All of it. Even what I told you back at the cottage." *I will do everything I can to free you.* I don't dare say those words aloud, instead keeping them in my heart. Hoping she can read them from my expression. Hoping that, somehow, she can feel them if nothing else.

The air between us is heavy and still. The night's chill is leaving thanks to whatever fire spirit they have called upon for the bonfire and the rising sun scaring away the cool dew. She opens her mouth to speak, but is interrupted by Bardulf emerging from his tent.

"And just what are you two doing? Scheming?" His voice is thick with sleep, still, and lacks its usual bite. But that doesn't mean the warning isn't there.

"Breakfast." Aurora finishes her fish with one large bite and tosses the wooden skewer into the bonfire. I follow her lead.

"And what about us?" Bardulf crosses with purpose. "Where are our fish?"

"In the sea?"

He grabs her elbow. "Well go get them for us."

"Let her go." I close the gap and grab his forearm, glaring up at the man.

"You. Let me. Go. Before my patience and kindness wears thin." He bares his teeth at me.

"I have no idea where this 'kindness' of which you speak has been." I narrow my eyes and don't move.

"You're breathing, aren't you?"

"Careful, the bar is so low you might trip."

Bardulf snaps at me, teeth slamming together so hard my own are stinging.

"All of you, let each other go." Evander is up. He throws his pack into the sand in front of him and begins to pull down his tent. "It's too early for this."

I keep my attention on Bardulf. "You first."

"You," he quips back.

Aurora rips her arm from Bardulf's grasp, which must've slackened while he was distracted. I release the lykin as soon as he no longer has his hand on her. I keep near Aurora as Bardulf goes to dismantle and roll up his own tent. Evander is already working on Aurora's. His tent has been condensed into a canvas bag identical to what he's stuffing Aurora's into.

"Are you all right?" I whisper to Aurora, hoping the flapping of canvas and Bardulf's unnecessary grunting with every movement distracts him and Evander from our conversation.

"I've endured worse." She gives me a tired smile. It doesn't offer me any comfort.

"Right, then." Evander slings the two canvas tent bags over his shoulders. "Faelyn, you'll be with me."

"For what, exactly?"

Rather than answering me, Evander shifts into his wolf form with a small hop. The tent bags and his personal pack vanish into the form along with his trousers. Bardulf follows his lead.

"We ride them," Aurora explains.

"I'm…sorry?" I look between her and the wolves.

"It's faster than walking." She starts for Bardulf.

"Would you like to—uh—*ride* Evander, instead?" I fight laughter at the absurdity of the question. Must my mind really venture to the most inappropriate of places?

Aurora bites her lower lip, holding back a chuckle. She must've known where my thoughts wandered. "He wants you on him." A snort escapes me. Her grin says the phrasing was on purpose. "Bardulf is fine with me. At least in this form they can't speak."

Bardulf's lips peel away from his teeth in a snarl. But he doesn't snap or change his form.

"Yes, that's much improved, indeed." I cross to Evander, who looks back at me from the corner of one large, silvery eye. I'm sure I'm imagining it…but I think I see amusement alight. I can't stop a slight smile. Though the expression falls from my face the moment I look to the wide swath of fur before me.

The inky blackness of Evander's coat mirrors a midnight sky on a moonless night—the same color as the wild tangles of his human hair. Unlike Bardulf's pelt, not a single streak of gray mars its dark expanse. My hands hover over the glossy fur, vaguely aware of Evander still watching me intently.

The gentle tickle of his soft pelt greets my palms as I finally make contact. It gives way to firm, unyielding muscle beneath. His ribs expand with a deep inhale. For some reason, a smile tugs wider at the corners of my lips.

"Are you all right?" Aurora is already perched on Bardulf's back, riding astride.

"Yes, sorry." When Evander eases his stomach to the ground, I take a fistful of fur and swing up awkwardly, ending up flat on my belly. One leg doesn't make it quite over. I shimmy, wriggling until it does and I'm astride as well. If I hurt Evander pulling on his fur to get into position, he makes no indication of it.

"You'll get used to it," Aurora manages to say through a giggle.

"I don't have much experience riding anything." I wriggle my hips, trying to settle into a comfortable position. It's odd to feel a living, breathing creature underneath me. One that isn't—now my cheeks are burning.

Luckily, Evander saves me from myself as he lurches forward and all I can do is hold on for dear life.

My hips are moving in one direction and my torso in an opposite one. I imagine I have all the grace of the fish I ate for breakfast after it was pulled ashore. When I try too hard to lean forward, I find I tip more side to side. Too far back and I'm off-balance constantly.

The world is a blur as I try to find the right combination of holding on tight enough that I don't lose my grip, while also being loose enough to move with Evander. As the initial panic of being tossed off subsides, I begin to pay attention to the ripple of his muscles. The strength that courses through his firm body. How every shift betrays his next movement.

My fingers sink into the fur by his neck. It's coarse and thick, giving me ample to hold onto. I begin to move my hips in time with what I predict his motions to be. One front foot before the other, back legs pulling in with almost a galloping motion, rear haunches rising and falling, one hip forward, then the next.

It's somewhere between running and leaping. Every step is a half jump—a push and pull. Each muscle pushing to give forward momentum.

The tall grasses of the expansive plains blur into an undulating, emerald sea. As I gradually adapt to riding on wolf-back, my senses are no longer consumed by keeping myself astride and I can drink in the breathtaking beauty of this new land. The horizon stretches unbroken, a pale blue dawn in serene harmony with the streaks of green and yellow that rush past. The expansive panorama renders me small. With every heartbeat, I'm swallowed by the untamed and hazy landscape.

A smile splits my lips. The wind whips my rusty hair against my face, teasing it out of the thick braid I pulled it into yesterday morning. Dawn has come in earnest as the sun breaks the distant, still horizon behind us and casts everything in a brief but sweetly honeyed glow. Even as the sun rises, it doesn't chase away the morning fog.

I unfurl one fist and shift my hold with the other. Tightening my legs to steady myself, I tip sideways and reach into the grasses, which are tall enough to brush Evander's stomach. If I were to stand, they'd almost be up to my waist. The blades tangle with my fingers, kissing my palm. Magic surges up my arms.

"Spirits of fields?" I ask. The grass shrinks away and I grab nothing but air. "Of grasses?"

The whole meadow suddenly ripples out from us in rings, like a stone thrown into a still pond. Suddenly the blades of grass thread through my fingers once more.

"Grasses, then!"

"Are you making friends?" Aurora calls over.

"Perhaps? If they would like to be my friends?"

Another ripple is my reply.

"Lovely to meet you…"

"Farah!" Aurora answers for the grasses. "Their name is Farah."

"Lovely to meet you, Farah!"

As if on command, the path ahead flattens. No longer does the flora smack at the faces of the wolves. Rather, the grasses and wildflowers weave themselves into a carpet that unfurls before us.

"They like you." Aurora smiles in my direction, though it doesn't quite reach her eyes.

The wonder I've felt turns sour with guilt. This is not a delight for her. It is not an exploration into a bold new world of magic—one that had only ever existed in storybooks.

This is a return to her prison. It is a place of pain. The one place she wanted to go anywhere but.

I will save you, I vow again.

As if she heard me, Aurora's eyes meet mine once more. They widen slightly. I give a slight nod. One she returns.

It takes a half day of streaking through sweeping plains before I see anything that resembles civilization in the distance. Large, six-sided tents are erected, rising into points at their tops, with small flags waving in the breeze. They are surrounded by smaller tents of all shapes and sizes—wedge tents like those Evander and Bardulf travel with, and larger ones with canopies that stretch out before them. They all have three crimson bands stretching up one of their sides.

Before we can get too close, three wolves rush out from the encampment. One is as black as Evander. The other is white, laced with silver. But the one in the center is the largest. It has an all-too-familiar set of fierce eyes that cause the day's warmth to flee the moment his gaze lands on me.

The one in the middle leads the charge. He leaps forward and lands as a man. Evander and Bardulf are beginning to slow also, and, with the world no longer reduced to a blur, I can make out his features.

He's a handsome man with lightly tanned skin. Tall. With long, dark, brown hair pulled back into a bun at the nape of his neck. Like Bardulf and Evander, he wears no shirt. His skin has been adorned with an intricate tattoo of a wolf's paw in the center of his chest. Around his brow is a circlet made of fangs, woven together by wrapped silver. It is a thorny crown that gives an uneasy edge to his overall appearance.

Evander and Bardulf come to a stop. Aurora slides down and I follow her lead. Luckily Evander doesn't change back to his human form immediately. The bones of my legs seem to have become jelly and I rely on his sturdiness to keep myself upright. As soon as I release him, the lykin takes a step and sheds his fur for skin.

"Aurora, what a relief it is to see you." Conri, king of the wolves, I can only assume, goes to her. He grabs her elbows and kisses both her cheeks, as though she is a long-lost friend returned.

The motion isn't returned by Aurora. If anything, she has gone completely rigid. She stares numbly, straight though the wolf king.

"You have no idea how much you worried me when you left like that." He wraps an arm around her shoulders and ushers her toward one of the two wolves that had run at his side. "Now, come, let's get you bathed and dressed properly."

Aurora digs in her heels. "I'm not going anywhere without Faelyn."

"Faelyn..." His attention swings to me. But Conri's arm is still around Aurora's shoulders in a possessive stance. "Yes, I had been intending to ask why my two best knights somehow thought it wise to bring a human to our lands."

"Not quite a human, a witch," I dare to correct him.

"Ah, so then we don't need to worry about the withering taking your life, as your body is already accustomed to, and linked with, the magic of this world. Good." The way he speaks, I don't think he actually believes that to be good. I don't think he cares about me at all. Which, oddly, might be preferable. But the longer he looks at me, the stiller he becomes. Comprehension lights up his expression. "You are the witch in the woods from that night…yes, I know that cape. You are the one who took my Aurora."

"I gave her shelter when she asked," I say curtly, pulling my cape around me tighter for strength.

He inhales deeply and exhales with a serpentine smile. "You know, this was all a misunderstanding. You thought Aurora needed help." *She did*, I want to scream. But I keep my mouth shut. "You looked after her, and now she is returned safely to me. I am feeling generous, this day. I think it is best for you to go back to your woods, little witch. Thank you for allowing me the option of hunting her, Evander, Bardulf. But I do not desire it. You may return her."

"My liege, there is more," Bardulf interjects.

"It can wait." Conri waves at Bardulf, as if the imposing man is little more than an annoyance. "Aurora, the ring. Now."

Her eyes turn toward me, and I can't ignore the fear that fills them. My throat goes thick and I swallow twice. I try to stand a little taller as Conri follows her stare. I'm not going to cower with a metaphorical tail between my legs.

"You." The wolf king closes the gap. This close, I can see the ring of black that lines his silvery eyes. He moves faster than I can react, his hand flying up underneath my chin. His fingers grab either side of my face tightly, forcing me to look up at him. "Do not try my patience, witch. I can be a generous man, but I am not without my limits. If you have the ring, give it to me now, and I will still allow you to return home with all your flesh intact."

"I destroyed the ring," Aurora declares, loudly. The two lykin still in wolf forms recoil back. Bardulf looks away in shame. Evander's expression is impossible to read. Though it is completely, and utterly, focused on me.

Conri's fingers go slack, but he doesn't quite release me. "You… *what?* Aurora, I don't think I heard you."

"I destroyed it," she says bluntly. "I went to a grove of one of the great redwood saplings—one that links to the redwood throne and all the way back to the Lifetree of the sirens, where the goddess of life resides. I begged for her to return my power and set me free."

The wolf king releases me, spins, and is upon Aurora in a blink. He grabs her shoulders, shaking her, growling, "You would dare to abandon your oath?"

Aurora ignores the mention of her "oath," instead saying, "I broke the ring on the wood of the redwood, but my powers didn't return to me. I doubt they could so long as I'm in this form—too much ancient magic for one mortal body to handle; only an old god could restore it properly. So the magic found a new home.

"My magic, my essence, lives in her now, Conri. So do take care not to tear her flesh from her bones. She's of far more value to both of us alive and well."

The king staggers back. He looks from person to person, as if searching for someone to have an answer. Expression shifting from shock, to rage, to numbness. Finally, his eyes land on me with an emotion that I can't quite make sense of.

The wind whispers through the grasses. Somehow, that solitary, quiet breeze reminds me of just how alone I truly am in this strange new world.

"Evander, take Aurora to her tent and tie her up. Ensure that she doesn't get away again." At the order, Evander shrugs his pack and tent bags from his shoulders. One of the other wolves comes to collect them, taking the straps between her teeth.

Aurora takes a step back. "No, I, Conri, please—"

Evander grabs Aurora, throwing her over his broad shoulder. She kicks and screams. My stomach churns.

"Don't. Please. Conri, I won't run," she pleads. "I swear it, so *please* don't tie me up."

Conri doesn't turn—his eyes are fixed on me.

"Bardulf, take the witch to my tent, bind her, too, and then summon my generals so we can decide what will be done with her."

ten

I WILL WEAR HOLES THROUGH THE SOLES OF MY SHOES IF I DON'T STOP PACING. But this nervous energy is relentless and unbearable, and it's not as if I have anything else I can do to relieve it.

As commanded, Bardulf took me to the tent of the wolf king and bound my wrists. Then, he tied me to the center tent post. I can spiral around it, winding my leash as tight as my nerves. But even when the rope has all its slack, I can't reach anything.

Conri's wickedness might be matched by his cleverness. He knew to have Bardulf remove my cloak and set it aside on the cot—out of my reach, but close enough to mock me. I am left in my simple, linen shirt. Lose-fitting and down to my upper thigh. It nearly covers the rips in my trousers from Bardulf's claws. My clothing is still streaked with blood. I realize my hair is likely a mess, too. Mud is caked by the roots from where I smeared it across my face to try and mask my scent when I first tried to save Aurora.

What a sight I must be.

Not that I care for appearances in general. Being regarded as an oddity at best, and a freak at worst, has trained me not to concern myself with the thoughts of others. I care even less around these lykin. All that matters to me is getting my cloak, my supplies, Aurora, and then getting as far from here as we can.

If these knots weren't so damn tight—old gods, Bardulf, did you seal them with paste?

I try everything I can think of, short of breaking my wrists, to free myself from the binding. I've lain on the canvas-covered ground, stretching out my toes after pulling off my shoe to see if I could grab my cape with my foot. When all that failed, I returned to pacing.

I've taken stock of everything here, several times over, looking for what might be used as a weapon against me. Or what I might be able to use as a weapon against them. Nothing stands out. Though, given that these creatures can grow fangs larger than my fingers, and claws the size of my hands, I don't know what good seeing no weapons does me. And it's not as if I have any real practice with combat. My strengths lie in my magic and summoning those powers depends on me getting my cloak.

Deflating to the ground, I heave a sigh and stare up at the heavy canvas of the tent. It's dim in here, even in daylight. My eyes fall to one of the candles on the lone table near the bed, unlit, in its holder.

An idea strikes me like lightning. I fish into my pocket and retrieve the tiny shards of brick and clay pot. Not all of my spirit links were stitched into my cloak. How had I not thought of this earlier?

Returning the pot shard to my pocket, I hold just the piece of brick and whisper, "Folost?" Nothing. I stand, moving as close as I'm able to the candle, focusing on it intently, willing it to ignite. "Folost, please, if you can—"

The candle sparks to flame. Two tiny eyes are barely discernible in the little flicker.

"Folost!" I keep my voice to a hush, hoping he can hear me. "Can you go find Aurora, please, and tell me if she's all right?"

One blink. I can't tell if the candle is too small a form for him to be able to speak, or if he just doesn't dare risk alerting anyone else to his presence. Either way, I choose to take it as a good sign when the candle extinguishes itself. He's going to find her. There must be some kind of candle or lantern in every tent—something for him to alight upon. And he can communicate with her wordlessly as I saw them do the first night.

I can't stop myself from pacing again as I wait. It seems to take forever, but is also only a moment. I rush to the end of my tether when the candle lights again.

"Is she…" I start my question and abandon it.

One blink.

I heave a sigh of relief. There are no shadows on the outside of the tent. I've heard movement and distant discussion this entire time, but nothing too close.

"Can you speak in this form?" I dare to whisper, keeping my voice as low as possible.

"Yes." The word is little more than the sound of candle flame flickering in the wind.

"Can you tell me where she is? Are you able to discern it from traveling to her?"

"She is—" The tent flap opens and Folost is snuffed on the breeze. Or he flees willingly. A small, thin trail of smoke is the only thing that betrays his presence, but it's gone in a blink with barely an aroma.

The wolf king doesn't seem to notice either. His eyes are solely on me. Fixed. Purposeful.

Evander is with him, hovering at the entrance with arms folded in a way that accentuates the bulge of his muscles. His stare is penetrating, filled with rage as he focuses solely on me through the shadows cast by his long bangs. The instinct to retreat nearly gets the better of me and I take a half step back. I did not think him fond of me, but given Aurora's lack of outright hostility, and after last night…I thought we had some kind of understanding. Right now, it looks as if he blames me for every ill to ever befall him.

I'm not sure who to focus on. The wolf king, who suddenly approaches me with open arms like a mother coming to console her child…or the knight, who, up until now, had been verging on decent toward me but now looks positively murderous.

"Faelyn, forgive me for this brutality." Conri begins to undo the bindings at my wrists. It's frustrating how easily he's able to unravel the knots with those strong hands of his. "You were quite the surprise following a tumultuous few weeks. First the howls of the Blood Moon, then denning down following, then Aurora…" Conri pauses; his face becomes a void, every muscle relaxing into a perfectly blank slate. His gaze softens, unfocuses. It is more unnerving than outright hate. Then, emotion and expression all comes rushing back with a smile that is too sweet for comfort. "And now you are here."

"What are you going to do with me?" I demand to know, not sure if I like his sudden fondness. No, I am sure. I don't like it at all.

"Come, I have a most exciting proclamation for all of us." Conri takes me by the hand as I am rubbing my wrists. His touch is cool and I find myself oddly aware of the placement of every finger against mine.

I dig in my heels. He tugs on my arm. I give a pointed look to my cape, still on the bed. "I won't leave without it."

"You do not need it here," he says smoothly. His voice has my shoulders relaxing despite the alarm I know I should feel. His hands run over them, as if he sees their slight slouch. Tingles shoot down my spine at the touch, making my body ease farther into him with his unspoken beckoning. "Now, relax, and come with me." His fingertips run down my arms to lace with mine once more. The hold is firm. "You will come with me, right?"

I find myself nodding, unable to break my gaze with his.

"Good." He escorts me out and, this time, my feet obey.

Evander follows in close step as we leave the tent.

I am caught off guard by the surreal nature of it all, accentuated by the blinding sun as my eyes adjust. Men halt their movements mid stir of pots. Women slowly stand, their sparring forgotten. Even children come to a dusty stop in their play, staring up at me being led with linked fingers by the king of the wolves. No, not me...*him*. They are all entranced by Conri. It is when their stares turn to me that the loving gaze is broken and twists into something that could be akin to mistrust, or even hate.

The only thing that I suspect keeps them from attacking me is Conri's fingers still wrapped around mine as he leads me to the center of camp. The bustling quiets to murmurs. Shuffling. We have gathered a crowd.

Behind me, Evander continues to exude a searing aura of tension. It clashes with the ease and safety I feel near Conri. There are times he takes an extra step and is so close that I can almost feel his breath down my neck. It summons sensations of last night, when he pulled me between his legs. The heat of all his muscles around me.

It has been years since I last sought out the bodily pleasure of a man. To engage in the most primal ritual of all. That is not to say I haven't had satisfaction—a woman learns how to care for herself and all her needs as she grows into independence. But my desire has always delighted in the feel of a strong body underneath me. Gripping me…

Am I really having these thoughts right now? I silently scold myself. I hadn't realized just how long it had been until I found myself in a pack of alarmingly handsome, shirtless men. Had I known this would be a problem, I would've satiated my needs during my time in town yesterday…

The lykin make a large circle in the center of the camp. I pull my focus back to what's important and scan for any indication of where Aurora might be, but I see nothing that would give her presence away. *What if they've removed her from this camp?* The thought is intrusive, but it is in line with what Evander mentioned last night: If Aurora and I are together, we can escape. But separated and we will always be stuck waiting for the other.

Aurora can't be freed without me and I won't abandon her.

Conri comes to a stop in the center of the circle formed by the wolves, still holding my hand. A hush falls over them. Without warning, the wolf king tips back his head and lets out a noise that is somewhere between a howl and a scream—a raw and primal sound that seems to call back to the first days when time was counted.

The other lykin join, letting out screams. Some change into their wolf forms, tipping up their chins to join the chorus.

They end abruptly and all eyes are back on me. I shift my weight from foot to foot, wishing I had my cape to draw around me. Or that I knew how I could use Aurora's magic within me to better protect myself, if that's even possible.

"Long ago, Bewulf the Uniter fell in love with the spirit of the moon. With her power, he brought together the squabbling packs for an era of peace. A time of triumph and domination by our ancestors in these misty plains. This time of unity and prosperity is what I have aspired to return us to as your king. One moon. One wolf."

Howling follows the statement. Some thump their fists against their chests. Others gnash their teeth with excitement.

"We have had our time of peace. Of living under one banner. But there has been something calling me. Drawing me toward a greatness yet unknown. I would see it in the stars and hear it in the whispers of the wind. But I did not know what it was…until she stood before me." Conri gestures toward me, still holding my hand.

I realize his grip has tightened some. He's preventing me from running. Not that I have anywhere to go. Surely he knows the threat Evander and Bardulf have both made to me.

"Like Bewulf the Uniter, I have been taken by a creature of astounding beauty. Whose meeting is one of unexpected serendipity and, now that she is before me, can only be described as my destiny. For hers is a kind vanishing from this world faster than our own. In her is the blood of a rare breed of human—those who had begun to master the dormant magic buried within them, gifted by the old gods but untapped."

Murmuring now. Women and men exchange confused and worried glances. Children are growing restless from the length of Conri's speech. Though no more restless than I am.

A creature of astounding beauty? Serendipity? What in the old gods' forgotten names is he talking about?

"In her is part of the moon spirit's power. I have little doubt it flowed into her because she is my destined mate. And, once I formalize our bond, we shall use our union to push our borders back into our ancestral lands. We shall have the ability to reclaim that which the humans have taken from us and, once more, our feet will run through the distant grasses across the Fade."

My ears are ringing. My heart is fluttering so fast that I can't seem to catch a full breath. One word…*mate*. Surely I cannot be comprehending it correctly. There is some meaning lost in culture of the lykin, or translation to the common tongue that I know.

"We shall return, far beyond the thickest mists of the plains, to the deep woods of Den. Come with me, my pack, my blood. Behold as I stand before the great wolf and forever bind us. For, once I make this human my bride and bind our bloodlines forevermore—we shall use her power to conquer the world beyond the Fade."

eleven

"No."

"Quiet," Conri hisses at me over the howling and cheering of the lykin.

I didn't realize I'd uttered the word. I thought it had been kept to my mind. My whole body is numb, I don't know if I could move if I tried, so I'm amazed my lips somehow managed to form a sound.

Conri still continues to hold me with white knuckles as he declares, "Break down your tents; we start our trek to Gualla this afternoon."

Most of the lykin jump to activity at his decree. But many are affixed to their spots. Never before have I had so many focused solely on me. Some bare their teeth as I pass. Others shift into their wolf shapes, hairs on end and muscles tense.

The announcement of our upcoming union is already an unpopular decision. Perhaps I can use the disdain of Conri's people to my advantage. I debate my next steps and best approaches the entire way back to Conri's tent. He releases me only to give me a light push inside.

"Leave us, Evander," Conri commands. The knight has remained diligently at our side. "Help the others ready to move. I don't want any delays."

Evander hovers in the entrance, his eyes darting from me, to Conri, and back again. He wears the same scowl as before.

Perhaps this loathing comes from the announcement Conri made. I wonder if the man loves his king or just thinks me unworthy.

"Yes, my king." Evander's nod is jerky and forced. It looks as if he has to expend a great deal of effort to force himself to leave.

"Evander is a good and loyal knight," Conri says with a note of approval. "I have a mind to appoint him as your sworn protector in all instances where I am kept from your side. He knows the world of the humans well, and the ways of witches. I think that would make you comfortable while you acclimate to your new home here in Midscape."

"Married?" I blurt, completely ignoring everything he said. "Mate?"

"Yes." Conri begins packing his things as though everything is perfectly normal. "I realize you must be stunned by the great honor I have bestowed upon you since you think yourself unworthy, no doubt. But I assure you that, with all the power you have to offer me, and Aurora's magic within you, you will be a fitting mate."

"I have no interest in being your mate," I say bluntly so there can be no misunderstanding. He pauses, mid packing. His back is still to me, and his shoulders tense slightly, drawing toward his ears. "Or your wife. Or being with you for any extended period at all in any way."

There's a long pause where the whole world seems to hold its breath, myself included. Then he begins packing again, hands moving before his mouth. When he speaks, his tone is placid, as though I've said nothing more than trivial notions.

"I had hoped you would find joy in the great honor that I am bestowing upon you." He hums. "Though, perhaps it can't be helped; you've still much to learn about our ways."

"I don't…" I can't say I don't want to learn. I'm genuinely curious about the lykin and all of Midscape. What I don't want to do is learn from the man who's kept Aurora hostage and seems to be trying to do the same to me. "I have other priorities."

"You will need to make me your priority now," he says, matter-of-fact.

"Excuse me?"

"Within you is half the magic of the moon spirit." He spins and stares down at me. "In you is the primordial power promised to my people—sworn to the rightful king of the wolves for centuries. Even if your human mind tells you that you do not love me, somewhere within you is Aurora's essence. *That* will love me, with all its might. And you will learn to follow its lead, in time."

"You honestly expect me to make nice to you so you can lead your pack to wage war on my homeland?" My voice rises slightly and I shake my head. If the wolf king marches through the Fade and into human towns and cities, what was all my effort maintaining the barriers for?

Though…Bardulf and Evander broke my barrier without issue. Perhaps it was all an illusion of safety from the start. Then again, Conri just said Evander has knowledge of witches, and he was the one to try and order the spirits Rhave and Gruvun. Maybe he's the man I really need to be careful of.

Danger lurks behind every silver eye here.

"Faelyn…"

Hearing my name from his lips stills me.

"The lykin are dying. Our lands grow more barren with every generation. Our numbers dwindle with every mating spring. We are a people without hope or future." Conri's eyes widen enough to fill with sorrow. The tension between my shoulders unknots some with unbidden sympathy. He looks…genuinely afraid. "We cannot push west or we will be crushed by the Elf King and his armies for extending beyond our borders. The mountains are well claimed by the vampir and fortified for centuries—it'd be a foolish effort to walk into the land of our mortal enemies. The lands of the Natural World are fertile, still. They were once our home; pack territories extended well beyond the current line of the Fade. We have as much of a claim to them as the humans do."

"The lykin struck a deal with the witches not to come into the lands of the human." A deal that, knowing they lost territory, makes so much more sense now.

"Not quite. The witches gained access to spirits and magic from Midscape by allowing the Fade to be opened from time to time, and the lykin gained a rich hunting ground of the woods nearest the Fade." It strikes me that not once have I ever questioned why the lykin were given the run of the woods when the witches, probably, could have just as easily held them at the Fade. "Can't you see? Your people and mine…we were meant to work together. Opening the Fade to us would help you, too. It would further restore magic to the Natural World, emboldening witches to reclaim their birthright, also."

"Witches work to protect our human brethren. We wouldn't sacrifice them for our own power." I regard him skeptically.

"Who is asking you to?" The corner of his mouth quirks up slightly. Amusement breaks through his kingly composure. "I never said anything of conquest."

"But…" I think back, repeating all he said in my mind. I suppose… he didn't. Not explicitly. I just thought it was so clear…

"I won't lie to you, Faelyn. There will be those who would ask me to raze human settlements. Just as I'm sure there are humans that would seek to hunt us. But we can make our own path—guide them, teach them." His words are soft, nearly tender. They soothe over my worries, easing them into the recesses of my mind. He holds out a hand and, despite myself, I'm compelled to take it. Barely audibly, under his breath, he whispers, "That's it."

Conri takes a step closer still. I'm acutely aware of his lean, muscular form. The heat emanating from him envelopes me, stirring that need deep within me that I tried, desperately, to push away. I am intoxicated by the pull that slips over my shoulders like the weight of my cloak.

"Think of all you could do at my side, as my wife." He brings a hand to my cheek. It pushes around to the back of my neck, pulling at my hair, dragging my face up toward his to whisper his words across my cheeks. "What were your prospects before you came to me? To be a witch at the edge of town for the rest of your life? Think of all you can do now for your people…for yourself. You have the power of the spirit of the moon in you. Immense. Power that could make the very foundations of the world tremble should you dare to harness it."

He's pulled me nearly flush to him, without me entirely realizing when or how. The distance between us is so small that a single shudder that threatens to rip down my spine would have me quivering against him. His right fingers lace against mine, sliding. Gripping. His other hand is at the nape of my neck, tangled with my hair. It closes into a fist as well.

"Be my mate, willingly, Faelyn. Harness your power. Claim this destiny I have placed before you. Perhaps, one day, you and I shall rule as mighty as the Elf King and Human Queen…perhaps even more so."

His eyes drop to my mouth and mine mirror the motion, looking at his. His closely cropped beard accentuates the dusky pink of his full lips. They are inviting. Tempting.

"It's all right, Faelyn," he murmurs, mouth almost touching mine. "Give in to me."

"My liege." Evander bursts into the tent without warning.

My eyes dart over toward the knight. I can't move my head because Conri still grips my hair too tightly. His face hovers close to mine. Expectantly.

Evander's expression darkens as he takes in the scene before him. His chin dips, ever so slightly, and his eyes are shadowed by the veil of his unruly bangs. His focus shifts from Conri's hand, entwined with my hair, to the perilous proximity of our mouths. Evander's smoldering intensity heightens to near ferocity in the silver of his eyes, like a thunderstorm on a distant horizon.

"A moment, Evander," Conri declares. I can't tell if he's oblivious to his knight's brewing rage or not by tone alone. When my attention shifts back to him, I'm once more enthralled by the still calm of his silver eyes, darkened by an almost black ring around the outer edge. "Kiss me, my future queen."

"What?" I breathe. The same squirming need I felt earlier is back in force. I've practically forgotten Evander is there at all.

"Kiss me." Those two words hold a power unlike any I've known before. For the command almost has me moving instantly. He relaxes his grip enough that I could move toward him. But I don't. I tremble with the exertion of not doing so, feeling my body brush against his in delightful and forbidden ways. I'm fighting with all my might not to give in to my basest of needs.

"It's all right," he whispers soothingly. "You can give in here. We lykin revel in our urges, our natural desires. Try it. Taste this life and you might find you like the flavor. Taste me, and you will never want anything else."

His right hand slides across my hip, grabbing right above my rear and pulling me flush against him. I feel his hard length as he presses it into me. There is no shame to his desire. He wants me to know the truth to his words with his deeds.

Something tells me that, were I to ask him to take me, he would strip me bare here and now and do it with Evander watching—with the whole pack watching—and not feel a second of shame.

A distant part of me that's somewhere far beyond my flesh is disgusted by my excitement. That woman who is in control of her thoughts and emotions screams from the corners of my mind for me to get a hold of myself. But is she right? I don't know anymore. The longer I stare into his eyes, the less sure I am of anything but the man in front of me.

"Kiss me," Conri says again, sultry and smooth.

And I do.

Our lips collide and his hips roll against mine. His thumb finds purchase at the hinge of my jaw, gently urging it to part and make way for his tongue. His mouth tastes uniquely of him—like dark fruit, ripe with passion, sour yet sweet.

I yearn for more. It feels as if it's been an eternity since I last felt a body moving against mine. Since I could last put to rest all thoughts and worries with the closing of my eyes. Allowing the strong hands of a man to ease away all of life's heaviness.

Without warning, he pulls away with a smug look of triumph. Conri cocks his head to the side slightly, eyes dragging from my lips—wet with his saliva—to meet my gaze. He does not have heavy lids, or a lusty stare. His expression is sharp.

He looks at me as little more than a conquest and I am instantly sobered by it.

"Excellent, you will be a good girl for me, won't you?" He runs a finger down my cheek as he releases my rear. "No trouble as we make our way to Gualla and the ancient wood beyond?"

"I..." I croak. Unable to find words. Everything is catching up to me with horrible clarity.

"No, no, you will be no trouble. You will be my good girl now, tomorrow, and..." He leans forward to whisper in my ear. "...in weeks from now when we arrive at the old wood and I bend you over in front of all my pack to take you beneath the moon, filling your belly with my heirs."

The words are so shocking that I can't react to them before he leaves—murmuring something to Evander and clasping him on the shoulder. I'm left breathless. Stunned. Horrified.

Utterly disgusted with myself.

Am I that desperate? That pathetic? It doesn't matter how sweet his tongue is, that man is Aurora's captor. And I just willingly handed myself to him.

twelve

My eyes finally meet Evander's. He has yet to move. He continues to stare at me as my finger drags across my still-wet lips, feeling the proof of what I've done. His eyes are still burning with hate. Well, now we share that emotion. Self-loathing fills me.

"And here I thought that you were a noble witch of character, powerful enough to resist his charm," he growls.

"Excuse me?"

Evander stalks over, his muscles rippling with tension. Fists clenched. He looms over me. "You…"

"Me? What?" I gather myself and stand a little taller. The only judgment I will accept is my own, and Aurora's. I'm certainly not giving that power to this brutish lykin.

"Did you like the way his tongue in your mouth felt? Did it set you ablaze the way you'd hoped it would?"

"What does it matter to you?" I snap. I continue before he can get in another word, "I've spent my whole life with people looking at me sideways—for good or ill. With people judging me for all I did and did not do. And you know what? Their assessments of me have made no difference. So what makes you think I will expend any effort to care about yours?"

He folds his arms and cocks his head back, pulling away slightly. "What about Aurora? I thought you cared about her."

The words strike me straight through the chest, as sure and true as a hunter's arrow. "My relationship with Aurora is between her and I alone. Stay out of it."

"Fine. If you wish. Then I won't concern myself with bringing you to her." He shrugs. "She would probably be heartbroken, anyway, to find out what you really are."

I still have several choice words for Evander. But there's only one thing he said that I choose to focus on. "You can take me to her? She's still here?"

"Of course she is. Conri wouldn't allow her out of his sight for long. Lest she try to run away again…or someone tries to steal her."

"Take me to her."

"Why should I?" Evander turns and begins to shove some of Conri's things into the rucksack the wolf king had started packing earlier.

"Because you would be escorting me as a knight, and that's better than being a king's butler." I take the opportunity to snatch my cloak off the bed, throwing it over my shoulders. Evander doesn't stop me.

"Better a butler than a whore." He goes to put the pack by the entrance. I move in front of him and stop him. "Move."

"No."

He opens his mouth to speak.

I cut him off. "Apologize."

"For—" Evander stops himself before he can say "what." He continues to glare down at me.

I glare back, unmoving. Unflinching. I honestly expect him to push past me, to repeat his offensive words, or defend what he said. But Evander sinks back slightly, glancing away.

His pale silver eyes are drawn back when he finally says, "That was uncalled for. My apologies."

Shock has my lips parting slightly. He actually apologized. I hastily try and recover, as if I was expecting him to heed my demand all along.

"You're forgiven. I'm sure your king deciding to marry a human, without warning, is a bit upsetting to you. It's understandable that you'd still be processing this turn of events."

A deep, rasping noise emits from him. At first I think he's weeping. But then he shakes his head and I see the almost crazed grin spanning his cheeks.

Evander takes a step closer, voice dropping with his chin as he levels his eyes with mine, a dangerous glint flashing in their stormy depths. "He might be the wolf king. But he is not—and will never be—my king. Not after what I have seen him do. Not after what he has forced my hand to do on his behalf."

My lips part slightly. Then why was Evander so angry? And what does this mean if he's my sworn knight by a king he so clearly does not respect? This man is like a maze. Every time I think I'm on the right path to understanding him, I have to backtrack and start all over again.

"Now, let's get you to Aurora before the pack moves." He starts out of the tent. I let out a noise of frustration and hastily follow.

The lykin packing up their camp mirrors my own thoughts—disorganized and chaotic. I'm in a daze the entire way through to the far edge, where I see Bardulf taking Aurora from a tent similar to Conri's.

My feet move on their own at the sight of her, picking up speed until I rush past Evander in a sprint. Neither knight stops me. I throw my arms around Aurora's shoulders. "Thank goodness you're all right."

She squeezes me in return. "They wouldn't hurt me; they need me too much to do that."

"I was still worried."

"I know, I saw Folost," she whispers before releasing me. Aurora wears a warm expression and that only makes me feel more guilty for my actions.

"I need to speak with you." I glance over my shoulder. Evander continues to hover, making no effort to hide his wordless judgment. Fortunately, Bardulf seems to have gone off elsewhere. I've had enough of him for a lifetime.

"I figured as much. It's why I sent Evander to find a way to get you for me."

"You sent him?" I link arms with Aurora, guiding us a few steps away from Evander and the bustle of camp being torn down. The knight sets to working on her tent.

"I knew he'd find a way to get to you. Conri trusts him, the fool." Aurora ducks her head slightly as she speaks, keeping her voice down. Evander had adamantly said that Conri was not his king.

"And do you trust him?" I ask.

She takes another step away from him and the camp. I've no doubt we're reaching the end of our invisible leash.

"Evander is...complicated," she murmurs.

There are so many meanings that can be wrapped up in that word. "Do you care for him?"

"Old gods, no." She laughs lightly, gaining amusement from the mere notion. "I've never loved another since my Bewulf, and I never will. I am far too old now to seek romantic companionship, especially not with a mortal." Her eyes shine with bittersweet sorrow.

"Then, he's a friend?"

"He's not an enemy." Hardly an endorsement.

"Even though he was the one who came and forced you back?" I shake my head, trying to reconcile what she's saying with what I saw. "He tied you up. He—"

"If not him, then it would've been Bardulf, who is far rougher. If not either of them, then someone else who's worse still." Aurora shakes her head. "The king has no shortage of knights on his retainer. But a grave shortage of halfway decent ones."

"But he—"

"Evander is a dog on a leash attached to an unkind collar," Aurora interrupts me. "He is a harsh man, certainly. But that is because it is how he has been made. The world has been cruel to him and returning that cruelty is the only way he knows how to survive."

"That is not an excuse," I remind her.

"But it is an explanation," she says gently. "Which can help us understand him. Evander is the very last of an ancient pack, one that was among the few who stood against Conri's father."

"How is he alive, then?" If he is part of such a lineage, I would've thought Conri would've made an example of him.

"I do not know the story of his past earlier than when he was brought before Conri six years ago...but he came to the alpha's pack with an astounding knowledge of spirits. He was able to find and commune with them. His pack had taught him old knowledge previously thought lost to the lykin—knowledge gained through study with your ancestors, I might add." There's a note of pride at the end, one I allow myself to briefly indulge in.

"And that knowledge was how you became close to him," I realize.

She nods. "Conri assigned him as my knight. He was responsible for keeping me safe."

"Then, how did you escape?"

Aurora locks eyes with mine and repeats, "He was responsible for keeping me safe."

It dawns on me, what she's saying without outright explaining. Evander took his duty to the spirits—to her—to heart. He sought to keep her safe and that meant setting her free.

"But, because of that…I escaped on his watch. Had Evander not been successful in retrieving me and making good on his folly, he probably would've been put to death."

I look back over my shoulder to where Evander continues to help break down her tent. He glances our way from time to time with that glower that never seems to fade. A thin stubble shades his chin today, giving his whole face an even more severe expression.

He is brutish, that much is certain. *Imposing and rude* are other words that come to mind. But I trust Aurora—she knows this world more than I do. And if he is the best we have for an ally…

"Faelyn, were it not for him I would not have been able to escape at all." She touches my elbow, summoning my attention back to her. "He never explained it, or said so, but I am certain he intentionally created the opening I needed to flee."

"So he could claim you for his own."

"If that were his intent, he would've pursued me the moment I had the ring and left Conri's watchful eye." Aurora pauses, staring out over the plains. "The moon only witnesses half the day. There are things that are invisible to even my sight. I do not know what Evander's motivations are and they don't always make sense to me. But I do believe he is a decent man in his heart. I've seen enough bad ones to know the good. His exterior has merely been twisted by the circumstances he's been given."

I sigh heavily and run a hand through my hair. It snags on tangles and I realize it is still knotted in my braid. I pull at the ribbon that ties off the end and begin to rake my fingers through. As if, by untangling my hair, I could untangle my thoughts. I desperately need a bath.

"Conri is going to try to marry me."

"What?" Aurora seems genuinely stunned. It's the first she's heard of it. I swallow thickly and nod. "If he can't possess the ring…he's going to try and own you." She grabs my shoulders, leaning forward to look me directly in the eyes. "You must leave. Get away, far, *far* from here."

"But you—"

"Don't worry about me, Faelyn. This has been my fate for centuries. It can be my fate for centuries more. I know how to endure." She wears a weary smile that doesn't quite reach her eyes. Her hands feel heavy on me. There is so much pain within her, so much hurt. I'm amazed she's not crushed into dust where she stands.

"I can't leave you," I say softly. "I won't." Aurora opens her mouth to speak but I cut her off. "Where would I go? Evander clearly knows whatever magic is needed to break through the thin barriers I put at the edge of the woods in my world. Even if he's a 'good man,' you said it yourself, he will hunt me down for Conri. He has no choice. He's not going to put either of us before himself."

I wait for Aurora to object, but she doesn't. How "good" can he be when he won't stand up for what's right?

"And it's not like I have anything to go back to…my family is all dead, save for me. My home is gone. And, clearly, I am not strong enough to keep the people of that world safe." I think of what Conri told me of his plans. Maybe he was sincere and has no genuine intention to bring his people to the Natural World, maybe it's just a ploy to keep me under his thumb and playing nicely. But the possibility of the lykin bringing violence to my home is enough to keep me here alongside everything else. "So no more of telling me to go. We leave together and I free you, or we stay. There are no separate futures for us now."

Her hands go limp, sliding down my arms until they fall to her sides, swaying slightly. "I should have never run."

I *shh* her. "I'm glad you did. Because, one way or another, I will find a way to help you."

"You are a good friend, Faelyn."

"I am not." My lips burn from where I kissed Conri. From what I still need to tell Aurora. "Conri… He… I…"

"What? What happened?" She knows something is amiss instantly and her concern makes it all so much worse.

"I kissed him," I admit, forcing the words.

Aurora jaw drops, then she closes it quickly and purses her lips. I can't stand to look at her. The shame is so great that I nearly step away to be sick.

"I should have warned you," she whispers finally. "This is my fault."

"What?" My head snaps back up. "No. I—"

"Conri is the wolf king," she says, low and fast. "He is the alpha of the pack, ruler of these lands, leader and protector of every creature that steps upon them...and one of his sole obligations is to see to the *longevity* of the pack." I think of him whispering how he will fill my belly with his heirs and my cheeks grow hot. "Part of the unique magic that comes with being the wolf king is ensuring his ability to do this."

"He has magic outside of your powers?" I ask, trying to keep my focus when the implication she's hinting at seems a bit outlandish.

"All the lykin have a unique power, just like all the other occupants of Midscape. They can commune with spirits and change into wolves, after all." Her mouth quirks into a slight smile as I give a slight nod of my head, acknowledging the obvious. "Their pact with the great wolf spirit of the old wood gave them some other abilities than just the gift of shape."

Grandmother always warned me of the lykins' keen senses, even in their human shapes.

"So his power is to...ensure the longevity of the pack?" I'm amazed I can ask the question when my mind is filled with words like mate, and filling my belly with—*stop, Faelyn*, I command myself.

"He is irresistible to mortal women because of a unique charm he possesses as the alpha." Aurora frowns, looking back at camp. Evander had mentioned Conri's "charm," too. I had thought it just a turn of phrase before. "I have seen proud women make fools of themselves in a desperate attempt for a moment in his bed."

"What can I do to protect myself from this 'charm?'" I ask.

"Your cape should help, some." No wonder Conri refused to allow me to have it earlier. The moment I had it back on, my head was notably clearer. "There's good protection woven in that fabric." Perhaps if I can get my grandmother's threads and dyes back from Evander, I could figure out some kind of spell to weave into the cape specifically to guard me from Conri. "Otherwise, it is a matter of allowing your head to be as clear as possible around him. The more excitable you are, the harder it will be for you to resist him."

“When you say ‘excitable’ you mean…” I can’t possibly have the right assumption. There’s no way she means what I think she does. But the way Aurora speaks leaves no room for doubt.

“Ensure you are satisfied, Faelyn, or you might give in and ask him to do it for you.”

thirteen

THIS IS WONDERFUL. *Absolutely perfect.* The most important thing for me to do right now is keep my wits about me and have me focus on anything other than carnal urges.

But I am astride Evander in his wolf form as he runs at Conri's right side. Even though I try, desperately, to focus on the breathtaking scenery unfolding before me as I had before, every bump and dip of Evander's spine hitting me right between the legs brings my mind right back to the thing I'm trying to ignore. I shift my positioning, which only makes things worse.

The whole pack runs behind us. We left the campsite a few hours ago and there's been nothing but misty, unbroken grassland since. I'm being taken farther into a vast unknown of Midscape—a land of magic. I should be focusing on deepening my powers, getting in tune with Aurora's within me, communing with spirits, studying the landscape to plan my escape.

Literally. Anything. Else.

But my mind continues to revert to wondering just how long it's been since I was last pleasured. I gather my cloak around me and grip Evander's fur tighter, trying to recall what I was told before we began to move.

We'll be at another pack's encampment by the end of the day. Conri is going to collect them on the journey to Gualla—the main city of the lykin, but that's not the place known as Den where Conri and I will wed. That means tonight, hopefully, I can find some time alone to satiate some of these urges… assuming Conri doesn't steal me away to his tent again immediately.

"Aurora," I say, loud enough that I trust Conri and Evander to both hear over the wind and thumping of the pack's paws against the ground. Conri was insistent that the moon spirit ride upon him. But I am kept expectedly close. "When we arrive at this other encampment, should I go to your tent so that you can commune with the powers of yours that are within me?"

She's confused for only a second. Comprehension lifts her brows. "Oh, yes, that would be important. Perhaps Evander can guard us from outside the tent during that time, as we must be alone for the magic to work."

Evander glances back, his large wolf head shifting with his run. Conri's attention is on us as well.

"I'm sure we will figure it out when we arrive," I say brightly. Not wanting to arouse too much suspicion by harping on the matter.

The grassy plains we run through are seemingly endless. An ocean of pale green, almost silver in the sunlight, shining through a thin layer of haze that perpetually hovers over. The tall grasses go on, and on, rolling slightly.

There are no trees, no shrubs, nothing. That makes the tall, unnatural structure in the distance stand out all the more. I squint through the fog, trying to make out what it is.

"Aurora—"

"It's a watchtower, left over from the days of feuding packs—every pack had one to mark their territory," she answers my question before I can ask. "In modern times, they're rarely used for more than anchors for the barriers and blessings on the land of the lykin."

My eyes follow it as we pass, until it vanishes once more into the fog. The next structure I see is the encampment. Like the tower, it appears as a dark dot on the horizon that grows into a grouping of tents and lykin.

The people are much the same as Conri's pack—as varied in appearance as humans are. But the tents are slightly different. Even though their construction is much the same, there are three red stripes on one side and two blue dots on the other.

I ask Aurora about the latter as we slow toward the center of the encampment. She explains a bit more on the history of the lykin—how every pack was once governed on their own, independent of all others. And how the packs that bent to the king were allowed to keep portions of their previous identities.

It reminds me of the townships in the Natural World. Each can govern themselves, to a point, but usually there are councils that rule over each region. I know there is one for where I am and, technically, its laws would rule over me. But I never gave them much heed. No lawmen would go all the way to the edge of the woods to ensure Grandma and I were heeding their arbitrary ways. The only others who lived remotely close to us were the huntsman and his son…and neither of them was going to turn us in. Not when Liam and I were…

The wolves come to a stop, blessedly jarring me from my thoughts. Aurora dismounts and I do the same. My legs are still stiff from the first day of riding on wolf-back, but I know better now how to manage myself on Evander to prevent too much stiffness. At least I don't feel like I'm about to tumble over on my way to the ground.

Most of the lykin change to their human forms, shrugging off their packs and handing them to others who approach to assist. It is convenient that all clothing and possessions on the lykin are held in some kind of stasis when they transform. It makes travel far easier than Aurora and I will face, whenever we run.

All the eyes of the pack whose camp we've entered remain on Conri, expectant. What I find truly fascinating is how their attention starts on me, then goes to him and sticks. I doubt they could look away if they tried; they're instantly enamored. His mere essence has them fixated on him even when the oddity of a human witch is in their midst.

I pull my cape tighter around me, even though its protection is the same regardless of how open or closed it is—all that matters is that it's on my shoulders.

Yet, even with it, I am drawn to him just like the rest of them. Even knowing of his magic charm and wanting to resist…I find myself looking in his direction more often than not. Admiring the way his long, brown hair has escaped the bun at the nape of his neck. The way sweat rolls down over the wolf's paw tattoo in the center of his chest, making my own tighten. My ribs compress on my lungs. My shirt is too tight. I might—

Aurora touches the back of my hand gently.

I blink several times and it's as though I'm waking from a trance. Conri must have been speaking for some time because all of a sudden there's a chorus of howls lifting to the dusky sky. He grabs my right hand and hoists it, as though we have accomplished an unknown victory. Aurora's hand is in my left.

It strikes me that we three are some kind of odd, singular entity. All separate individuals, yet three parts of one whole. Aurora and I share the magic that Conri needs. He offers us protection and a place in this society. I'm an anchor between him and Aurora…and possibly the rest of the spirits alongside the Natural World.

Maybe another woman in my shoes would be elated by being so needed. So wanted. To have the possibility of not just one partner, but two.

Unfortunately for me, I am not that woman.

"Let us retreat to our tent, my future queen," Conri says to me.

"I need some time with Aurora," I say, glancing away to avoid looking into his eyes. The haze of the charm is worse when I do.

Conri doesn't allow it, resting his fingertips on my chin and guiding my attention to be solely on him. I can almost feel the crackle of magic over my skin as the cape tries to protect me from his forced charm. Disgust can beat out obsession. It must. So I root myself in that emotion.

"What is it you need to do together? Be my good girl and tell me true." He's trying to worm out any kind of deceit or lie. I can't tell if he is actually suspicious, or if this is just his nature.

You owe him nothing; he's trying to manipulate you, I remind myself. "She is going to spend time with the part of her powers within me. It is important for her to have time to commune with them to keep up her own strength."

"And I will help ensure Faelyn can leverage those powers to continue defending against the withering," Aurora says. "Along with whatever else you desire of her."

"Shouldn't her magic as a witch be enough to protect against the withering?" Conri glances over at Aurora, but only for a second. I wonder if he knows that my resolve will be easier to break than the spirit's. That assumption only makes me want to be even stronger. "I had thought the withering was not a concern since she already possesses magic within her?"

"We can never be too careful." Aurora keeps her tone serious. "This world is not made for humans—the opposite, in fact. Save for the Human Queen, of course. I would like to keep a close eye on her to be safe."

"Well, I can have nothing happen to my blushing bride." Conri gives me a warm smile and squeezes my hip lightly. "Go on, then, I'll see you later." He glances around, his hand lingering on me. "Evander! Keep a close eye on them."

The lykin knight approaches, abandoning helping the others set up camp for the night. "My liege."

"You are responsible henceforth for my dear Faelyn. See to it that nothing happens to her or else the consequences will be yours to bear."

"Yes, my king." Evander bows his head, hair falling in front of his face. He looks subservient at a glance—and Conri is merely glancing. But I see the hard press of his mouth into a line. Almost like a grimace.

Aurora is right… He holds no love for Conri. But that doesn't mean he's a natural ally for us by default.

The longer I try to make sense of Evander, the harder he is to understand. There's so much to him. Every turned stone reveals deeper secrets still. Never have I met someone so frustrating, but also so intriguing.

"This way. Your tent was set up first," he says to Aurora.

"Don't be too long." Conri gives me one more squeeze and a wink before releasing my hip. "I'm not a man who likes to be kept waiting." Even though the words are coy and playful, there is a note of warning underneath them that I can't ignore.

I merely nod and follow Evander to Aurora's tent, relieved to be free of Conri.

The lykin knight remains poised outside the tent. Arms folded. A statue of grumpiness and muscle. But an oddly comforting one, given the alternative.

"Evander." I pause, tent flap in hand. His eyes swing in my direction. "You still had my things when we arrived at the first camp. Do you think you could get them and bring them to me?"

"I will look into it." He nods and I disappear inside the tent.

As soon as Aurora and I are alone, the air seems lighter. The fading light somehow brighter, despite being filtered through the thick canvas. Her tent is as nice as Conri's—a cot instead of just a bedroll, a small table and chair that look like they both can fold up to be carried on someone's back.

"What is it that you need?" Aurora asks.

"My grandmother's sewing supplies." I dare to take off my cape.

"Ah, right, weaver witches," she says with a slight smile. "The first instance of humans ever being able to harness magic was with a thread of it. A shame you were broken away from Midscape and all its magic so prematurely. Who's to know what could've happened for humanity, otherwise."

"So, all humans can have magic?" I ask.

She nods. "The dryads did not make the humans with the intention of being magic-less. They just were poor teachers and magic is variable. Every creature must come into their magic in their own way, making it hard for one to effectively teach another."

"Dryads?"

"Yes, an early folk of the forests. Not quite fae, not quite primordial spirit. An early iteration of life made by Lady Safina's hand, more or less in her image."

"Lady Safina…" The name strikes a vague memory, a folklore I learned long ago. "Old Goddess of Life—the one you wish to go to?"

"Just so." Aurora nods and sits on her cot. "The only one who could build a mortal body that could house a spirit, *and* split my magic so that I could occupy that body."

I sit beside her, listening as she speaks.

"The spirits were friends with the old gods when the world was small. We all existed side-by-side. Think of the spirits like small gods of this world…and the old gods the keepers of the Great Beyond, of the universe in its whole."

A small laugh escapes me.

She's understandably confused. "What is amusing?"

"I find it incredible…old gods, spirits with true forms. Though I wish you were not in the situation you are stuck in now."

"That makes two of us."

Evander ducks his head inside the tent and holds out my two satchels. “Here.”

I quickly retrieve them, confirming that all the contents of my basket are inside. Everything is, save for one potato. Though I suspect that more likely rolled out when Bardulf tackled me rather than being thieved.

“Thank you,” I say earnestly, allowing him to see the sincerity in my eyes.

It seems to startle him. “You’re welcome,” he mutters hastily and then leaves.

I sit back on the cot, unfastening the button and opening the top flap of the embroidered satchel. Inside are bundles of thick thread, undyed and tightly wound. Atop them is a thin, fabric folio, where smaller loops of colored thread are coiled and buttoned behind flaps. I run my index fingertip over the lengths of four needles.

“What is each needle for?” Aurora asks.

“Bone is for the body—protection of the flesh, healing. Silver is for objects—mending, sturdiness. Redwood for the spirits—evoking, summoning. Gold is for the heart and mind.” I take the gold needle. “We spun the threads in spring and summer…after the sheep were sheared in the village. I would brush out the wool and Grandmother would work the wheel. We both would collect the dyes from the forests throughout the year—me more so at the end. She would boil the ingredients in her cauldron over Folost, who always knew just what heat would draw out the best color. Mary helped with the recipes and guiding me in the woods.”

“And the thread held on to the magic you summoned through the ritual.” Aurora pulls a length from the folio, inspecting it. I can almost see the wool shimmer underneath her fingers in the same way that it would in Folost’s flickering light. “It’s such a clever leveraging of the magic for a people who found it slippery to hold on to.” She smiles faintly and I wonder just how many early humans—early witches—she would watch over in her moonlight.

“The right combination of ritual, thread, and needle makes all the difference. But it also requires a skilled, magical hand.”

“One you have.” It sounds like she’s reassuring me of my doubts. Either I am transparent, or Aurora knows me all too well already.

"Let's hope so." I take the cape in my lap, gathering a small section at the base of the hood, and begin to sew.

I've chosen a yellow thread. We dyed it last summer with onion peels, the sharp scent to fill the mouths of any who would speak ill, rhubarb to purify the mind, and turmeric for trusting in one's gut. The cottage had smelled of warm spices, like a stew was cooking all day. As I pull on the needle, I bring it up to my face and inhale deeply, trying to get the last dredges of that aroma to remind me of those times with my grandmother.

It only smells like the stale fabric of her sewing folio now.

"What are you singing?" Aurora asks, interrupting my focus.

"Oh." I hadn't even realized I'd begun to hum. "I'm not sure. It's just something Grandma would always do when she worked on the cape."

A slight smile curves her lips. "It is like a siren song."

"I don't think I'm luring sailors to their deaths anytime soon." I grin in reply.

Aurora chuckles. "Sirens use songs to draw out their magic. They are often the music of the soul—which is in the tongue of the old gods that came before us all. A very ancient form of magic, that."

"I didn't learn any words of old gods, either." I keep focused on my stitches. I'm nearly finished.

"That you know of." Aurora leans back, resting her palms behind her. "To think, the mystery of unlocking human's magic was merely to apply the right combination of all the others…"

I don't respond, keeping focused on the design. It's an eight-pointed star, each point in the cardinal directions a little longer than the other four points. I shift slightly, ensuring I am facing true north like the star it's meant to represent.

Keep me on my course, I will into it, *guide me. Ensure my thoughts are true and my heart is steadfast. Let none lead me astray from my true desires*.

When I finish, I tie off the thread with a sturdy knot and cut it with the small blade in Grandma's kit. *My kit now, I suppose*, I think somewhat sadly as I roll up the thread. I shake my head to try and shake the sorrow that clouds my mind. She wouldn't want me to be sad, and this was mine to inherit, anyway.

"Did it not work?" Aurora straightens, looking over at my stitches.

"I think it did." I try to sound optimistic. It'd be stronger if I had some kind of spirit binding to also weave into the spell. But I know of no spirit that would help me with this goal. "There's one way to find out for sure."

"Let's hope it does work, because the hardest part is ahead." Each word is heavier than the last, her expression more severe.

"What is it?" My stomach tightens, making me slightly nauseous. What could possibly be harder?

"Being alone with him tonight." She catches my worried gaze with one of her own. "It is likely that he will make you remove your cloak… and that he will suggest that things don't stop there."

A scarlet heat rises in me, fueled by panic. I quickly grab the thread, choosing red like my cape, yellow like the star I just stitched, and black to ground me. I braid them together, humming again as I do. When I'm finished, I grab my larger hunting knife to tear through all the threads at once. Then, I hold the strand out to Aurora.

"Tie it around my wrist." I thrust out my hand. "It's a small thing so he might not know what it is. It won't offer as much protection as my cape but—"

"It's something for while the cape is off," she says with a nod of approval, fastening it around my wrist. Her eyes fall to the blade. "May I see it?"

"What?" I follow her focus. "Oh, this?" Without a moment's hesitation, I hand her the knife. It's a simple blade, unadorned, not special in any way, but she twists it, watching the light flash off the flat as though it is a relic.

"I've never been able to hold a weapon before…" she murmurs.

"Because Conri is rightfully afraid you would attack him?"

"Yes. Though, as in most things, his paranoia isn't rooted in reality. So long as I am kept within the barriers of the lykin's plains, my oath holds and I can't harm the wolf king," she says solemnly. "Still… May I keep it?"

"Sure." I hand her the leather sheathe, which she returns the blade to and slips into her boot. It seems an odd request for a woman who's magically bound to not bring harm to the one person she'd no doubt want to…but I imagine after being captive and helpless for so long, even the imagining of being able to fight back is an indulgent fantasy.

“Thank you.”

“You’ve helped me so much, it’s the least I can do.” Besides, I have another blade in the sewing kit. Smaller, but still effective. “What else can I do to fend off his charm? I won’t allow myself to succumb to it again; I will not give in.”

“Keep your cape on for as long as possible. Seek out my magic through this. Let it ground you.” Her fingertips touch the hastily made bracelet. “And, if you can…you should try to find your own satisfaction before he can elicit the need.”

That suggestion is back. My cheeks are surely blazing now. “Could you…step outside?”

Aurora purses her lips. “I don’t think I could without suspicion. But I have an idea.”

“What?” I’m ready to take any suggestion, any advice that might help. I will not betray Aurora again by giving into Conri.

“Evander,” she calls to the entrance of the tent.

Oh, old gods…anything but that.

fourteen

The lykin ducks into the tent. He has a single, dark eyebrow quirked slightly with a questioning expression. His attention darts between us but I can't keep his gaze.

This can't be happening. Aurora can't honestly be suggesting what I think she is…

"Evander, can you find Faelyn a quiet tent where she won't be disturbed for…" Aurora looks to me expectantly.

"Ten minutes—no, five, five should be fine." I'm fairly certain I'm going to melt, puddling onto the floor with embarrassment.

There is no shame in personal pleasure, I insist to myself. It is a normal, understandable need; I have no reason to hang my head. Even if I personally wouldn't usually talk about it so brazenly with others. Especially not people I still hardly know…

"Somewhere she won't be disturbed for five minutes?" Aurora finishes her question.

"I can probably manage that," Evander says uncertainly. His eyes dart between us. I purse my lips, not about to offer any additional explanation. "Conri is still held up meeting with the alpha of this pack. He should be distracted for a good while yet."

"Good. But don't do it too early. She should have her time as close to when you return her to Conri as possible."

The furrow of Evander's brow deepens. He is clearly confused by this request and I can't decide if I want to laugh or decide that I need to go for a long, long walk far away from here, right now.

"Very well," he relents finally when neither Aurora nor I say anything more. "Let's go."

"Now?"

"Yes, it's best if I have more time to maneuver you through the camp to shake any wandering, curious eyes, otherwise it might look suspicious if we leave here and you go immediately to my tent."

"Send Conri to me if you need to buy time," Aurora says as I stand. "Tell him I need to revitalize his magic." Her eyes dart my way and she gives a wink. "Don't worry, I won't actually."

"Thank you," I say as Evander leads me out of the tent. Aurora gives me one more look of encouragement, one I leech off of as best I can and hold close to my heart. My gut tells me I'll need it.

"We'll take a walk around the camp," Evander announces. "Give you a lay of the land."

"Won't the camp change every time we move?"

"Some of it will, but much remains the same. The tents are set up in the hierarchy of the pack…" He explains how Conri's tent is always set up adjacent to the central area of camp—but not quite on the inner ring that circles the bonfire. His preference. Next to Conri's tent is the pack alpha—or alphas, in case of multiple packs gathering at once. In circles out from there are the knights and favorites of the leaders. Then families. Then the footmen and more knights on the outer edge to protect the pack.

That's where we end up: on one outermost edge, staring out at the grassy sea as the sky turns a blazing orange.

"Is there anything Conri doesn't control?" Everything Evander said was hedged with, "so long as Conri wishes."

He shakes his head, staring over the grasses. "The king is just that…a king. He rules all of us. The one true alpha, caretaker and life giver for all the packs. All he asks for in return is complete, and utter, subservience."

I note how he doesn't say loyalty. "Is that all?" I mutter.

Evander huffs with slight amusement at my dry tone. "That's it."

"Tell me, what was it like before the wolf king?" I think of Aurora's story, that there was a time before the packs were united as one. That Evander was born in one of the last such dissenting packs.

"I wasn't born then. I'm not that old." He must be thinking the same thing.

"Are you sure? Given how curmudgeonly you are, I'd guess you're at least a few thousand years."

He snorts and shifts his weight, facing me. "How old do you think I am, Faelyn?"

I bring my attention to him, making a leisurely assessment from toe to head. He boasts the physique of a man in his prime. Those black trousers trace the contours of his formidable strength, an asset that would elude both younger and older men. The scars on his chest and back are old wounds, turned white, puckering along the skin and crafting constellations that tell stories of traumas long past. His face is mostly unmarred by the lines of age, though a shadow of stubble graces his jaw.

But it is his eyes that my attention sticks on and refuses to move from.

They are alight with the intensity I've come to associate with him alone—an insatiable hunger that I have no doubt has been gnawing at him for decades longer than he's even been alive. As if he's been searching for something, or someone, he will never be able to find. Left forever needy and yearning. Gifting him with a wizened gravity that men half a century his elder could scarcely even dream of.

"Answer me one question first," I finally say, before giving my guess. He raises his brows and says nothing. "Do lykin age in the same way as humans?"

He hums. "I'm not sure if I should answer that."

"You should, if you don't want me guessing you're in your hundreds."

Evander grabs his chest, fingers pressing into the bare skin. "You wound me. Hundreds?" He chuckles, shrugging it off at my smile. "All occupants of Midscape live and die in the same way as humans. None of us are blessed with lifespans greater than your kind. Save for Aurora in her unnatural state."

"Then, I would say you are…twenty-eight."

He grabs his chest again, more sudden, and sways back as though he has been physically struck. "You wound me again. I look so old?"

"Twenty-eight is not old." I laugh from the bottom of my stomach. I'm reminded of a time when I was younger, when I told Grandma that I couldn't wait to be "old"—and, by old, I meant in my twenties. She howled with laughter to the point that I thought the roof shingles of our hut shook.

He grins, recovering from the mock offense. "I'm twenty-three."

"Only a year older than me?"

"Is it that surprising?" He looks back out across the grasses.

"You seem…older."

"Now you're making a game of offending me."

"More grizzled than a man of twenty-three."

"You know, you're not helping the situation." He glances at me from the corners of his eyes.

I try to fight a sly little smile and lose. "Some men would be pleased to hear they come off as mature and stately."

He huffs. "I am not 'some men.' I have nothing to prove to anyone."

"No? No partners in your life?"

"I swore to Conri I would take no bride and father no children," he answers, all levity vanishing like the last vestiges of daylight. "It was the deal I made—to keep my life, I had to sacrifice the ability to make life."

"You…gave up your ability to have children?" I can't help it; my gaze falls to his groin.

He snorts. "All the parts are still attached." His slight amusement at my boldness doesn't reach his eyes. "The bargain was of a more magical sort when I swore myself to him and became his knight."

"I…see." It's a cruel cost to ask of someone, if such things were among their priorities. I can't bring myself to ask Evander if children were something he wanted. That pain might be too much to bear.

His expression turns grave once more. "Not that I would be a deserving father or husband in any case."

"What makes you say that?" My chest tightens slightly on his behalf. I can't help it. The words he says are filled with such pain and turmoil.

"I am not a good person, Faelyn. Everyone whom I love ends up getting hurt. It is a kindness for me to not have to worry of such things."

"A kindness for you, or what you perceive as a kindness to others?" I take a slight step forward, angling myself to look him in the eyes.

"Both." He shifts to face me once more, meeting my gaze. For the first time, his expression is open. Evander isn't hiding behind anger or brutishness. For the first time…I think I truly see the man behind his prickly demeanor. "I do not deserve that sweet, nearly sacred touch of a woman in love. Not anymore." His voice drops slightly as he speaks. The way Evander looks at me is almost as if he seeks my forgiveness. As though I could be a proxy for every woman he's ever hurt—every woman alive.

"Evander, I…" I don't get to finish.

A group of wolves crests the slope of the hill in the distance, ten of them. They race back to camp. Each of them has a limp animal hanging from their mouth. As they near, I can make out a fox and two hares.

"Dinner." Evander starts back into camp, trusting me to follow.

I do, and we leave the conversation at our backs.

Everyone gathers in the center of camp, where a large fire has been erected. The flames burn in the center of a collection of small stones that in no way could keep the fire from jumping…were it natural. However, this fire is not natural. Much like the bonfire at the beach, it doesn't burn any kind of fuel.

I'm overcome with a vague sense of familiarity, even though I don't see a pair of golden eyes in the roaring fire. It's a sense of looking at something you've seen before, even though it's different from anything you've ever laid eyes on. Squinting slightly, I slow to a stop a bit farther away from the fire, trying to settle on what this sensation is before drawing nearer. The sensation is clearer than on the beach, easier to parse out.

"It is a spirit," Evander affirms my suspicions. "His name is Devlan. He's a fire spirit much like your Folost."

"But much larger."

"There are many types of fire, many types of spirits." He takes a step forward to approach the flame with the gathering pack.

I catch his wrist, a bolt of clarity surging through me. "This spirit, was he the one you used to set fire to my barriers and burn down my home?"

Evander's eyes widen a fraction, but are quickly narrowed again by his furrowing brow. His expression borders on disgust. Hatred, even. My grip slackens.

"I told you that I am not a good person." He leans forward slightly. "Don't be surprised when you are presented with proof of it."

Evander rips his wrist from my grasp and starts toward the bonfire. But I am rooted. Stuck. Staring at the broad back of the man who was capable of burning down my home even after he had Aurora. I rush forward, stepping around him before we reach the rest of the pack. We're still in a mostly secluded place between two tents. Not private, but no one seems to be focusing on us—they're all too drawn to the flame and the food being placed before it.

"Why? You had her, didn't you? Why burn down the house? Did you do it because you wanted to—because you could? Or because he told you to?" I demand to know, even though nausea is rippling through me, riding on waves of fear at the answer.

His rage at being stopped again dissipates instantly at my questioning. It's a slipping of his angry mask once more, betraying the more guilty man beneath. Brief, but there.

"It doesn't matter," he mutters, looking away. His body language, expression, tone…it's all the answer I need.

But I want to hear it anyway. "It does to me."

"It will be easier if you hate me," he whispers, deep and low.

"I'll decide who and what I hate."

Evander presses his eyes shut and pinches the bridge of his nose. "Goddess help me. You are relentless."

"I know." Why does that bring a tired smile to my face?

Evander looks around, somewhat nervously. There must be no one he can see or sense to be alarmed about because he finally says, as quietly as possible, "Conri commanded it. He saw you that night when you took Aurora. He wanted to hurt you. I tried to refrain, but Bardulf had heard the order. We had…a minor disagreement over it. But there was no getting around it."

A minor disagreement… The bruise I saw on his cheek when I first laid eyes on him is so faint it's hard to see now. But it looks like someone might have punched him.

"Were…" The thoughts take a second to form in my head. They're darker than I imagined and my mind doesn't want to believe them. "Were you supposed to kill me?"

He says nothing. Once more, it's my answer. My blood is cold. I will be forced to marry a man who had ordered my death.

"Were you going to tell him that you had done the deed when he asked? That you had killed me?"

"Bardulf knew the truth." Evander shrugs. "I would've said you weren't there—the truth. Conri wouldn't have faulted us for not pursuing you when our focus was Aurora and we had her."

"And if Bardulf hadn't been there?"

"What does this hypothetical matter?" He sighs.

"It matters very much to me." *It matters if you're protecting me or not, in your own way.*

"I told you, I have done horrible things. Things that would make your throat burn with nausea. I will continue to do horrible things, so long as that man is in power." The words are direct and angry. Yet, as soon as he finishes his outburst, his expression softens. "But…it is not because I want to. I desperately, desperately cling to whatever shred of decency I can. Because…"

"Because?" I breathe, hanging on his words.

He takes a small step forward, voice dropping even further. "Because I like to dream that, one day, I might be free of him. And, when I am, I would like to be a man that can sleep at night."

The words slowly sink into me. His expression is somewhere between tortured and desperate. Seeking. Asking me for a forgiveness that I would've never even contemplated giving a man who had wronged me in the way he has.

But…things suddenly don't seem so simple.

"We should join the rest before they wonder." Evander breaks the moment by backing away. "If I'm going to sneak you away later, we can't have people already suspicious of us, and there are enough eyes on you already."

"One more thing." I stop him for a final time. "Really, it's the last thing," I assure his agitated expression. "My barrier, how did you—"

"You suspected correctly. I used the fire spirit to burn through it," he says, matter-of-fact. Never have I hated being right. "Almost couldn't do it, though. No physical items worked and the spirit was nearly not strong enough."

"So my magic wasn't bad," I whisper.

"Quite the contrary." The corners of Evander's lips tug slightly, as though he is fighting a smile. The expression is quickly abandoned. "Now, let's move along."

"Right," I murmur as he steps around me.

Once more I'm looking at his back. At those scars gouged by Conri, the wolf king who leaves nothing but damage and heartache in his wake. Evander might have been the one to break my barrier, take Aurora, and burn my home to ash, but it was at the direction of the wolf king. As he tells it…he almost was trying to protect me the entire time.

But can I believe him? I answer my own question when it occurs to me that Aurora trusts him, too. At least some amount. Evander was the one to free her, more or less.

I start to walk, falling in at Evander's side, our strides matching in length and gait. I fight the urge to look up at him. To continue studying this strange man that I only think I'm just beginning to know.

Unbidden, the sensation of his fingertips running down my arms and wrists, settling on my hands, crosses my mind. I'm back in that dark tent on my first night here. My skin puckers.

There's a gentleness to him. But also a hunger. And a darkness that is equal measures intriguing and terrifying.

fifteen

THE MEAT IS DISTRIBUTED AMONG THE PACK ONE TINY STRIP AT A TIME. Children are brought up first with their parents hovering over their shoulders. But the adults don't take any. They return to their places in the greater circles to wait until it is their turn to come up to eat.

I didn't think there were that many people in the pack until I see how quickly what little food there is goes. I grab the strap of my satchel at my shoulder tightly, thinking of what little rations I still have inside. Evander could've taken them when he had possession of my effects. But he didn't. I glance up at him, and then back to the line.

He mistakes the look. "It'll be our turn soon. We'll go up following the knights and other alpha, with Conri."

"And Aurora?"

"Conri has decided that she won't be allowed to leave her tent while we are in camp, save for when we're moving from place to place."

"I see." A frown tugs at my lips. I suspect the moment he's back to their permanent settlement, he'll have shackles fashioned for her. We'll have to leave before then. Which means, no matter how badly I want to dip into the supplies, I must preserve what rations we have. "Why is there so little food?"

"Have you seen any game on these plains?" Evander asks. I shake my head. Nor have I seen any of the hallmarks that larger game would need for life—like regular watering holes or a variety of animals in the food chain. "There used to be many animals—elk, bison, others…but the ancestral packs hunted them to extinction. They burned and deforested the lands of their enemies to starve them. Those early days of fighting and destroying without care for each other or our lands was part of what prompted Bewulf to unite the packs. It worked, for a time. Until it didn't and everything went back to the way it was. Now we survive on the scraps left behind by our forefathers."

Conri was telling the truth, I realize, when he spoke of venturing into the Natural World to seek more fertile land for his people. I tuck the information away, unsure of how I want to process it yet.

"Is all of Midscape barren like this?" I ask, thinking of what else Conri said—about not being able to venture past his borders for fear of the Elf King and vampir.

Evander shakes his head. "There are mountains to the south, southwest of here where the vampir live, forests beneath them that have always been contested territory between us and the vampir, and more land farther west. But the lykin have long demanded that others stay out of our misty plains and hills so we do the same for them."

"Much like the early treaties between lykin and the witches." I think of the barrier.

He nods. "Our turn for food."

The conversation ends as we approach the central fire. Meat is cut from bone with deft skill to ensure nothing goes to waste, and handed to me raw. I can see why Aurora grew weary of meat…and why she'd want it well cooked were she to have it.

"I think she would prefer it seared." Conri steals my thought, reaching around me to take the meat and skewer it on a long dagger. I am caught between his arms as he moves, dagger flashing in the firelight right in front of my face. I wonder if it is intended as a threat, because that's the message I gather.

"Thank you," I say politely as he holds it out to the fire, Evander taking a step back to give him room.

"You are most welcome." Conri singes it for only a few seconds, bringing it back before me. He plucks the meat off the dagger point with his free hand, holding it in front of my face. "Eat, my future queen."

Stomach churning, I force myself to take a bite from his hand.

Everyone is watching him feed me this chewy, gamey strip of meat. It is a show for my benefit and theirs. A display of ownership.

I barely resist the urge to push him away. The dagger still near my throat is good motivation. I swallow down the meat and with it my pride. Fortunately my cape seems to be protecting me from his charm, for now. But I'll need to act like it isn't if I want to have any hope of keeping it on my shoulders.

"My future king." I tilt my head back with a languid smile, pausing to admire him. As though he is the most beautiful creature I have ever beheld. Sad thing is, he could be…were it not for the disgusting nature he hides underneath his handsome face. "Have you brought food for Aurora yet?"

"Not yet, my love." He leans down and kisses the exposed part of my neck lightly. The touch stirs me in a way I do not wish for. Words, and looks, my cape might be able to protect me from…but touches? Especially skin-to-skin ones? I am already ablaze. He will turn me into a puddle with another peck if I'm not careful. "Though I feel I have a hunger for something other than food now. I shall send someone—"

"No," I say quickly. Perhaps a little too forced. But I had to overcome the haze that was overtaking me. I brace myself as I turn to face him and dare to rest my hand on his upper thigh. The contact doesn't affect me. I'm not sure if it's because I initiated, or because there is the cloth of his trousers between our skin. Something to test in the coming days and hours. "She needs to see you. We shall have time later. Do what must be done for the spirit that looks after the great pack."

Conri smiles sweetly and kisses my forehead. Elation surges through me as he says, "You will be a good queen, looking after our kin so attentively. Very well, I'll see what Aurora needs, and then return to you."

He steps away and my chest is straining against my shirt underneath my cape. I am near breathless, just from that. Ready to beg for sweet release. Aurora was right…I can't go to him tonight without some kind of relief. Even my cape wasn't enough.

"See to it that she is ready in my tent within the hour," Conri commands Evander.

"Of course, my king." Evander bows his head.

Conri takes a strip of meat in hand and walks off. The absence of the wolf king prompts the pack to relax, the thrall of his presence leaving them. Some wander off; others choose to lounge by the bonfire. Many shoot me wary and angry looks.

Have him, I want to scream. *Old gods, take him from me and Aurora; we do not want him!* But no one will. Because they can't. We have been claimed by the king and there is nothing any of them can do to change it.

"Let me show you more of the camp," Evander says. "If you are to be our queen, you should know more about us."

"Thank you." I smile and follow him away, listening attentively as he gives me more facts about how the different packs roam the lands, maintaining the towers that keep the barriers strong, defending the few permanent settlements that are usually clustered near them. Whereas other packs stay in the cities and towns of the lykin permanently, focusing on the craftsmanship that helps support the rest of their people.

All the while, we're both looking over our shoulders. Keeping track of all the others near us.

Without warning, Evander says, "Now," and lifts a tent flap.

I duck inside and he follows closely behind.

The night closes in around us at an instant, filtered through the heavy canvas, unfettered by any light or candle. The distant bonfire casts an orange-tinted glow on one side of the tent—on one side of Evander's face as he stares at me intently. I am well aware of how alone we are and I draw my cape closer around me, the act making me think of his arms around my body the other night and not of Conri's proximity only a handful of minutes ago.

The bedroll is familiar, even though the tent is large enough now for us to stand in. No longer is he sleeping in a simple triangle tent; the king's knight has been upgraded to a tent large enough to properly stand in.

"Do what you need quickly; we shouldn't linger or someone might take notice." His voice has dropped to a hush. I can't tell if he truly has no idea about what the goal of this little escape is or not.

"Then can you please step outside for a few minutes?"

"No." That brings my attention back to him. At my pointed stare, he elaborates, "I can't linger outside and risk being seen without you. Conri has charged me personally with your care."

"And sneaking off with me into a tent, alone, is better?" I ask, somewhat curious, somewhat annoyed that he isn't just doing as I want. This would be so much simpler if I could just be done with it.

"No one saw us come in. Others will likely assume that we're in another area of camp." He folds his arms. "Don't let me stop you from doing whatever magic it is Aurora has charged you with." As he speaks, my cheeks are warming. "I assure you, I have seen all manner of magic and—"

"It's not magic," I interject. The heat has nearly reached the tops of my ears. Thank goodness for the near total darkness of the night. I hope his lykin sight isn't keen enough for him to behold my embarrassment.

His arms fall to his sides. "What, then?"

I inhale deeply and exhale any traces of shame. "I need to relieve myself."

He blinks. "The camp latrines are—"

"No, you dense man, I need to satisfy myself in a carnal way to remove some of the temptation of Conri's charm." I lock eyes with his and say the words slowly and clearly, refusing to allow for any misconceptions.

He holds my gaze. "I see."

"I think I would find the task much easier, and faster, if you could just step outside."

"I told you, we can't risk it."

"Not even for five minutes? I assure you it's not the first time I've done this, I won't be long," I say with a soft laugh.

"Is it worth the risk of me being flayed?" He takes a small step forward, staring down at me.

"Of course not," I say, less demanding than the last.

"Because that is what you're asking me to risk. If Conri sees that I have abandoned my post at your side, I cannot trust all my flesh will remain attached to bone."

"Why does anyone follow him?" I breathe in horror.

"Because some are as cruel and wicked as he is. Most know nothing else, or they have no option because he controls Aurora and therefore has powers none of us can challenge. Pick one, or a mix, they're all viable explanations and the outcome doesn't change." Evander sighs. "I can go over here and cover my ears." He steps toward the entrance, putting his back to me and raising his hands to the sides of his face. "I swear, my eyes are closed and I will not look."

It's the best option I have. I slowly sit on the cot with his bedroll… the bedroll I slept in just last night. Lying back, I stare up at the top of the tent. The canvas is stained a deep blue with the starry shades of night.

My hand slides down my side, over my hip, finding its place between my thighs. It moves slowly, lacking momentum, trying to find its purpose. This is as straightforward as a spell, I insist to myself. I do the right motions, create the right sensations, breathe in the right way, and things should begin to go…

I force my eyes closed and focus. All I need to do is find that rising need in me. It has been forever since I was last touched. It shouldn't be hard to summon.

But right when I have it, my thoughts wander to the wolf king. Conri's lean body fills my mind. Hard and strong. His brown hair slicks to his neck, curling over his shoulders, framing the tattoo at the center of his—

No. *No, no, no*. My eyes snap open and I sit. I will not pleasure myself to the thought of that man. I am doing this to free my mind from him. Not to allow him to worm deeper into it.

Try again.

My back is against the cot once more. Hand in position. I force my eyes closed and try to think of anything—anyone else. But the innkeeper's son I sneaked into an unused room with slowly morphs into Conri in my mind's eye. The traveler I met on the road and lay with underneath an old oak becomes the king atop me.

It's not as though I have a deep swath of sexual experiences to draw from. Liam, the only man I ever loved, he left me with nothing but kisses and a broken heart. Neither of which are enough for me to shake the visions of Conri that plague my every thought. It's as if the wolf king imprinted himself on me in a mere day's time.

Think of someone else, literally anyone else…

Then, my mind takes a turn I wasn't expecting.

Perhaps it is the smell of the cot. The location. His proximity…but the phantom sensation of Evander's arms slipping around me overtakes me once more. I feel his breath, hot on my neck. As if he's really there…

My hand moves with more purpose. I shift, leaning into it. Allowing myself to get lost in my body.

In my fantasy, I turn. My legs wrap around Evander's waist and I tangle my fingers into his black, silken locks. He bites at the base of my neck, as though he were a vampir, but then lets out a growl that's all lykin.

Yes, my love, my mate, that's it, he would whisper in my ear as my hips rolled against his. *That's it...don't hesitate. Let yourself go. Give yourself to me.*

Yes, my every movement says in reply. *Take me. Undo me. Make me yours.*

A soft whimper escapes my lips. I can't tell if it's real, or my fantasy. I'm so lost in the sensations...every motion sweeter than the last. My other hand is assisting in the pleasure, underneath my shirt. Working me to a delicious breaking point.

Come for me, the Evander of my imagination commands. I've never received such a deliciously crude request before. So outright. So bold.

It snaps me in two. My back arches off the cot. I bite into the bedroll to keep myself from calling out or moaning as my body trembles and shudders. Luckily, I learned how to keep myself silent, and as the haze of pleasure leaves me, I'm fairly confident that I made no noise.

Swinging my feet off the cot, I stand and adjust myself, ensuring nothing is out of place. Clothes smoothed over and my composure collected, I take the few steps to Evander. But my hand hovers just short of touching his shoulder. My thoughts are still in my fantasy. Of him. Of all that bare skin against mine...

I swallow thickly and tap him. He turns to face me. Somehow, that's worse because now I can see his sharp, hungry eyes. As though he really could devour me whole.

Come for me, the rogue whisper echoes through my mind and I fight a shiver.

"We should go," I force myself to say, voice level. I'm not sure how long I took, but it's probably better to move faster rather than slower.

He nods. "We should take a few laps around camp, make sure any smell of me has time to air out of your clothes."

"Right." I glance back at the cot as he leads me out of the tent. My thoughts continue to wander back to what just happened. Why, out of everyone, did I have to choose him? No, that question I can answer. He's achingly handsome in almost every way that has ever appealed to me. And he's a relatively unknown person to me, still. I can impose whatever fantasy I need upon him like a blank canvas.

The better questions is why, out of everyone, out of all possible fantasies I tried to conjure, was Evander the only one that Conri's magic charm couldn't break through?

sixteen

My thoughts and wondering persist long after Evander leaves me alone inside Conri's tent. I think I managed to act normal enough around him during our walk around camp. Whatever "normal" means for us.

I bury my face in my hands and steal a breath to myself. What am I doing pleasuring myself to thoughts of the man who burned down my home? I should feel disgusted with myself for it, but all I feel is more hatred toward Conri. Were it not for him, none of this—not one thing—would be happening.

I cling to that hatred when he finally enters the tent. As he does so, I catch one glimpse of Evander positioned outside. Our eyes meet, briefly, and then it's just me and the wolf king.

"My love." Conri holds out his arms and walks over to me.

My love, my mate, fantasy Evander whispers from the back of my mind.

I shiver as Conri embraces me. He chuckles and pulls away. Judging from the gleam in his eyes and the somewhat triumphant smile he wears, he thinks the shiver was solely because of him. It's for the best that I let him continue thinking that.

"I am so sorry to keep you waiting," he says. There's no indication that he smells Evander on me. Though, I trusted Evander to know what the keen senses of his kind would and wouldn't pick up.

"It's all right, darling." I try to add sweetness to my words and admiration to my gaze. Though all I feel inside is simmering loathing. "I took the opportunity to learn more about those that will soon be my people."

"Yes, the ones you will rule over with me." Conri sits and motions to the cot next to him. "How are you finding these lands?"

"Incredible."

"Truly?" He chuckles. "We are a humble people. But I am glad you find us to be so astounding."

"Even though I am familiar with magic, the powers of the inhabitants of Midscape are still astounding to behold. The spirits are so alive and well here. That alone is enough to make me never want to leave," I say, rooting my words in a kernel of truth. There are incredible things here. Conri not among them.

"I would desire to show you more incredible things…" He trails off, the air pregnant with the words unsaid. Conri takes my hand in his and then runs his fingertips up to my shoulder, tucking hair behind my ear as it slips around to the back of my neck. "Should you let me."

I feel no pull. No tug toward him. Be it my cape and the added protection I've stitched into it, the threads around my wrist, or the relief I just had—probably a combination of all—there's no desire to give in to Conri's touch. I can only hope this clarity lasts through the night.

"Forgive me, but the day was long and I am exhausted," I say gently, shifting my grip to pat the back of his hand. "Perhaps tomorrow? I would so love to see these incredible things," I add with a sultry note that sounds fake to my ears, but he seems to buy it. "But I want to ensure that I will satisfy you as well."

"Very well. Allow me to help make you more comfortable for slumber." It's not a question; he's already reaching for my cape. Conri rightfully suspects it's what's helping me resist him.

"There's a bit of a chill in the air tonight. I would like to sleep with it on."

"I will keep you warm." He's undoing the pin at the center of my neck. I swallow thickly and allow him to take it off, not seeing a way I could fight further without arousing suspicion. "There," he murmurs, guiding my face back to his, "isn't that better?"

"Yes, of course," I say.

"Now, kiss me."

I do. It is frustrating how, even still, with all this rage and all I know about the rotten inner core of this man, it is easy to kiss him. With the edges of his charm smoothing across my mind, reminding me just how handsome he is, it's almost enough to have me not caring about all those other things. Almost, but not entirely.

There is no overwhelming mindlessness that comes with the kiss this time. While I kiss him, I am fully aware of myself, and my actions. And the disgust that accompanies them. But I am in control of every movement. Including when I pull away, much to his confusion.

"Forgive me, my king, but I really am weary from the day. I'm not accustomed to this sort of travel."

"Yes, of course." He's forcing the smile. I can tell by how it pulls at his cheeks yet fails to reach his eyes. "Let us rest, then."

He stretches out in his cot, shifting and inviting me to lie next to him—my back to his front. I oblige, knowing I have little choice. The act is what's going to help me free Aurora and myself. The less Conri suspects, the easier it will be to break away. I just have to bide my time and wait…

Conri shifts behind me, pressing himself against me. He inhales deeply against my neck. I swallow thickly as the sensation sends a tickle down my spine. It's as if he can feel even that subtle reaction to his movements. He shifts again, grinding into me not so subtly.

"You smell delicious…like I could devour you," he says with a growl.

"I'd prefer not to be eaten." I try to laugh it off with a joke. The chuckle comes easily on the relief that he really can't seem to smell Evander.

"You don't have be shy. Here, you can engage in your deepest carnal acts without fear of judgment or reprisal. The lykin are not like most humans." His hand snakes around my stomach, grazing up my ribs.

I bite my lip and press my eyes closed. One small touch and he has me fighting a gasp. Conri can feel it. He kisses my neck lightly, the hand grazing the bottom of my breast.

It would feel so good, a voice whispers in the back of my mind, *give in, you can still escape later…if you want.*

No. I won't give in. I can't. But his hand shifts, threatening to make my mind go blank. If I'm not careful, he will reignite my urges. I have to fight this magic taking hold. I can't let him win. I won't.

My thoughts race, trying to focus on anything else. It's a war of my mind against his hands. His mouth. Nothing seems to distract me from thoughts of him. He's going to consume my last shreds of willpower if I don't—

Evander.

The fantasy that saved me earlier returns to my mind with force. But rather than imagining Evander moving as Conri is…rather than allowing myself to get worked up faster…I think of every reason I have to hate Evander—of him taking Aurora, burning my home, taking me to Conri and putting me in this position. And that dovetails my mind back into all the reasons I have to hate Conri.

My thoughts are my own again. I grab the hand groping me, lacing my fingers firmly with his so that there cannot be any other movement on his part without my permission. He stops his kisses. His body goes still behind me.

"I am too weary," I insist, leaving no room for debate in my tone. Though, I do hold my breath, just a little. With all I've heard of Conri… will I have to defend myself more from him? How far will he go?

"Of course, darling." He kisses my neck lightly one last time and his hand relaxes in my grip. "I would never force a person to give something they had not otherwise freely given."

I almost point out Aurora, myself, Evander, everything else that I don't know but I've no doubt is evidence to the contrary. The words are so close to escaping. But I somehow manage to hold them back and continue playing nicely.

Conri settles at my back. I stay alert. Waiting. But his breathing slows and steadies. It's even and deep. He actually fell asleep.

I release a slow sigh, my muscles easing their tension. I did it. I somehow actually managed to thwart him and his charm. It's such a small thing…but it feels like a monumental triumph.

That being said, relaxing enough to sleep is a completely different story altogether.

Morning breaks not with the cry of birds, but a howl. I jolt upright, startled. My heart hammers in my chest.

Conri roars with laughter. "Faelyn, you are a delight, even when you steal all the blankets." So I have; they're on the floor, thrown off by my movement. "There is nothing to worry for. It is just the pack alpha alerting everyone that today is a day to move."

"I see." I place my hand on my chest, as if trying to force my heartbeat to slow.

"Don't be afraid; we are surrounded by my most loyal knights—men and women who would die for me. You have nothing to worry about ever again. I will be responsible for you forevermore."

"Thank you. It is truly a relief," I say and force a slight smile. He intends it to be reassuring…but all I hear is that I am surrounded by people loyal to him. People who will follow his every command. *Save for one man.* "How long will it take us to get to the old wood where the great wolf spirit lives?"

"We will cross the Lykin Plains to Den. On the way, we'll gather a few of the other packs that roam these lands so they will bear witness to our union. Gualla is our halfway point—the lykin's largest city. After resting there and resupplying, we'll continue to Den. In the grove there is where we will say our vows before the altar of the great wolf spirit and…" He trails a finger up my spine as the words trail off. "…we will consummate our union for all to see."

"And this journey will take us…days? Weeks?"

"Hasty, are we?"

"Can you blame me?" I glance over my shoulder with a slight smile. "I will become the queen of the lykin. It is an honor I look forward to."

"I promise, I will not keep you waiting long." He sits and kisses my temple, holding the other side of my head as he does. Every movement seems to immobilize me, reminding me that I am completely in his hands and control. "You shall be my bride before the seasons change."

Before the seasons change… It is nearly midsummer. If he is basing his timing off the autumnal solstice, then I should have nearly three months.

But Conri said "before" the seasons change. Does that mean it's sooner than that? I can't keep pressing the matter, so I sit and stew until he bids his farewells. After he's gone, I make a slow count to thirty. Pacing with every second. And then I collect my things, throw my cape over my shoulders, race to the tent opening, and push out the tent flap just enough to catch a glimpse on the other side.

Evander is there.

"Have you been there all night?" I ask. His eyes turn to mine and I'm reminded of every fantasy I had to leverage of him to keep my mind clear against Conri last night. Who would've thought that the only way I could find to ward against the wolf king's charm is fantasizing about his sworn knight?

"I slept. Bardulf took the middle night position," Evander answers.

"I hear we're moving." I take the lead, striding out of the tent.

He gives me a curious look, but falls into step beside me. "Yes, another three days of running until we get to the next pack. Likely a week to the pack after. Then a few days to Gualla. After that, two weeks to Den. Depending on the pace Conri wants to set and if he wants to go to every pack personally."

There's almost a month of traveling there, plus whatever time we spend in Gualla. Then if we're in Den for a while to prepare for the ceremony…maybe I have two full months?

We come to a stop before Aurora's tent. Luckily they haven't started breaking it down yet.

"A moment." I excuse myself and enter.

Aurora is seated on her cot, pleasantly surprised to see me. But worry has her brows upturning slightly in the middle. "How did last night go?"

"It was all right," I say, taking my seat next to her, just as I did last night. "Let me rephrase. It was horrible being next to him, but I didn't give in. Though I did kiss him again, just so he wouldn't be suspicious. But I managed to keep my head about me."

"A smart play." A genuine smile cracks her lips. "I'm relieved to hear our plan worked."

"Me too." I take her hands in mine and give them a squeeze.

Aurora's expression falls with her gaze. "Though, I wish I hadn't put you in a position where you had to do these things."

"You didn't," I say firmly. I'll say it a thousand times, if that's what she needs to hear. And then a thousand times more. "All of this is Conri's doing; and that's why we're going to escape him." Her head jerks back towards mine, as if she's surprised I'm still adamant about this. It's my turn to give her a slight smile.

"I've heard our travel plans," I continue. "I think it's best if we wait till we get to Den and then make our move. I still have the supplies I gathered for our journey and they'll keep. We might be able to gather more in Gualla. I have Folost and Mary who will come to our aid if I call for help. And on the journey to Den, you can teach me how to use the magic of yours that's in me. I'm hoping I can use it to find more spirits to bring to our cause."

Her eyes widen slightly, the dark voids threatening to swallow me whole. Her words quiver. "There is no escaping, not for me…"

"Those are Conri's words, not yours," I say firmly. She opens her mouth to object, but I speak over her. "You escaped once."

"But I had help."

"And you'll have help again," I insist, squeezing her hands as Evander calls in that it is time for us to go. I stand. "Don't lose faith, Aurora. I made you a promise and I intend to keep it."

Bardulf is waiting on the other side of the tent flaps to take Aurora away. Other lykin begin to break down the tents. I leave in the opposite direction with Evander. Walking slowly as we make our way toward the center of camp where everyone is beginning to gather. The pack is markedly larger than yesterday.

"Evander," I say softly. He slows his pace as well, showing me he's listening. "You helped Aurora once; will you help her again?"

He says nothing, gaze drifting from the ground to the distant horizon. He's silent for long enough that I look up at him expectantly, bracing myself for what is to come. Will he deny it, thinking that I am firmly under Conri's spell? Will he be aghast that I would even dare ask so boldly?

It is bold. But I have to be. I'm trying to thwart a wolf king.

I pause, shifting to face him. That brings his eyes to mine. He can't look away. I command all of his attention and it sends a tingling rush across my skin.

"I need to know if you're really on our side." I still don't know why he would be. But his actions suggest he is. Evander's motivations are obscured, but I'm not going to question them when we need all the help we can get.

Finally, after what feels like forever, he offers me a slow nod. “I will always be on your side, Faelyn.”

The side that isn't Conri, is what I assume he means. The best option we all have.

I nod. “Good. We start laying our plans in the coming weeks.” I start walking again, feeling somewhat like a general charging off to war.

“What do you need of me in the meantime?” He wears a slight smile, as if he finds all this amusing. I suppose if he's risking his life, amusement is better than complete and utter terror.

“I'll let you know as the time comes. For now, hold until further orders.” I embrace this new vision of myself. Conri has his knights and alphas. But I have a knight of my own, the moon spirit herself, and hopefully, soon, an army of other spirits ready to get Aurora across the world and returned to the sirens.

“As my lady commands.”

We arrive in the center of camp, where everyone is amassing. It isn't long until the lykin have taken their wolf shapes and Aurora and I are back on Conri and Evander's backs.

I grip the fur between his shoulders, right at the nape of his neck. He glances back at me and our eyes meet once more. My heart skips a beat. My breath catches.

With a brief howl and a leap, Conri is off, leading the charge. I suck in my core, and lean forward slightly as my wolf knight and I charge toward the horizon.

seventeen

It is a miracle that Aurora, Evander, and I somehow manage to avoid Conri's suspicions during the three days between the two pack encampments. We struggle to navigate time with Aurora and myself so I can begin learning how to better tap into the magic that is now within me—and make some small progress in so doing—as well as finding time for me to sneak into Evander's tent to take care of other matters.

Perhaps it is the chaos of the temporary camps that helps us go undetected. The tents are less permanent—though Conri's is always set up to the point of maximum comfort. There is less of a schedule and more of an organic flow to the pack. People are rarely in the same place twice, so they don't take note of where you are or what you're doing. Which allows Evander and I to continue what have become our evening walks with enough time for me to see Aurora and slip away before being returned to Conri with the wolf king none the wiser.

Strolling with Evander in a late dusk has proved… surprisingly delightful. So long as I can manage to set aside how awkward I feel knowing what the capstone of my evening is. But Evander shares with me the mythology of the lykin and vampir—stories that I can tell are the grandmothers to the tales I was told growing up. He explains how young lykin do not come into their powers in full, transformations included, until they go before the great wolf spirit. We seem to effortlessly talk about anything and everything, so long as it doesn't have to do with either of us.

He doesn't ask. Neither do I. It's an unspoken agreement that suits us both.

But I know our habits will need to change the moment I see the next camp, larger than the last pack's. We can't be too consistent here or people will take notice. Which is why when I am dismounting Evander I make it a point to pretend to twist my ankle and fall dramatically.

Conri is there in an instant, shifting from his wolf form to his human form and wrapping his arms around me before I can hit the ground. He's on one knee, clutching me to him. When he studies my face, what looks like genuine worry is alight in his eyes. No doubt a show for all the others that are gathered.

"Faelyn, are you all right? What's wrong?" he asks. His attention shifts to Evander, now a man standing over us. His eyes narrow slightly. "What did you do to her?"

"No, no," I say hastily, suddenly worried my ploy has turned sour. "It wasn't him. Merely my own clumsiness when dismounting."

Conri continues to give Evander a hard stare. For his part, the knight stands there passively, expression unreadable. I lift a hand and rest it on Conri's cheek, guiding his face back to me.

"Truly, my darling, it is just a small sprain."

"We shall stay an extra day, no, two days here," he declares. "That way you have ample time to heal."

"I might be able to assist as well." Aurora steps forward. "I could activate my powers within her to help her flesh mend, as it helps mine in this form."

"Yes." Rather than releasing me, Conri slips his arm under my knees, the other still holding my shoulders. He hoists me up and I can't stop a small noise of surprise. My hand grips his shoulder for balance; the strong muscle is as hard as rock under my fingers. "Set up the tent for the moon spirit," he barks, and lykin immediately begin moving. "I will take my future queen there myself." Conri gives Evander a side-eye as he brushes past.

"It truly wasn't his fault." I dare to rise to Evander's defense, keeping my voice light and playful. "If anything, it is your fault for deciding to take such a clumsy woman for a bride."

"I am the wolf king, I do not make mistakes," he says with a slight smirk. Thank the old gods my jest worked. "And I know Evander is a good man and would never go against my wishes." I work to keep any reaction to that proclamation to myself and just keep smiling. "It is simply that I do not wish to see any harm come to what is mine."

What is mine… The words sit as uneasy with me as the majority of Conri's other statements. They're small wordings, little things that betray his true intentions and the way he actually perceives this relationship. I am as much a thing to him as the ring was. Nothing more.

By the time we arrive at the usual placement for Aurora's tent, it is nearly finished being set up. Conri walks inside and sets me down on the cot. Aurora is close behind. Bardulf is positioned outside the entry.

"Ensure she is mended." His eyes remain on me as he speaks, fingertips trailing down my jaw. "For I wish her to be in top form for tonight."

"Yes, my king." Aurora bows her head as he leaves.

As soon as the tent flap closes behind Conri, I make a gagging expression nearly at the same time as Aurora. We both share a look, and the snort of a barely contained, bitter laugh. She quickly sobers and sits on the cot next to me. We don't exchange a word for another minute. It's a good thing, because Conri's voice is muffled by the canvas as he exchanges low words with Bardulf that I can't distinguish. But, after another few moments, he's gone.

"I assume you're actually all right?" Aurora nods to my ankle. She keeps her voice low.

"I am." I move my foot in a circle. "I wanted to ensure I had some time with you and our routine was likely to be thrown off by the new camp."

She nods. "Luckily, Conri should be meeting with the alpha of this camp tonight, so we have some time."

I shift off the cot, sitting on the grass. My left hand, I place out on my knee, fingers up. My right hand I dig into the earth at my side. It's the meditative position she's put me in for the past few days as we've been traveling. A hand on the earth. Fingers to the sky. Ears and heart open with a large inhale, my eyes fluttering closed.

"Today, we shall actually attempt to call upon a spirit," Aurora says softly, shifting behind me. She kneels, resting both hands on my shoulders.

"What?" I whisper. So far I've spent days just meditating, feeling the flow of energy through my body, her energy through her, and our place in the world.

"You're going to call her to you," Aurora says. "But not with your voice…with your magic and mine."

My pulse quickens. "What will I do first?"

"Clear your mind and find the magic as you have before. Find the threads of my power woven into you and pull upon them," she instructs in a slow, steady tone.

Within my mind's eye, I imagine my soul as a large swath of canvas. Every experience, every meeting, is carefully embroidered in colorful thread. There are the threads that still smell of woodsmoke from Grandma's hearth—from our home burning to dust. Threads that are too hot to touch that stretch out into oblivion, connecting me with Folost, wherever he might currently reside. There are threads of bright red, the color of passion and blood and all the ties that bind. Threads of deepest blue, of starless nights consumed by endless tears and hollow heartache.

Among them all is a thread of pale moonlight. Lightly looped into me, stretching behind to tie into Aurora's soul. My fingers twitch as I imagine myself grabbing it.

"Her name is Brundil, and she is the spirit of the earth."

"The spirit of the earth?" My eyes nearly open with surprise, as if by seeing I could somehow ensure my understanding of what she said. Aurora has positioned herself behind me. "Someone so grand? I'm not—"

"Worthy?" Aurora finishes for me. I can hear the slight grin to her voice. "Faelyn, you are most worthy. You are bound with the spirit of the moon, someone equally grand."

"Your might is not my own." I look over my shoulder and back at her. "I would never presume to take credit for your greatness; I am merely its temporary steward."

"And that is what makes you all the more worthy to carry it within you." She dips her chin and her eyes meet mine. "Now, I would like to see my old friend, if you don't mind?"

"Of course not. But…could you not just call upon her?" I ask.

"Not split as I am." A sad, slight smile graces her lips, only for a second. "When I had the ring in hand…it was barely enough connection to my full might to make my way across the tides and through the Fade."

I know she doesn't intend it, but I can't help the guilt that streaks through me. As if it is somehow my fault her powers weren't returned to her that night. If I hadn't been there…

"But you have enough to do it, with the magic you already possessed." Aurora squeezes my shoulder warmly. "Now, Brundil."

"Right." I shift, facing forward again, and close my eyes, returning my focus inward. Once I have my mental fingertips on Aurora's power, I speak. Even though I use my voice, it feels as though the words are not formed with my breath but, instead, formed by the power within me. "Brundil, I, Faelyn, a humble weaver witch, call upon you with an open heart and good intentions." As if with a mind of their own, my fingers sink deeper into the earth. "I seek you not only as an ally, but as a friend."

At first, nothing happens. But I feel a shifting deep within. An unfurling of magic, like a line cast out far, far beyond myself. And then a tug. A connection was made. A metaphorical fish took the bait.

But there is nothing fishlike about the creature that emerges before me.

The ground sags, prompting my eyes to open. The earth has turned to liquid, swirling before me, grasses churning into hard dirt, and richer, deeper soil beneath. And from that primordial churning, a figure rises.

It is childlike in nature. The mighty spirit of the earth looks like a girl no older than ten. Her skin is cracked mud and patches of moss. Her legs are wooden, fingers spindly roots. From her head, long grasses grow, tangling with flowering vines.

She sits before me, cross-legged and head tilted to the side. Her eyes, two smooth river rocks, revolve in their sockets as she looks from Aurora to me.

"I was wondering when you would call on me, Faelyn the witch," she says finally. Her voice is deep and cracking, like wood splitting the silence of a winter's day.

"You…know me?" I whisper. Not just because I don't want anyone else to hear, but also because I am drawn to reverent silence before this primordial creature. Vaguely, I wonder how different Aurora might look and feel when she is freed from her mortal form and reunited with her power. Will she resemble the woman at all as I know her? Even if she doesn't, I know my heart will recognize her.

"Mary has told me much of you over the years."

"Is she well?" I immediately ask.

"She is."

"I'm so glad." I can't stop a smile at the mention of my dear friend. "She has always been a good companion to me."

"And you to her, it would seem." Brundil's eyes shift again. "Aurora, it has been some time since you last called upon me."

"A few millennia, yes. Forgive me, friend." Aurora releases my shoulders, shifting to my side. "But I could feel you in every sodden earth of summer, every flower-filled day of spring."

"It is truly a crime against nature itself, what they have done to you." Brundil reaches out, cupping Aurora's cheek gently. "I miss our dances."

"As do I."

"I am going to restore Aurora's power," I dare to interject.

"Says the person who currently holds it." Brundil releases Aurora and casts a suspicious tone my way.

"It was an accident," Aurora speaks for me. "Faelyn has only been good to me. I believe her word that she will be the one to finally free me."

"And when we make our move, I would like to call upon you again," I say to the earth spirit. "If you would let me."

Brundil leans back, looking mildly offended. "I am not some minor spirit to be at the beck and call of a little witch."

"I…" My gaze drops. Little witch. That's always been the fear, hasn't it? That everything I am and everything I could be won't amount to much. The protections I tried to keep for the humans in the Natural World…the barrier so easily shredded.

But my magic wasn't *bad*… Quite the contrary. My conversation with Evander returns to me. Not just anyone could break it—it took a lykin, a magical being, with knowledge of witches *and* with the aid of a strong spirit. I try to remind myself of what I have accomplished and sit a little taller.

Meeting Brundil's eyes with purpose, I say, "Even someone of the least skill, and smallest stature, can do incredible things. I might be a 'little witch' but I am also your friend's ally and currently her best chance to be free. Do not mistake stature for capability."

The earth spirit tilts her head in the opposite direction.

I continue, "And I would not want you at my 'beck and call.' I respect you, Lady Brundil. I wouldn't waste your time. But I do not think asking you to help us escape would be a waste."

A slight smile curls her lips. Mud cracks and flakes off to the ground with each of her movements, landing as petals that are instantly decomposed into the soil. She's a constantly growing and changing spirit.

"The trees and stones of the forest by the redwood offshoot spoke highly of you, as did Mary…and Aurora. I suppose I can put my faith in you, little witch." When she says it this time, it no longer sounds like an offense. But, rather, a term of endearment.

I reach into the satchel at my side, pulling out my grandma's—my sewing kit. I take out a length of thread, and hum softly as I loop it around my fingers. I only ever watched Grandma perform this act once. Yet…it's imprinted on my soul. I know the motions as if on instinct.

When I raise my hand, the thread lifts into the air, fighting gravity itself. Brundil mirrors the motion, lifting her spindly hand as well, too many rooty fingers to be human. The thread loops around her digits, pulling our wrists together until our fingertips touch.

Locking eyes with her, I say, "Brundil of earth, I bind myself to you. Let there not be a day that I do not bask in your wonder, am not satiated by the creatures of your lands, and am not comforted by the magic that courses from you, all around me."

Her fingers lace with mine and the thread explodes into stardust, fading from view. Tiny flowers pop up along her roots. She gives a smile and nods before sinking back into the ground.

I stare in wonder as the grasses return to their previous positions. There is no sign that she was ever there.

Aurora rests her hand once more on my shoulder. "Well done."

eighteen

I sit on the cot in Conri's tent, waiting for him to arrive. He demanded I be delivered earlier tonight, leaving no time for Evander to sneak me off. I briefly consider trying to take care of my needs before Conri can arrive. But the idea of doing it on his cot…where he could walk in at any moment… The thought makes me gag.

Instead, I keep my hands busy and my mind focused on other things.

My cape is draped over my knees, thread beside me. I slowly embroider a tree in the same thread I used earlier to bond with Brundil. It is a reminder and a memorization. It is a physical manifestation of tying her magic to mine…and to the children I don't yet have that I dream of someday passing on these names and powers to, just as my grandma and mother did for me.

Without warning, the tent flap opens. I knot off the thread and quickly snap it with my fingers, returning the needle to my kit.

"I'm sorry to keep you waiting. But I see you found a way to entertain yourself." Conri smiles and approaches, kissing both my cheeks.

"It's good to have hobbies." I try and fling the cape around my shoulders, but I don't have a chance before Conri takes it from my hands and sets it aside. I have to bite my lip to keep myself from asking him not to touch it and clench my fists to stop myself from grabbing it back from him.

He glances back in my direction, noticing the former. "Oh, allow me."

Conri takes my face in both of his hands again, leaning forward to kiss me slowly. He sucks my lower lip between his teeth, biting lightly. The movement almost elicits a moan from me. I force my thoughts instantly to Evander—the only thing that can break Conri's charm. I think of Evander's mouth on mine. Of him next to me in his cot where I have pleasured myself for the past few days.

It keeps my head about me enough to break the kiss from Conri when there is a moment and pull away. "Forgive me, but travel still makes me weary. I do not think I will be a worthy bed companion for you while we are on the road. And you, my king, deserve nothing less than the most enthusiastic partner."

There's a glint to his eyes that complements the wickedness in his grin as he says, "I know what you're doing."

My blood runs cold. Those words. So simple. As sharp as a knife's edge running down my throat.

"My king?" I look up at him, trying to have nothing but confusion on my features. Play the part. Don't give too much away until I must.

Conri, wolf king, drops to one knee before me. The cot is low and he is tall, so our eyes are nearly at the same level. I can't clear a knot in my throat. My mouth is bone dry.

He seems to enjoy the silence. No, he enjoys what it does to me. Conri allows me to steep in it a little bit longer until he lets out the soft rumble of a chuckle.

"I know someone must have told you of my charm and you are doing all you can to resist it. I know you are most likely conspiring with Aurora to use her magic, in some way that I do not understand, to help subdue the influence."

I open my mouth to object, not wanting Aurora to be dragged into this. She's already on thin enough ice with him. The last thing I want is for her to face more unintended consequences.

He stops me by raising a hand, that sly smile still curling his lips. "I don't have to know. In fact, I think I like it better not knowing."

"What?" I'm too surprised to think of what my gasp of a word might be giving away.

"You see, Faelyn..." Conri rests both his palms on my knees and slowly slides them up my thighs. He pushes open my legs, placing himself between them as he shifts and leans forward. "It has been years since I last could enjoy the chase of a woman. Years. It's all well and good to have people throwing themselves at you. But it grows…dull." His lips split into a smirk, teeth shining. "I am a predator by nature; the hunt is in my blood."

His chest presses against mine. It compresses my breath. My head spins with his proximity. Every breath I take is on his exhale. The world has become so very small.

"So continue resisting me. Let me work for you. Let me show you how deep my desire runs. Make me ache for you—yearn for you. Show me your ferocity and watch how hard it makes me. It'll make the taste when I finally do have you that much sweeter." His lips almost brush against mine as he speaks. But he doesn't kiss me. The quivering of my lower lip nearly leads ours to touch. But still, he doesn't close the gap. Instead, with another low noise of amusement, Conri pulls away and stands. He goes to the lantern, snuffing it for the night as though this is just another evening…as if he hasn't found out the truth of my protest.

"What if I never want you?" I whisper into the darkness that comes crashing down around me.

"You will." He shifts around me, situating himself behind me in the cot and pulling me down with him. "They all do, in the end."

"I might never," I insist, instantly wishing I said "will" and not "might." How is it that I already sound weaker than I intended?

"If you are trying in a roundabout way to ask if I will force you to bed me, Faelyn, I will not." He runs his fingertips up my arm. "I have not forced anything of you yet, have I?"

"Nothing other than forcing me into your bed. And becoming your wife."

"Ah, yes…I will not sacrifice the well-being of my packs and my stability as king for anyone, not even my future queen." Conri seems genuinely…contemplative about the matter. "However, the bed. Would you like your own?" He seems genuinely surprised, as if he hasn't considered that I might.

"Yes." I test the ever-evolving limits.

"Very well." Conri shifts suddenly, standing. I fall back into the cot without him there. He crosses to the entrance of the tent and barks an order at Evander. In a matter of minutes, there's another cot brought in by two knights with another bedroll. Conri motions at both the cot I'm in and the new one. "Pick. I care not."

Moving to the other cot feels like a daze. The bedroll smells mostly fresh—unused. But I can still smell Conri near me. In the small tent, our cots are only a finger's width apart. But, still, it is my own…

"Better?" Conri asks as he settles.

"Yes," I admit, still shocked by what's happening. It breaks every expectation I've cultivated of Conri so far. We both lie, side by side, but apart. I stare at him through the darkness and, even though my eyes aren't good enough to see, something tells me that he's staring back. "Conri?" I dare.

"Faelyn." He is still awake.

"Would there be another way to ensure stability for the lykin other than marrying you—"

He stops me. "Faelyn, a mere few days without the moon spirit in hand and someone moved against me. Pups were killed—*children* were killed merely because they were of my pack. That is one matter I cannot compromise on. I need the power of the moon spirit to keep the peace."

"And if that power were to be set free? Where would that leave me?"

A pause. "Do you have a way to do that?"

Freeing Aurora of her bonds and restoring her as a full spirit. But I'm not going to say that aloud… "No."

"Well, then it sounds like you have little to worry about. So, yes, you will marry me, Faelyn. That I am afraid I need. But"—he reaches over, taking my hand in his—"I hope that I can be a man you would consider yourself honored to have as your husband. That perhaps one day you will learn to not only tolerate me in your bed, but, infinitely better, to welcome me in your heart."

The words seem sweet, and pure. Simple. Could it really be that simple?

"I know how my pack speaks of me. But I ask you earnestly, give me the chance," he continues. "Learn who I truly am for yourself. See my love for my people—love that will extend to you. Let me win your heart. If you give in you might find you enjoy the chase, too."

My heart flutters as he releases me. Conri rolls over, putting his back to me. But I continue to lie on my side, facing him, peering into the darkness. As if, somehow, I'll be able to figure out what in the forgotten names of all the old gods just happened.

nineteen

EVEN THOUGH CONRI CLEARLY SUSPECTED MY WOUNDED ANKLE WAS A RUSE, HE STILL WILL HAVE THE PACK STAYING AN EXTRA TWO DAYS IN THE CAMP. I learn this when Evander comes to collect me in the morning. Conri was up with the dawn. I pretended to be asleep as he left. Even though I don't usually sleep late, I dozed for an extra few hours. It's been impossible to get quality sleep next to him when I'm so on edge from his presence.

"You are quiet today," Evander observes as we take a morning walk. I make it a point to favor my "good" ankle a little more, but not overly so. Given our conversation last night, the ruse is up.

"Sorry," I murmur.

"You've no need of apologies." He slows to a stop at the edge of camp, staring out over the grasslands that sway in the breeze, shimmering silver and gray among the low mists that permanently blanket these plains. "Did he… Is everything…" Evander shifts to face me, an expression of steely determination and deep concern etched into his face. "Did he do anything untoward last night?"

I look up at the knight. "My 'sworn protector,'" I say softly. "Tell me, would you even protect me from him, if it came to it?"

"Without doubt." There's no hesitation. Hardly a delay at all, even. I don't know if he would've had the same answer when we arrived at Midscape almost a week ago.

"Evander—"

"I know what he is, what he's capable of. He has asked me to do and defend many heinous acts, but there are some that not even I will abide."

"What he's capable of…" I repeat softly, my gaze drifting back to the slowly sloping hills. "He didn't hurt me, Evander. Quite the contrary. The extra cot was to make me more comfortable because he expects nothing of me."

I can see Evander's lips purse from the corners of my eyes. He looks back out over the grasses as well. There are things he wants to say. The words are a weight in the air, but he doesn't alleviate the pressure.

"If I wanted to go and see what is over that hill"—I point to the distant horizon—"could you take me?"

Evander glances over his shoulder, back at the camp, no doubt looking for Conri. The king is nowhere to be seen. "If we were to stay in sight of the camp, it should be all right…"

"Especially if I demanded it of you for the sake of my magic?" I grin slightly.

Evander returns the expression. "Definitely so, in that case."

"Good, take me there."

On my request, he changes into his wolf shape. There's a ripple of magic and a curling of smoky haze in the air, like the last sigh of a soul leaving this mortal world. Fur ripples out from where there was once skin and broad muscles become strong legs that could carry me farther than the horizon.

Evander's silvery eyes meet mine. His wolfish expression is relaxed. Almost like a pup… I can't stop myself; I reach out. My hand hovers over his head and our eyes remain locked. Until his dip closed and he tilts his chin up, pressing the soft fur between his ears against my palm.

A slight smile crosses my lips as I scratch between the ears. He seems to enjoy the act as much as a dog would. After a moment of savoring, Evander folds his legs under him, sitting in a manner that turns his body into a furry loaf of bread.

Grabbing his fur between the shoulders is almost second nature now, as is swinging my leg over. When he stands, I shift once, feeling him do the same. I change my grip and press my knees gently but firmly into his sides. We've been traveling for days, but something about leaving the camp feels different. It feels like the first time I was astride him all over again.

Evander can apparently sense the precise instant my resolve crystallizes, because he launches forward like an arrow let loose, soaring through the mist-laden morning. I incline slightly, pressing my abdomen and chest into the rippling strength of his back. My hands glide forward and loosely grip the fur on either side of his neck, rather than his shoulders. I imagine myself as one of the couriers I would see from time to time racing across the old streets and trade-ways, carrying letters and parcels for those privileged enough to purchase their services.

Except Evander is sleeker and faster than any horse I have ever beheld. He is half the size but three times the muscle. Every pounding of his feet against the earth hammers away my worries. The sensations of the wind tangling in my hair, his fur tickling my skin, the aroma of dew-kissed grasses…it strips away the layers of fear and worry from my bones, replacing it all with clarity the moment we arrive at the crest of that once distant hill.

Even though Evander was the one who ran, I am breathless. My eyes sting from the biting air and thin rivulets of tears streak down my cheeks from his pace. At least, I believe them solely the speed and wind's doing.

Evander eases himself to the ground and I hastily brush away the dampness before dismounting. Though I do not turn to face him—instead, I take a few steps forward and stare out over a landscape more breathtaking than any I have ever seen before.

My instincts about this particular crest of earth were founded. The land slopes gently down and away, providing a stunning vantage. To our left, soaring mountains loom like slate sentinels. A dense forest clusters their feet. Between here and there, and all around, is a large expanse of grass and mist, spotted with towers and small encampments with vast swaths of desolate beauty between. And at my right, so far in the distance that I must squint, is what appears to be a coastline.

"Is that the sea?" I point to the water in the distance.

"No, it is a lake."

"A lake?" I repeat, shocked, given its scale.

"Yes, the largest in Midscape. It is called Calduwyn. As some stories go, there was once a massive dragon that made that lake its bed. When it took to the skies, the hole it left behind filled with a hundred years of rain that watered the early earth," Evander says. "Though, I think most believe that to be an old legend that's more fiction than fact. Especially since other tales conflict."

"We have legends of dragons in the Natural World, too," I say.

"I know."

"Do you?" I lift my brows.

He shrugs. "I know some history of humans and the Natural World they occupy."

"And of witches," I point out.

Evander glances at me from the corners of his eyes. He could see the gentle probe into his history, but is clearly uninclined to proffer any information. Instead, he points to the mountains and shifts the topic. "Those are the mountains of the vampir. Though their ilk hasn't been seen for a thousand years. Not since the lykin had to sequester them to their frosty peaks to prevent their blight from sweeping across the lands."

Despite my fascination with the vampir, I return to the lake. I suspect I already know the answer, but I must ask anyway. "The siren, do they live there?"

"No, they live in the Eversea, which is in the waters far, far to the northwest. The most direct route would be to cross Calduwyn and then traverse the marshes that separate the northern fae wilds from the very edge of our world."

"Sounds easy enough," I murmur sarcastically.

"If you are asking for the sake of your plans of running away with Aurora, then I would say that your best chance would be to head to the southwest, not north." He points down at the forest, finger tracing up to beyond where my eyes can see. "The land route will be far easier than daring to brave the magic-steeped and strange waters of Calduwyn. Once you pass the edge of the forest, you'll be out of lykin land—which should free some of Aurora's powers."

"They were not freed from coming to the Natural World?"

He considers this. "You'd need to ask her. But my suspicion would be not, since that was once lykin territory as well."

Frustrating.

"Farther still," he continues, "you'll reach the large wall of the elves' territory. If you can make it to them, you could plea for an audience with the Elf King.

"They say his heart is made of ice, but you could try and beseech his Human Queen to take pity on you—she might out of fondness for her people, and he might warm out of pity for Aurora. If you can make it to the elves, I believe you would be safe. Conri would never dream of going against the Elf King."

"This Elf King is that powerful?" I am not keen on dealing with another king whose reputation is a heart of ice.

"He is the ancestor of the ones who made both the Veil and the Fade, the barriers of the worlds. His power is monumental," Evander says with a note of reverence. "In the land of the elves, Conri's knights couldn't reach you. And if you have the Elf King's agreement, he might send an escort with you all the way to the siren. You'll want his help to cross through the fae wilds, too, given the rumors that they have become as bloody a landscape as the lykins' plains before our uniting."

"Midscape seems a dangerous place," I murmur.

"If the rumors are to be believed…but who knows what's to be true. Historically, all our peoples would work together, leaders meeting in Evalon for the Council of Kings to exchange information and work for the benefit of all peoples. But in modern times…Midscape is a fractured land. Every people keeping to themselves and deeply suspicious of the next."

Somewhere beyond the horizon, in a land that's as full of magic as it is danger…is our best chance of safety, locked behind an elf wall and in the hands of another king. But if there is a human queen then, surely, she too is a witch like me. She would take pity on us.

I might not place much stock in kings after my experiences with Conri, but I would bet on a fellow witch.

"How long will it take to get to the elves? How many days?"

"On two feet? I would guess four—no, five days, at least."

I bite my lower lip and sink to the ground, pulling my knees to my chest and settling them in the crooks of my elbows as I stare out over the hills, forest, mountains, and lake. Evander sits next to me. Close enough that I feel his warmth breaking through the morning's chill, but far enough away that there is no risk of us touching. I wonder if he's still aware of Conri's attention landing upon us.

"Evander, do you think that there is a chance that, maybe, Conri could help free Aurora?" The question is quiet. Small.

"No." The word is void of doubt.

"Even if there was a way to keep the lykin strong and united without her?" The conversation from the night prior continues to play in my mind.

"Conri would slaughter half the packs if it meant keeping Aurora's power solely to himself. He'd be a king of bones before being just another man."

"It's hard to reconcile what you tell me with what he says," I admit.

Evander grabs my arm, pulling my attention to him. He locks eyes with me. "Do not be drawn into him, through charm or whatever honeyed falsehood he espouses. Conri is not someone you can trust. He is not your ally, Faelyn."

"But he hasn't hurt me, so far," I point out.

"Other than forcing you to marry him."

"Given the position he's in, it's—"

"Do not make excuses for him," Evander cuts me off coldly. "He is a king; there is always a way for a king to make what he wants happen, if he deems it important enough. He is the one who holds the power and makes the rules. If he wanted you to be free—Aurora to be free—you both would be. But instead he keeps you hoarded like treasures that are for him alone. Ready to kill anyone who so much as looks at you for too long."

I sigh and shift uncomfortably, keeping my attention over the landscape. "Perhaps what's happened with Aurora has scared him? Maybe he wants to start fresh with a new way of leading?"

"No. Not Conri." The words are bitten out.

"You truly hate him."

"The first thing he did, the moment he got his hands on Aurora's ring, was demand every alpha in the grasslands submit to him. Those that didn't were slaughtered. At just seventeen, he killed pups in their dens with his own claws and teeth." Evander draws his knees to his chest, mirroring me, gripping his hands around them to the point that his knuckles are white. The flexing of his muscles highlights the scars that cover him.

"He hurt you, as well," I say softly.

Evander slowly turns to face me. His expression is hollow. Void enough for ghosts long dead to live in those eyes the color of the morning's fog.

"He took something from me far more precious than my flesh." His tone has gone quiet, low, slow.

"Aurora told me about your pack," I whisper.

"Yes, my pack, my history, my father, right before my very eyes." The shadows over Evander's eyes darken. "And he took from me the woman I loved."

Ah, love and revenge. I give a small nod and turn back to the landscape before me. I wonder if Conri killed this woman. Or if he "took" her in other ways. Regardless, Evander has plenty of reasons—good reasons, I admit—to hate Conri.

But I need to focus on myself and Aurora foremost. Evander's motivations for hating Conri are his own, and I can use them to our advantage. They're worth considering and keeping in mind. But if there's a way to get Conri on my side, I must try. Seeing the seemingly endless expanse of Midscape has cemented that for me.

I don't know what "getting him on my side" will mean yet…but if there's a chance, I will take it. Not just Aurora's sake, but also for my own. Perhaps all of the lykin. If I can help temper his ways, then maybe there will be a benefit for us all.

twenty

If Conri is aware of my venture out with Evander, he says nothing of it later that night. He makes no mention of my returning to Aurora, either. Or of my evening walk around camp with Evander—where I sneak off, again, as I have been.

Again, there are two cots set up in the tent. Side by side. We sleep apart and he makes no movement toward me. Not even for a kiss.

I find myself staring up at the ceiling of the tent for most of the night. Sleep comes intermittently. Time passes fast enough that I know rest was gained. But it was hardly of quality. How is it that I am more unnerved when he has stopped trying to seduce me?

When morning finally comes and he begins to rouse, I realize the night has been wasted. I am no closer to a plan to get Aurora out. No more confident in what the best course of action is for me to take. As a result, I'm hardly sure of what I want to do next.

"You're awake," Conri observes as he sits and stretches.

"I woke early today," I lie.

"Fortuitous for me."

"Oh?"

"I had half a mind to invite you on this morning's hunt." He sits and, as the blanket pools around his lap, I realize he decided to sleep without trousers.

I look instantly away, but not without seeing the top of the curve of his shapely rear as he stands. My cheeks flush slightly and I bite the insides, hoping that the pain clears my head a little and prevents him from noticing by the time he turns back around. "I am not much of a hunter."

"No? How did you sustain yourself, then?"

"There are many ways to sustain one's self that do not involve the flesh of other creatures." When I hear the gliding of fabric over skin, I dare to glance back. He's fastening the laces at the front of his trousers and, fortunately, I see nothing else.

"I suppose that is true. But what a sad existence to not indulge in meat regularly."

I snort. "The opposite is as much true. Perhaps your lands would still be rich with game should your people have taken a more balanced approach."

Conri gives me a hard look at the comment. I swallow thickly. That probably shouldn't have been said.

But he speaks before I have the opportunity to backtrack. "Perhaps you're right, and this is yet another way you can bring wisdom to the lykin. Though, I do not envy the battle you have ahead of you when it comes to convincing the lykin to indulge in less meat."

"Vegetables can be equally nourishing and twice as delicious if prepared right." I stand, deciding that I will go with him on this hunt. It's a good opportunity to continue getting a feel for the land. And, if I can see where game hides, it is an opportunity to help sustain Aurora and myself when we're on the road. The provisions I've kept hidden away will only last a few days as I had been planning on having other townships to stop into as we ventured through the Natural World. Here, we'll have to be much more self-sufficient.

"But much more boring to hunt." Conri smirks. "I do not think there is the same satisfaction in chasing down a carrot."

"Then you have never had the pleasure of a particularly good forage," I counter.

His expression spreads into an outright smile that lights up his eyes. "I shall show you the joys of the hunt this day, and you shall show me the joys of the forage."

"What?"

"Was I unclear?" He pauses, halfway to the tent flap. "We can both do that which we enjoy and share in it together."

"You want to learn how to forage?"

Conri turns and takes the two steps it is to close the gap between us. He rests his hands gently on my shoulders, meeting my eyes. "I don't think you understand, Faelyn. My main goal is to look after my people. Yes, sometimes that requires blood, and sacrifice, and brutality. Sometimes, there are perhaps gentler approaches I've yet to see. Maybe you can help me see them. I am willing to learn."

"Right," I murmur as he releases me and leaves the tent. The words ring in my ears. Another reminder of this strange man who continually leads me to believe in a pure and gentle nature despite my first impressions…and despite everyone else warning me against him.

"Evander, come, we hunt," Conri commands as we step outside. Evander's eyes dart between Conri and me. There's a silent question to them when they briefly meet mine. But there's no way for me to answer. "You will take the queen, as you have been. Ensure that no harm will befall her. I know how the scent of blood can rally the other alphas and knights."

"Yes, my king."

I fall beside Evander, dealing with the awkwardness of the radiating tension from him. Is he upset I'm doing this? Is there a danger I don't know of?

Within a few moments we've gathered with one woman and two other men. Bardulf I know already. Conri introduces the man as Weylyn, another alpha. The woman I've seen around camp, lingering in the same circles as Evander and Bardulf. Her name is Mell, another of Conri's knights.

"I will lead," Conri announces before taking on his wolf form.

Once more on Evander's back, we speed across the grasslands, fanned in the shape of an arrow point. Conri is at the front. Evander and I over his right shoulder. Weylyn is at his left. Bardulf is behind Evander and me with Mell behind Weylyn. The pace is blisteringly fast and all I can focus on is clutching Evander as tightly as possible.

Conri veers, shifting course without warning. His muzzle lowers and lifts, shifting positions as he runs, smelling earth and air. He's tracking something and I find out what over the slope of a nearby hill. The lykin's eyes catch the movement before I do. Gnashing teeth and excited snarls have my attention locking on to what they are all already focused on—a depression in the grasses, racing away from us.

Conri is faster than the creature. He leaps, jaws open. They clamp around the small creature and a horrible whimper fills the air before being cut short. The wolf king lifts his head, a gray hare caught between his jaws. Red seeps into the poor creature's fur around the fangs that have punctured its neck, killing it instantly. The wolf king's eyes meet mine and he trots over, placing the hare at Evander's side, by my foot, like an offering to me.

I force a beaming smile and nod my head for the sake of the others. I'm sure this is an important gesture in the lykin's culture and instinct tells me not to offend. Just as I'm sure Conri is looking for approval for his kill on my behalf.

It was an impressive feat, how he picked up the smell of the creature, found it, and killed it with such speed and accuracy. But in that dead hare I can't help but see a subtle warning. *See*, the seeping blood seems to say, *look at how easily a life can be ended. Look at how fast and efficient I am at hunting and killing.* The message is clear. But what I do not know is if it was intentional.

Swinging down off Evander, I do as they had instructed me before we left. I take the knife from my satchel and make a careful slit at the creature's throat. My larger hunting knife would've been more effective, if I still had it. But the small one does the trick. Then, I tie the hare upside-down to the strappings around Evander's neck so it will bleed out as it swings against Evander's side.

We repeat this process for three more hare and one fox. I am in the process of stringing up the last when Conri shifts out of his wolf form for the first time since we began the hunt. He helps me tie off the last of the knots, giving a hum of approval as his fingertips brush over mine.

"You're rather skilled with managing the kills of hunting for someone who claims not to do it much."

"I…" My hands still for a second as memories I've not thought of in a long, long time threaten to overwhelm me. For a flash, I am back in the forests. Another set of hands are on me as I clutch a bowstring. Two strong arms around me. The first time my heart fluttered. *Deep breaths, Faelyn, easy, steady…* I quickly recover, hoping Conri didn't notice my brief departure from the present. "Not many humans lived near the edge of the woods. The only others that did were hunters. Growing up so secluded was lonely, so having a companion was a welcome friendship, even if our lives were very different."

Liam. My first true love. My only love. The first day we ever met was one of the worst in my life: the day my mother died. But he was something good to come of all that grief. A shoulder to cry on. A new friendship blossomed out of trauma. And, eventually, something more…or so I had thought.

"You were close with this hunter," Conri observes.

I glance in his direction, finishing the knot that affixes the fox to Evander's side. The wolf knight glances over his shoulder at us. I wonder if he, too, is listening to this part of my history that I would sometimes rather forget. I've no doubt he is, given how little we've shared with each other about our origins.

Conri laughs, no doubt mistaking my hesitation. "I have had many lovers before you, my future queen. I assume the same to be true of you. So worry not for modesty and answer me true."

"I did care for him," I admit. "But then he left, and that was the end of it." Such an oversimplification of what actually happened. But also…so accurate. Liam's and my story isn't more complicated than that. I had given Liam all my heart. I was ready to give him all my body, and every year that was left ahead of me.

And, without a word, he left me waiting alone in the dark night.

"A fool to leave a woman such as you." Conri steps away from Evander. "Now, show me this foraging you so love."

It takes no small amount of mental effort to shift my focus from those old wounds and bring my attention back to the present. I haven't thought deeply of Liam for years. But it seems even a world away, there's so much that makes me think of him. Briefly, for the first time in a long time, I wonder what he's doing now. Did he find happiness separate from me?

"All right," I say, and kneel, pushing my fingers into the ground. "But I'm going to ask for the help of a friend, as I am unfamiliar with the best places to do so in these lands." I take a low, slow breath, and summon the magic that sleeps within me. It's easier to find that latent power since working with Aurora. Or perhaps there's just more of it to grasp at. "Mary, I seek your help."

Small marigolds bud around my hand, the largest blooming in place of my palm when I pull my hand away. Tiny vines stretch up in impossible ways, forming a doll-like humanoid. Mary's form is much smaller than I last saw her. But there's a sturdiness to her magic that I have never sensed before. Having her leave was the best thing that could happen for her.

It causes me to briefly wonder, yet again, what the true depths of Aurora's power might be, were she able to be free.

"Hello, Faelyn," Mary says in her sweet, whispering voice. "It is good to see you again."

All the wolves have gathered around us, even though they cannot understand the words. Conri looks on silently, a proud smile on his lips. I focus on Mary rather than the rest of them.

"And you as well. Do you think you have time and energy to help me forage? I don't know where to look, or what to look for in these lands. But, based on the terrain, I'm hoping for perhaps some root vegetables?"

"It would be my honor." Mary dips her chin and the vines sink back into the earth. Another marigold pops up a few steps away. And another beyond that.

"We'll follow her," I say to Conri in the common tongue. Shifting between the language of spirits and that of other mortals is instinctive and effortless.

Conri looks over his shoulder. "The rest of you, take the kills back to camp. They should be shared with the pack, sooner the better."

The four wolves lower their heads at their king. Evander's muzzle doesn't dip quite as far as the others, I notice. Following their king's command, they race off.

"It is impressive to watch a witch work," Conri appraises as we start walking in the direction of the next marigold bloom. "Your ability to summon spirits is uncanny."

"Evander summoned a water spirit for our passage."

"Evander is an odd lykin." Conri laughs lightly. "It is best not to use him as a measure for the rest of us. And he is far less graceful than you with these skills."

"Odd how?" I ask, trying to sound casual despite my deep curiosity.

"Careful, Faelyn, or I might be jealous of you inquiring about another man." Conri says the words easily enough, but I see the flash of warning in his eyes.

I laugh and link my arm with his. "I am only asking if I need to be worried about my sworn protector."

"Ah, nothing like that, my dear." He pats my forearm. "While the lykin can see spirits, we cannot commune or bond with them in the same way as a witch. It is what makes our oath to the great wolf spirit so unique, and a notable exception—we cannot simply call upon spirits as we please, or communicate with them."

I imagine that is also what makes Aurora so valuable to them… If they cannot call upon spirits, then they hoard what power they do have from them.

"There are some lykin who have an easier time harnessing our power and seeking out spirits than others, for one reason or another. But even then, it is not guaranteed the spirits will oblige. We cannot command their loyalty as you can." His wording grates.

"I do not command spirits."

"No?" He motions to the small flowers we're following.

"Mary is a friend."

"Are you not bonded?" Conri arches his brows at me.

"Yes, but—"

"And a bond is a sworn oath to a witch that the spirit will lend you their powers as they are able, is it not?"

"It is," I admit, feeling somewhat backed into a corner. "But to be given a bond is to be deemed worthy of it. And while it is, admittedly, almost impossible to unravel a bond once tied, I would pursue undoing one if asked."

He's silent for a few steps. "You think I should free Aurora."

When I look up at him, he wears a slightly amused expression and an easy smile. If he's taken offense, it's not showing. So I dare to be brave. "I do."

"And what happens when she's freed and we lykin no longer have the strength to change into our wolf forms on command? When we are relegated to the moon's cycle? You know now that we have no other powers than this, as mighty as they are. How will we defend ourselves or keep the vampir's blight at bay in their mountains?"

"I am sure—"

"How will a king be determined from among the alphas if not for control of the moon spirit? Without a method, we would inevitably return to the years of warring packs, fighting and squabbling amongst ourselves to the point that we lack any sort of real say or sway among the other rulers of Midscape should the Council of Kings ever reconvene?"

It's my turn to be silent for a few steps. I know I should stop talking and let the matter drop...but my bravery continues walking with me, whispering in my ear.

"I do not know," I admit. "I don't know the politics of Midscape or half its magics." I pause to look up and meet his eyes. "But what I do know is that a king who is only able to be king because of entrapping another is no real ruler. He is a coward."

Conri stops as well and lifts his brows. The dull but somehow simultaneously dangerous look he gives me almost sets my hands to trembling. Almost. But I continue to stand tall. As long as I have Aurora's powers, I am immune to many repercussions. I hope.

To my surprise, he says, "Then perhaps, as a witch, you can assist me in finding a way to do that without risking my people's well-being."

"What?" I say, utterly flummoxed.

"A king has never been wedded to a witch before. Perhaps, with your magic, we can find a way to sustain my people, keep the peace, *and* free Aurora."

"You really think so?" A slight breeze picks up over the hills. It smells of fresh grass and surprisingly of hope.

"If you are willing to truly be at my side, Faelyn, then I think we could accomplish anything." The muscles of his arm tense around my hand. Somehow, I'd managed to forget that I had grabbed on to him.

Evander's warnings are loud in my mind. The sense of betrayal toward Aurora is sharp. But is it truly betraying her if the end result is the same? I am not going against what she would want...merely exploring another way.

twenty-one

That night, I'm able to cook for Aurora on a small fire, off to the side. I take the scraps of meat given to us by Conri and roast them until the juices run clear. Evander has found me two bowls—better suited for mixing than for eating from, so the leafy greens I foraged earlier look like a comically small amount. At the fire's edge are two root vegetables. Some kind of potato, so far as I can tell, that I rotate on occasion while preparing everything else.

"What did you two talk about?" Evander blurts after Conri leaves.

"Ah, thank you for finally asking," I say without looking up from tearing leaves.

"Pardon?"

"I could feel you had something you wanted to say ever since I returned to camp."

"I wasn't about to ask with him here," Evander mutters.

"Why do you want to know what we talked about?" I poke at the potatoes.

"I'm afraid he's trying to win you over, and that he might be succeeding." Severity and fear line Evander's words, accompanied by an undercurrent of disgust.

I sigh. *Is that what's happening?* In my effort to use Conri, is he using me?

"This is how it always goes…" Evander crouches next to me. "His charm wears everyone down in the end."

"Evander, my goal is to free Aurora." I drop my voice to

barely a whisper, eyes flicking toward him. "My *only* goal is to free her. I will do whatever it takes to accomplish that. I will explore every option and opportunity. And if you resent me for that, I'll have to ask if you were ever really on my side to begin with."

Evander leans forward, putting his face in mine. I don't move. I don't back away. If there's one thing I'm starting to learn about the lykin, it's that they're constantly struggling for power—constantly looking for who has the upper hand and control in a situation. I can't show any trace of weakness or doubt.

"Other than Aurora herself, I am the only one here on your side. And I think my actions have proved that."

He makes it sound like I should be able to trust him without a moment's hesitation. I purse my lips, willfully ignoring the fact that I have, up to this point, found it dangerously easy to give him the benefit of the doubt. "If you're on my side, then why wouldn't you—"

"Be willing to work with Conri?" Evander raises his brows. The firelight glows on half of his face, casting the other half in a deep shadow. "Because that is one of the few things that would be worse than death. Don't give in to him, Faelyn. His words are lies. His actions are a smokescreen for his intent. He can't be trusted."

"Yet, he continues to give me space. He listens to me when I speak. He even knows that I am working to resist his charm," I speak hastily, getting the words out before Evander can launch another objection.

"He what?" Evander hisses.

"He knows I am resisting him and he is not forcing the matter," I say. "That is why he gave me another cot. Why he is allowing me space and time as I need and please."

Evander purses his lips, brow furrowing into a severe expression. He murmurs, "That is not good."

"So far my life has been much improved here since my hesitation toward him came out."

"Faelyn, he is not a man who does well not getting what he wants."

"He said he likes the hunt." I pull the meat from the flame and turn the potatoes again.

Evander grabs my wrist, bringing my attention back to him. "Yes, he loves the hunt. But what do you think will happen if he doesn't get his prey at the end of it?" Evander continues to pin me with his stare.

His expression is more demanding than his question. "Don't know? That's because, one way or another, Conri always gets his prey. He might be playing nicely with you now, but the moment he grows bored of this game, his tactics will shift, and the facade of a nice man you know will be gone."

As someone walks between two nearby tents, Evander immediately releases me, head jerking in that direction. But the person doesn't even so much as spare a glance our way. I use the moment to stab the potatoes, throwing them into the wooden bowls.

"You've been heard, Evander. Now I need to take this to Aurora."

He escorts me to her tent without further word on the matter. Though I can feel his frustration steaming as hot as the potatoes. Aurora is expectedly pleased to see us both and the warm welcome she gives Evander makes me feel a touch guilty over doubting him. She truly does trust him.

Her excitement doubles the moment she lays eyes on what's in the bowl. Evander leaves us to it, taking his position just outside the tent.

"Greens, vegetables, properly cooked meats?" Aurora sits cross-legged on the ground, situating the bowl in her lap. "How did you manage this miracle?"

"Conri went foraging with me."

Aurora pauses mid grab of a handful of greens. She shoves them in her mouth, chewing over them for a long minute.

I continue in her silence, "He knows what's been happening—more or less. That I've been resisting him…" I quickly recap her on the events of the past day. Her expression is impossible to read the entire time I speak. "… But I'm thinking that, if he's sincere, maybe there is a way for us all to get what we want."

"Not with him. Not Conri," she says finally, shaking her head slowly. "He will want you to believe it's possible. But there is no way he'd ever give in."

"And maybe he doesn't have to, not really," I say hastily. Her words echo Evander's and I feel more and more foolish by the moment for starting to trust Conri. "Maybe we can use him long enough to get what we need. If he thinks we're on his side, we can use that to our advantage."

Aurora considers this. "I'd rather you didn't."

I sigh heavily. "You and Evander…you both have given me such warnings about him. And I do believe you both." I glance toward the tent flap, hoping my voice is low enough that Evander doesn't overhear. "But Conri hasn't been the man that you've claimed. At least not to me. Maybe he really is trying to change and grow?"

"I have stood beside hundreds of wolf kings, and each one of them becomes as corrupted by their power as the last."

"Aurora, we mortals aren't a monolith. I know you have endured hundreds of years of hardship. But every single person has the capacity to change, if they want it."

"*If they want it*," she repeats, emphasizing. "He never will."

I rest my elbow on my knee and sink my head into my palm. "I just don't know how to free you without his help. I saw Midscape, or just this portion of it… This world is expansive. I don't know if I could get us free of him and I fear his wrath should we try and fail."

"You are not alone in fearing his wraith." Aurora rests her fingertips on my free hand that is on my other knee. "Which is why we will not fail. We will continue gathering spirits to our cause and we will call on them when the time comes for us to make our flight. We will plan carefully and only act when we're sure."

I nod and straighten, trying to exude more confidence than I feel.

"So let's finish our meals and then we work on your magic again."

We spend one more night in the camp with Weylyn's pack, and then the tents come down. There are almost a hundred wolves now, running as one, thundering across the sloping plains. I do not find the same joy in the rides as I once did. The wind doesn't smell as sweetly with hope.

Every night between the two pack camps, we set up temporary tents. Yet Conri's remains the most established. Every night, I have my separate cot and he bids me to dream well.

Come the dawn, I am only more conflicted.

I watch Conri's every movement in search of betrayal. A hint of deception. But I can find none.

Given his past, all that Evander and Aurora have said, I don't think I could ever love him…but if he is trying to change, perhaps we could be friends. Or friends enough that he would be right and we could accomplish something meaningful for both our worlds.

Helping lykin and human alike is a far greater purpose than defending the woods. And when I am successful in restoring Aurora's power to her, I will need a purpose after. A goal.

Every morning I wake, thinking I will have more clarity than the last. But I only feel more muddled and confused.

"Faelyn," Conri says, announcing his presence as he enters the tent on our first night in the new pack's camp. "Are you awake?"

"I am," I say, even though he can plainly see as much.

Conri sits on the edge of his cot, near the foot. "If you are not too tired, I would love for you to hear our songs."

"Songs?"

"Yes, they will be sung around the bonfire." He extends his hand. "Come with me? But only if you wish."

I am curious enough that I accept the invitation. Conri escorts me out of the tent, Evander at his shoulder. We head to the large bonfire at the center of camp. Half of the pack sits or stands in a circle around it. I see pan pipes and simple, flat drums.

A man I recognize as one of the other alphas gives a respectful nod to Conri. Then he tilts his head back and lets out a noise that is not quite singing and not quite howling, but something between. It comes from deep in his gut and rises up the back of his head. Others lift their chins and howl in reply. It's a call and repeat, soon joined by slow and steady thumping of the drums.

The pack is soon breathing as one, sharp inhales part of the sound that is quickly becoming music. Each person seems to sing-howl one sound, but they do so in such quick succession that, together, they begin to form words.

"Evander, if you would?" Conri commands in so few words.

Evander steps forward. I think he is going to sing, but instead he approaches the bonfire. He holds out a hand, as if reaching for the flame, and closes his fingers. As his lips move, I watch the flames dance, eyes appearing within them.

Folost? I have never seen the little fire spirit look so mighty. Mary hasn't been the only one who's benefited from time in Midscape.

One blink of golden eyes. *Yes.* But yes to what? My question is answered as the fire burns low, Evander lowering his hands as if smothering it. The lykin then raises his right palm, fingers shifting, pulling it out to the side. Folost moves with Evander, as though the lykin is conducting the fire spirit.

The flames make shapes, of wolves and fanged crowns, of a glowing orb that looks like the sun but I can only assume represents the moon.

It is their history being told through the flickering yellows, oranges, and reds. A story echoed by the primordial, guttural howls that form words in an ancient tongue I don't understand. Yet…I find myself swaying with them. Breathing with them. The thrumming drums and sharp trills of pan pipes sustaining high notes gives a sweet dizziness akin to too much mead. Heart racing, slightly bubbly, but also the air thick with anticipation.

"Come," Conri says, just that one word. A command. Yet I heed it anyway when he extends his hand. "Dance with me."

He pulls me away from the crowd, yanking me toward him. His palm smooths over my hip, grazing around my rear, gripping firmly. My cheeks flush instantly and I glance around. There are so many eyes on us…

"Look at me," he orders. "Only at me."

And I do.

The movements are unlike any dance I've ever known. I never considered myself much of a dancer. But I have had my share of naked twirling under the full moon. This…is not unlike that. When I would dance in the woods I felt as light as the air itself. Here, now, I am heavy and hot, moving with words and howls and pulsing drumbeats.

Conri wraps his arms around my waist and leans forward. I tip backward, bending at the small of my back. My hips press into his. Conri growls low against my neck. I burn like the fire and my thoughts swim, swirling into an oblivion, leaving a void behind in my mind.

It would feel good…

The voice is back, the one egged on by Conri's charm. By the magic that makes all the men and women of the pack behold Conri with envy and lust. Conri pulls me up, our chests pressing. He spins me. Lifts me.

Drums pulsing. Sweat rolling down my neck. Howling in my soul and silver eyes that threaten to consume me… I am a ship at sea, being pulled away in the current. A leaf from a tree, helpless of where I will land.

My arms fly out and pain sears through the haze.

I blink, regaining focus. At first, I think I've gone too close to the fire. But I should be far enough away. A spark?

My gaze shifts, meeting Evander's dark stare beyond Folost's golden eyes. He had the spirit burn me intentionally, I realize. He wanted me to regain my focus.

"Forgive me." I rest my hands on Conri's shoulders, playing up my breathlessness. "I grow weary."

Conri's smile doesn't falter. His eyes hold the same burning passion that caused me to almost give in entirely to him seconds ago. "Of course. Let's take you to bed."

I am escorted back to the tent. As I sit on my cot, Conri leans over me, placing a gentle kiss on my forehead.

"Thank you for dancing with me," he whispers in my ear, lips brushing my cheek. "I cannot tell you how deeply I enjoyed it. Though I do wish I could show you how many more ways our bodies could move together."

"I—"

"Not right now." He leans away with a slight smirk. I wonder if he thought I was going to give in this time. After that dance…I can't fault him for it. "I have some matters to attend to with my knights and alphas." Conri cups my cheek, dragging his thumb over my lips. I shiver. "Though, perhaps later, if you are still so keen."

I don't have a chance to respond before he leaves the tent. I'm left breathless. Molten at my core. Sweat still rolls down my neck. The insatiable urge to touch myself is mind-numbing. But I resist leaning back onto my cot. If I pleasured myself now, I would be thinking of Conri…I'd be giving in to him.

But would it truly be so bad?

As if to answer the thought, the tent flaps open, revealing Evander. "We need to move quickly."

"What?"

"Don't fight me and just follow. There's something you need to hear. Now."

Something in his voice compels me to do as he says without delay. I step out and Evander draws me instantly against his side. His left hand on my hip. My flesh is still aflame and I am hyperaware of how his fingers press into me. Of the feeling of his body moving next to mine as he leads me through the camp.

We slink from shadow to shadow. His every motion possesses a grace I've yet to see from him. Evander's eyes shine in the growing moonlight. Sharp and alert. He seems to know who's around every corner before they say or do anything. I'm confident no one has seen us by the time we round the camp and slow to a stop at a tent on the inner circle—opposite from Conri's. A tent that seems as normal as the rest of them.

Evander raises a finger to his lips and crouches down, leading me closer to the wall of canvas. We stop and he leans an ear toward the canvas; I mirror the movement. While the tents are sturdy, they're still just fabric and I can hear almost every word without issue.

"...truly marry her?" a woman muses with a note of disgust. I don't recognize the voice.

"Would it be so bad?" Conri asks with a soft snort, as if he knows the answer to his own question. "A witch for a wife."

"A *human*," she corrects with malice. "The wolf king cannot be having litters with a human. Even a weaver witch, the idea is unthinkable."

"I know, but I have little choice for the time being; so long as Aurora's magic is within her, it's a game we all must play." He sighs.

"You didn't look like you were playing a game with her when you danced." I recognize Weylyn's voice from the hunt, alpha of the last pack we collected.

"Good, then my performance was convincing enough." A chill, colder than winter's grasp, courses through my veins. The voice belongs to Conri, yet it's a stranger to me. His tone is unfeeling, calculating, and shifting. It is the lift of a curtain—a reveal behind the facade. As if, for the first time, I can hear the depths of his malevolence. "She thinks she can resist me. It's adorable, really, that she believes she can thwart me with magic when at the end of the day she's just a simple woman and giving in to her urges is something that her nature will compel her to do. No magic required. I'll make her bend before me in more ways than one."

I don't know which I'm more disgusted by, that he thinks me so basic, or that I've been playing right into his game.

"I have her in the palm of my hand. She'll play nicely enough and let us take her to Den."

"Where you will marry her?" the woman asks. She's this pack's alpha, I assume.

Conri snorts. "You really do believe that, don't you, Drena?"

"But you—"

"I will take her to the old wood and bring her before the wolf spirit. There, we will cut out her heart and feed it to the great wolf, who will be ready to receive Aurora's power from the act. Then, that power will be passed from the wolf to me, as the king, where it will live forever in my bloodline," Conri says, matter-of-fact.

He never meant that the power would be in his bloodline by bedding me…

He is going to kill me.

twenty-two

STRENGTH ABANDONS ME AND I FALL OUT OF MY CROUCH, MY REAR MEETING THE COOL EARTH AS SHOCK WEIGHS DOWN MY SHOULDERS. *You shouldn't be surprised*, a soft voice scolds from the back of my mind, *this is what they told you he was*. No…I'm not surprised at Conri. I'm surprised at myself. Even if I told myself I was indulging him for the purpose of manipulation, I was actually falling for his charm.

"Do you think she will catch on to your intentions?" Weylyn asks.

"No, she thinks herself clever, but I have her right where I want her. I'll let her believe she's in control until it's too late," Conri says nonchalantly.

"And if she doesn't follow your plans?" Drena asks.

"That is what he has me for," Bardulf speaks, sounding a little too excited. "Her presence is already an insult enough; it would be my honor to remove her stain from our lands."

A light touch on my elbow pulls me from the conversation. Weylyn is saying something else but my attention is back outside the tent. On Evander, who is gently wrapping his fingers around my arm and pulling me up.

I allow him to guide me back through camp. Conri was right. I thought I had control. But, in reality, I was a puppet, dancing under Conri's fingers. Now my strings are cut and I am limp under Evander's grip.

As the camp blurs around us, my daze slowly turns to rage. That gives my mind sharpness and clarity again. The only thing that has changed is I now know, without doubt, that there can never be reasoning with Conri. Aurora and Evander were right. I should be thanking Conri for removing any doubt or second thoughts surrounding my path forward.

By the time we reach Evander's tent, slipping through the flap and into the darkness, my thoughts are moving again. I take the two steps the tent can afford me to reach the back wall. Turn, walk back to Evander, turn, and repeat. Pacing.

Evander tries to speak. "He does not—"

"Care for me?" I make a noise of disgust. "That much is obvious." I stop, my back to Evander. Fists clenching. "You know, I didn't think he cared for me. Not really. But I had thought that *maybe* he would respect me enough that we could work together toward a common goal. That perhaps time had worn him down, fear over Aurora's loss had shown him vulnerability and he wasn't quite the man you both knew… That he could be—"

"Reasoned with?" It's Evander's turn to finish my sentence. "Conri doesn't know the meaning of those words. It's his way or nothing. By resisting him, even daring to try, you committed a cardinal sin for which there is no forgiveness." Even though he speaks at barely a whisper, Evander's voice grows louder as he draws near. He comes to a stop right behind me and I think he is about to rest a hand on my shoulder, but it must be my imagination, as a touch never comes. "I am sorry you had to find out that way. But I couldn't let you go on thinking there was hope for an alliance with him. Not when I learned of his plans."

"The only thing I am sorry for is that I was gullible enough to give him the benefit of the doubt." Rage, not sorrow, softens my voice.

"Hoping for reason and seeing the best in people are hallmarks of a good heart. They're not a reason to be upset with yourself."

Perhaps he's right, but in this moment I'm searing the truth into my mind with a red-hot branding iron. I will never forget this lesson.

"Thank you for taking me there," I say. "I needed to know. Now I will fight him with all I am."

"Good. Because he's going to do everything in his power to ensure that you will continue to fall for him."

"That I will still be in the palm of his hand." I hatefully paraphrase his words.

"For Conri, admitting his charm isn't working would be akin to a loss of his manhood. It'd make a fool of him."

Has anything ever sounded better than the mere idea of making a fool of an egotistical king? I think not. My fingers relax and my head tips back slightly as I bring my gaze from the lower wall to the ceiling of the tent. It's washed in a pale haze from the growing moon. I've been here nearly two weeks. Enough time for the moon to swell to almost its apex.

Aurora's might grows in tandem with the heavenly body. Perhaps that is what is feeding my boldness. Or this fiery resolve is all my own. A strength cultivated out of necessity, nurtured by the wisdom and sorcery that was gifted to me by my mother and grandmother, that was hard won across every triumph and setback across my years. Seeds from which my power continues to blossom.

"I think I would like to do that," I whisper.

"Do what?" Evander sounds legitimately confused.

"Make a fool of him." The words taste delicious.

Evander does grab my shoulder now, turning me to look me in the eyes. His brows are furrowed. Shoulders pulling with tension. I feel his fingertips well into my flesh through my cloak and shirt.

"Did you not learn anything?" he growls. "Challenging Conri is a deadly game."

"So I am to give in to him?" I lift my own brows and tilt my head slightly. "Just allow him to do with me as he pleases until my use to him expires?" I chuckle softly and shake my head. Evander's expression only darkens. "That's not going to happen."

"You need to keep your head about you."

"I agree." I rest my hand on his chest lightly. The sculpted contour of his pectoral fits seamlessly into palm, like proof our forms were designed to complement one another. Even through the thin shirt he wears, I can feel every curve of his rock-hard muscle. A playful little smile dances upon my lips. Enough with holding back. I look up at him through my lashes with purpose. "That's why I need your help."

"Of course." He steps backward, ready to move away as he has all the other nights.

I catch Evander's wrist with my left hand and bring his attention back to me, my right palm still against his skin. My heart is pounding with such force that my breathing quickens. But nerves aren't the cause…it's anticipation. Excitement. I've thought about this enough times that it is a relief to imagine it finally coming to pass. "I need… more."

His lips part slightly. Body relaxes. Shock only, I hope, and not disgust at my obvious implication.

"If you're willing to give it," I hastily add, hoping that was already assumed.

"You want to…" The words are so breathy and faint that they fade completely by the end.

"I want you to help make it so that I do not think of Conri. I want to—need to be satisfied in a way that I have not been in years."

He searches my face. "Have you known many men?"

"Not many. But enough that I assure you I will not be a disappointment." I take a small step forward, our bodies nearly flush. "Enough to know what I'm doing and what I'm asking. I don't go in blindly, or in haste."

Evander chuckles deeply. "Not in haste? How is moving on me to spite the man who you just learned is laying plans to kill you anything but haste?" He shakes his head and pulls away. The palm that was on his chest grabs the night air, icy after touching him. "I will not be a thing for you to use."

"You're more than that," I blurt. He stops, but doesn't turn back to face me. I instantly regret this choice to try and persuade him. I should have let the matter drop.

"Why?"

I have to tell him. Not just for the sake of trying to convince him, but because he has a right to know what I've been doing. Especially if it is something that he would prefer I stop. Given how he's acting, he might find the idea nauseating.

"Because…" I gather all the courage I'd just found. *Don't leave me now*, I silently beg that braver side of me. "Because you are the only thing that has allowed me to break free of him."

"Yes, and you can still do what you need here."

"That's not what I mean. Evander, you—I think of you."

"What?" he whispers, finally turning to face me once more. Evander searches my expression.

"Every time I've had to resist Conri's charms. Even when he is right there, exerting all his effort and magic to try and claim me, if I bring you to the front of my mind then all thoughts of him vanish." As I speak, Evander's expression is impossible to read. But it isn't one of disgust. So I dare to continue, hoping that perhaps he believes what I'm saying. "I've fantasized about you every single time these past two weeks. I tried to think of someone else—of my past partners, of a man I fabricated entirely in my imagination. But none of them worked. None of them could cut through the haze of his charm. Except you."

"You're saying…" It's his turn to approach me. And the strong glide of his hips through the air, the sway to his shoulders, the movement is more like a prowl than a step. "That when you lie there, pleasuring yourself…that when he is whispering in your ear and attempting to exert every bit of his magic force upon you…you think of me?"

I manage a small nod. My throat has gone thick with anticipation as he condenses the space between us into nothing but buzzing heat.

"Tell me," he commands, stopping just shy of touching me. Having him this unbearably close has me aware of every inch of exposed skin that yearns to be touched. Every hair stands on end. *Touch me*, I want to scream, to beg. "Tell me everything you've thought of."

"I thought of…you, and me…"

"Oh, Faelyn." He chuckles darkly. The man is enjoying this. If the torture weren't so delightful, I might resent him for it. Evander hooks my chin with his fingers, guiding my face to his. But he does not kiss me. His lips hover just off mine. "You have to give me more detail than that, or I might misunderstand."

"I think of you, touching me." My words quiver slightly.

"More." Evander's other hand grazes up my thigh, to my hip, hooking on my shirt and slipping under it. With the heel of his palm, he smooths his hand over my waist. An involuntary gasp escapes me at the sensation of his touch. My lids grow heavy and hazy, as if I am drunk off the sensations of him. "Tell me more. Give me every, last, vivid detail."

"I've thought of you with your hand where mine is as I pleasure myself. Nibbling on my ear, whispering of how you will ravage my body. You, hot and naked beside me, my hands on your length. Of you between my legs—your face and your hips. I've fantasized about you mounting me like a beast and relentlessly pounding into me. Taking me. And I've imagined you kissing me with all the tenderness of the world." The words come bursting forth; every fantasy and half-baked daydream is rushing out of me as if this is my one and only chance to speak them into existence.

Evander leans forward, expression still unreadable. He tilts his head, cheek brushing against mine as he whispers into my ear, "And how do I taste?"

My knees have turned to jelly. I quiver, not knowing how much longer I'll be able to stand. I doubt it will be very long, if he keeps this up. I want to melt into him. To collapse into this vortex of passion that has opened at our feet, threatening to swallow me whole.

"In my fantasies, you taste as sweet as you are forbidden."

"And do I leave you satisfied, yet yearning for more?"

"Always," I breathe.

He pulls away, locking eyes with mine. "Good. Then I shall have no problem living up to these desires of yours."

I don't have time to respond before he claims my words and my thoughts with his mouth.

twenty-three

My hands are on his shoulders in an instant, gliding around the back of his neck for a better grip. Evander wastes no time in deepening the kiss. He drops both hands to my hips and pulls me toward him with breathless force. His palms skate around to my rear, groping and kneading. When he shifts, our mouths part just enough for a soft moan to escape me.

"Quiet now, no one can hear us," he rasps against my lips, even as I am still trying to kiss him. "I don't want there to be any suspicion. That way, I can take my time with you."

Without warning, he leans forward slightly, takes a firm grip of my rear, and pulls up. His strong muscles contract, bulging from the shoulders that I hold on to fiercely for balance as my legs wrap around his hips on instinct. A soft yelp of surprise escapes me, both from the sudden movement and from the hot firmness that presses into my heat.

"I said quiet," he growls, kissing me again. Evander sucks my lower lip between his teeth, biting and nibbling on it almost to the point of pain, *almost*. I fight moans as he releases and returns to kissing me, tongue in my mouth.

I am putty underneath his hands. He is the sculptor, and I am the clay. I want him to make me, mold me into an entity that was made for him and him alone. My weightlessness in his strong arms is a surrender of all my better sense. The muscles of my back relax. Pent-up tension is unraveled, pooling into my lower abdomen. Kissing him is both relief and frustration. I have had the bare minimum of satisfaction and now I want it all.

Evander drops to his knees, one at a time. My ankles are locked behind him. One hand releases me and fumbles off to the side. I'm too distracted with kissing him to pay attention to what he's reaching for. But the question is answered when, without breaking the kiss, my back meets the ground, hastily covered by his bedroll.

He lays me down, freeing his hands from underneath me. We move with desperate haste. His shirt is off. The ties on his trousers are no match for my skilled fingers. I've untangled too many threads that knotted from storage to be thwarted by a few finger-lengths of leather cord.

"May I?" he whispers huskily against my throat, right under my jaw. One hand is positioned at the clasp of my cape.

Somehow, it didn't occur to me that for him to take me, he would have to remove my greatest source of magical protection. Foolish, really. But lust is so rarely logical. When I don't immediately respond, he shifts, dipping his chin to meet my eyes.

The world stills, holding its breath in unison with me. I study his expression. Ablaze within the molten mercury of his irises is unbridled passion, yet, at the center of that fiery tempest is a sanctuary of unspoken gentleness. The atmosphere surrounding us shivers, filling with tension, tightening with every second that slips by where we do nothing but study each other, wondering if we have the strength to cross the line and finish what we started.

"Will you hurt me?" I whisper.

A tired, slightly unhinged smirk crosses his lips. There's an almost wicked shine to his eyes brought on by the ghosts that dance through his gaze. Specters that I don't understand. Perhaps these are the phantoms that relentlessly hound him, chaining him to the belief that he's only a burden to those he loves.

Not that I need this to be love…

"I warned you that my touch is like a mark of hardship." He leans forward once more, brushing his lips with mine.

"I can't believe it," I murmur.

"No? Then why do you hesitate? Your body knows to fear me, even if your mind says otherwise." Even as he warns me against him, his hand moves down my side, catching on my breast. Thumb flicking over its peak that has my back arching off the ground. "Perhaps it is the danger of me that excites your desire."

"You wouldn't hurt me." I settle on that truth, surprisingly confident. Those words resound in me with perfect clarity, not a trace of doubt, cutting through the heady haze of my immense need.

"No?" He growls as he leans forward to kiss me again. This time fiercer. Almost angry. His tongue has turned bitter. "I have killed the heart of a witch before."

My heartbeats slow, every one resounding in my ears, echoing the words ominously. Yes, there's a danger to his movements. Yet I find myself more intrigued by it than afraid.

"Are you sure you want to bed a man such as me?"

I study him, searching those haunted eyes for an explanation I know I will not find. It's too closely guarded. The facts have been muddled to obscure the picture.

"You are what I want." Even with all the unknowns that surround him, even with fear and doubt trying to cut through my resolve, those words ring true. "When you are near, thoughts of you eclipse all others. Only you can make the world melt away to nothingness. I want you to ravage my body until I can't think. There will be nothing for Conri to claim if I allow you to destroy it."

His smirk turns into a grin. Satisfied and triumphant. I wonder if he is gloating to himself that he will take the woman Conri claimed. Let him, if it ends the talking.

"Good. For I have dreamed of feeling you under me since the first moment I laid eyes on you." He kisses me again and unfastens the clasp of my cape with a single hand. That hand moves from my collarbones to my chest, grazing over my breasts, to the bottom of my shirt, where it slips underneath the hem and reaches back up. He grabs my bare breast, gently, caressing and grazing over every sensitive spot. Then, firmer.

Evander lets out a low growl into my ear. "But I should warn you, Faelyn. I might not be the monster that Conri is, but I cannot promise I am a gentle lover. If you tell me to ravage your body, then that is what I shall do."

"I don't need you to be gentle." I surprise even myself by saying so. But it's true. I've been so twisted and bent and strung to the point of near breaking by the endless teasing and tempting that I want nothing more than raw and simple satisfaction. "And I meant what I told you."

He takes me at my word.

Releasing me, his hand leaves my shirt and grabs my hips and yanks me to him. Evander's lips seek out mine, claiming them in a kiss that threatens to break me. I moan into the kiss, it escapes as a gasp as his hands explore the curves of my body once more, pushing away fabric and pulling off my clothes.

Quivering against the night air, my own hands are pushing down his pants. They have a mind of their own, moving with a need that I've never had before. Never have I needed release so badly. Never have I ached for a man's touch upon me with every trembling fiber of my being.

Coming up for air, we pant against each other. His shining eyes threaten to consume me and, as they do, I'm aware of how naked I am even though his own pants are still clinging loosely on his lower hips, hanging in a frustratingly modest manner. Evander grabs my face, thumb under my chin.

"Tell me what you want," he growls against my mouth.

"You," I say instantly.

"You know that's not good enough. Be specific."

"I want to taste you." My voice is not my own. It's deep with desire and heavy with need. "I want to feel you against me. I want to have you fill me to the point that I can't worry about anything else." *Make the world fade away.*

"I will give you all that and more." Evander places a kiss on my mouth that's almost so sweet it could be called love. It's contrasted as he leans away and I get my first look at all of him. He shifted just enough to shed the last of his clothes while kissing me.

He's as stunning as all my imaginings. My attention follows the dark line of hair from his chest down his stomach, framed by the divots of his upper hips, all the way down to the object of my focus. Two words cross my mind and manage to escape my lips as a breath.

"Yes please."

With a chuckle, Evander pushes me back. I shiver as his lips kiss a trail down my neck, nibbling and licking all over the swell of my breasts. My body goes as rigid as him in response. He returns to my face, clearly savoring every aching, smothered moan and hitching breath.

"Are you ready for me?" he whispers into my ear.

"More than."

Evander's body presses against mine, his arousal pulsing against me. His hands and tongue continue to explore my body greedily. Right when I'm about ready to scream for him, he grabs my hips and adjusts our positioning. Without another warning, he pushes into me. Slowly and purposefully. All the while, eyes locked with mine.

The moment all the space between us has collapsed, he sets a rhythm. His fingers dig into me, lips never leaving mine as the pace works nearly into a frenzy.

This, every ragged breath seems to say. *This!* every beat of my heart screams. At long last I have him. I feel him. And it is better than my imaginings. Every wave of bliss that crashes over me, leaving trembles in its wake, is better than the last.

As the passion builds in my body, I find myself trying to hold back. I'm not ready for it to be over. But Evander knows me, somehow, as well as I know myself. He knows just where to bite on my throat, just where to push, and pull, and pinch.

"Give yourself to me," he commands, looming over me.

"Everything." The word is little more than a gasp as pleasure crashes over me. It's enough that my mind goes blank. That all doubt and fear is erased—if only for a few blissful seconds. But even as the rush fades, there's still him there and I find I don't want to push him away.

When he finally leaves my body, I expect him to dress without word. To act as if what we just did didn't happen at all. Wetness drips between my thighs. I hope Conri never comes in this tent because I imagine our scent has soaked into the canvas. At the very least, Evander's bedroll.

But, despite my expectations, Evander stretches out on the bedroll beside me. He lies slightly on his side; one arm beckons. The other reaches up toward me.

"May I hold you?" he asks. "Not for long…but I think we have time. I doubt Conri has even noticed your absence yet."

"You want to hold me?" A slight smile curls my tired lips. All the muscles in my face, so recently twisted in pleasure, in the pain of keeping in my moans, relax. "I didn't think this was that type of relationship?"

"If I am completely honest with you, Faelyn, the warmth of a woman next to me is more satisfaction than the act of having her," Evander says. "But to answer you directly, yes, I want to hold you. I want to know a different kind of intimacy with you."

After searching his face for any hint of deceit and finding none, I lie down next to him, shifting until I am settled within the crook of his arm. He is against my back—it seems to be the most natural position for us to fall into—and that thought causes me to wear a satisfied smirk as my eyes flutter closed, mind already filling with ideas for the next time. Evander is pure heat and it soothes my delightfully aching muscles. His left arm wraps around my waist, pulling me closer. My legs curl and tangle with his. I use his right arm like a pillow.

For being a man who threatened to break my heart an hour ago, he is nothing but sincerity and tenderness now.

Evander's soft, steady breaths on the nape of my neck cause my own breathing to slow. And, in turn, my heart. All that muscle behind me is like a wall that is strong enough to block out and hold back the horrors of the world…if only for a little while.

A sigh escapes from me, taking with it my consciousness as I slip into an unintentional, but complete and dreamless slumber.

twenty-four

I AM JOLTED AWAKE BY A LOUD, SHARP HOWL. Even though I am no lykin, I know something is wrong by the sound alone. And I suspect I can reason what it is since I am still naked, in Evander's arms, and not in Conri's tent where I am meant to be.

Evander is up in a blur, tugging on his trousers.

"How long was I asleep for?" I ask as I follow his lead and hastily pull on my clothes as well.

"I don't know, I was asleep, too." His worried expression only heightens my panic.

"You said it wouldn't be long, that you would—"

"Well you wore me out," he snaps. Though there's a flash of amusement in his eyes, briefly chasing away the agitation.

"The howl?"

"Conri."

"Shit." I situate my cape around me. I had been hoping my instinct and guess had been wrong. "What are we going to do?"

"I'm trying to think." Evander rubs his temples.

Another howl. It rips through me like the night I met Aurora. The noise of a predator. Of warning. *Run*, it causes a voice in me to say. But there is nowhere to go.

"Mary," I say, leaning toward the grass. Two marigolds bloom like eyes. "I need you, many of you. Perfume the air, then neutralize your aroma, make this place void of all other scents."

A thousand tiny marigolds carpet the tent. I bury my fingers in the ground between the buds, pouring my magic into it. There's the sharp aroma of flowers, followed by an atmospheric ethereal haze of almost too fresh air. It'll do...*I hope*. It'll have to.

"Thank you," I say to my friend. "That's all."

The flowers disappear.

"What are—"

"Can you smell our sex?"

Even Evander is surprised by my bluntness. "No."

"Good." Hopefully it works on Conri too. "You are going to go outside your tent and pretend to have fallen asleep."

"What?"

"You're just waking up, you heard the howls," I keep instructing, short and to the point. "You're going to run to him and say that he must come quickly. That you were unable to get through to me."

"Conri is—"

"Unless you have a better plan now is not the time to argue," I interject. Evander opens his mouth and promptly shuts it. Answer enough. "Right then, trust me."

"With my life," he says, and leaves the tent.

For a second, I stare at where he was just standing. There's something odd about the knight that's been sworn to protect me saying that he trusts me with his life. But we are playing a dangerous game. One that will threaten both of us, should it unravel.

Shaking my head and dismissing the worries for now, I kneel and draw my cape around me. Lightly, I grab at the small tree I most recently stitched among all the other embroideries. I sigh heavily. I truly hate to go back on my word.

"Brundil, I need you," I say softly as I press my fingers back into the ground. "Please, come to my aid."

Nothing happens for a long, held breath. Hope threatens to leave me. But then the earth shifts. A clay figure wrapped in roots emerges, drawn up by invisible hands. Brundil has taken a slightly different shape this time—more plant and less human. But I still know her in my bones.

"You don't seem to be fleeing with Aurora." She tsks, looking around the tent. The weight of her final judgment lands on me. "Witches. All the same, wasteful."

"What I will ask of you will help me flee with Aurora," I say quickly. She blinks her river stone eyes. The dull look is all the prompting I get to continue my plea. "I'm going to summon you for all the lykin to see. I need you to come and make some kind of grand display."

"What sort of grand display?" She sounds mildly intrigued.

"That's up to you. Just…don't hurt anyone?" As much as Conri has proved to be my enemy—alongside some of his alphas and knights—there are innocent lykin here, children. I'm not going to risk harming them.

"You ruin all my fun."

"Apologies." I hear a raucous collection of voices nearing. Conri's chief among them all. "Will you do it?"

"My power to impact the world, while great, is limited," she cautions. Grandma had warned me as much with spirits, especially greater ones. Spirits aren't meant to take corporeal forms and influence the world. Doing so exhausts their powers—much like how Folost and Mary were worn down from having to exist in the Natural World. Different spirits have different strengths, and limitations. "Are you sure you wish to exhaust my strength, here and now? It will take some time for me to recover."

"Yes." I hate to say it, but if I don't get out of this predicament then Brundil's strength won't matter.

"Very well then." She leans forward, her unseeing eyes peering into mine. As if she can look into the very fabric of my being and judge me. "I will. But you'd best live up to your word and get Aurora out of this mess. Or I will make sure that, when you die, not even the maggots will touch your corpse. You will lie cold, dead but undying, never returning to the earth from whence you came. Your flesh will rot, but the soil will not absorb its nutrients. I will place a curse upon your body so great it will taint your very soul."

I shudder. She leans away with a look of approval. Her words had the desired effect, I see.

"Good, then we have an understanding. I will await your call, little witch." Brundil seeps back into the ground. Leaving me in the cold darkness.

But I've little time to process the threat. The voices are almost upon the tent, close enough now for me to make out individual speakers.

Conri is among them. I stick all my fingers into the ground and hunch over. Luckily, my hair is still a mess from Evander's pulling and raking through my tresses. It will help sell my claims.

The tent flap is nearly ripped in two when it's yanked open. I can feel Conri there. His charm slams against me like a wave crashing upon the shore. But I am a breaker rock. Steady and unyielding. The magic pools around me but doesn't seep in. The feeling of Evander within me, of his mouth on mine, of the sweetness of his skin, is far better than any fantasy I could ever concoct and it fights off the charm.

But I do not look up, as tempting as it is. I stay hunched over, swaying slightly. I murmur to myself old chants Grandma taught me. They're words of protection—old spirit names for those long gone, she said. Hopefully Conri does not recognize them.

"What is the meaning of this?" Conri barks.

"She said she needed time and space," Evander says, unflinching, even in the wake of Conri's palpable rage.

"Time and space in my tent wasn't good enough? I demand an explanation. *Now!*"

I tip to the side, letting my body go limp. Conri moves, but he's not quite fast enough. My teeth slam together with the impact but I don't let the stinging pain show as he pulls me off the ground. Instead I murmur incomprehensible words, forcing shivers, fluttering my lids.

"What is wrong with her? My queen? My queen!" He has the audacity to sound worried. As if he wasn't just plotting my demise with his other alphas.

"C…Conri?" I finally crack open my eyes as if coming to after a long dream. "My king? What…Where…" I make a show of looking around the tent. Widening my eyes as if clarity is dawning on me. "Oh…" I begin to laugh, like I have some monumental relief easing my muscles. "It worked."

"Worked? What worked?" Conri's grip tightens on me. He leans slightly in and drops his voice. "You are verging on making a fool of me, Faelyn. Something that no amount of love for you can spare you from the consequences of."

The words are harsh, void of any concern or compassion. It's a cracking of his facade and I am relieved to finally see it. Not that the rest of them can, or do. Conri wouldn't allow that.

It's easy to smile at his threat. Making a fool of him was what I wanted. How easily it came to pass. But I try to hide my mockery, instead keeping my expression serene and joyful—as if there is nothing for us to worry about even though my insides are knotted.

I hope this works…

"I thought about what you told me of these lands and I have a gift for you. For all of you." I finally turn my attention to the tent flap, where the rest of them huddle, looking in. Evander is doing a good job of being composed. But I can see the worry behind his eyes. The skepticism. "Let's go to the center of camp."

Conri agrees, albeit reluctantly. I keep waiting for the moment he can smell Evander still hot on my flesh. But my spell seems to have worked. When Conri stands and faces the rest of those gathered, he wears a bright smile. He helps me out of Evander's tent. I feign weakness in the process, as though I have exerted great effort and can barely stand without support. However, my wobbly knees aren't entirely an act…

We make our way to the center of camp, where the bonfire has begun to burn low. To think…hours ago I danced around that fire with Conri. I thought that perhaps there could be a path forward together. I almost gave in to the sweet words he was whispering to me—that there was a way I could do right not just for me, but for Aurora, the spirits, and even my home.

I almost fell prey to him once. I won't let it happen again. I will make him regret ever thinking he could use and discard me.

"I am looking forward to seeing this surprise, future wife," Conri says loud enough for them all to hear, then, just for me, "For your sake, I hope it's exceptional."

He releases me and steps away. The whole pack has gathered, no doubt brought to alarm by Conri's howls. Now held in place by curiosity. They all stare at me, some genuinely interested, while others ooze a sense of satisfaction, as if they are waiting for the moment I fail and this all comes tumbling down. I wonder what they think Conri will do to me should I continue to disappoint him. Judging by the hungry gazes and wicked, satisfied grins, it wouldn't be good, and they will be delighted to watch.

I kneel and press my fingers into the ground. I spare one thought for how this all might have been had Conri been genuine. What might we have been able to accomplish? Great things, I dare to think. But I don't need him to achieve my goals. I am strong enough to do it on my own.

"Brundil, great and ancient spirit of earth, hear me, I summon you to my cause," I intone, low and slow, trying to give the air of authority and mystery at the same time.

All those gathered hold their breath. Total silence. I join them. Waiting in anticipation. Nothing happens.

Brundil will come back. She'll help me. I believe it with all my being.

The ground rumbles. Murmuring breaks into outright shouts and screams of surprise and horror as large cracks rip through the camp, racing toward me. The ground around me splits, lifting slightly, as though I am on a pedestal. Lykin jump, avoiding the cracking earth. It rises in places and lowers in others. Whole tents are consumed into the rumbling earth—tents I hope are empty. But I can't do anything to stop Brundil now. Not that I would want to.

The bonfire is swallowed whole. It falls deep into the depths, the orange consumed and reduced to a puff of smoke. As the last curl of gray rises to the air, the lykin catching their breath, clutching each other, and murmuring in shock and horror, the earth begins to groan anew.

Screaming now. They think I have brought about the end times. Or that I am attacking them. The knights change into wolf shapes, trying to find their footing on the earth. What do they think they could really do to me if I was attacking? From my vantage, I'm the one in control.

I stand, wobbling, but Brundil keeps the column under me blessedly still.

"Brundil, come to me!" I thrust out my arms, tilt my head back, and shout to the heavens, my voice echoing across the plains like thunder.

The earth rumbles with the reverberation of my words. A geyser of mud shoots up from the large crack before me. But it doesn't rain down around us. Instead, it hovers unnaturally, slowly melting into the shape of a mighty golem with two smooth boulders for eyes.

"Hello, witch." Brundil's voice rumbles like the deep earth. I appreciate that she decided to leave off "little." "You have summoned me?"

"I would like to ask of you a boon—a blessing on these people of your lands, should you have the strength," I shout so that all can hear.

Brundil displayed her might. Now I want her to display her utility and, by proxy, my own. "Will you create a copse of trees here, somewhere that game might thrive for generations to come to feed the lykin of these lands?"

Brundil gives me a hard stare. My stomach squirms as if I have swallowed worms. If she refuses, it will show that I have precious little control of the situation. My ruse will be up.

But she comes through. "Very well. But it will be paid for by your power as well."

"Done."

The word is still reverberating in my ears when she collapses back into the earth. There's rumbling again, but of a calmer sort. The grasses ripple with a wave that pulses underneath them, out from me.

An invisible hand pulls on my ankles. I sink into the earth, the pedestal around me cracking as though I am suddenly an immense weight. My power is pulled out through my feet, down and into the earth. It is the sensation of wet fabric being yanked underneath my skin. Ripped from me with ruthlessness.

I tip my head back, gasping, as if trying to break the surface of invisible water so that I can catch a breath. But my lungs are being pulled with the rest of me. They are collapsing inward. It's impossible to catch a breath. My very soul is being ripped from my body.

Yet, I cling to consciousness. I fight to keep my eyes open, even when all I want to do is give in to this bone-deep exhaustion. From my periphery, I can see the ground continuing to ripple out. And, in the wake of the magic burst, trees shoot up from the ground. Not saplings, but full-grown sentries as tall as the old wood that grew near the redwood by my home.

They dot the landscape around the camp, becoming denser where the tents stop. Their mighty roots span the cracks in the earth as if trying to mend the broken rock and soil. They shore up like bridges, vines and overgrowth carpeting them. The deep smell of fresh earth accompanies the rich aroma of pine and cedar. The cracking and groaning of wood slows.

I am finally freed of the pull. I double forward, losing my balance, and tip off the side of the column Brundil had placed me atop. Wind rushes around me briefly, ended by two strong arms.

For some reason, when I look up, I hope to see Evander's eyes. But I am met with Conri. Even exhausted, I manage to force a smile and hide my disappointment.

"You are an astounding creature," he whispers in awe. Gently, Conri sets me down. I wobble. Not an act this time. But he supports me with an arm around me and a firm grip on my hip. With his free hand, he motions toward me. "Behold, the might of your future queen!"

The lykin erupt in cheers and howls.

twenty-five

CONRI WASTES NO TIME IN TAKING ME BACK TO HIS TENT AFTER THE JUBILATION DIES DOWN. I try to glance at him from the corners of my eyes as subtly as possible. He's unreadable.

"I'm sorry for disappearing, and for worrying you." It's easy to have a pained expression on my face as I try to walk. My muscles burn and joints ache as though I have been running without stop for days. "I really wanted to show how I could use the spirits to help your people. I sensed the spirit of the earth and I thought I could bond with her—that it'd be a marvelous opportunity! And, well… I lost track of time."

"Hush, hush. Yes, I was worried. And, in the future, you absolutely must tell me what you are doing. I never want to be unaware when it comes to you. I have a right to know."

The way he speaks makes it sound as though these mandates are from his concern for my well-being. That he is afraid out of love. But I see it for what it is: He wants to control me. Not just because of Aurora any longer, but to know that this power I have demonstrated will be his and his alone.

"I know," I say. "I'm sorry."

"Why could you not just commune with the spirit in our tent?"

"Truthfully?" I look at him with wide eyes, fearful of reprisal.

He stops to cup my cheek gently. "Sweet one, you are my sole priority. My responsibility. No, my light and love and hope for our people. Yes, I always want you to speak true."

"It is because…" I drop my eyes. "Your powers are so mighty, my king." He preens at the flattery. Old gods, he's easy to manipulate when I want to make the effort. "Brundil is an old spirit—mighty, but she hides deep within the earth. I had to find somewhere farther from you, as painful as it was, to keep my senses clear. I knew Evander had your trust, and would keep me safe, so I could think of no better place to do what needed to be done."

Conri looks between me and Evander, slowing to a stop before his tent. He sighs deeply. "Forgive me, Evander. I thought the worst of you."

The apology surprises even me. I'm surprised Evander doesn't fall over.

"Your reaction was understandable, my king. One such as me doesn't deserve your apologies." Evander lowers his gaze, bowing his head slightly in subservience.

"I give them gladly anyway."

I bite my tongue and resist the urge to stand up for Evander. That he is worthy of Conri's apologies. And so much more.

Conri turns his attention back to me. "Now, tell me, Faelyn, would it be possible for you to find more spirits like this to help us in other ways? Can you call upon Brundil again to reforest our plains? Perhaps commune with others to prompt game to return?" His eyes shine with excitement. He genuinely wants to do this for his people. I hate that it's admirable.

"I could…" It's time to launch the next stage of my plot. "But it was hard enough to find Brundil among your powerful magic, and the powers of all the other lykin. Plus, a witch must go to where the spirits reside to call upon them, meet them, learn their names, and bond with them. We cannot summon spirits, especially ones we've never met, out of thin air."

Conri considers this, stroking his chin thoughtfully. Luckily, it's also the truth. So even if he knows how the magic of witches works, I've given him no reason to doubt me.

"So, if you know where spirits might reside," I continue, "I could go to those locations, take the time to learn their names, and bond with them. Then, we could call upon their powers for your glory." My eyes dart over to Evander's, meeting his for a second and holding them with a pointed stare. Conri doesn't see the look; he's too absorbed in his own thoughts. *Please, read my mind,* I silently beg Evander. Though it's probably futile. I'll have to feed something more. I open my mouth to speak again.

Evander cuts me off. "I think I know where some might reside."

"You do?" Conri looks to his knight. Then a bright smile lights up his face. "Of course you do! My witchlike knight. You're the one who's always known these sorts of things. To think I have both of you in my possession. It must be fate blessing my rule."

Conri claps his hands together with excitement. It causes him to release me and I sway slightly. Evander takes a half step forward but I lift my hand just a little at the wrist, stopping him. He heeds the silent command.

"If you would permit, my king. I could take Faelyn to find more spirits for you while you join with the other alphas in Gualla. It'll be plenty of time for us, and we would meet you there within a day or two of you arriving in Den," Evander casually suggests.

Conri looks to me. "What do you think, my dear? Could you survive a week without me?"

"It will be hard, but I think I can manage." I force a smile.

"Exceptional, then it's settled. In the morning you two will split off and, next we meet, you will bring me an army of spirits."

An army… The words stick with me, enough that my cheeks burn from the effort of holding my smile. No matter what he says or does, the implication of conquest is always around him.

As long as I breathe, I will never let spirits be used for his ambitions, Aurora included.

Evander takes me to Aurora's tent first thing in the morning. I didn't have to ask. He rightly assumed that I would want to see her before we left.

I suspected she might be cross with me, but the air in the tent feels colder than the outside. As icy as her stare and as unflinching as the back she puts to me.

"Aurora—"

"I trusted you."

"Aurora, please—"

I take a step closer. She spins in place and spears me through with a look. I don't dare proceed. She is the forest on a dark, cold winter solstice. When the last light has died and there is nothing that keeps the spirits of a more wicked nature at bay. She is a barrier set up by another witch that fizzles against my skin, that cautions against progressing. She is primordial strength, fate itself turning against me.

Not welcome are the two words the whole sensation of being in her presence can be boiled into.

"I told you of my powers, of my past. I taught you how to harness your gifts and mine together. I…I introduced you to one of my oldest and dearest friends and you used up so much of her power that now she must lie dormant to recover." Her voice cracks and she looks away, as if frustrated by the betrayal of her mortal body showing how deep her wounds are cut. "You're just like the rest of them, in the end. All you care for is yourself. All you want is your own benefit."

"Aurora…" All I can manage is a weak whisper of her name. Silenced when she looks away, as if offended I would dare even speak it.

"And you know, Faelyn, I might have been able to tolerate it if you wanted the power for you, but to share it with *him*…"

"No." I burst forward and push past the invisible barrier she's tried to place between us. I take both her hands in mine, which brings her attention, and her ire, back to me. I speak before she can this time. "Not with him. Never for him. I will die a thousand painful deaths before I let him use my powers or any spirits. I vowed as much last night."

My conviction stills her. The air shifts. She's inquisitive. But still skeptical.

"I don't blame you for what you thought of me, not after all you've been through," I start. "And I know how it looks—how I wanted it to look."

"Wanted it?" she repeats softly.

"Yes. I…I was going to be caught in a compromising position. Which was my fault, and I'm sorry." I can't bring myself to tell her that the "position" involved Evander. "I had to think quickly, and I thought that if I showed Conri Brundil, he would realize my merit and give me a longer leash. Which would, in turn, give us a better chance of escaping."

Aurora withdraws her hands, folds her arms, and continues to look skeptical. But I take her silence as a good sign and continue.

"I privately asked Brundil before calling upon her, and she agreed. I let her choose her initial display of power and what I asked her for was a gift that I wanted to give to the lykin. Even if we hate Conri, we can still help the lykin, especially if it also benefits us."

"That bastard," she mutters under her breath.

"What?"

"Conri said it was all his idea." Aurora sighs heavily and rests her forehead in her palm a moment. "I should know better."

"It's easy to get sucked into his aura." I touch her arm lightly in reassurance. She attempts a smile, but it vanishes quickly. "In any case, it all worked. Conri is going to allow me to go off so that I can 'find other spirits.'"

"You're…leaving?" Her tone is wounded in a completely different way and it nearly cleaves my heart in two.

"I'm going ahead." My voice drops to a whisper. "I'm going to figure out the best path for us. I'll use what you taught me and what I know to find whatever spirits I can that might help us. Not for him, but for our escape. I'm going to take extra supplies than what Evander and I need—Conri already agreed since the pack will be restocking soon in Gualla. I'll set up supply caches for us along the way, hidden. I'll make some shelters so we don't have to slow down to make them later. Then, when I meet back with you in Den, and decide when the moment is right, we'll be ready to leave." My words speed up with excitement toward the end.

Her eyes widen slightly. "You really think we can escape him?"

"Evander already showed me the way. Or, some of it… We're going west, to the elves. Once we're behind their wall, we'll be safe from Conri and I'll beg the Human Queen to help us. We just have to get there. And if I can give us a head start on supplies and a path for our journey then we'll have all the better chance of outrunning Conri. I know he's going to chase us, but we'll be one step ahead."

"And once I'm out of the lykin borders… I'll be that much closer to freedom," she whispers. Without warning, Aurora yanks me close, throwing her arms around my shoulders. I readily return the embrace, clutching behind her back. Aurora draws a shaky breath. "I'm sorry I doubted you."

"I already told you, I don't blame you. Especially not given how I was acting..." I press my eyes closed and sigh softly. "I was being taken in by Conri a little, if I'm honest."

"Then it's good you're leaving." She pulls away. "Give you some space to be free of his charms for a while. Even though I will miss you terribly. I've grown fond of having company."

"I'll be back soon enough," I reassure her hastily. The sorrow in her eyes is almost enough to make me want to stay.

"I'll be fine. Don't worry too much for me. Just keep yourself safe."

I nod. "You too."

I can only imagine that Conri will keep Aurora extra close in my absence. I wonder if she will be sharing his tent in my cot while I'm gone. If he doesn't have both of us, he will no doubt keep the piece of her magic he does under his watchful eye.

"And Aurora?"

"Yes?"

"You know I will come back, right?" I search her face for any traces of doubt. There is nothing but a reassuring smile.

"I absolutely do."

"Faelyn?" Evander lifts the tent flap. "We should be going."

"Look after her, Evander." Aurora locks eyes with him. "She's yours to care for."

"With my life," he vows.

The words still me. He means them. He's always meant them. Beyond Aurora. Beyond Conri. He will keep me safe no matter what...I can feel it in my marrow. Part of me wants to write it off as last night clouding my judgment. But I feel like, if anything, I'm seeing clearer.

Evander cares for me.

"Let's go." I give Aurora one last squeeze and follow Evander out into the dawn.

There is little fanfare to our goodbyes. I wonder if Conri is going to attempt to keep my absence a secret. Leaving is nothing more than walking to the edge of camp and slipping between the new trees.

Before I know it, I am soaring across the plains. Charging toward the great unknown of Midscape.

twenty-six

EVANDER RUNS WITH THE SPEED OF AN UNBROKEN STALLION. My knuckles are white, fingers numb from clutching and from the cool morning air battering my body. But even as tears prick my eyes from the wind, a smile cuts my lips.

This time, when we crest the ridge in the distance, we don't stop. Evander keeps running down the sloping hills and past where Conri's prying eyes can see. I smile even wider.

He slows not long after, though, coming to a complete stop and settling his belly on the ground. I take it as a sign to dismount. As soon as I'm off, Evander rolls onto his back, changing back into his human form. He still pants loudly, sweat coating his body atop a ruddy flush.

"He really…let you…go," Evander finally manages, staring dumbstruck at the heavens above. The rise and fall of his chest draws my eyes to it and I barely resist the urge to place my hands on him here and now. It's especially hard when he tilts his head and flashes me a dazzling smile. "You really are brilliant."

I lie back in the grass next to him, watching the sheeplike clouds dance across a field of blue. "'Brilliant' wouldn't have been caught in the first place. It would've never been taken in by his charm."

He takes a deep breath and lets it out slowly, recovering his breath. "You're right. But better men and women have fallen for the lull of his charm. And as far as being caught, you used it to your advantage well."

I sigh softly and rest the back of my forearm on my forehead. "I had to give up an advantage to get one."

"So he knows about Brundil. What of it?" Evander looks over to me. "He can't summon her without you. And I know you would never abuse her power on his behalf."

"You have so much faith in me." I meet his gaze.

"You're someone it's easy to have faith in." Evander shifts in the grasses, looking back to the sky but only for a moment before closing his eyes and taking another deep breath.

I've never seen him so relaxed. So…free. I'm not the only one who shed weight by escaping Conri. It's a monumental relief for me and I've only been trapped with the wolf king for a short time. I can only imagine what Evander must feel any time he gets away.

"Evander," I start delicately, "what was your life like before Conri?"

He opens his eyes and stares up at the sky. I wonder if he sees his old pack, the people he loved, dancing among the clouds. During the stretch of silence that follows, I begin to doubt he'll tell me at all. We've been so careful about sharing little when it comes to anything too personal. Even though we've crossed many lines, it is a different sort of intimacy than what I'm asking now.

"Peaceful," he says, at long last. Never have I clung to what someone might say next so tightly. "We lived near the forest at the edge of the lykin's territory. I never realized what…what my circumstances were." A frown tugs on his lips slightly. "I grew up without pack politics and the wolf king. I got to live the life most pups would only dream of. Until the day he came for us."

The pain in Evander's voice draws me to him. I shift slightly, reaching through the grasses to find his fingers. But even as I make contact, he continues to stare up at those old ghosts that peer down at us through the Veil between here and the Great Beyond.

"Conri killed… He took everyone I ever knew and loved from me. He should have killed me, too, but he didn't. I was worth more to him alive."

"Because you know about spirits?" I ask, barely refraining from adding, *And witches?*

"That, and because I was the last male of my pack—by rights, I was the alpha of a pack of one. Me. But that is symbolic enough for him to make me his knight and take my ability to have children from me in the process. Showing the other alphas what he can reduce a pack to—a man to."

My ribs feel too small for my lungs. I suppress a whimper. This pain is his, not mine. I feel it in sympathy, but I cannot allow it to manifest because it would shift the focus off of him in this moment.

"It is…so cruel," I whisper.

That finally brings his eyes to mine. Haunted but sharp. Distant, and yet somehow able to look right into my very soul.

"He is cruel," Evander says. "Every day, I cursed his name. I wasn't sure why I allowed myself to be taken alive. There were nights I wished I would never wake from. Days I would push every boundary in the hope that Conri would just end it."

"Evander…"

"But now…now I am grateful for every breath. Every gnarled scar on my flesh and heart is like a map that led me to here, now, with you. I wouldn't change any second of pain because forsaking it would also mean forsaking the pleasure of your company, your smiles, your body." He speaks every word so plainly. So earnestly. He's so suddenly laid his soul bare before me and I've no idea what to do with it.

I thought I knew what love was…but now I know it was nothing more than a childhood infatuation. It was real, but as real as it could be for a young woman whose world was small and who knew so little. Real looks different when your perspective on the world changes with time and experience.

"Do you mean all that?" I ask, even though I already know the answer.

Evander rolls onto his side, propping himself up on one elbow. His other hand reaches for my face, cupping my cheek. He leans in but holds off kissing me long enough to say, "Every word and more."

My eyes dip closed and my chin rises slightly on instinct. His mouth meets mine in the slowest, most glorious kiss I have ever felt. I don't have to kiss him. Conri is nowhere near. I don't have a pent-up urge threatening to be the thief of my better sense.

I kiss him because I *want to*. Because it feels so good when his mouth is on mine. Silken lips gliding on instinct. The roughness of his stubble.

He pulls away and I rise for one last peck, stealing it right off his lips. Evander chuckles at my preciousness and lies back with a smile.

"So, where is it that you want to go? We have about a week."

"Do you actually know where any spirits are?" I ask, still genuinely curious about the extent of what he knows when it comes to the magic of witches.

He nods. "I have some prospects. But I've never been able to look into them too deeply."

"Do these prospects take us to the forest?" I sit up and nod down to the forest that walls off the lykin's territory from the rest.

"Some could."

"Good, that's where I want to go."

"You're going to prepare an escape path for you and Aurora… aren't you?" He sits as well. Our shoulders brush and I relish in the easy familiarity that comes with someone you trust—someone you've shared your body and intimate secrets with.

"That's my plan," I have no trouble admitting to him.

"And how are you going to escape Conri to get you and Aurora on this path?" Skepticism weighs down his words.

"I'll figure that out at Den." I glance his way with a slight grin. "Or, you will."

He huffs. "How did I know I'd be a part of this escape?"

"You already were once." A thought occurs to me, something that's lingered in the back of my mind since coming here. "Why did you help her on the first new moon after the Blood Moon?"

He doesn't answer for so long that I end up looking in his direction to make sure he heard. But the moment I see the severe expression on his face I know he did. His brows are furrowed in what looks almost like confusion…as if he doesn't quite know the answer.

"Because…it was the right thing to do," he says, finally.

I shift to get a better look at him. This is important to me, I realize. I must know why he did what he did because, if I do, then maybe I can fully trust him without any trace of doubt. I'll know, unlike Conri, he's not just pouring honeyed words into my ears. "Even though you were risking everything to do it?"

"I thought I was pretty explicit that my life has meant very little to me over the years." He doesn't look at me when he speaks. He continues to stare past the forest. “Once I was on Conri’s leash, little else mattered, even myself.”

“What kept you going?” I dare to ask.

“I…” He dips his chin, staring at the ground. A slight smile curves his mouth. “Someone I loved, or the memory of her, perhaps.”

“The witch?” I dare to seek confirmation of my suspicions. His head jerks in my direction. Eyes wide. I laugh softly. “You’ve made it kind of obvious… You know so much about witches, so you had to be close to one, or had one captive. And I don’t think it was the latter.”

“How can you be so sure? Didn’t I warn you I killed the heart of a witch?”

“I remember.” I shrug. “There are many ways to ‘kill’ a heart. Perhaps you did what you had to do to protect her.”

“I…hope she’d someday see it that way,” he says softly, raising his gaze once more to meet mine.

“I know this might be difficult, and I’m sorry for asking, but do you think you could take me to her? If there are witches in Midscape, I would want to meet them. They might prove valuable allies,” I carefully explain in the hopes that he doesn’t think I’m trying to inflict torture on his poor heart.

“There aren’t any.” His body language shifts, closing off. It makes me wonder if he truly means “kill” in the literal sense. Evander stands. “We should keep going to make the most of our time.”

“Evander—” I stand as well and take his hand to draw his attention back to me. “If this journey will be too hard on you, you don’t have to go.”

He snorts. “You think I’m going to let you go on alone?”

“I’m perfectly capable.” I motion to the field around us, dotted with all manner of wildflower and lupine. “You could have a lovely vacation from all obligation for a few days. Enjoy the sunshine.”

“I am not a man who sits still well.” Evander grins.

“Forgive me for trying to be nice to you.”

He smiles and takes a step forward, resting his forehead on mine. “I appreciate it. But I don’t think anywhere would be ‘hard on me’ if you are at my side. Don’t worry so much, Faelyn. I know there is a great deal to accomplish, but you should also try to rest and relax, too. When we return to Conri you will be fighting for your life—and Aurora's—every second. So breathe easy while you can. Gather your strength."

I nod as he pulls away. Evander gives me a slight but genuine smile before changing back into his wolf shape. Once more, he places his belly on the ground, I mount, and we're off again.

We reach the edge of the woods by the late afternoon. Midscape is larger than I thought—larger than it appears. Even with Evander running as fast as he can, it still took us the better portion of a day to make it to the forest. But the moment we cross underneath the trees, all doubts as to if this venture was worth it or not vanish.

"Evander, stop." I don't even wait for him to be fully still before I'm dismounting, jumping off. I quickly cross to the nearest tree and place both hands and my forehead upon it, shutting my eyes. This place hums with ancient energies, like the woods back home. "I greet you, sentries and spirits of this forest. I come as a friend—hopefully an ally. I hope you will welcome my companion and I and aid our path."

There's a faint humming in the back of my mind. Like the buzzing of a bee, or the flapping of a small bird's wings. It's brief, almost melodic, and ripples under my skin. I straighten with a smile and say, "Thank you."

"The woods welcome us?" Evander asks, back in his human form.

"Yes, I think so." I step away from the tree. The earth is soft, carpeted with mosses and small leafy plants that can survive in the wide spaces between the trees; this is not a condensed forest. I reach out a hand and Evander takes it without my having to ask. With his support, I pull off both of my boots and socks, resting them atop my satchel. I wiggle my toes against the lichen. "That's better."

"Would you like to lead from here?" Evander offers.

I nod. "I would, if you don't mind. That way I can focus on sensing any magic."

"I don't mind at all. I have a keen sense of direction, so don't worry for us getting lost."

"Sometimes…getting lost for a while is the best way to be found." I start walking, pulled by the beats of my heart, the feeling of the living earth beneath me, the shifting breezes, and the animals that scurry and flit between the trees.

"You're more right than you know." Evander falls into step beside me.

As I keep my senses open for spirits, and my eyes open for potential points of shelter, Evander and I make hours of conversation. He tells me more of the ways of the lykin. How, in the primordial forest of Den, there is a Grove where the lykin can speak with the great wolf spirit—one of the few spirits they can commune with. I tell him of how my grandmother taught me, as a girl and as a woman, to identify the magic in everything—traces of spirits—and how to use that combined with the power within me to perform small blessings and feats of magic.

I ask him about how the lykin's magic works, how it feels to be a wolf, how they determine their hierarchy and what the markings on the sides of tents mean—different packs, as I'd begun to surmise.

He asks me about the most mundane things in reply. What I ate from day to day. How I occupied my time. How long it had been since my grandmother passed the Veil to the Great Beyond.

The day passes effortlessly.

"We should probably bed down for the night." Evander stares up at the stars winking through the canopy. The moon is nearly full and offers a great amount of light, even filtered through the tangled boughs above.

"Evander…" I stare up at the moon as well, at what it means beyond merely light for us to see by.

"Yes?"

"When I free Aurora"—*not if, when*—"what will happen to the lykin?" I know Conri has claimed it would be the end for them. But I don't trust him to be entirely forthright.

"It's impossible to know," he says softly. "Perhaps we will go back to as we were before Bewulf the Uniter swooned her and we will no longer be able to transform at will, but only when the moon is full. Perhaps she has been one with our kind for so long that her magic is as much in our blood as the old wolf spirit's is, and we will remain as we are. Perhaps, somehow, even after all we have done to her, she'll take pity upon us and give us that boon, however undeserving we might be of it."

I continue to stare up at the sky. My insides knot. I'm heavy with the weight of all he's told me. Of his people and their ways and history. A history that, one way or another, I will be forever entrenched in. I doubt I will be known as anything more than a villain.

"Faelyn." Evander places a hand on my shoulder, grounding me back in the present. My eyes are drawn to him. He's cast in moonlight. A silhouette outlined in silver and shadow. Both suit him, the light and the dark. "The lykin will survive. No matter what. We're a tough people. Born of the moon and of the wolf. Both will always be a part of us, one way or another. So do what is right. Aurora is a stain on our legacy as she is now. That is why I tried to free her, and continue to do so. This chapter is a disgrace in our history books. If you can liberate her…then it must be done."

I nod. *If only Conri wasn't the wolf king and you were*, I want to say. But I can't bring myself to. Evander has been through enough. The hardships of ruling shouldn't be yet another weight upon his shoulders.

"I won't falter," I vow to him, and to the moon above.

"Good." Evander steps away and begins to set up the tent.

"It's a lovely night; I don't think that's necessary," I say. The air here isn't too hot or cold, despite it being summer. There's a nice breeze, but not too rigorous.

"Are you sure?"

"Just the bedroll is fine," I insist.

He rolls out two bedrolls a modest amount apart. I fold my arms as he finishes and give him a dull look when he turns in my direction. His brow furrows. I can't stop a grin.

"What?" Evander asks.

"You're really putting them like that? After last night?"

"I…didn't want to assume." The moonlight mostly hides what I dare think is a blush. "I wasn't sure if last night was a moment or…"

I kneel on the earth next to him, sitting back onto my ankles, so I can look him in the eyes. "Do you want it to just be a moment?"

"Old gods, no," he breathes like a desperate prayer.

He wants me. Still. Even now. I can feel it as much as I can see it in his eyes. In the twitch of his hands as he refrains from touching me. It swells like a rush of too much sugar, surging through me. It takes my head like too much mead. Before I know it, my hands are on his cheeks, my mouth is on his. His hands are on my rear. I'm maneuvered into his lap, straddling him.

"Have me again," I whisper against his mouth, raking my fingers through his silken tresses. "Not because of Conri's charm. Or because of unfulfilled urges. Have me because you want me and I want you. Because you feel this draw as much as I do."

As I talk, his hands slide up my back. They spread across my shoulder blades. One slips up to grab my hair at the nape of my neck, pulling my head back, as it makes a fist.

Evander draws a quivering breath against the soft skin of my neck. "I could have you a thousand times, and only want you a thousand more."

"I welcome the challenge," I breathe.

With a growl, he takes my skin between his teeth. His hips rock against mine. My nails dig into his shoulders as he grabs at my shirt.

The moment our flesh meets again, the world is right. The second of pain when he fills me, followed by the bliss of my body accepting him, is enough to make my mind go blank. My arms around his shoulders. His body atop mine.

Tonight, we are not quiet. The sound of our bodies moving, our moans and ragged breaths, fills the woods with shameless abandon. Tonight, we have nothing to hide, and nothing to pretend to be other than each other's.

twenty-seven

EVANDER'S ARM IS TIGHT AROUND MY WAIST WHEN WE WAKE. My back is pressed against his chest. His breath is hot on the nape of my neck.

But unlike before, when we woke violently thanks to Conri, this morning we're greeted by a gentle dawn spilling across the land, carried on a misty haze. Cool dew has settled across the ground like scattered diamonds. It coats my shoulder, exposed from where the bedroll we unfolded and used as a duvet slipped off me in the night.

I blink slowly, unsure if I want to wake, or continue sleeping. I savor the deep aches in me as I wiggle my toes, tensing and relaxing my thighs in the process. The movement sets him to stirring.

Evander kisses my shoulder and grumbles sleepily, "Good morning."

"It's early yet," I reply with a yawn.

"We shouldn't waste the day."

"We shouldn't."

Yet, neither of us moves. We continue to relish in these sweet, uninterrupted moments of simplicity. Of pretending that our obligations are not as overbearing as they are.

Finally, he pulls away. Our skin sticks from being pressed together for half the night, and him peeling away has cool air rushing in on my back. I groan softly, yanking at the blanket.

Evander chuckles and leans over, kissing my temple lightly. "We must."

"It's cold."

"It is not, you are merely a little stove." He stands, collecting his clothes. I roll onto my back to watch him, resisting another groan when his trousers rise over the pert curve of his rear. Evander catches me staring and smirks. I don't look away, smirking back. "You know, early lykin would often go without their clothes, preferring to be as 'natural' as possible. I could bring back that tradition."

I laugh and sit. If he's getting ready then I should as well. "Do what makes you the most comfortable."

He wraps his arms around my waist when I stand, pulling me close. A low growl rises up the back of his throat. "Perhaps I would enjoy it if you embraced the tradition, too."

I snort and push him away. Evander releases me without a fight. "I would not be comfortable roaming naked."

"And here I thought witches danced in the woods in the nude." He begins collecting the bedrolls.

"Sometimes we do." I finish dressing. "But only on particularly important days of the year. Otherwise I prefer not to accidentally brush a tender part against poisonous vines or brush."

"Did you dance for the Blood Moon?"

I pause, my hands freeze midway through grabbing my crimson cape. "No," I say softly, "my grandma had just died. I was still in mourning."

"I'm sorry," he murmurs. "I should have remembered."

I shake my head. "You don't need to remember everything about me. I don't blame you for forgetting."

"I *want* to remember everything about you." He straps the bedrolls onto the bags with purpose, as if trying to also strap in the facts to his memories.

"Even if that hadn't been the case, I wouldn't have gone out on the night of the Blood Moon. Grandma warned me before her death that it was a night of great power for lykin, vampir, spirits, and more." I force my voice to stay light so he knows that I'm not cross with him over forgetting about my grandma.

"Wouldn't that mean it's a better night to go out and perform your witchy rituals?"

I shake my head. "If I am opening myself to spirits and magic on a night like that, I might end up inviting some I don't entirely want to meet. The Blood Moon isn't a night meant for humans."

"Well, speaking of spirits, where to today?" He shrugs the packs on his shoulders but doesn't yet change into his wolf form.

"I could carry one."

"You have your satchel, and I hardly realize these are here." He shrugs. I frown. Which only makes Evander chuckle. "Really, if it becomes inconvenient I'll change into my wolf form. These muscles aren't just for show."

"Suit yourself." I laugh and sink my toes into the earth and moss, shifting my focus off of him and onto the magic around us. The woods are alive, but I don't feel drawn in any particular direction. There's no calling. Which means I must be the one to make the decision on our headway. "Which way is the edge of the lykin's territory, closest to the elves?"

"Parallel to the mountains." He points in an eastern direction and I follow his finger, focusing through the trees.

"Then we'll keep carrying on in that direction. I want to go as far as we can as fast as we can, that way we can set a more leisurely pace on the way back." If something catches my eye on the way, we'll stop. However, I want to see how far Evander and I can get at an aggressive pace. It will be farther than Aurora and I will be able make it on our own in the same amount of time. On our own… "Evander?"

"I'm still right here."

I turn to face him, taking him in for a moment. The dark hair that falls into his eyes. The slowly growing shadow of stubble that lines his cheeks, the same color as the hair on his chest. He is every bit a woman's fantasy and I take a moment to savor the fact that—at least for now—he is mine.

"What?" Evander chuckles and crosses to me, hooking my chin. He pulls my face up, almost kissing me. "You see something you like?"

"I do." I grin and rise onto my toes to kiss him lightly and then withdraw. The light expression evaporates off my cheeks, fast enough that he takes notice.

Evander's brows furrow slightly. "What is it?"

"Come with us?" I dare to ask, not knowing what he might say.

Evander promptly looks away, staring back in the direction of the lykin's plains and Conri. I reach up to guide his attention back to me.

"Why do you want me to come?" he asks—no, demands. I'm almost taken aback by the tone.

"There's nothing for you back there, is there?" I almost stammer, surprised by his sudden intensity.

"You're dodging the question. Why do you want me with you and Aurora?"

"You've helped both of us so much that—"

"Ah, you still want your bodyguard." He starts walking deeper into the forest with purpose, like he's running.

"Evander, it's not that." I chase after him.

"What, then?" He spins in place, looking down at me. "Do you want me there because you're fond of me? Because you *love* me?"

Do you want me to love you? The question almost slips out. Keeping it trapped behind my lips nearly burns. He almost…looks like he does. I didn't take him for a hopeless romantic.

"I don't know," I admit softly. "Love can take time, or it can be a whirlwind. I don't know if this is either, or nothing, yet."

"How could you?" He scoffs. "You don't even know me."

"I know enough," I insist back.

"Hardly anything. And there's so much I don't know about you." He says it like it should be dismissive. But…

"Exactly," I counter, taking a step forward, hands on my hips, getting right into his space. "There's so much we've yet to learn about each other, and rather than futility, I see possibility. There's an uncharted course we both could venture down. A future of our own making."

"Must you always be so optimistic?" His eyes shine with amusement, but his tone is dejected. Heartbroken, even.

"Evander—"

"Let's not trouble ourselves with such things now. We should be making use of our time. We're burning daylight." Without giving me a chance to get another word, he turns into his wolf form.

I sigh and scramble up onto his back. "You know…"

He glances over his shoulder and back at me.

"Some people consider optimism a virtue."

Evander huffs and launches forward, taking us deeper into the woods.

It's easy for one tree to look much like the next, especially when racing through the woods on wolf-back. But I'm so accustomed to navigating my way through forests, on and off trails, that I have little mechanisms to help me know where I am. Landmarks are fallen trees turned into hollow homes for animal families, massive boulders covered in moss, the slope of the terrain. There is also a unique feeling as I move through the forest, of grounding myself in the greater powers that curl between the trees and reach out to me with invisible hands. I leave my mark on them as much as they leave their mark on me.

At night we make camp in the hollow and rot-worn remains of a small hamlet. I avoid discussing any difficult topics. Evander isn't keen to, either. So we spend our hours around a small fire ignited by Folost, discussing our favorite foods and telling tales to each other woven into what stars we manage to see.

All the while, I add a few stitches to Mary's symbol in the cape—something that will hopefully neutralize Evander's and my scent like she managed to in the tent for when we inevitably return. A sort of tether for the spell. Evander assists, giving me pointers until it seems just right.

The next day is much the same as the last. Even though, once or twice, I think I can sense the presence of a spirit shiver across my magic, I decide not to stop. Our focus is to get as far as we're able, as fast as we're able.

The day after, we cross over a large river, fed by a breathtaking waterfall that tumbles off the mountains in the distance. But we don't pause to admire it. All I manage is a glimpse. Evander is tireless, running the entire day. He doesn't come to a stop until, sides heaving, he reaches the remnants of a large, abandoned town, hollowed out by time.

I take it as my signal to dismount. Evander promptly changes back into his human form, flopping on the ground in much the same manner as he did yesterday.

"This…is…as far…as we should go," he manages to say between ragged breaths.

"Thank you for pushing so hard." I crouch down next to him to lightly pat his shoulder.

"I needed a good run."

What are you running from? I want to ask. But, once more, I resist. I've encountered a wall with Evander and instinct tells me that trying to overcome it with force will only make him fortify the ramparts. I have to show him that I'm someone who can be trusted. Not just with his body, but with whatever secrets are engraved on his heart as deep as the scars on his back. He has to let me past his defenses willingly.

"I'm glad you could have one—many, with this excursion." I stand once more and take another step into this ruined town. The houses made of stone are still standing, roofs collapsed in. Those of wood have been mostly reclaimed by the forest, creeping vines and decay consuming them. It's been abandoned for some time. "Was this another lykin outpost?"

"In part. Vampir also lived here. And elves…" He sits, continuing to catch his breath. "The middle of town is the edge of the lykin's territory. The southwestern part is vampir. This place was abandoned when the vampir turned into monsters."

"We're out," I breathe, inhaling a little deeper than I have before in Midscape. The air is fresher here. Cool off the mighty mountains that stand guard to the left of this town as we face south. "Do we need to worry about the vampir?"

"One hasn't been seen in centuries, my ancestors saw to that, so we should be fine." He stands. "And if there is one, I'll protect you."

"My hero." I lean into him, batting my eyelashes.

Evander chuckles, but I do think he looks the slightest bit flattered. "This way."

I follow as he leads us through the town. Past two large buildings that I imagine were once an inn and perhaps some kind of town hall. Perhaps a market. I slow to a stop.

"What is it?" Evander pauses as well.

"There was a town not far from where I lived…" I murmur.

"Corwall," he blurts.

I look in his direction, startled. "You know it?"

"I'm the only one who knows anything really about the other side of the Fade."

"Because of your witch love?"

He pauses. I don't think he's going to answer. But at last he says, "Yes."

I purse my lips. The only witches I knew near Corwall were my grandmother and I. Perhaps there were others up the forest on the other side?

"Where did she live?"

"By the woods."

"Obviously." I resist rolling my eyes, partly in frustration. "All witches live at the edge of the Fade. But where, specifically?"

"It doesn't matter now." He starts walking again.

I quickly catch up to his side. "It matters to me." He says nothing. It's as if he didn't hear me at all. "Do you have any idea how lonely my life was? If there were witches out there that I missed then—"

"It would make it worse," he interrupts with confidence, silencing me. "Trust me, Faelyn. There are few combinations of words more horrible than 'what could have been.'"

I sigh as he continues. So much for trying to respect his boundaries. Of course he wouldn't want to talk about his lost love. I know that hurt all too well.

We reach the edge of the town. At the far end are the remnants of a road. Cobblestones dot the tall grasses, carving a path up and into the mountains.

"It's paved." I step out into the abandoned road. There are still carriage grooves in the rock. "Not many roads are paved like this in the Natural World."

"The vampir were master craftsmen. Moreover, their full moon festivals would draw everyone from common born to the highest of nobility into their mountaintop citadel. This road takes you to the great bridge that leads to the heart of their lands." He points in a western direction. "Most of the vampir's lands are on a peninsula. It's part of what made it so easy to drive them back when they turned feral."

"The lykin forced them to abandon their homes?" I look back to the town.

"Just what was on this side of the bridge. It was necessary." His tone is grave. "I wasn't there, of course. This was thousands of years ago… But all the stories speak of them turning into monsters. Of their blood rotting from within and taking their minds and sense with it. A shame for creatures that used to create such beauty."

"All the stories I've ever heard are of their more monstrous nature," I say softly. "Never anything about them as craftsmen or artists."

"Their decline happened around the time the Fade was erected; it makes sense that all humans would know of them is stories of their horrors. Fortunately, the western sea separates the vampir from the Natural World, just like it does the lykin. I doubt any crossed," he says optimistically.

I merely nod. The sorrowful history of the vampir. A cursed people… Perhaps, once Aurora is saved, I could try and help them, somehow…

Evander points in the opposite direction of the vampir bridge. The road curves through the woods to the southeast. "That way will take you to the main road that leads from the territory of the elves. If you can make it this far with Aurora, you will be out of the lykin's territory and it will become significantly more difficult for Conri to follow out of his lands. From here, it is a straight shot down into the land of the elves. Make it to the gate, and you both will be free. Conri wouldn't dare to trespass on their territory uninvited."

Free… The word sounds glorious to me and I haven't even endured a speck as much as she has. Or even a fraction as much as Evander has.

I look to him. Take a step closer, and slip my hand into his. "And you will be with us," I say in no uncertain terms. I'm not asking this time. I'm telling, if that's what it takes. If Aurora and I escape on Evander's watch, Conri will kill him this time. There will be no second chances. "I'm not leaving you behind to face his wrath. If you truly do not want to journey with us, then escape and go off on your own, after. Find a cute cottage in the land of the elves. You deserve freedom, too."

His lips part lightly with shock. I hope also with appreciation. But sorrow wells in his eyes, nearly threatening to overflow. Evander cups my cheek and presses his forehead against mine.

"If only you knew how deeply undeserving I am of your kindness."

"Quite the contrary." I meet his eyes and hold his gaze. "You are worthy of all the goodness in the world; you are worthy of second chances at happiness, of paths forward you never expected." I speak these words as much for myself as for him. "And I will prove it to you, Evander, however long it takes."

twenty-eight

We debate staying in the village that night, but I decide it's best for us to start back. I still need to find at least one spirit along the way or I risk Conri's suspicion about our venture into the woods. Then there's the matter of making outposts for Aurora and myself. Given that it took Evander and me almost three days to cross the woods, I expect it to take Aurora and me at least four.

For that reason, I ask Evander to slow his pace. Riding on wolf-back is still faster than walking and it is worth saving the time because I am stopping frequently.

The trees are no longer a blur. I can track every ancient line of gnarled bark. The changing scents of the forest—wet earth as we near streams, rot of fallen trees, fresh leaves that fall like snow when the breezes catch the upper branches—are no longer muddled across my senses.

My lips arch into a smile as I sink my hands deeper into Evander's fur, feeling it stretch between my fingers. I pat his shoulder and he takes the signal to stop. Dismounting, I cross to one of the larger trees. Despite its size, there's nothing particularly impressive about it. I reach into my satchel and retrieve my sewing kit, select a strand of deep yellow thread, and tie a length around a jagged remnant of a long, broken branch. The strand of gold is barely visible when I walk away, but I feel it like a beacon, even within these enchanted woods.

I hold in my heart a spool of magic that unravels as Evander and I speed away from the tree. I imagine it whirring like

Grandma's yarn, twisting and tightening as she twirls it between her fingers, the wheel squeaking with its age, the movement instinct. My magic connects to the next yellow thread I tie around another tree branch a little farther down. That one connects to the next…and then the next, as the process repeats.

Despite my being adamant that Evander will come with us, I am not naive. I know all too well that it is possible something might happen that will prevent him from doing so. Though the mere thought makes my hands grip him tighter. Or he might be sincere in his wish to stay. If so, I would not dream of actually forcing him, even if I know in my heart it'd be for the best.

I am left to my thoughts for most of the day and find myself feeling all the more relaxed for it. I'm accustomed to having the limited company of Grandmother and spirits. Musings and magic. What more could a woman need?

It is late in the afternoon when a whisper of power tangles with my own. The sensation is like brushing up against the bendy boughs of a sapling and nearly breaks my focus. I sit straighter and stare off in the direction from whence it came. Evander feels the shift in my stance, slowing. He glances back over his shoulder, a silvery eye meeting mine. Then he stares where my head is turned.

"Please, if you don't mind," I say.

Evander bounds off in that direction. I tug on his fur gently, guiding him left and right, as the sensation ebbs and flows. At once, it stops, and I pull back, Evander skidding with a huff.

Whipping my head around, turning at the waist, I try to pick back up on the feeling. But I cannot seem to grasp it again. I dismount, stepping away from Evander, hoping that without his presence I might be able to have clearer senses.

"What is it?"

I didn't even notice him changing back into his human form. "I thought I felt something."

"'Something?'" he repeats with an audible note of worry to his voice.

"A spirit, I thought," I say quickly to put his fears to rest.

"*Ah.* A spirit of what?"

"I'm not sure. Something flighty. Bird? Bug? Wind? Perhaps… It was faintly there and disappeared without warning. Then reappeared… then gone again." I dig out my grandmother's threads, crossing to a nearby tree. The chase went on longer than I thought and my last marker is dangerously distant. As I tie a short length of gold around a lower branch, I let out a heavy sigh.

"We'll find it again, I'm sure," Evander offers optimistically.

The threads in my little folio continue to stare up at me. There's still a good amount left…but they'll run out eventually. I'll have to make more, without Grandma.

"What is it?" Fallen twigs and leaves crunch under Evander's foot as he takes a step closer.

I still don't turn. A slightly sick feeling has lodged itself into my throat, making it difficult to speak. Evander approaches, but it's not him I imagine drawing near. Instead, it's a shapeless shadow of faceless gray. A mass that's been haunting me for weeks now, sneaking up whenever I least expect it. Wrapping its tendrils around my throat and heart. Trying to pin my feet to the ground with roots that skewer through the meat between my toes. It's heavy, and yet so ethereal that I can almost, *almost* forget it's there. Especially when I insist all is well and keep my focus anywhere else.

"Faelyn?" He's right behind me now. His hands rest on my shoulders, jarring me from the thoughts.

I shake my head, jostling myself back to the present. "Sorry, we should carry on."

"No." He doesn't move, replacing his hands on my shoulders when I turn.

"No?" A frown tugs on my lips. I swallow. Somehow, his concerned expression has only made the knot in my throat worse.

"No," he repeats again, gentler. "Tell me what has you so shaken?"

I sigh heavily, looking back at the folio that still rests in my hands. Open. Staring up at me. The thing that summoned that lurking shadow to the fore.

"I'll have to make more threads—sooner rather than later—and it'll be the first time I'm making them without Grandma," I admit, surprised at how level I manage to keep my voice.

His brows lift briefly with surprise, and as they settle back into place, a slight smile rests on his lips. "You'll do excellently, I'm sure."

I run my fingertips over the threads. "There's so much she never taught me. I had a lifetime with her, and it wasn't enough time."

"We could live two lifetimes with our elders and still feel there wasn't time to gather their wisdom. By the time we have enough wisdom of our own to appreciate theirs, twilight has already settled upon them," he says with a heavy tone. There's a knowing sadness in those words.

He lost everyone he cared about, too. He knows this pain. If anyone could understand, it would be Evander, wouldn't it? Yet, I can't muster the strength to continue speaking.

He continues in my silence, "But I'm sure you have nothing to worry about."

"It's not that I'm worried about doing it right…" I murmur.

"What is it, then?"

I close the sewing folio and slip it back into my bag. But I still can't bring myself to look at him. Maybe a slow and steadying breath will help?

No. I still feel as jittery as before.

"Faelyn—"

"I'll be doing it alone." I jerk my face in his direction, feeling vulnerable the instant our eyes meet. I have given this man my body, and—dare I admit it?—pieces of my heart. But this is a part of me that isn't lovely. That's difficult and tender to touch. I'm afraid to offer this part of me to him for judgment. "She was always there; since the moment I took my first breath, she was there. She carried me into this world as I left my mother's body. She held me when I mourned her loss. These are the first few weeks—months—that I have ever been without her."

His arms tighten around my shoulders and he pulls me to him. Evander says nothing. The silence begs to be filled.

"I am no stranger to grief; my mother died when I was young. She went into the woods and never returned," I say hastily, my breath catching on almost every other word. "I know she died—she wouldn't have left us. Word was brought back of her passing. We mourned her together."

"Together," he echoes, emphasizing it for me more than him.

Together. The word continues to resonate in me. Louder and louder, rather than softer. "Yes…she was always there for me. And I knew she would leave. I knew the end was coming as it comes for us all… She would not want me to mourn—she told me as much—and I am trying so hard to be strong but…"

"You are strong," he whispers in my ear. "Grief is not a simple or fast process. Every loss hits us differently."

"But I have mourned her, I have said my goodbyes." I press my eyes closed as my arms wrap tightly around his waist, locking by gripping my elbows. "Why does that shroud of death continue to haunt me?"

"The pain manifests in ways we least expect, at times we least expect." He kisses my temple gently.

It's a tender gesture, one that whispers to me, *Evander cares for you.* A few tears escape despite my best efforts. I draw a shuddering breath, trying to collect myself. But, for some reason, it only seems to make things worse. More tears fall.

I've begun to care for him, too. I hold him all the tighter, as though I can keep the realization safe and pressed close to my heart, not allowing it to escape. It is not safe to care. Not safe for my fragile heart. Nor is it safe for us when we return to the wolves' den.

"It's all right, Faelyn," he soothes, stroking my hair. "It's all right."

"When…when Aurora is freed, she will be gone too. Everyone I've ever loved has left well before I was ready." The words stumble over the tears I'm fighting. Evander flinches. My wits return at the sight. What am I thinking? He's endured far worse than I. "Evander, I—"

His grip slackens, hands returning to my shoulders as he leans away. I expect to see an expression of disgust. Of anger that I could be so inconsiderate to him and his hurt.

But that isn't the expression he wears. Instead, Evander's brows pinch with what almost looks like pain. As though he is somehow the cause of *my* pain. Anger would be easier than guilt.

"I will be there," he says before I can get a word of apology in for my careless disregard of his suffering.

"What?" I whisper.

"I will be there," Evander says again, with emphasis. "I will be there when you bid Aurora goodbye. I will be there when you need to spin more threads, and dye them in your vats of turmeric and pine. When your fingertips are stained yellow and you reek of onion peels for two weeks." He chuckles softly, almost sadly. "I will be there when you loop them after they've dried and I will be there when you need to start the process anew with spring's fresh wool."

"Evander…" I can't formulate a response. What he's saying is barely comprehensible to me. I understand the words…but the meaning. *What is he really implying?*

"As long as you wish for it, I will be there with you."

"Why are you saying all this?" I breathe, searching his silvery eyes, shadowed by his dark hair and the fading light. He looks dangerous in the twilight. Yet I am not afraid. This danger is on my side, protecting me.

"Because I do not want you to think for another second that you will be alone ever again." He's deathly serious.

"Please don't make promises like this unless you intend on keeping them." My words are no stronger than the last. It's as though all the strength I've been relying on to prop me up is fading. As if I can finally rely on his support at long last.

"I have every intention of keeping it." Evander locks his gaze with mine and doesn't let go. He holds me as much with a stare as his arms and as my own grasp.

Somehow, despite all odds, I believe him.

twenty-nine

THAT NIGHT I DECIDE TO MAKE A SHELTER FOR US TO SLEEP IN, ONE STURDY ENOUGH THAT IT COULD SERVE AURORA AND ME. Evander lends his assistance at my guidance.

"I would think you would be better at this." I chuckle and take the branch from his grasp, showing him again how to weave it with the others to form a roof of saplings for the hovel we're making.

"You've seen the Lykin Plains; there aren't a lot of trees there. Ask me to set up a tent and I will have it done for you in seconds." Evander makes another attempt, with much better success than the last four.

"This is not that much different than setting up a tent."

He huffs. "A tent is vastly different. It has a precise way it comes together. There's far less of all these fiddly bits." He struggles with another branch. This time I let him and he figures it out. "How did you learn to do this, anyway?"

"My mother taught me," I say.

"I'm sorry. I didn't mean to bring up something difficult for you." He tries to hide a flash of guilt in his focus as he twists the small, soft branches.

"Don't be sorry. It's all right." I flash him a smile as proof. "You said it yourself, grief can be strange. I'm fine to talk about her—and Grandma. I *want to*. I don't want to let grief become fear of their memories. I love them far too much for that."

He shares in my smile before returning his focus to weaving. We're making good progress and this shelter should hold not just for days or weeks, but possibly months. Though I hope it won't take me that long to escape with Aurora…

"My mother taught me how I could use the forest for protection and sustenance. So did my grandma, after. But she was older, then, and her hip was already starting to ache so she couldn't go as far or want to be out for as long," I explain. "What my mother didn't have a chance to teach me, I learned myself in the wood as I went out to collect supplies for Grandma and me. Even though I couldn't sense all the spirits—or there were no other spirits in my world to sense—I was still connected to their remnants. To the world itself."

"It wasn't magical or spirit related…but my father also taught me about how I could thrive in the forest," Evander says so softly I almost miss the words. His hands still, but I don't encourage him to continue weaving. I give him the moment and the space by focusing on my own hands and my own branches. I'm surprised when he continues, "We would go out, sometimes for a week at a time, into the woods. He never seemed like he wanted to go—he'd exhaust himself telling me how dangerous it was. How I had to be so careful. The days leading up to our trips, he would spend hours planning and fretting. Scouting ahead. But…"

Evander sighs softly and drops his hands to his sides. He tilts his head upward and stares at the darkening sky, as if offering his cheeks for the first rays of moonlight to land upon. I slow my own movements, straightening as well, my focus narrowing to him.

He truly is the sort of handsome that can lead one to believe in the gods, because, surely, a man like him had divine intervention in his crafting. Ignorantly and effortlessly, Evander wields the kind of allure that whispers dark temptations, impossible to resist even when you know there's danger lurking beneath. And yet, for all his beauty, he is equally tortured. A veil of heartache shrouds him, clinging to him like a second skin. A constant companion that I wish I couldn't recognize.

"All that stress leading up to our departure, and, yet, when we were in the forest…Father moved like he was home. All those worries, those fears, melted away. They collapsed into long hours of trekking down hidden paths that felt like nature made solely for us. He could walk and walk for hours, as if he was trying to get back to somewhere…"

Evander hangs his head, shaking it, rubbing his eyes. "Somewhere that no longer existed."

"Because of Conri?" I dare to ask.

Evander's eyes meet mine and he nods. "Conri took everything from my pack, whittling us down until it was, well, only me."

"We will get our vengeance," I swear.

"I know." He shifts closer to me. "And I thank you with every breath for it."

I nod and return to working on the shelter. Light is fading. But, more than that, there's an irresistible draw to Evander in this moment. The pull is so strong that if I were to move for him now, I might stumble and fall into his arms and never be able to escape him again.

I will be there as long as you want me.

His words from earlier resonate in me. I slowly bring my eyes back to him to find him waiting, staring. As if he knew my attention would return if he merely waited.

Would it be so bad if I fell for him? Not just for the necessity of fighting off Conri's charms, or for the bodily pleasures we can give each other, but for the man himself? I try to shift the way I look at him and find it easy to consider him as a prospective partner. Perhaps it's been shifting for a few days now.

"What is it?" He chuckles. "You're looking at me like I've changed my shape into something other than a wolf." Evander steps forward and reaches out to cup my cheek.

I hadn't realized I'd actually tilted my head to look at him differently until his palm meets my skin. I'm grateful for the night to hide the dusting of blush that coats my cheeks. Though I wonder if he can feel the warmth. It almost makes me blush more.

His lips part slightly. Evander takes a small step forward, hand landing on my hip—feather light, as if, somehow, now of all times, he's afraid to touch me. His palm quivers slightly. It seems as if every time we step apart, we come back together, faster than the last. My heart hammers. The way he's looking at me now…like I am everything…

"Faelyn, there's so much I need to tell you. So much you should know," he whispers huskily.

"We'll have time for you to tell me as you're ready." I raise a hand to cover his, holding it against my warm cheek. "You're coming with me, remember?"

"As long as you want me there," he reiterates.

"There isn't any world I could imagine where I wouldn't."

"When you learn all of who I am, what I've done…"

"Things you had to," I insist to him. "To survive Conri and this harsh world you were born into."

"If only that were the extent of it." He sighs and releases me, going to move away.

I don't let him. Both hands on his face, I keep him in place, and kiss him firmly. Pulling away just enough to form words, I whisper, "Stop being so afraid."

"But—"

"You've spent so much of your life afraid. Sacrificing joy. Chasing one fleeting happiness after the last. You don't have to be afraid with me. I'm not leaving."

He groans and claims my mouth, arms tight around my waist. Evander leans forward, as if he wants to devour me whole. I lean back, but only slightly, struggling to match his sudden fervor though desperately wanting to.

Moving hands. Shifting gasps. Tugs on the hems of clothing and the chill air of night against his bare skin that prickles it to gooseflesh under my hands. Never have I wanted to help someone relax more. I want him to take me. To use me for his relief this once. The joy I would find in seeing his unburdened smile and knowing I am the cause…

Evander reaches forward, grabbing my rear and pulling me up. I move on instinct, knowing what he wants. My legs lock around his waist and my back presses into a tree.

His one hand is in my hair. The other caresses down my side, grabbing my breast on the way before gripping my hip. His thumb makes circles, closer and closer, until it hits my most sensitive spot. I moan into his mouth, suck on his tongue, and grind my hips against his.

"Woman." The word is somewhere between a gasp and a growl as he frees his lips from mine, burying his face in the crook of my neck. His teeth sink into my skin, thumb moving relentlessly, working me to a fervor. "You make me mindless. You make me hasty and hot. You make me want like I have never wanted before—like I never thought I would ever want again." He almost sounds angered by it.

"It's all right to want me," I whisper reassuringly. "Because, Evander, I want you, too."

"Damn these trousers," he growls, hand fumbling at the fastenings at my waist.

I laugh. "You should have taken them off first."

"I will rip them off with my teeth if I must." Evander steps back and loosens his grip enough that my legs unravel from around his waist and I stand on my own once more.

"I would like to see that."

He slides down my body, determined eyes locked with mine, hands on my sides and returning to my rear as he kneels before me. Evander takes the fastenings between his teeth with purpose. Immediately, my mind is filled with all manner of lewd imaginings of him with his face between my thighs. His tongue as relentless down there as I know it to be in my mouth. My hands holding his head in place until I am screaming and he surfaces with that smug grin that delights me so.

Evander pulls on the string between his teeth, slowly pulling the loop through the knot. He releases it and I feel my trousers loosen. At the same time, another sensation ripples through me.

"It's back," I gasp. Every muscle tenses. I don't move, for fear I'll lose the feeling again.

"What—" Evander doesn't have a chance to finish his question.

I'm off, running through the dark woods, trying to hastily tie up my trousers on the way. I can hear him behind me, pulling on his own pants, stumbling with a curse. He falls heavy into a tree. Another curse.

But I can't afford to pay him any mind. My focus remains on the whispers of spirit magic that are tickling my arms, like raindrops rolling down my skin. I sprint through the woods. A wolf is soon at my side, Evander no doubt gave up on attempting to get his pants properly on.

At once, the sensation changes. I stop. Sway. The magic hits me with force again, this time from a different direction. Then nothing. Then another pulse. Like a call and response. An echo? Or…

"Evander, use your nose, take us to the nearest stream or river," I command. I can't get a sense of where this spirit is, but I think I know *what* it is. And if I'm right, then this whole excursion will be worth it for this spirit alone.

He dips his muzzle and bolts through the trees.

I nearly trip over myself, multiple times, trying to keep up. The first time he hears my clamor of almost falling, Evander pauses, looking back. After that, he sets a slower but aggressive pace. He must've heard the desperation in my voice or seen the haste in my eyes because he doesn't slow too much.

Without warning, we break free of the trees and nearly fall into a small river. The moonlight beaming through the rippling current illuminates the smooth stones of the bed, making them shine like diamonds.

Here.

The sense of power nearly physically pushes me back, keeping me from falling in the water. Better for it, as I wouldn't want to enter a spirit's domain unbidden. I shift my stance, collecting myself, and stare in awe of this raw essence.

Right before my eyes, the current shifts. The water flows backward.

"Don't go," I say quickly.

The current slows, but does not stop.

"I am not your enemy." I take a step forward and Evander hangs back. He remains on the grass near the trees as I approach on the rocky bank. Slowly, I kneel, staring into the deepest part of the water. What I first thought were the inky outlines of two fishes seem to shift to look at me. Not unlike Folost's eyes. "If you are willing, I would like to speak with you."

I bow forward, stretching out my fingers and doubling over my knees. I bring my forehead to the backs of my hands in the deepest kneel possible. When I speak next, it is without moving from this position. The only way I know that the spirit is still present is by the sense of it.

"I am but a humble witch. I come with an open heart. But I do seek you out for my own gain."

Honesty is the heart of magic, Grandma would say. *No true power is gained by hiding or smothering truth.*

"There is a wicked king. I know he holds one of your primordial cousins captive." Aurora. "And I fear another might be twisted by his sway." The ancient wolf spirit in the old wood. If the wolf kings somehow managed to keep Aurora captive, who's to say that they aren't doing the same with the wolf spirit? "I am working to free any spirits he keeps unjustly, and end his reign in turn. But I cannot do this alone. So I seek your name and your bond. I seek your help when I call upon you—and your trust to know I will not do so without great care and consideration."

When I am done speaking, there is no movement. The river is nearly perfectly still. Then it begins moving again. I lift my head.

The water is normal. I've failed.

My ribs collapse in. I suck in air but can't seem to get a good breath. There's so much I never learned about meeting spirits. About dealing with them. Grandma never had a chance to teach me—there weren't enough in our world. I'm treating these ancient beings like I would the old wood. No wonder they care little to deal with me.

Sitting up, I lean back onto my heels and sigh heavily.

"I'm sorry." I can't bring myself to turn back to Evander. My failure will not only risk us both, but also Aurora. Our whole plan… "I wasn't enough."

"You are but a small witch," another soft voice says, as whispering as water against rock. Evander's eyes go wide and I follow his stare over my shoulder, back to the water and the source of the voice. "But you are more than enough."

Tiny bubbles float from between the rocks of the riverbed, foaming on the surface and rising to form a mound of water. The spirit emerges as the loose shape of the torso of a man. It's constantly shifting and changing as the water rises and falls, foam creating a strange sort of outline in the moonlight.

"Hello, spirit." I halfway bow. I should go deeper but I don't seem to be quite in control of my body. It refuses to move. I'm stuck between shock and awe of what's before me.

"Hello, Faelyn." When he speaks, water falls away from the face of the visage. It's the sound of it hitting against the surface of the river combining with the babbling current that forms cohesive words.

"You know my name?" I blink.

"Gruvun told me." Spirit of the tides. I recognize the name from when I first arrived in Midscape.

"Is Gruvun well?" I haven't seen him since the ferry ride after crossing the Fade.

"He is. Ever moving. Ever changing. He is the busy one, and I am more the still. Constant." The spirit speaks with forced, almost stilted words. Each seems difficult to make and I worry that I am unnecessarily taxing him with this conversation.

"You are the spirit of water," I whisper. As soon as I say it a feeling of rightness floods through me.

The water collapses, the spirit falling with a splash. I worry somehow I've harmed him with the outright identification, until he takes his shape once more before me.

"Yes, witch, I am Volst, the spirit of water eternal." Those two shadowy eyes bore into me. Yet, I do not feel afraid. Something about this spirit is just as familiar as Brundil. Without being aware, I've known him all my life. "You may call upon me in your cause."

With a final splash he returns to the river. The magic darts away like fish, carried on the current. I imagine him and Gruvun dancing endlessly across the world, carving mountains, circling islands, exploring the far corners of the earth.

"What did he say?" Evander asks, reminding me of his presence, and that he can't understand the spirits—save for Aurora, given her human form. Even though he has some affinity for the spirits thanks to the witch he once knew.

"His name is Volst. And he'll help us," I announce, standing. My trousers are soaked up to the knee. I didn't realize, but the water must have risen when Volst drew near. I turn to face Evander and halt. His expression has me stopping in my tracks.

Evander leans against a tree. A slight smile curls the corners of his lips. He looks at me with pride and admiration.

"I hope you know, I never doubted you for an instant."

thirty

THE TREES ARE THINNING. We did not return the same way we came. Instead, we've turned farther north. Heading directly to Den.

We've walked most of this final day, dragging our feet toward the inevitable. But now that I can see those seemingly unending plains through the trees, I've slowed almost to a stop. Evander halts beside me, his hand slipping into mine.

"How much farther is it?" I ask, my voice soft and small. The vastness of the plains feels like it could swallow me whole. The only things that mar the emerald surface are two towers on the horizon. Even though Evander said most of them were abandoned, I feel like there is someone there, watching me right now, relaying to Conri and the rest of the wolf packs that I am not far.

"Two days? If that. I can set a fast pace." Evander's thumb gently caresses my hand like a reminder of his promise to stay by my side. I won't be going alone. And Aurora is waiting for me, too. "We have time. We can spend one more night out here, if you'd like."

I nod with a slight smile. "Reading my mind now, are you?"

"Lucky guesses."

"Indeed." I start walking again through the trees, running my hands along them as I pass.

The magic I've been stringing along still pulls out of me. It's thinner now, like a spider's strand clinging stubbornly despite the breeze. Stopping at a tree near the edge of the woods, I take a longer strand of yellow thread and tie it around a particularly bulbous knot in a way that leaves a majority of the length in one end of the knot. I cut the remainder with my small knife, feeling my power thread against the strands of wool.

"Evander, will you help me?"

"Me?" He sounds surprised. I suppose I haven't asked him for help so far.

I nod and he approaches. I hold out my hand, the thread draped over my palm. Even though the wind picks up more readily through the trees, it doesn't move. It's perfectly still. Weighted by magic.

"Take the ends, and loop it around one of my fingers. Tie it off," I instruct.

Evander reaches out and hesitates, fingers hovering around the ends of the strands. It's impossible to read him but, after a moment, he takes both ends, lifting the threads. His movements are deliberate with intention. He slips the thread between my fingers, choosing one to wrap it several times around. It's only on the third loop that I realize what hand I've given him—and what finger he chose.

"Make sure you fasten it well," I say softly as he begins to tie the knot. "I don't want it coming off."

"I don't either," he murmurs, and I lose my fight against the blush. Evander finishes the knot, tucking in the tiny bit of extra length underneath the loops.

I lift up my left hand. The yellow thread looks almost like spun gold around my ring finger. The knot is subtle, yet prominent, like a set stone. The sight of it is…beautiful. Yet simultaneously too much to bear. I drop my hand to my stomach, trying to quell the near-instant nausea, and turn away.

"Faelyn?"

I inhale slowly through my nose and then out through my mouth. Trying to reclaim my emotional balance. The shuddering breath helps.

"It's so, so silly." I try to force a laugh, lighter than what I feel.

"I doubt that's the case." He steps forward. I can feel him draw near as much as hear his footstep crunch against the forest floor. "But if you don't wish to tell me…"

"When I was younger, I met my soulmate. Or, I *thought* I did. From the moment I laid eyes on him, I thought I knew that he was the one I was destined to be with. I could feel it with every fiber of me. Every strand of time and fate drew me to him. I was just sixteen, him not much older, but I knew I was ready to swear myself to him." Glancing over my shoulder, I dare to look at Evander, pleased to find he doesn't look too shocked. "You must think that to know such a thing at sixteen is far too young, but—"

"Sometimes it is fate," he whispers. I shift to face him, my fear of being judged for this confession fading. "The lykin have these beliefs, too. That there are old gods who made every spirit and crafted every soul. Sometimes, the souls and spirits were too mighty to be one being, so they were split into two."

"I suspect Gruvun and Volst are examples of that." Tides and water, two beings moving as one.

"What happened to your mate?" he says, forcing the question. I wonder if Evander is jealous of my lost love. Part of me hopes he is, because it would mean he cares. While another part of me wants to reassure him he has nothing to fear from a long, long ago flame.

"In truth, I never could confirm if he was my soulmate or not." I tilt my head and stare up at the puffy clouds that backdrop the swaying trees. "We could wait on human marriage and formal ceremonies, but I wanted to promise myself to him. I wanted to know that what I felt—and suspected—was real. So I invited him out one night into the woods. I planned to take him before the ancient redwood on a new moon and ask the spirits to give me clarity. If we were truly meant to be one, to bless and unite us. Give us a sign our union was meant to be."

I'm back in the thick that night. Back in the woods waiting…and waiting. Alone all night.

Wet grasses soak my trousers as I trek down the hills and along the paths to the hunter's home. The windows are dark. The door ajar. The scent of the morning's dew is so clean and crisp that I can't even pick up on the aroma of him. His bed is cold.

"But I was wrong," I finish softly, pulling myself from the memories. "He wasn't my soulmate after all."

"You confirmed this?"

"He never came." I shrug, trying to play off the dull ache the memories still cause me. "A soulmate wouldn't abandon their partner."

"Perhaps something prevented him from coming?" Evander offers.

I close my eyes, huff, and shake my head. "He was a hunter's son. A fighter who knew the lands and the woods. And I went to his house—there was no sign of a struggle. All their things were packed. It wasn't a hasty departure; it had to have been planned. He knew he was leaving and…didn't even tell me. He let me believe he would come and meet me. That he loved me."

Silence as heavy as standing in that abandoned cabin settles upon us.

Lowering my gaze from the sky, I bring my attention back to the thread looped around my finger. "It had been years, really, since I thought about all this. But ever since my Grandma died and I came here, I can't seem to escape the memories. Perhaps I never really accepted what happened."

Evander closes the gap and takes my hand, running his thumb over the knot that he tied. "That means what you felt was real."

"Don't," I whisper. "It wasn't. It couldn't have been. He wouldn't."

"I am sure that he desperately, *desperately* wanted to come to you that night," Evander assures me with all the confidence in the world.

"You don't know anything about it." I try to pull my hand away but he holds fast.

"I know that it is the honor of any man to merely stand in your presence. But to be your mate?" He chuckles deeply, and there's a bitter note to it. Almost sad. "That, that is an honor worth more than the names and bonds of all the spirits in the world. That would make one's days worth living and every hour a delight."

He loves you. The words strike true right between my ribs. They echo across my whole body like lightning sizzling under my skin, causing me to take a breath. *Evander loves me*. He isn't telling me in so few words. But it's there. I can hear it in the weight of everything left unsaid. In the heaviness of his stance. In the slight edge of fear that clouds his gaze and is no doubt tainting my own because…

…because…

I think I might be falling in love with him, too.

The realization makes me want to throw my arms around his shoulders. To place my mouth on his and kiss him until we are breathless. Until he pins me against a tree and takes me time and again—to the point that we collapse alongside our walls and fears and are left with nothing but that singular, all-important truth.

But, with the game we play, that is a deadly truth. Conri might convey that he sees Evander as a loyal general that wouldn't dare cross him. Yet, I've already seen how quickly that facade can drop. Conri knows anyone would kill for his position. And few have more reasons to slay him than Evander. I can't be yet another.

My fingers thread against his. I grip Evander's hand with all my might and lock my gaze with his. His eyes widen slightly. For a second, it's as though we breathe in unison. I try and tell him everything that he needs to know with that look alone.

Let's not say it now; it's too dangerous. If it's meant to be, let's wait until we're free.

He gives a slight nod and cups my face with his other hand. Evander kisses me and the taste is almost salty…like unshed tears. When we pull away, I don't think I imagine his silvery eyes are shining more than normal.

"Let's stay here, at the edge of the forest, one more night," I whisper, our faces still close. "Just you and me for a little bit longer. The world can wait, right?"

He nods. "It can." Evander tilts his head and leans forward to whisper in my ear. His breath moves my hair, sending shivers up and down my spine. "I will enjoy having you all to myself for one more night out here, where I can tremble the stars with your cries of passion."

thirty-one

We move together as though our bodies were built for this singular act. I know his movements, his points of passion, as well as my own. We tumble—him on top, me on top, on our sides, him behind me—until I am dizzy and breathless. His hips slap against mine with such force that it's almost as if he's trying to compete with my cries of passion. Evander grabs for me as if I am his only lifeline—the tether to his entire existence.

We are shameless and needy. He takes me like I am the last woman on earth and he is the last man. Like his one goal is to consume me.

Evander bites my neck where it meets my shoulder, growling, pinning me down by my wrists as he furiously pounds into me. I allow each thrust of his hips to push a thought out of my mind. There is nothing left but blurred visions, his low moans and rasping breath.

Never have I been with someone like I am with him now. I have never felt so…animalistic. Every shred of decency is gone and I do not feel the least bit ashamed. I feel free. This passion fills me, lifts me. It allows me to let go of everything else and savor this one moment. To be a primal and sensual being.

The climax comes swift and fast, rolling over me as I shudder with a cry. Evander slows, kissing me through it, before he finds his pace again. And again…and again.

Finally, when we are sweaty, breathless, and spent, he

collapses next to me. Neither of us says anything. But when he stretches out an arm, I know just what to do. I shift closer to him, using his bicep like a pillow, leaning slightly and continuing to look up at the sky above.

"Thank you," I whisper.

"I should be thanking you." He twists to plant a kiss on my forehead. It is so tender compared to the beast that just ravaged my body. Two sides of this man—gentle and ferocious. I love both. "That was…the best I've ever had."

I sit and slap his shoulder playfully. "Oh stop, now you're just trying to butter me up to get me to go again."

He smirks. "Is it working?"

Laughing, I stand, and my legs wobble, which only causes me to laugh more. Evander sits quickly and I wave him away with a grin. "I'm fine. But that thing you did with your tongue…it has my knees a bit weak, still."

"So do that first, that way you have the most time on your back to recover. Noted."

I laugh harder. "You are insatiable."

"Only for you." There's a faint dusting of heat still on his cheeks, accented by an easy, satisfied smile. I pause, taking a moment to admire him in the moonlight.

"Contentment suits you, Evander," I say softly.

"Glad you think so, for I so often find myself content when you are near." He stretches. The sentiment fills me with a gentle warmth. "But is everything well?"

"More than well. I have a strong desire to rinse off after that and saw a stream not too far away earlier."

"Are you saying I'm dirty?" Evander arches a brow.

"I'm saying the things you did to me were." I grin to convey I am not upset by it in the slightest.

"I can't argue with that. Hurry back." He yawns and lies back down onto the blanket we've stretched out. A blanket that I think we'll have to leave behind instead of bringing to Den. It smells too much of our sex. "I sleep better when you're here."

"Then I'll be sure not to delay."

My feet are light, even if my knees are a bit wobbly. That was what I had needed. A satisfying culmination of our trip away and a reaffirmation of everything I've been suspecting. Speaking with bodies, rather than words, to convey the depth of our feelings for each other.

The stream is only a few minutes' walk. I hesitate for a second before stepping in, thinking of Volst, overcome by the uncomfortable sensation of washing myself in the home of a spirit. But then I think of all the people and animals who do that, and much worse, in the rivers, lakes, and streams he presides over, and…

I cringe and stop worrying.

The water is icy and clears my head. It quenches the fires of desire and allows me to focus with a level mind, replaying everything to see if it truly was how I remember…or if I'm imprinting meaning that isn't there from the heat of the moment. Every motion, every time his hand was behind my head to ease it down to the ground. The moments he hesitated out of worry he'd been too rough, pausing to check on me.

"He loves me." The thought is as clear as the moonlit water. A surge of elation nearly has me soaring to the heavens.

Only to bring me crashing down when a rough voice says, "Yes, you certainly seemed to enjoy yourselves."

Winter itself sweeps through me, coating my bones in frost. The urge to drop into the water and curl up into a ball of horror and shame is nearly overwhelming. I am naked and alone and the man's voice is that of a predator.

But I don't cower. I'm not going to give Bardulf, of all people, the satisfaction of my fear or the power that comes from my shame. My danger doesn't truly lessen if I bend before him.

I slowly turn to face the source of the voice, confirming what I already knew from the sound alone. Bardulf stands off the side of the creek, leaning against a tree like Evander had when I communed with Volst. But unlike Evander, who radiated warmth and approval, Bardulf is danger. Disgust competes with hatred as it fills me.

This man will hurt me. He has already so casually violated my privacy. Even if the lykin have different notions of modesty…there's something in his aura that feels as if he wants me to be uncomfortable. It is a gut instinct of danger that I would be a fool not to listen to.

Even though my muscles are trembling with every step, I work to keep myself calm and composed as I emerge from the stream. I must play nicely to get back to Evander.

"There is nothing quite like a dip in a cool creek." *Why didn't I bring my clothes?* I groan internally. Oh, because I didn't think I was going to run into one of my least favorite people in the entire world as naked as the day I was born.

"You enjoyed a lot more than that." He pushes off the tree, walking quickly. I try to pick up my pace as well. He steps in front of my path. I halt to avoid walking into him. The only thing I want less than Bardulf seeing me naked is my bare skin touching his. "What do you think Conri will say when I tell him that his prized bitch is rutting with his knight and looking like she's enjoying it a whole lot? The same bitch that has refused to lie with him. Even better, that she thinks that cur knight *loves* her. Is that true? Does that bastard love you?" Bardulf leans forward, looming over me.

"Let me pass." I bite out the words.

"You think you can order me? No, no, you are mine now. If you don't want Conri to find out what you've done then you'll do exactly as I say." A thin, sinister smirk slithers across his lips, arcing with the sharpness of a sickle.

"Go ahead and tell him." I use Bardulf's moment of surprise to step around him, trying to exude more confidence and nonchalance than I feel. I know how bad this is. But I can't tackle it alone. I must get back to Evander. "Tell Conri whatever pleases you to say. We'll see if he's inclined to believe you when I'm the one that shares his bed and has his ear in a way you never could."

Bardulf lets out a growl. A fist closes around the back of my neck. I gasp, cut short by the press of his too-large fingers, which wrap around the front of my throat with a crushing grip. He pulls me back and draws near. I stumble but keep my feet, hands going to my throat, trying to dig underneath his grip.

"You will spend every day of the rest of your short life regretting challenging me," he snarls. "I'll give you one more chance. Tell me you'll be my good girl and maybe I can overlook this."

"Let me go." I can't tell if the words are soft and raspy from the grip he has on me, or the rage I feel.

"Or what?"

"You saw what I can do in the last encampment. I'll have the earth open and swallow you whole."

It's an empty threat—Brundil's magic is still too weak for me to ask anything more of her. But Bardulf clearly doesn't understand that component of spirit magic, because his grip slackens some. *That's right*, I want to say, *you lykin aren't the only ones with teeth.* Then, his hand tenses again, firmer than before. I can feel my heart throbbing against the pads of his fingers. Pain blossoms behind my eyes.

"You wouldn't dare hurt one of Conri's knights."

"Try me."

He doesn't move and neither do I. We both take two breaths, seeing who will snap first. He has me by the throat, literally and metaphorically. But he thinks I have powers he can only dream of. Though, if he changes into his wolf shape, he's faster and stronger than any spirit I could think to summon. Do I keep trying to talk down the situation or do I try and make the first strike?

Bardulf grunts, frustrations boiling over. I open my mouth to speak. But neither of us gets to make whatever move we've been planning.

Out of nowhere, a blur of shadow crashes into Bardulf. I am pulled down with the tumble of muscle and fur, at least until Bardulf releases me as shock slackens his hand. I tumble over leaves and roots. They dig into my flesh, scratching but not causing major damage.

I collect myself to the sounds of snapping maws and growling. There isn't one wolf on the ground now, but two. They tumble and roll. Claws and jaws and blood.

"Evander!" I shout as Bardulf pounces on him. Crimson explodes across the ground.

Evander bares his teeth with a sound that resembles more a roar than a snarl. He snaps at Bardulf's throat. Bardulf narrowly dodges but Evander still rips off a chunk of meat from Bardulf.

I have to help him. The creek babbles behind them. I can't push Brundil again so soon. But Volost…

Scrambling up, I dash past the wolves. Bardulf takes note and snarls but Evander pounces upon him, taking him down before he can charge after me. Splashing into the water, I kneel, folding my hands and closing my eyes.

"Volst, I call upon you. Please, I beseech you, help me." At first, nothing. Just the sounds of the fighting wolves and the running water. My hands tremble as I clutch them tighter, reaching out with my magic. Feeling the strand of thread Evander tied around my finger. I can't let something happen to him—not before I tell him what he means to me. "Please, Volst, Gruvun, anyone. *Please*."

The current stops completely. I peel one lid open and then the other. The water looks the same as normal. Except, it is unnaturally still.

"Volst?" I whisper.

A ripple thrums against me, its source unseen.

"Help him. Please, save Evander."

The stream diverts, flowing through the air as a geyser. A fist of water plows straight into Bardulf, knocking him against a tree and pinning him there with one mighty wave. Then the water seeps back into the stream, flowing like nothing happened.

Bardulf doesn't move.

"Is he…" I stand to try and spot the rise and fall of his chest. Did I just kill a man? The thought shakes me to my core and I begin to tremble all over.

Evander rushes over, changing into his human form on the way. My cloak is on his shoulders and he quickly unties it, placing it upon me. Fastening the clasp into place.

"Are you all right?" he asks hastily.

"You…" I look Evander up and down: he's covered in bruises and cuts. Deep gashes line his shoulders where Bardulf pounced into him. "You're hurt."

"Oh, this?" Evander smiles. It's forced and doesn't reach his eyes. I can see him hiding winces with every movement. "It's nothing. I've had much worse."

"We need to tend to those wounds. And Bardulf—"

The man in question jolts back to life. In the process of rolling onto his side, he changes from his wolf form back to his human one, coughing up water. Sputtering.

"It'll take more than that to kill the bastard, unfortunately," Evander says darkly, his words ripe with anger.

"Evander," I whisper quickly as Bardulf is still composing himself. "He saw us."

"What?" Evander fixates solely on me.

"He saw us," I repeat, making sure to emphasize every word. "Together. He knows."

"She's right." Bardulf heard anyway, despite my efforts to be quiet and speak while he was distracted. "I saw everything." He twists onto his other side to face us, slowly sitting. "I give you credit, Evander, I didn't think you had it in you. Going against Conri like that when you've always been such a loyal cur on the outside. You think just because you are graced with some of the king's charm as his knight, you can steal his bitch?"

"Call her that one more time," Evander threatens, hands balled into fists so tight the massive muscles in his arms bulge.

"King's charm..." I repeat softly, my brows knitting. It's been so many days since I last felt myself slipping under Conri's aura that I had almost forgotten about it.

"Oh, you don't know?" Bardulf's attention lands solely on me. A smirk slides across his lips. "He didn't tell you, did he? Of course he didn't."

"Enough," Evander snaps.

"We knights make our oath to the wolf king and, sure, he takes our ability to have children. But for our loyalty, we don't come up empty-handed. No...we might not be able to have children, but we're not denied the pleasures of partners. In fact, it's made easier. Our oaths make us an extension of the wolf king and so we gain part of his powers."

"I said enough!" Evander roars, charging toward Bardulf.

"Let him speak!" I snap. Evander stops in his tracks. My heart is hammering, but no longer out of fear that I killed a man or of what Bardulf is going to do. I'm drawing my cloak around me as if I can defend myself from this truth.

Bardulf howls with laughter. "You dog, she didn't know. Yes, Faelyn. Your protector, darling knight has been using powers he's kept hidden from you to lure you into his bed."

thirty-two

I DRAG MY GAZE TO EVANDER, MEETING HIS EYES. "Is it true?" The words are nothing more than a trembling whisper. Fear for what the answer might be nearly silences them completely.

"Faelyn, it…" The pause is unbearable.

"Yes or no."

Bardulf interjects himself. He's clearly getting too much glee from my torture to leave it be. "Didn't you ever wonder why you were so drawn to him? Why you so readily fell into the bed of a man you just met? You probably felt attracted to him from the very first moment you laid eyes on him, didn't you?"

I'm back in the tent on the beach, on the very first night. Wondering why I wasn't as disgusted as I should have been when he touched me.

"Most of us knights have the decency to try and suppress the charm. Especially around bitches the king is interested in."

"I said don't call her that!" Evander snarls and tries to move toward Bardulf again.

"Answer me!" I stop him with a sharp command. Evander looks back and his expression tells me everything. "It's true… isn't it?"

"It's not what you think," he tries to say hastily. "Faelyn, I would never—"

"The first night you took me into your tent…" Goose bumps run up my arms where Evander touched me that very first night. Not from pleasure, now, but horror. I remember how good he felt. How much I wanted him, even then, despite myself. He was so ready to accept me when I propositioned him later. He had no problem taking me to his tent so I could… I thought it was just the pressures of Conri's charm weighing on us both. That they were actions of necessity. But, no.

I've been such a fool.

"I always thought, one day, sooner or later, I'd finally be able to show your true colors to Conri, Evander." Bardulf stands slowly, using the help of the tree he was just slammed against to get upright. "Show him that you couldn't be trusted. But I never thought this was how I'd be able to do it."

"Do you really think I'd do that to you?" Evander whispers, focused only on me.

"What am I supposed to believe?" I ask him. Anger and hurt vie for control of my words. One wants to scream. The other wants to say nothing at all. "You lied to me, Evander."

"No, no. I…I didn't tell you about the charm but—"

"That's all I need to know, then."

"I can suppress it!" He takes a step toward me now. Not Bardulf. "Magic is a choice, always. I haven't been using it on you, I swear."

"You've fallen in love with the king's queen or tricked your way into her bed; either way, it doesn't look good for you," Bardulf says with glee.

I get no enjoyment from this. There's no satisfaction, twisted or otherwise, to this exposure. And his enthusiasm only makes me loathe Bardulf all the more. He doesn't care about me, he cares about taking down Evander and bringing me to heel. Evander only cares about… I don't have a clear answer. My heart and mind are too murky for it. The only thing I can land on is himself—Evander only cares about himself.

"How can I believe you when I already know you lied to me?" I ask Evander.

"I never lied to you." His tone has become pleading. He's begging for me to understand.

I don't. I can't. "A lie by omission is still a lie. You didn't tell me the truth and I wouldn't have known to ask. You had to have known that this was something I would've wanted to be made aware of. It's not fair to me otherwise."

"Faelyn…"

"If I were you, Evander, I wouldn't say another word until you stand before Conri. Save your breath to defend yourself. I think you're going to need it." Bardulf approaches, focusing on me instead of him. "Faelyn, Conri sent me because he sensed you returning to the plains and asked me to come and ensure you were well and to escort you back. If you would care to leave, we can go without Evander."

"I would," I say coldly. The only person I can trust is back with Conri—Aurora. She's the only one I should have ever listened to in this brutal world.

But, Aurora… She trusted Evander. Spoke well of him. She never mentioned the charm. Does that mean it's not real? Or that Evander is speaking the truth about suppressing it around me?

The only way to know for sure will be to ask her. Then, whatever Aurora says is what I'll believe. The sooner I get back, the better.

"Why don't you go on ahead, Evander?" Bardulf tries to wrap his arm around my shoulders. I step away with a glare, not about to let him think we're friendly. I might be angry with Evander, but that doesn't mean I suddenly like Bardulf. He just gives me a thin smile and returns his attention to Evander. "I'll finish escorting her to Den. I think she'll be safer with me."

"Conri told me to protect her, and to stay at her side. To look after her." Evander barely manages words, his jaw is clenched so tightly.

"What a job of 'protecting her' you were doing." Bardulf takes another step closer to me. I take another step back.

"You're making her uncomfortable," Evander says on my behalf. I want to tell him not to, but I am still secretly grateful for him getting Bardulf to step away, even if I'm still disgusted.

"Here you are, trying to lecture me, like you have some moral high ground, when all I'm doing is trying to offer you the opportunity to save yourself. You really want the first word Conri hears of this to be from me?" Bardulf's threat is clear.

"I'm not leaving—"

"Go, Evander," I interject curtly. Evander's attention swings toward me, his expression wounded, as if I were the one who had dug claws into his flesh. "Get to Den and mend yourself. I'll see you in a day."

"Faelyn…"

"I do not want you by my side." The statement is calm, cool. But I can see the havoc it wreaks within him. Evander takes a step back and visibly deflates. He said he'd always be there, as long as I wanted him. Well, now I've made it clear. I've drawn the line in the sand.

"I... Very well." Evander works to compose himself. It's marginally successful. "But I will see you tomorrow." He encroaches on Bardulf's personal space, Evander's muscular mass nearly encapsulating the other man. "I'd better see her tomorrow in one piece. If any harm comes to her—"

"Unlike you, I haven't forgotten my oath to Conri." Bardulf glances at me. "Let's go."

"I'm not going anywhere until I get my clothes and my things." I draw my cloak tighter around me, glaring at them both. They both have the good sense not to challenge and I trudge back to the campsite Evander and I had made.

The blanket is still out. Indents of both of our bodies lay side by side like ghosts. With all the dignity I can still muster, I dress. And I work to ignore the memories somehow even my clothes fill me with—visions of Evander peeling them from my body that blend into the feeling of his hands on me. Him kissing me.

I dress faster and when I am done, I turn to face them both. "Right, then, let's go."

Bardulf steps forward. He still has a bit of a limp, but he's already recovering well. He changes into his wolf state and sinks low, clearly expecting me to climb on. The idea of riding on his back makes my stomach churn.

"You can't honestly trust him." Evander steals my thoughts, giving them sound.

"At least I know that with him," I hiss back. "You...I don't know what to think about you."

He takes a half step toward me, dipping his chin, locking eyes with mine. Unlike Bardulf, I don't move away. Even now, knowing what I know, there's no part of me that wants to move away from him. I'm still drawn to this man...but is it because of an instinct I can trust? Or a magic charm that pulls on my heart? I might never find out if I don't somehow get away from him and give myself a moment to clear my head.

"If you want or need me, all you need do is call. No distance will be too great, no power insurmountable. I'm not afraid of the cost, anymore, Faelyn…I will find you."

The sentiment would be sweet, were it not for the circumstances surrounding it.

"I will not call." I know the words will cause him pain—and they do—but I am wicked because I do not find it within me to care. The want to hurt him, as he has hurt me, is an ugly urge but an insatiable one.

Bardulf turns his head over his shoulder and lets out a gruff bark. I move for him, leaving Evander behind. Evander doesn't make any other motions for me. He stands there, watching, as I awkwardly position myself on Bardulf's back.

I sway slightly, struggling to situate myself as Bardulf stands. He's a bit smaller than Evander as a wolf. Leaner. It's awkward to hold on to him and difficult to figure out where I want to sit. Just being astride him fills me with an unwanted sense of intimacy.

Glancing back over my shoulder, I meet Evander's eyes once before Bardulf charges off into the night. All too soon, the trees and night obscure Evander completely and I feel as if a part of myself is being ripped from me.

Is this sensation the charm leaving me? Is it magic that I feel slipping from my being? Or is it the feeling of heartbreak I know all too well?

The wind batters my face as we emerge from the woods and out onto the plains. It pricks my eyes, drawing out salt. I try to fight the tears. I don't want to be so vulnerable around Bardulf. If it were up to me, I'd be completely alone right now. I'd go back to my hut, set a simmer pot over Folost, and spin Grandma's wheel until my own thoughts grew as orderly as the thread between my fingers.

But the comforts of home are a luxury I no longer possess. And they are not luxuries Aurora has had in centuries. I channel my pain and anguish into thoughts of her—into what I'm doing here in the first place. I'm going to save her. No matter what pain I feel, what heartache, it is only a tiny fraction of what she has endured.

With the dawn will come Den, and, once we arrive, I'm not holding back and I'm not wasting time. We're leaving Conri, the lykin, and Evander all behind.

thirty-three

Bardulf slows his pace. It's still well before dawn and we have only just crested the slope that leads up to the Lykin Plains. The forest shadows the valley beneath us. There's no sign of Evander at all. Bardulf sinks to the ground and I dismount.

"Is everything all right?" I ask when he changes back into his human form.

Bardulf places his hands on his lower back and tilts left to right, forward and back. "I'm still aching from our tussle, and you're not exactly light."

I bristle at the way he frames the remark. While I appreciate my full hips and plump rear and am not about to let him change that, it's clear he intended for the sentiment to offend.

"Perhaps you should become stronger, then." I fold my arms and look over the plains. "How long until you're ready to run again?"

"You are relentless," he grumbles, glowering at me. "You should be thanking me for freeing you from Evander. Bowing down to kiss my boots."

"That's not happening," I say flatly. I bring my attention back to him with a pointed glare. "Don't mistake my being here for any kind of fondness for you. I still find you brutish and utterly intolerable. You are only a means to get back to Conri faster." I add in the last bit, emphasizing that I am still under Conri's protection. Evander is right, I'm not safe with Bardulf, and I know it.

"I am surprised you'd want to get back to Conri. You didn't look like you felt any haste to return to him when you were straddling Evander, moaning his name." Bardulf pulls no punches. I purse my lips and feel a scarlet flush rising with anger and embarrassment. He doesn't miss it. "Yes, Faelyn, don't forget before you open that smart mouth of yours that I still hold power over you. You're either the poor victim of Evander's treachery, or a treasonous wench. It's up to you what you want me to tell Conri when we return."

I glare up at him, keeping my mouth shut until I can trust myself not to snap. When I do speak, my words are soft. "Perhaps you should focus more on regaining your strength than running your mouth. I don't think you'll enjoy finding out who Conri listens to between the two of us."

Bardulf snorts and sits where he stands, situating himself back on the grass. "First smart thing you've said. Take your own advice, bitch."

I bristle, but don't rise to the insult, instead keeping my focus. "In an hour we begin again?"

"Den is still too far." He yawns. "We'll sleep, then carry on after sunrise."

"It's not that far."

"We'll go in a few hours," he reiterates with force.

"Fine." I take a few large steps away from him and lie back as well. I keep my back toward Bardulf and rest my head on my arm. I stare at nothing, waiting for sleep to come to me. But it doesn't.

Instead, I pass the time thinking about what I'm going to do first when I reach Den. Aurora is my only priority now. Will we immediately leave? There could be an element of surprise to quickly running off. Conri wouldn't be expecting it in the slightest, and the longer we stay, the more suspicious he might become. Moreover, it sounded like Evander would have some kind of trial immediately on return. We could leverage the chaos…

The mere thought has my insides squirming. It's so heartless. Could I really leave him behind like a sacrificial lamb? *He was heartless first*, I remind myself. But when I do, his wounded expression returns to me. The pain in his eyes.

Was he really using me?

I bite back a sigh. The urge to get up and walk back to the woods nearly overwhelms me. I press my eyes closed, as though I could somehow get rid of the urge by shutting out the world.

But in the darkness behind my lids, a new urge creeps into my mind. It sneaks in like an ant, crawling over the edge of a picnic basket, scouting, inviting friends. A shiver rips through me, dragging stillness over my shoulders in its wake. I am as heavy as a cloud over the moon. My consciousness is as clear as twilight.

It felt good, giving in to him…it truly did. It had been so long. It could feel good giving in again… My breath hitches, catching in my throat. I can almost feel his fingers running down my shoulder and arm. Feel his breath on the back of my neck.

Give in…

The voice in my mind is no longer my own. My brow furrows. Something's wrong.

Relax. You want this.

No. I don't. I force my eyes open and the world comes crashing back around me. With it comes the awareness of a presence at my back. I sit quickly, spinning.

Bardulf looms.

"What do you want?" I snap, rubbing my arms. It helps shake the slimy feeling that's crept into me like a chill of winter. It's then that I become aware that my cape has slid off my shoulders. Or perhaps… the feeling of fingers on my arm. Did he remove it? I keep my eyes on Bardulf, looking at him with a fresh awareness of just how menacing he is, as I purposefully slip my cloak back into place.

"You looked like you were having a nightmare." He crouches down. "I was worried."

No you weren't. "I'm fine."

"Are you sure? You look pale." He reaches out a hand to touch my face and the feeling is back with a force so violent that it nearly knocks the wind from me. I lean away and Bardulf's face twists from a mask of worry into a far more sincere scowl.

"I said, *I'm fine*. Go back to where you were sleeping and leave me alone," I snap, hoping there's no room for misinterpretation.

"I said, I'm worried about you." He speaks slowly, as if I somehow had misunderstood him. "Let me comfort you."

The sensation is back. It batters against me, pressing on my shoulders as if it's trying to break my bones and sink into my marrow as entry. The swiftness of the assault almost makes it to my head. Almost has me relaxing as he reaches for me again.

Almost. I push off with my heels, propelling myself backward on the ground. His face twists back to that of hatred.

"How are you…"

"Touch me and I will hurt you," I threaten.

"Come now." He chuckles. Bardulf's demeanor changes again as effortlessly as a pendulum swing. He shifts his weight with a coy smirk. He has the air of a man trying and failing at seduction. The sight of it makes me sick. "Let's not play coy. I watched you with Evander, I know what sexual creature you are. I can fill you better than he can."

"Say another word and I'll vomit all over you." I add a gag for good measure. The mask falls from his face once more. The only consistent emotion in Bardulf right now is the hunger in his eyes. "There is no world in which I would ever, *ever* want you."

"But you already do want me." He speaks the words like one would a chant—a spell. Another battery of magic. It becomes perfectly clear what he's doing.

I draw my cape tighter around me and fight off the assault of his magic. He's trying to leverage the charm with all the finesse of a butcher using an axe. These are the edges of Conri's powers that he spoke of? This is the charm that the knights possess? Did Evander have some kind of greater mastery, or did he speak true and he never used it to lure me into his arms? There's no way I could've missed this.

"I will not repeat myself again." I stand tall. "I do not want you. I have never wanted you. I will never want you. Now get out of my sight."

"It's that cloak." He stands as well. "That's how you're resisting."

"Don't come near me." I hold out a hand, as if that alone will stop him. Of course, it doesn't, and he takes a step closer.

"Oh, now I have all the information, don't I?" He chuckles and takes another step. I take two steps back. "I'll tell Conri of your magic cloak and of you falling onto Evander's prick."

"I said, don't come closer." If he doesn't stop, I'm going to have to make good on my threats. My heart begins to race again. What was I thinking coming out here with Bardulf alone? I clearly wasn't thinking. I was just hurt and foolish and now I'm going to have to defend myself.

"I'll out you for what you are to the wolf king unless you give me some satisfaction, too." He smirks. It's so clear that he fully expects me to give in. The bastard.

"Never."

"Old gods! You would rut with Evander but not me? That pathetic, mewling sycophant?" Bardulf's hands ball into fists. "Let me guess, you think he's on your side because he lived in your world."

What? I don't have a chance to ask the question. Nor would I trust the answer. Bardulf starts walking faster. I can't put enough distance between us.

"Now I'm going to show you how a real man takes a woman."

"Don't touch me!"

He ignores my threat and reaches out. I stare at the offending hand. He's not going to stop. Bardulf is going to rip off my pin, and my cloak, and then…

I reach into my bag, pull out the piece of the hearth that had been Folost's home for years, hold it before me, and call, "Folost."

The spirit sparks into life, hovering over the small shard of brick. Bardulf stops short, looking at the little spark in confusion. Folost's eyes swing to meet mine as Bardulf roars with laughter.

"You think that pathetic little flame is going to stop me?" Bardulf lifts a hand, about to slap the brick from my palm.

I completely ignore him, focusing only on the spirit before me. He's not mighty or primordial, but I knew he would come no matter what.

"I need you to bring Devlan." I lower my chin and lock eyes with the spirit, making my intention known in a way that only Folost would understand—knowing that I can speak a language with him that Bardulf cannot understand. Even if I could call on one of the greater spirits outright, there would be no time to beg, to explain. I only heard the name once from Aurora—on the beach when we first arrived. I've no bond with this spirit, and I have to rely on Folost speaking for me.

Bardulf's palm slams into mine as he slaps away the brick. Folost tries to cling to the stone. Sparks. And is snuffed by the damp grasses.

"Enough games," Bardulf snarls. "Now give me what I want!"

I don't move. I stand as tall as a mighty redwood. As unyielding as a spirit before its essence. I will not cower before a creature as pathetic as him.

"Devlan," I say as Bardulf lunges for me. My words are calm. Deathly quiet. "Please, I summon you."

A spark from the scrap of brick, discarded in the grass. I feel the presence of Folost. A surge of magic. And then…

Flame.

It is a torrent of fire that billows out like a scream. The cone shoots from Folost's brick shard and consumes Bardulf whole. I stand a mere breath from its wall. The heat is staggering. Yet, no tongues of flame leap to me. They lap around me as I stare into the blinding light where Bardulf once stood.

His cries are cut short. They are accompanied by the stink of burning flesh. Then, nothing but fire and smoke. Devlan burns until his flames are as golden as sunlight. As quickly as he came, he disappears.

Before me is a charred stretch of earth. Blackened to dirt. There are not even bones left of Bardulf. It is as if he never existed at all.

I blink away the blue haze that lingers in my vision from the blinding light, breathing slowly. Turning, I take a few steps, collecting the brick that Bardulf had slapped from my hand, and return it to my pouch. My hand is shaking. Not quivering, or trembling. Shaking.

The cone of burnt earth stretches out from my feet like a tombstone. His final monument. Like an arrow pointing to me that says, *She did it.*

What was I supposed to do? I want to ask. I had to defend myself. He wasn't exactly a good person. I want to explain everything for my own ears to hear. But all I manage is a croak.

I will not allow myself to feel guilty. Not for that. Not for him. Not after the brutal intentions that he had made so clear.

"I will not feel guilty," I manage to say. Though every word trembles like my steps.

When I try to walk away, I stumble and fall to my knees. I dig my hands into the damp earth, trying to find purchase—something solid and real and stable. Because I am none of those things. I am going to shake apart.

I killed him.

I killed a man. I used my magic. The magic of my ancestors. The magic that Grandma taught me to use to protect and serve. A spirit that is innocent of mortal conflict. I used it to end a life.

"Evander," I rasp. Then, I scream to the heavens, "Evander!"

The tears come unbidden. It is a torrent of emotions unlike any I've known. It is somehow as consuming as the grief that I felt for Grandma, yet worse. What am I becoming? What is this world making me?

It's too much. My arms give out and I go to collapse to the earth. But my face doesn't meet the grass. Instead, I fall into a wall of muscle. Of warmth and comfort. Of familiar smells and reassurance.

"I'm here, Faelyn," Evander whispers into my ear through ragged panting. "As long as you want me, I'm here."

thirty-four

I CLING TO HIM AND CRY.

I cannot say for how long. But long enough that my fingers have cramped by the time I compose myself. Long enough that when I peel myself away from his chest, our skin sticks and my eyes are dry. There aren't tears left within me. I have cried oceans.

"He… He…"

"It's all right." Evander smooths my hair away from my face. It clings to my wet cheeks. "You're all right."

I didn't realize how badly I needed to hear those words until they were said. Somehow, between the waves of guilt and nausea, the memories of Grandma, and the shroud of death that haunts me at every turn…there was still fear. It all happened so quickly. He was there, and then not, and then…

"Why…" I stare up at Evander, his silver eyes shining as if he, too, wept. "Why did you come?"

"You called."

Two words. So simple. Somehow better than every "I love you" that could've ever been said.

"Even after what happened?"

"Do you really think that would change anything for me?" Evander gives me a tired but sincere smile. "My feelings for you are not so fickle."

"I still don't know what I should feel about you," I admit.

"You've had a long night," he says softly. "Let it be, for now. We can sort it out later."

"No." I shake my head, pulling away slightly. His arms slip from around my shoulders, hands running down to rest by my elbows as I clutch on to him as well. "I have to know now. This long night will continue to chase me if I don't just know and settle it."

"Then ask what you need to ask. I won't lie to you or obscure the truth, I swear it."

I lock my gaze with him, hunting for any whisper of deceit. "Is the extension of the charm that the knights possess real?"

"It is."

A twinge of pain at that. But I ignore the sensation, pressing on. "Did you ever use it on me?"

"Never. Nor anyone else, for that matter. I am not a man who could gain satisfaction from coercing another into my arms." He has enough disgust in his tone that I believe him, especially combined with how the charm felt when Bardulf used it. Everything I've thought to be true about Evander, I still hold in my heart.

"Then you and I…" I can't finish what I want to say. But Evander doesn't step up to do it for me. He just waits, staring. Holding my gaze as I work up the courage on my own. As if this realization—these words are a line he's been waiting for me to cross this whole time. "Why, why did I fall for you so quickly?"

I'm all but admitting it now—this passion that I have for him is more than carnal. The need isn't just satisfaction, or trying to protect myself from the charm. It's deeper than that.

"You know why," he whispers. His thumbs gently caress me. "You just closed your heart to it long ago."

"These feelings are not because of the charm?" Another knot is working its way into my throat. I'm regretting doing this. I don't want to admit what's right before my eyes. What's been haunting me without my realizing for so long that it's now upon me.

"No."

"How can I be so sure?"

"You know how." He holds me in place with his stare. His grip has become comically loose, as if Evander is giving me the option to bolt should it be too much for me. And it nearly is. But there's nowhere I can run from this.

I love him.

"It's not possible," I whisper.

"It is." He dips his chin slightly, leaning forward. Not close enough to kiss me, but close enough to look right into my eyes. "Because I love you, too."

"I can't believe you." I shake my head. "I can't believe any of this."

"That's the fear talking," he says knowingly, with a glimmer of understanding in his eyes. "You know it's true."

I keep shaking my head. As if I can keep blotting out the realization that's creeping upon me like the dawn. I don't fall in love that quickly. It's been years since I even considered a man remotely in such a way. This can't be…

"Faelyn." He whispers my name with sorrow and pain. The roots of which I don't want to recognize.

"No," I breathe. "It's going to hurt."

"It will." Evander pulls me close again, kissing my forehead and temple tenderly. "And you have been through so much. I cannot ask enough forgiveness for all you've had to endure because of me."

I close my eyes and press my face into his chest, breathing deeply. The smell of his skin is still calming. The feeling of his arms. Even when his presence is the very thing that threatens to tear me apart…it's the only thing keeping me together.

He's asking for the world from me. And, yet, asking for nothing at all. There are a thousand thoughts and a million emotions that I don't want to recognize.

"Why?" So much wrapped up into that one word. There are endless questions I want to ask but can't bring myself to.

"Because you love me."

I pull away enough to look up at him. Our faces are close enough that I could kiss him. I nearly do. I should have, to prevent him from saying what comes next.

"Or…you did, once. What feels like a lifetime ago. You loved a foolish and naive young man enough to sneak out and meet him underneath the redwood tree to swear yourself to him."

Evander's face changes right before my eyes. In my mind, his cheeks fill in some; the stubble thins. He has much, much less muscle, and the streak of gray is gone from his dark hair. His eyes aren't silver, but blue.

The change is significant enough that it's little wonder I wouldn't have seen it right away. Especially since I'd be looking for a young man I thought was human and very far gone—possibly dead—in the body of a lykin man. But now that I've allowed myself to see it…I can't see anything else.

I raise a hand to his cheek. Evander doesn't move as I gently press my fingers against his high cheekbone, smoothing over the stubble.

"It can't be," I whisper.

"My words the moment I laid eyes on you in the woods that night." His control breaks. He pulls me close again, half situating me on his lap, arms tight around me. I'm unsure of what to do with my own hands. Do I want to clutch on to him? Or do I want to push him away and scream for what he put me through? "I can't believe I found you. That you're here, with me. I know I don't deserve you, Faelyn, not after what I did to you, but—"

I pry myself away, the latter emotion winning. I glare up at him. My heart feels like two hands have grabbed it and are twisting. "Why? I waited for you. I wanted to be with you. You… You had my whole heart, Liam. If that's even your name?"

"It is—was." He releases me. A wise decision on his part, as I can't decide if I want to run and never look back, or kiss him. "It was the name my father gave me when he brought me to the Natural World to hide me. Evander was the name my mother gave me here, in Midscape, where I was…born. Back in the woods, as I told you." It's odd to hear him struggle with that truth even though he's lived with it for years.

I inhale slowly and hold out my hand, stopping him before he can say anything else. "Start at the beginning, the very beginning. Tell me even the parts you think I know—that I was there for. I want to hear it all. From you."

Evander takes a deep breath and confesses everything.

thirty-five

"I DID NOT LIE TO YOU THAT I WAS BORN INTO A NOW EXTINCT PACK, NOR ABOUT HOW I AM ITS LAST SURVIVING MEMBER." He turns his head back toward the forest. "We were a pack of vampir hunters, tasked with keeping them in their borders as they turned into monsters from some unknown blight. This was well before my time, of course…but my pack settled in those woods at the edge of the lykin territory. Just out of the Lykin Plains, and somewhat separate from the other packs, who were more under the eyes of the wolf kings. We were beyond the towers of the plains and that afforded us some autonomy."

I can imagine it in vivid detail, as though I were actually there. I can see a pack of lykin sent into the woods thousands of years ago during the combative time with the vampir. Their ghosts fill the streets of that long-abandoned little town that we came across, right at the very edge of two territories.

"I think, after a time, the pack was forgotten by most of the lykin—or they believed we had succumbed to the vampir. And the alphas—my forefathers—liked it that way."

"It kept your ancestors safe."

He nods. "No one came looking. No wolf kings wanted to impose their rule or draw my ancestors into whatever squabbles they were currently enduring. So my kin could live in peace and harmony. The pack used their skill of hunting vampir to track game in the familiar woods. They traded with the few, rare travelers who weren't afraid of coming so close to the vampir mountains and closed-off lykin. It was an opportunity to learn about how to commune with the spirits, as the spirits realized my ancestors weren't like their kin on the plains and had little interest in their subjugation. There were humans who had gone to meet the vampir and they learned alongside us."

"It must have been peaceful," I say softly. The description of his pack reminds me of the stories of the early witches Grandma told me. Of men and women working together in collectives, pooling their power and resources. Back before the Fade was erected and magic was plentiful among the people.

"I never knew that time, but, in my imaginings, it was." He stares down at his hands in his lap, folding and unfolding them, looking more like an insecure boy than a confident man. "My father always told me those were some of the best days. But I never even saw the homes of my kin before I was brought back to Midscape as a man."

"Let's get to your story." As fascinating as the history of the lykin is, the sky is already lightening and we'll need to be off soon.

"When the wolf king before Conri came to power, he uncovered evidence of our pack—a group that had been thriving outside the reach of the wolf king for centuries. He demanded we come to the plains, abandon our homes, and submit to him completely."

"And they didn't want to." I saw the remnants of their homes in the woods. What overgrown husks that remain.

"He tried to eradicate our people and, in the process, was mortally wounded. During the chaos, my father escaped and brought me with him." His pack's knowledge of the spirits must've been the key to their escape. "My mother was not so lucky. She stayed behind to give us a path, draw their attention."

"I'm sorry." The pain of losing one's mother is all too real.

He shakes his head. "I was just a babe. I didn't know her. Not like you and your mother…"

"I was so young, too. As you know," I hastily add. There's still a part of my mind that is reckoning with the notion that Evander and Liam are the same person. All the things I told him about my life as if he didn't already know them… "You really let me talk to you as if you had no idea about my story."

"I'm sorry." He cringes slightly. "I didn't know what else to do. Was it better to tell you who I was and risk your standing with Conri—the only thing that was keeping you safe?"

"I don't know," I admit. "Carry on with your story, and I'll tell you how I feel about it all when you've had your chance to fully explain yourself." Hopefully, by the time he's finished and I know everything, my own emotions will be clearer.

"Right… Well, my father made it across the Fade with me, obviously. As I told you, lykin aren't born with the power to change our shapes. We are gifted it when we reach maturation by swearing an oath to the great wolf spirit and connecting with the power in our bloodlines. I grew up with no idea who I was—what I was." Evander leans forward slightly. "When I met you, I truly was nothing more than a hunter's son. In my mind and heart, I knew nothing else."

I study his face and find his words to be true. Dipping my chin, I say, "I believe you." Evander sighs with relief. "But, then, how did you come back here? When did you find out?"

"Most of my years, I had no idea." He shakes his head. "Father mentioned nothing. The only time I had any idea something might be… off, was when your mother died."

"Mother?" The word is dry on my tongue.

"We were in the woods. Father told me he heard a fight even though nothing reached my ears. Now I know that, if he heard it, he heard it with the keen ears of lykin. But, even more likely, he sensed Conri's presence."

"Conri was there?" I go perfectly still. These words, truths, are probing into wounds I thought long healed and scarred over. "My mother…" *Died in the woods*. The one place she was at her most powerful. Where she was most at home. I had always believed it to be a simple explanation because that's what Grandma had told me—what the hunter who found Mother's remains had told her. There wasn't the slightest bit of concern that Grandma let show.

"Father tried to save her." Evander reaches slowly for me. I don't move away and he rests his hand on mine, squeezing gently. "I'm so sorry we couldn't."

I shake my head, trying to suppress the emotions that are fighting their way up from the deepest pit of my heart I long ago threw them into. "It's not your fault—but how?"

"She had gone deep into the woods."

"Looking for more spirits." It was something Mother did often. She was determined to find a spirit on her own. Grandma had two. She wanted one. Perhaps to pass down to me… The notion floods me with guilt.

"She went as deep as the edge of the Fade. I suspect she did something that somehow alerted Conri—piqued his curiosity, at the very least. He sent a knight through the Fade for information."

"Who?"

"Bardulf."

I blurt laughter that has a crazed edge. Looking back to the charred patch of earth where he stood a mere hour ago has me laughing more. I laugh until I rasp, "Bastard."

"A fitting title for him."

"So much for feeling guilt over his death." I turn back to Evander and leave the remnants of any worry over killing a man behind me on the burnt grasses.

"I'm glad you were the one to do it."

"Now I am, too." Thoughts of my mother fill my mind. "Why would he hurt her? She wouldn't have attacked him."

"Conri sees witches like spirits—as tools that can be used. But if they're not with him and his mission…"

"Then they're against him," I say softly.

"Bardulf escaped through the Fade before my father could kill him, obviously."

"And, in the process, he told Conri of you and your father. That someone from the pack survived." I try to keep my focus on him and not on the revelation of my mother. I'm reeling. But nothing changes. Mother is still dead. Grief has long been settled in my heart. Any vengeance I could've wanted has been claimed. Save for maybe Conri, the man behind it all…

"Conri didn't believe him at first. Especially when he sent another knight through the Fade and found no evidence of lykin or witches."

"Why not?"

"Your grandmother gave us protection." A warm smile crosses his lips.

I remember that day…the day I met Liam—Evander. It was after the hunter had come to our hut to deliver word of Mother's death. Fate had brought us together, and from one of the worst days of my life, something beautiful would grow.

After our mourning and putting Mother to rest, Grandma said we were going to the hunter's cottage. That they needed our gratitude for their attempts to save Mother and for bringing us word of her death. The best way to give them that was our blessings.

I give words to my realization. "Grandma knew what you were."

"She was clever." He nods. "Father told me she knew the moment he came to break the horrible news."

"I'm sorry I didn't realize." If I had, I might have been able to save us both so much heartache.

"Faelyn…you were a young witch, had no reason to suspect, and didn't know what to look for." He hooks my chin and guides it back to look at him. "I had no idea, either. If I had, I would've told you."

"When did you know?" We spent years together following the death of my mother. Endless afternoons in the fields. Late evenings on the thatched roof of my hut, staring at the stars. "Accidentally" running into one another in the woods when I was out collecting herbs. The early mornings and long nights and any excuse to see each other until it became so obvious that we could drop all pretense.

"It wasn't until much, much later," he says, affirming my suspicion as he drops his hand from my face. Evander leans back and stands. He walks over to the ridge, looking down at the forest. "My father brought me back to Midscape to reclaim my birthright."

"The night you left." Even saying it puts my heart in a vise.

"Not quite." He glances back at me with an apologetic look. Mention of that night seems to hurt us both in no small measure. Knowing the pain is shared makes it somewhat easier to bear. "I performed the rites just before. You and I were to meet on the new moon, but to perform the rites, Father and I had to go when the moon was full."

"You came to Midscape to make your oath to the great wolf spirit."

He nods and then turns, crossing the gap between us in a few hasty steps. Evander scoops up both my hands in his and holds them fiercely, looking into my eyes with equal intensity. "If I had known what was going to happen—what misfortunes were about to befall us both—I would've never. Faelyn, if I could go back, I would have never crossed the Fade and made my oath."

"But you…"

"I would've rather lived a lifetime, ignorant as a human man, and have forsaken the magic of my forefathers—I would've forsaken all the magic in the world to be with you… rather than where we find ourselves now."

My grip on him tightens, as if I am trying to hold on to both our magic. The idea of someone giving theirs up is gutting to me and I am helpless to do anything but stare for a long moment.

"You can't forsake your destiny, because…you are the last of your pack," I say softly.

"And it will die with me anyway because I cannot bear children," he nearly speaks over me.

"There are many ways to have a child, Evander, and only one is by your own blood."

"In any case, my father brought me across the Fade and I made my oath. We couldn't go all the way to Den. But, thanks to the connections our pack had made with the spirits, we could summon the great wolf from the grove of Den," Evander continues hastily, clearly eager to change the subject. I let the matter of children drop, for now. It's clearly a sensitive topic, understandably so, and not the most important thing at this moment. "The full moon had enhanced not only our powers—but all other lykin's as well. Including the man who was most connected with the wolf spirit."

"Conri. That was how he found you both."

"It was hard for him to ignore the sensation of a young lykin making his oaths when there was no one in Den. After that, it was a matter of getting the information of who it was from Aurora."

"You knew Aurora?"

He shakes his head. "Aurora could consult with the wolf spirit and confirm which pack had just made oaths."

I realize why Conri forces all lykin to Den to make their oaths; it prevents any packs from resurrecting themselves quietly, away from his prying eyes. His wickedness seems only to be matched by his cleverness, and there are clearly no limits to what he'll do to ensure his power.

"Then it was a matter of Conri remembering what Bardulf had said, and coming for you and your father," I say, filling in the gap. "Which, if he had to consult Aurora, and then was coming from Den, would've taken him a few weeks."

Three people moving in tandem, each oblivious to the true actions of the others. Evander had gone to take his oaths and become a full lykin in magic as well as blood. Conri was gathering his information and his knights. And I was preparing to go before the great redwood to ask the spirits to confirm my suspicion that the young man I'd fallen in love with was, indeed, my soulmate.

"He crossed the Fade the night of the new moon. Risky for a lykin to do when his powers were weak, but he suspected, rightly, that he had the upper hand on us from numbers alone, and we were too weak ourselves to sense he was coming until it was too late. We had no warning. One moment, my father and I were going to bed—me secretly preparing to sneak away and meet you. The next moment, Father told me we had to run. He'd prepared everything as if he'd known it was a risk from the moment I took my oath." Evander drops his chin and slowly shakes his head. His shoulders droop some from the weight of that night. "I begged Father to let me leave word for you, but he said we couldn't risk it. I wanted to meet you first, but he refused that as well. Faelyn, I am so, so sorry."

"Evander, you were trying to keep yourself and your father alive. I understand." The words are surprisingly easy to say. There's still a child in me that wants to shout at him for the pain he caused me. But it is easy to ignore her.

She was a girl who saw the world in such simple rules. If someone wasn't with her, then they had left her forever. Gone. Abandoned. A girl who was afraid of losing everyone precious to her and spending her days alone.

"Faelyn—"

"Let your guilt go," I stress. I hear it lingering in his tone. Ripe with pain. "It serves no one. Not you. Not me—I don't want it."

Evander sighs and straightens some. He turns toward the dawn that lights his face orange. "Conri found Father and me in the woods. He killed my father, and nearly killed me, too. But, in the end, I think he liked the idea of having me under his control more than he liked me dead. I was the last survivor of the pack that had eluded so many kings. And Conri was the one to bring me to heel."

"Like some sick trophy," I mutter.

"Conri brought me back across the Fade while I was unconscious and bleeding out. Burning with infection and trauma. By the time I regained my wits, I was in Den. Scarred and vastly outnumbered. I was offered the choices of serving him, or dying by his hand."

"What made you choose to serve him?" I ask delicately. "Obviously, I am glad for this choice," I add hastily, with a small laugh. Evander huffs amusement as well. "But…you had just seen that man kill your father. Before then, you had spent your final moments with your father trying to run from him. No doubt being warned of the dangers. I…" I'm beginning to regret the question. But I'm in too deep. "I don't know if I would've made the same decision," I admit and leave it at that.

"You."

"What?" I blink.

Evander shifts, moving closer to me. We're both sitting angled toward each other, facing the sunrise. It reminds me of when I would slip out through the window in the loft and meet him on the roof of the hut. We'd spend the night talking, just like this, until sunrise. Though the topics were usually far lighter.

Still, like then, I can't take my eyes off of him. The rest of the world is distant and blurred. The only thing in focus is him in all the watercolor hues of dawn.

"I chose to serve him because of you."

I blink, startled. Evander continues before I can say anything.

"If I had died, it would take a lifetime to meet you again in the Beyond. As long as I drew breath, it meant I had hope of our paths crossing. I would endure whatever pain that meant, just for the chance to see you one more time."

The vise that was put on my heart tightens, causing it to beat harder, shortening my breath. Everything he endured. Everything he went through. Was because of me.

"My love," he whispers. The two words are like honey in my ears and I shiver before his hand even cups my cheek. "There is no more need of tears anymore, not now that we're together." Evander brushes away a rogue rivulet with his thumb.

"You went through so much."

"And I would go through it all again, ten times over, if it brought me back to this moment—to you."

Even though we never were able to stand beneath the redwood tree and bind our hands…I have my answer, as undeniable as the sun's rise or the wind in my hair. It was him. It has always been him.

Every gaze that lingered on another was in search of his face, even when I knew it would be impossible to find him in those moments. Every embrace I sought from others was a futile attempt to rediscover the warmth I once knew from his arms. Every kiss was in search of the taste of him.

"It was you." I lean in and press my forehead to his, as if somehow I could walk him through the sacred corners of my heart that were made for him, and him alone. The truth has been laid bare before me, each strand of choice and fate woven like a tapestry—a map, to guide us to each other.

"There are no others you want to return to?" he asks as if he's afraid of the answer.

"There were others." I've already admitted to as much. No wonder his reaction was so visceral at the time. He even winces now.

"You thought I was dead. Or, worse, that I had abandoned you," he says quickly, sounding like he's trying to rationalize it to himself as much as me. Funny that he thinks him abandoning me is worse than death.

"Yes. But…they never meant anything," I assure him. "Even when I was with them, it was nothing more than a need, a whim, or trying to fill the void you left. But none could compare. I could've walked the world and met every man, and it would've never been enough. None of them would've been you."

"I love you, Faelyn."

"And I love you, too, Evander."

Our lips meet in an unhurried caress, as though we're both allowing the words to imprint upon our very souls. The sensation courses through me like a surge of magic, making my head spin. For a breath, the fates have finally aligned in our favor. The stars and spirits themselves have conspired to bring us together. Even if the world beyond us is fraught with uncertainty, we have this stolen instant, and every other yet before us. We have each other.

Evander pulls away with a quivering sigh. "I wish I could stop the sun from rising."

"I might have some of Aurora's powers...but I can't make the moon rise again. Nor would I want to."

"No?" He pulls away, still holding on to me, to blink into the sunlight as it crests the grass in the distance.

"No," I breathe. The word is as light as the soft breeze that sweeps over the plains. "I don't want time to stop where it was. I want to go forward because that's where we will exist."

The sky is awash with color, turning the grasslands into a dark silhouette. The sun is as bright as hope. The sky is the color of all the blood that was spilled to bring us here.

"We have to go, though," I remind us both. Something in the glisten of his eyes tells me I need to be the strong one in this moment. "As much as I want to run off with you—"

"We can't abandon Aurora," he finishes for me, stands, and offers me his hand.

I take it, letting him half pull me up. "What will we do about Bardulf?"

"I'll think about it on the way. For now, we should get moving."

Yet, neither of us do. We stand, fingers intertwined, eyes locked. I would bet that if I were to put my head on his chest, I would feel our hearts beat in time.

"When we arrive in Den, you're going to have to keep up the illusion with Conri." Pain and anger make his words low, filled with gravel.

"I know. If he becomes suspicious, it's a risk for all of us." Evander, Aurora, and me. "We'll leave as soon as we can, together, and we'll never look back."

"So long as you want me at your side." The sentiment reminds me of what I told him earlier, the harsh words I used to push him away when my heart was breaking for what will be the final time in my life.

My face relaxes into a smile that it hasn't made in years. One that only he can bring out in me. "Always, Evander. Stay by my side, forever and always."

thirty-six

Being on Evander's back again erases the last thoughts of Bardulf. The wrongness of that man is left on the breeze. Left for the grasses and wind to reclaim. A chapter of my story that I didn't even realize I was writing has been closed—a burden lifted of questioning the unknowns surrounding my mother's death that I hadn't known I was asking. The only thing about it that matters now is how we are going to navigate Bardulf's disappearance when we arrive in Den, and how we'll take Aurora away.

Which is what Evander and I debate as we walk, side by side. He dropped out of his wolf form not long ago, saying we're only about an hour from Den, and this will be the last chance we have to talk before we arrive.

"Could we say he never met up with us?" I'd been turning the idea over in my head for the better portion of the morning. "Say that he must still be in the forest. Perhaps you could use that as an excuse to leave for the forest to find him and then—"

Evander lifts a hand. "I must stop you there. Conri already knows he's dead."

"He does? The oath?" I ask. Evander nods and I curse under my breath. "What do we do, then?"

"You're going to have to admit to killing him," Evander says plainly.

"Have you lost all your better senses?" I stop in my tracks, too stunned for a moment to continue.

"You're going to have to trust me." Evander stops as well and takes my hand.

"Obviously I do." I force myself to keep going. Even though we're not sprinting, we need to keep making progress toward Den if we want to make it back without Conri suspecting anything more than he already will. "What I don't trust is that madman who clearly has been murdering innocent people and retaining power at all costs."

"Nor should you trust him, outright. But there is one thing about Conri that we can trust."

"And what is that?"

"That he is going to always be looking out for himself. You're right, he'll retain power at all costs, and we need to make sure he sees Bardulf's death as a price of that." Evander shifts his grip on me, fingers lacing against mine.

"Because that doesn't sound risky at all," I mutter under my breath.

"Oh, it'll be very risky."

I stop without warning and yank him toward me. Evander lets out a noise of surprise before our lips meet. With my free hand I grab his hip, pulling him closer, feeling the hard length of him against me. My fingers slip over the curve of his rear, giving it a firm squeeze. Another noise of surprise that drops into the back of his throat and becomes almost like a growl as I pull away.

"What was that for?" he asks, as lazily as the smile that slips across his lips.

"Because I could—because I won't be able to soon."

The smile falls. His expression becomes gravely serious. "No matter what happens, know that I love you."

"So long as you don't forget the same." I search his gaze, trying to find any trace of doubt. There's worry. Fear. But not doubt. I am reassured by its absence.

"I will find a way, again, to come to you. We figured it out before. We will again." His conviction is more worrying than reassuring. Before, Evander was a relief, amusement, mild interest that could be something more, but I wasn't too bothered by the idea of it evolving or not.

Now he's everything.

"Let's just keep focused on staying safe and escaping. Once we succeed, we'll have the rest of our lives to enjoy being together." I force a reassuring smile, for myself as much as him.

Evander returns it and releases my hand as we begin walking together again. "Now, here's what will happen when we arrive at Den, and what you're going to need to do…"

We spend a little less than half an hour walking and going over all the plans. I practice lines and commit them to memory. Then, he returns to his lykin form to make up the time. For that last half hour as we're racing through the rolling grasslands, my mind is as blank as the fog that is perpetually settled on the land of the lykin. The farther northwest we go, the thicker the haze gets, to the point that I must believe Evander is navigating on memory, magic, and lykin senses, because I can't see much beyond my hand in front of my face.

He warned me that the fog grew thicker the farther north one went in the plains. But I wasn't expecting it to be this severe. We could be about to topple over a cliff and into the sea and I would not know until we were in free fall.

So it's all the more striking when, out of nowhere, the fog parts like a breath. A sharp inhale where the claustrophobia of the thick clouds is lifted and a column of sunlight warms my shoulders from the damp chill of the ride. Even in sunlight, my teeth are nearly chattering. We're far enough north that the day can't sweep away the cold that sank into the earth in the night.

A forest has fossilized in the dip of a valley. Large, stony trees, each the size of the mighty redwood I grew up revering, shelter the ancestral home of the lykin with boughs of glistening silver leaves. Reaching out, I press my palm into the bark of a tree as we pass. It's as smooth as a polished river rock, as cool as crystal. Though it looks and feels like a sculpture, it hums underneath my hand like a real, living tree would. They breathe in sunlight and the crisp, cool air and exhale life.

Underneath their dappled shade is what could, loosely, be described as a town. The majority of the structures are tents, only a few permanent collective homes and buildings. I recognize some of the tents as what I saw when we were out on the plains. Stunning feats of cord and tarp—manor houses, practically, made entirely from canvas and tension.

What structures are permanent are mismatched, added onto, and clearly constructed by different hands over different times. Stone buildings lined with moss, crumbling on one side, have new additions made of wood so fresh that it still smells of sap. Some buildings are more like halls that snake around the trees, room after room added on.

Every structure has lykin occupying it. They emerge from doorways and tent flaps. Halt their fire tending and sparring. I feel as though it is the first time I have arrived at the lykin all over again. The surreal sense of repetition grows as Conri races over to meet us.

Evander slows his pace, stopping before Conri reaches us. Evander sinks to the ground so I can dismount, then stands as a man. I adjust my cape around me and immediately begin walking, leaving Evander behind, as if I am all too relieved to see Conri. The wolf king changes into his human form and runs the rest of the way to me on two feet, throwing out his arms as if he is genuinely worried. Genuinely fearful for my well-being.

"Words cannot express how relieved I am to see you." He crushes me against him so tightly that I'm forced to exhale. It's like he's trying to absorb me into him. I'm sure if he could squeeze out Aurora's magic, he'd press me until my ribs cracked and eyes popped.

Still, I have a role to play. "My darling king, I missed you immeasurably." My words are almost shrill, as though I am fighting back tears. Luckily, I've had enough practice fighting back actual tears recently that I know how to adjust the tenor of my voice to make it convincing.

"What happened to Bardulf?" He releases me to look me in the eyes. Searching for a lie, no doubt.

In my periphery, I can see Aurora's shape. She's too hazy to make out her expression. But she's here. *Good.* I steel myself for what's to come next.

"I killed him," I speak plainly. No trace of guilt or remorse. I do not shrink away.

Conri stares at me, the words settling upon him. He blurts a noise of disbelief and shakes his head. He steps away, hands on his hips, and shakes his head again. Those who have gathered begin to whisper amongst themselves.

I'm forcing air in and out of my lungs. Breathe. Normally. How do I do that again? All I want to do is hold my breath, or let it quicken with the pace of my heart—a pace that I am also trying to keep slow.

He killed your mother. The thought sobers me and helps me keep calm despite my nerves. It sharpens my focus on the whetstone of revenge.

Conri turns to face me again. His eyes narrow slightly, as though he's working to bring me into focus. "How?"

That question alone tells me Evander's suspicions were right. Conri isn't asking why I killed Bardulf. He doesn't care one of his most loyal knights is dead. And my motive is secondary to finding out *how* I overpowered the man—a knight that killed another witch without issue.

"You sent me to find spirits that I could call upon for your causes—to bring glory to your name. That is what I have done."

"And how is killing Bardulf bringing glory to my name?" Conri cocks his head to the side. The air is still. As if this whole place is in tune with his every movement and the ebb and flow of his emotions.

"Forgive me for being the bearer of this news, my king, but Bardulf was not loyal to you," I say, still holding my head high. "I had to do it, because I was not about to let him take what is yours."

"What is mine?" he prompts me to continue. I can't read his expression, though, and his tone is neutral.

"Bardulf came to us in the woods and he saw my command of a new and powerful spirit that I was bringing back for you. I believe he intended to use it to usurp you."

Conri shakes his head. "Bardulf, no…no, he wouldn't."

"He followed me when I went to bathe. He attempted to seduce me and when that failed, he attempted to lay his hands upon me." None of it is a lie, so as Conri continues to probe me with his stare, I can meet it evenly. "Throughout it all, he attempted to use what felt like magic on me to coerce me to his side. I can only imagine that he intended to convince me to use the power of the spirits against you."

Aurora's power, too, I leave unsaid. Though, judging from Conri's expression, he hears it. This is the risk of the angle Evander and I have decided to put on our tale. There was no hiding the matter. Conri knew

Bardulf was dead the moment that we entered Den. The best outcome would be to convince Conri that I was the one to kill him and that it was for a good reason.

But that reason is going to emphasize that Aurora's power is split, and as long as it is, there might be others who will try and claim me to challenge Conri. His power isn't secure until he marries me or, better, returns Aurora's power to some kind of object he can easily keep in his clutches. Which will only hasten him doing the former or trying to kill me for the latter.

And there's the other danger of this plan. He now sees me as someone who is capable of killing. Who not only has the means, but the will to wield them thusly. That might push him in a single direction:

Kill me.

Not that he wasn't already leaning that way…but I've likely removed all doubt. Conri has spent his entire existence removing possible threats to his rule and now, in a way, I've become one.

Conri's eyes shift to Evander. "Is this true?"

"Every word." Evander doesn't miss a beat. "I had been moving to protect her from Bardulf's aggressions, but she acted before I could. Forgive me, my king, I had been asleep when it all started, or I would've been faster and Bardulf might have been able to face your judgment alive, as it should have been." Evander's tone ventures into disgust that I can feel directed at my back. We position ourselves at odds, and paint Evander as even more loyal in the process.

Conri stares at me for a long, tense minute. I think if he could end me here and now, he would. But he laughs, diffusing the tension, and claps his hands before opening them and motioning between the gathered lykin and me.

"Behold, your future queen! Is she not magnificent?" He crosses to me and wraps an arm around my waist. It reassures me that even though he no doubt sees me as a threat, he also sees me as a tool to continue having the other lykin fall in line. "Defending me and my crown from any who would dare act against us." He looks to me. "I cannot wait to make you my wife."

"Truly, you are not upset?" This is the only time I allow a trace of insecurity to sneak into my voice. I have made myself seem strong and dangerous enough. Now I want to reassure him that, even though

I might be a threat, I am not a clever one. He doesn't need to worry about me scheming; I'm too afraid of upsetting him for that. This was all simply an unfortunate set of circumstances…

"Upset? No. I am grateful to know that you would defend yourself and that, above all else, you are loyal to me and me alone."

"There is no future for me but one by your side." Disgusting.

"Do not forget it." He hooks my chin and guides my face toward his, as though he is about to kiss me. But he doesn't and instead smirks at my forced expression of yearning. "I am everything and you are nothing without me."

I smile languidly. "Everything for you, my love."

"Now, you must display this spirit that was mighty enough to kill one of my strongest knights."

"It is a spirit of water, unfortunately. So I wouldn't be able to without—"

"The great lake of Calduwyn is at the edge of Den, not far. We will go there now." Conri releases me and steps back.

"The great lake isn't a place where a spirit could—" Aurora tries to interject.

"We will go there now, I said," Conri stops her abruptly and changes into his wolf shape, leaving no room for debate.

I mount him as he clearly wants and brace myself. Not for the pace he sets. But for the hope that Volst will come again so soon, despite my recently having asked him for power. For if he doesn't, Evander's and my careful planning could all unravel.

thirty-seven

There isn't an opportunity to speak with Aurora. She rides on Evander, casting wary glances my way. I try and catch her eyes as inconspicuously as possible. But there's little hope in attempting to convey anything other than confidence and reassurance. A confidence that wanes slightly when her own expression is twisted with worry.

Her being on Evander's back also gives me an excuse to look in his direction without risking any suspicion from others who might see. My attention toward Aurora can be explained. But Evander is harder to have excuses for.

He looks tense. Though perhaps I'm projecting my own worries upon him—my own fears for him. I finally found him. He's returned to me despite all odds. I won't let anything happen to him now.

The silvery trees of Den go right up to the water's edge. There's no thinning or shrinking of the magical flora. Their mighty roots stretch right into the water, shimmering beneath the perfectly clear surface. The lake itself is miraculously still for its size. Despite what must be considerable winds whipping across its vast surface, there isn't so much as a ripple.

As my feet touch the ground, a jolt of power shoots through me, even greater than the magic of the living trees. I suck in a breath and exhale a faint cloud. Even though we have not gone far, the air is colder here.

"What is this place?" I whisper.

"The stories say that long ago there was a kingdom here,"

Conri answers, stepping to my side. I appreciate that he understood what I was asking and did not simply repeat that it is the great lake of Midscape. "This is well before the wars of magic that resulted in the Fade being erected. Back when the world was very young and the first peoples were inhabiting it alongside the old gods and spirits."

"What do the stories say happened to the kingdom?" I ask as the others arrive, slowing to a stop in an arc around Conri and me.

"That depends on whose stories you are listening to. The siren sing that the city sank far below the earth—that its people became the first spirits their old gods shepherded to the Beyond, and, perhaps, monsters of the deep. The fae's stories say that their kind destroyed the ancient city, for its kings couldn't be trusted as they dabbled in forbidden rituals." Conri stares out over the vast expanse of water. It's so wide that it touches each end of the horizon. Wide enough that, if not for what I am told, and its unnatural stillness and deep magic, I would think it was a sea.

"And what do the lykin's stories say?"

"Quite the opposite of the siren's claims." It's Evander who answers, and I work to keep my face passive as I look to him. It helps that he's not looking at me, either. He stares out over the lake, his expression a bit dull—as though he's a bit exasperated that he is explaining this at all to me. "The lykin's stories say that we lived in harmony with this kingdom. That we taught them about how to commune with the spirits and the sirens to their west taught them how to revere the old golds. The tales say forgotten kingdoms were the greatest among us and, for their splendor, they were rewarded. They were carried with the old gods as they left this world, ascending beyond this mortal coil to eternal glory."

Conri begins to chuckle as Evander finishes his story. He shakes his head. "Such foolish tales."

"You don't think there's any truth to them?" I ask the wolf king.

"The fae's account I suspect to be the most true. A kingdom—or kingdoms—that refused to follow the rules of the King's Council as it assembled. I find the fact that the lake extends from Evalon to be supporting evidence of this theory. I could see the other kings combining their power to eradicate a group that wouldn't stand with them and their rules…like cutting off an unruly limb," he adds with a sour note.

It makes me wonder what Conri's goals actually are for his rule.

To keep control of the lykin, obviously. But does he truly want to venture into the Natural World and claim the realm of the humans, as he suggested? Or does he simply want the power to keep himself independent of the other peoples of Midscape?

"But enough of histories and tall tales." Conri motions between me and the lake. "Show me this spirit that you've found."

All eyes are on me as I step forward. There is no getting around this. To object now would raise suspicions that I cannot invite.

Removing my shoes and setting them on the narrow, pebbled beach, I step into the water with a slow and bracing inhale. It is as cold as ice. My flesh immediately prickles, though I wonder if the sensation is from the deep magics that swirl in the lake, or from the chill. I square my shoulders and ball my hands into fists, trying to keep the instantaneous shivers from taking control.

Let's get this over with. I reach deep into my magic—into the well of power that is from Aurora. In a tongue reserved only for spirits, I intone without hesitation, "Volst, come to me."

The words send a ripple across the water that extends out from me. It speeds away with purpose as a visual representation of my summons seeking out the spirit. I watch as it fades beyond the realm of my vision.

But there is no reply.

My heartbeat quickens. "Volst, please," I whisper. The spirit seemed nice enough. But it is as mighty as Brundil and I suspect equally uninclined to be put on display. Or perhaps what I asked of him was too much. He can't return so quickly.

"Is there a problem?" Conri asks.

I glance over my shoulder. "No, no, it can take a moment."

The wolf king's expression is hard to read. The trembles begin to take over my shoulders. No doubt making me look even more guilty.

"Then why has this mighty spirit not yet come?" Conri demands to know.

"The spirits do have their own minds," I try to explain delicately, "and their roles to play in the world. We cannot always summon them on our mortal whims."

Conri closes the distance between us, his boots splashing into the water. They make short-lived ripples, the water actively refusing to be disturbed. He ducks his chin and lowers his voice, speaking only to me. "I am the wolf king; everything in this world will bend to my will. And if it does not…then I will have to break it." He leans away slightly, looking me dead in the eyes. "Do you understand, Faelyn?"

You included, is what he doesn't say, but wants me to hear. I manage a nod.

"Now. Try again." Conri steps back onto the rocky shore and out of the water that I am left to turn back to.

Never have I felt more alone than in this moment. Standing apart from the rest of them—completely unlike them. Having them all watch me like I am some kind of entertainment.

I take a steadying breath and roll my shoulders back. I am not alone. Back among them is Aurora—part of her magic is within me. In a way, right now, we are kin. Evander is there, waiting for me to come through for all of us. I can do this. Not for me, but for them. For the people who are going to be by me to the end.

"Volst," I say with purpose. My voice seems to carry across the still water, ripples chasing after the sound. "I ask for you to come to me, merely for a moment."

The words leave me and sink into the water. For a moment, I think I feel the slightest bit of magic brush against mine. A vague awareness that there is something else out there. But it's gone. He's too weak.

"Well," Conri says after a minute that feels like an hour. "I see that your expedition was a failure." I turn, looking back at him in shock. Even if it's only ever been for appearances, he's never spoke to me in such a tone in front of the others. Conri smiles. It's smug. He's gleeful at my shortcoming. I've little doubt it will be used as yet another reason to kill me. "Don't worry, though, my queen. Not all can be as powerful as me."

"She's probably exhausted." They're the first words Aurora has said and the glare that Conri immediately shoots her tells me the reason behind her silence. But she steps forward, away from Evander and toward me. "You sent her out and she not only found spirits, communed with them, learned their name, but had to defend herself, so the spirit is probably exhausted, too. She's been apart from me for too long and so our connection has wavered some, making all this harder."

Conri's glare does little to stop Aurora as she approaches me. She stops right at the water's edge. Her gaze drifts out across the surface and a frown that I think belongs to something more than Conri and the lykin tugs on the corners of her lips.

"This is a hard place he's brought you to," she whispers hastily as we meet at the water's edge. "This is a scar of great magic from long ago; it will be difficult for any spirit to come to you here, even if you and the spirit were at your best."

"What do I do?" I try to keep my face hidden behind Aurora as I ask so Conri can't see.

She leans forward and rests her cheek against mine, whispering in my ear. "I'm going to help you. Use my power—give it to Volst. Then I'll need you to help me recover after."

"What do I do?" I ask again, moving my lips as little as possible.

"Just being near me will help me recover from my magic within you."

She shifts and, with a press of her forehead into mine, a surge of magic flows through me. Aurora leans away, looking instantly exhausted. Her usual pallor has taken a worrying gray hue. Even the shine of her hair seems to have lost some of its luster.

"Auro—"

"There, now she should have the strength." She won't let me finish my worry. She steps back and turns to Conri. I wonder if the wolf king can see the immediate decline in her. If he can, I suspect it will only make him yet more inclined to kill me. Conri will see me as a leech to her power. I'm not doing a great job of giving him reasons to keep me alive.

"Well, then." Conri motions for me to make haste with a gesture of his open palm toward the water.

I force my expression to stay passive. Though, when I turn back to the lake, I can drop the mask. Disgust twists my stomach and my lips.

Kneeling, I submerge myself nearly to my breasts. I've grown accustomed to the chill and am no longer fighting shivers. Perhaps I have just been given enough motivation to steel myself.

I reach into my satchel and pull out a length of gray—nearly blue—line of thread. It's already soaked, but the tools of a witch's trade are no strangers to nature. If anything, they are further empowered the more patches of earth they fall into, the more grasses that stain them, and the more waters they soak up. They will draw from the power of my experience, and from the living spirits that live in everything.

With a firm knot, I tie the cord into a loop and rest it upon the surface of the water. Be it from my magic, or the powers in this lake, it floats in a nearly perfect circle. I cup my hands and lift, catching the circle on the upper rim of my palms. The thread rests along my pointer fingers, thumbs, and heels of my hands.

Purify, I think, pushing my powers into the thread. As pure as water cleansed by moonlight. The water bubbles and hisses, spilling over the sides of my hands. The power that the lake has been steeped into drips away with heavy plops, leaving nothing but plain water behind.

I just hope it is enough.

"Volst," I whisper into the tiny surface gathered in my palms. "I thank you for your help so far. Now, Aurora needs you. This is for her, not me. Leverage her power within me, if you must, with her blessing as well. But come to me here and now, if only for a second."

The water goes perfectly still. Then, it feels as if I am holding a pool of lead. My muscles strain with the weight of the spirit that I know has taken residence between my hands.

Forcing myself to stand, I turn, lock eyes with Conri, and say, "Behold, the might of the spirit of water."

The water lifts above my hands, hovering in the air, to the amazement of those gathered. There are gasps and wide eyes all around. Even Conri's scowl softens to something that I'd dare say could be wonder as the water takes the shape of a reversed raindrop, arms and head extending out from it.

Volst turns his head, looking at each of them. The lykin gasp and shrink back. I think it because of the weight of a spirit staring upon them…until I see the shadow rising behind me.

Daring a glance over my shoulder, I see that the water has vanished from around my still icy ankles and now stands suspended, like a frozen wave. It looms ominously over the shore. Quivering as Volst's eyes land on Conri.

The threat is palpable even to me. This is a warning. A display of power with the whisper of who this power might be used against.

But the threat doesn't snap the tension. Volst retreats into my palms, the water calmly shrinking back to its original place and settling. I feel it subside to my ankles and, when I return the water from my palms to the lake by kneeling down, Volst is no longer there.

"Thank you," I whisper, collecting the blue thread and looping it around my wrist. With any luck, it will make it easier to call upon him in a moment of need. We are connected now.

As I straighten, my eyes meet Conri's. He is staring at me with a mix of wonder…and horror. There is no doubt, he truly sees me now as the threat I am. I need to leave as soon as I'm able.

thirty-eight

"DID I NOT TELL YOU ALL THAT SHE WAS TRULY THE EPITOME OF MIGHT AND MAGNIFICENCE?" Conri wraps his arm around my waist, beginning to lead me back up the shore. He speaks as if they all hadn't just heard him literally saying the opposite not moments ago. But the truth of the lykin is shaped by their king, not by objective fact. "Her power is breathtaking, is it not?"

Whispers and murmurs accompany the polite nods. The lykin clearly don't know what to make of me. And Conri notices as well.

"Bewulf, our great uniter, gained his might by entering into a union with a spirit. The lykin's history is made mightier when our kings marry those with power to make it our own. Which is why, in just three weeks, we shall be married beneath the full moon!"

Some nods of approval. Polite cheers. They're still not won over to me. Not that I care. The only person whose perception actually matters is Conri.

"Truly, in three weeks?" I ask him.

"Does this upset you?"

"I only wish it could be sooner!" I laugh and lean into him with a forced smile. "I am glad that I could show you the might that I am bringing to you."

"The might that killed Bardulf." Conri chuckles darkly. "No wonder he was tempted by that power. Were I not the one marrying you, I would be tempted by you, too." His eyes turn to Evander. "Should I be worried about you next?"

The question is asked in jest. But there is a moment where both Evander and I fight a flinch. Luckily, I don't think Conri sees it, because Evander recovers instantly.

"I would never dream of betraying my king." Evander dips into a low bow. "And besides, the mere scent of a human is mildly repulsive to me after all this time in Midscape. I do not think I could ever bed one." He then adds hastily, "No offense to you and your bride, of course."

Conri laughs again and pats his shoulder. "Part of me thinks I should punish you for saying such things about my mate. But I am too reassured by your loyalty to do so." He glances at me. "Assuming you do not feel slighted?"

"Evander has been a loyal soldier to you, my king. It is a relief to know that you have such good men in your care after what happened with Bardulf."

"I would hate for you to have to kill another of my knights," he agrees. "I do not know if bringing me a powerful spirit could make up for it a second time." The warning is clear.

But my focus is on Aurora, who sways slightly at Evander's side. "My king, might I spend this night in Aurora's tent?"

Conri chuckles. "We are in Den, we shall not stay in tents."

"No?"

"You'll see." Conri leans forward to kiss me gently and I expend a monumental effort not to shrink away in disgust.

There isn't the warm feeling of Conri's charm, not even the slimy feeling that Bardulf created when he tried to leverage the magic. There's no haziness to my thoughts. No urges to give in. In fact, I work to return the kiss. When he pulls away, I lean forward slightly, as if I wanted more. But it is all a conscious choice. And a disgusting one at that.

The charm doesn't seem to be having the same effect on me as it once did.

"It is good to see you eager." He chuckles. "But save it for the night and I will keep you up past the dawn."

I smile, looking up at him through my lashes. "I would be so honored."

Aurora is back on Conri and I am on Evander for the short return into the heart of Den. I run my fingers through Evander's fur, pressing and squeezing—like a massage. Anything that could show him that he still has my heart. That there is nothing to worry about despite how I must act with Conri. I wish we had figured out some kind of communication system for when no words could be spared.

The lykin disperse as we trot through tent and building. Conri takes us farther through the trees, to a slope that an earth-bermed structure has been constructed into. Its doors and windows are nestled between the roots of the mighty trees that cascade down the slope. Wildflowers, lupines, lichen, and moss trellis down around it.

We enter through an archway into a large, central hall. In the center is a firepit, burning happily with individuals I recognize as other alphas lounging at its edges. They all look our way when we enter, but Conri waves off their formalities.

He leads us off to the side and into a tunnel that stretches deeper into the hillside. I quickly realize that the cave system that makes up the innards of this structure was naturally formed and merely polished by mortal hands. The adornments of carved pillars embellished with engravings of running wolves and the phases of the moon were certainly not naturally formed.

Led by the faint glow of torches, we plunge deeper into the hillside. In the distance, I think I see a speck of white light that suggests another entrance, but we stop well before reaching it. Conri leads us under an archway—one of the few branches off this hall.

It opens into a modest cavern. A fire crackles in a hearth on the opposite wall with blankets and pillows laid out in a divot in the floor before it, the sunken area no doubt catching the warmth of the flames to fight against the chill of the caves. To the right and left of the hearth are two other archways, their openings obscured by curtains, rather than doors. On one curtain is the embroidered visage of a wolf, a full moon on the other.

Conri explains the obvious. "The chambers of the king are to the left, the moon spirit on the right. So there will be no concerns about you having ample time with Aurora."

I glance in her direction. She emphasized that I needed to find time with her, despite knowing this setup of rooms. It underscores what is already clear—this place is not safe, or private.

Aurora confirms my suspicions. "I would like to spend the night in the grove."

"The grove? Is your weakness truly so bad?" Conri seems concerned, but not upset, which I take as a good sign.

"It is not grave, but my weariness is significant enough that I feel it'd be for the best. One night and I shall be as strong as I have always been," Aurora says without hesitation.

"And of course I will need to stay with her there," I add so there's no doubt.

Conri's frown deepens. "But we were just united, my darling. This evening I had planned to take you to bed."

His fake display of compassion truly disgusts me. "I know, and we will have days and days together, a lifetime. But I am weary, and so is Aurora—we should have some time to rejoin her powers," I say delicately. He does not seem to be easing his disapproval. I shift tactics. "What about this: We merely spend the day in the grove and then I make my way to your bed before dawn?"

The wolf king considers this.

"I could escort them both, my king. That way you can get the rest you so deserve, or attend to other necessary matters, until your bride and spirit are ready," Evander offers.

My insides tighten. Would Evander have offered to escort us before? Does his outright asking give away too much?

"That should be fine." Conri finally relents and I bite the insides of my cheeks to keep myself from exhaling an all too obvious sigh of relief. "In fact, take them there now, will you? You are right in that I have important matters to discuss with the other alphas."

Important matters like planning the details of killing your future wife...

"Yes, my king." Evander bows his head.

Conri grabs my wrist and leans in. "I'm looking forward to seeing you later," he whispers, and leaves. I manage to hold back my shudder until he's gone.

"Faelyn—" Evander moves for me.

"We need to get to the grove," I interrupt him and wrap my arm around Aurora's waist, positioning hers around my shoulders. She slumps into me with a sigh. Evander's eyes widen slightly as he grasps the severity of the situation.

"This way." Evander leads us back into the passage.

Conri had turned left, no doubt going back to the main cavern we first entered into. Instead, Evander turns right and guides us down the hall to the speck of light I saw earlier. Sure enough, my suspicions about it being another exit were correct.

We emerge into a dense copse of the silvery trees of Den. A well-worn path slopes down between them to a large, grassy clearing. At the far edge of the clearing is a large boulder, nearly the size of a small cliff. It is as tall as the hut I grew up in, and twice as wide. At the center of the clearing is another, flat rock. This one large enough for the three of us to stand on together.

Aurora sinks onto the stone the second we step onto it. I ease her down all the way into a laying position when it becomes clear that's what she desires. Shifting, I place her head in my lap. Her eyes are already closed.

"What is it?" Worry is apparent in Evander's tone.

"She's just tired," I answer on Aurora's behalf. Her breathing has become slow and steady—she's already in a deep slumber. "She'll be all right." I hope. "She just needs to rest."

"I've never seen her like this before." Evander steps off the central stone, glancing back up the pathway to make sure no one has followed us.

"She's never had her power split before." Our discussion doesn't seem to disturb Aurora. I rest my hands lightly around her face, fingertips brushing against her cheeks, neck, and shoulders. "And she had to help me to summon Volst. He was too weak to come otherwise, since I'd summoned him so recently."

"I suspected."

"I wonder if Conri is with the other alphas now, plotting my death."

Evander folds his arms and his muscles tense. His mouth is pressed into a hard line. "If they so much as lay a finger upon you…"

"The three of us will leave before they get the chance," I say optimistically. Allowing him to fantasize about hurting Conri too much could be dangerous; he might act on those impulses. "We knew this was a risk of our approach to the circumstances…just like we knew we had no other choice."

"I still hate it." His words and tone are in direct contrast with his body language. Were someone to emerge from the caverns and lay eyes on us, Evander would look bored but attentive for possible threats against Aurora and me. "It's probably the only thing I could hate more than seeing him touch you—his mouth on yours…"

"I'm sorry."

"Don't apologize," Evander says firmly. "You're keeping yourself safe—all of us safe. We have roles to play, still, unfortunately."

"Does keeping us all safe even matter if it breaks us in the process?" The words are faint and small.

The question prompts movement from Evander. He drops to a knee beside the stone Aurora and I are on, tilting his head to meet my eyes. It briefly draws my focus from Aurora and the depth of his stare steals my breath.

"Nothing, *nothing* will break us. Fate has tried, the wolf king has tried, but we continue coming back together despite it all. You are my mate, Faelyn. The other half of my soul. Not even the hands of the old gods can break that."

The furrow of my brow relaxes as a small smile curves my mouth. "Your optimism is infectious."

"It's not optimism, just simple truth." He returns my smile. "I will spend the rest of my days at your side, so long as you will have me."

"It would be my life's joy to spend every breath in your company."

"Then it shall be so," he says.

"It shall be so," I echo. As I speak, there's a gentle tingle—like a thousand butterflies settling upon me and then lifting all my hopes and wishes on their rainbow wings. Evander feels the same, I think, as his gaze softens into something akin to elation.

"I wish I could kiss you," he whispers.

"We shouldn't risk it out in the open." I hate to be a voice of reason.

"I know."

"So, you two finally figured it out." Aurora startles us both. I look back down at her to find her eyes open.

"How long have you been awake?" I ask, fighting a flush that's smoldering behind my cheeks.

"The whole time." She grins slightly. Her expression is still worn thin. "Think of it more as meditating than sleeping."

"You were intentionally eavesdropping." I purse my lips and narrow my eyes at her.

"You made an assumption, it's not my fault." She closes her eyes, wearing a little smile. So smug.

"It's true, then?" Evander doesn't seem bothered by Aurora's actions in the slightest. Instead, he has the air of excitement. "We are actually soulmates?"

"Why do you ask questions you already know the answers to?"

Evander shifts his attention from her to me. All doubt is gone. All pretense with it. The barriers I had built within me, the doubt, it crumbles. The feeling that's been there all along flows between us as freely as the magic between Aurora and me.

"How long have you known?" I ask Aurora without taking my eyes off Evander.

"From the first moment." She scoffs, though doesn't sound truly offended. "I am one of the oldest spirits still roaming this world. Do you think such a thing would escape me?"

"Why didn't you tell us?" I'm surprised at how I don't feel upset with her concealment in the slightest. Perhaps it's because of the pure joy that continues to surge through me.

"I've been around long enough to know that there are some things that mortals must figure out on their own. You tell a mortal something, and they fight it. Guide them to their own conclusion and they'll accept with open arms." All the little suggestions suddenly make sense. Her openness to suggest Evander as an outlet for me, her insistence that I could trust him despite appearances…

"Did I ever really need to 'relieve the tension' to fight Conri's charm? Or was that just a way of pushing Evander and me together?" I ask out of curiosity.

"The charm is very real, as you both know. And relief did help fight it."

"But?" I prompt her, feeling somewhat guilty when it's so obvious that she's still recovering her strength.

"But the connection of a soulmate bond, once accepted, is something that can prevent the charm altogether."

"How?" Evander and I say nearly in unison.

"Think of the charm like a false mirror of a genuine soul-mate bond—it is trying to recreate the pull. If you do not have that connection already, you are potentially open to receiving it. But, if the bond is there, there is no need for more. Like a peg in a hole, there is no space for other magic," Aurora explains.

It all begins to make sense. I see the past months with new clarity. When I first arrived in Midscape, I had shut off my senses to such bonds. By trying to ignore them, I had inadvertently made myself more vulnerable. Ever since returning—since knowing the truth of who Evander is and accepting the depths of my love for him—I've felt that Conri's charm has been nonexistent.

"It's true." The two words summarize so much. "When I was with Conri earlier, I didn't feel the barest edge of the charm."

Evander's brows tip up slightly in the middle, and his mouth parts with a smile that can only be described as relief. I return the expression wholeheartedly. *You don't need to worry about me falling prey to him*, I say without words. *I am yours, and yours alone.*

thirty-nine

THE REST OF THE DAY IN THE GROVE IS SPENT QUIETLY DISCUSSING AMONGST THE THREE OF US—OR JUST EVANDER AND MYSELF AS AURORA MEDITATES.

I learn more about the history of this sacred place. The grove is where the first lykin communed with the great wolf spirit underneath the full moon. It is also where Conri will make me his bride. That realization prompts some imaginings of what it might look like. Would I be dressed in finery? Or wear nothing at all?

Of course, I imagined my wedding to Evander when I was young, both the informal ceremony under the redwood and the more mortal one later on where actual vows would be said and rings exchanged. Here would be a fitting place for me to wed, in concept. I would've wanted such a ceremony to take place in nature, communing with magics old and new, swearing myself to my partner before gods and spirits alike. But if—when—such a day comes, it will not be to Conri. Nor do I suspect it will be here.

Evander and I will find another redwood to marry beneath, well after we escape from this prison.

The escape plan consumes the majority of our discussion throughout the fading hours. Aurora gives her own input, as she's able. Evander and I brainstorm and debate between her moments of consciousness.

As the moon rises, so does Aurora. My feet have long gone numb—I didn't dare move them while she was recovering—

and I stretch them slowly, wincing as feeling returns with pinpricks. But any discomfort I feel is dulled by seeing her revitalized and well.

Aurora takes my hand and squeezes it. "Thank you."

"You have nothing to thank me for." I squeeze her hand in return. "I would do it all again, gladly."

She flashes me a bright smile and I realize how much lighter I feel now that the worry is gone. Relief at having her back to normal floods me. This elation isn't just from the strengthening of the magic between us… A twinge of pain mingles with the joy and relief at seeing her well, changing up the mix of my emotions. Making it sweet, yet bitter.

Aurora will leave soon. And then I will never see her again. I want so badly to see her leave—to be free. But the mere idea of it is already carving an Aurora-shaped space in my heart. She was one of my first friends in a long, long time.

"We should probably head in." I turn my attention to the pathway that leads back into Den. "Conri will be waiting for me, and if I can return earlier, rather than later, it would probably be wise."

Evander and Aurora both sigh in unison, prompting them to lock eyes and share a smirk. The expression even slips onto my own face. Though it's short lived.

"Trust me, I share the sentiment," I murmur.

"My apologies, Faelyn. You're the one who's enduring the worst of him right now. We shouldn't be lamenting it," Aurora says.

"Lament away." I shrug. "It helps me feel not alone."

"You will never be alone." Evander rests his hand on my knee. It's the most outward contact he's made all day and my stomach flips. I want to lace my fingers against his and bring them to my lips to kiss his knuckles. But I don't dare. Judging from the almost tortured knit to his brows, he feels the same.

"Thank you." The best I can give him is a small smile that I try and pack all of my adoration into. "Besides, you two have served your time suffering at Conri's hand. It's my turn to share the burden."

"If I could make a world where no one had to suffer at the hands of a wolf king, I would." Evander's hands ball into fists and relax.

"Perhaps we might," Aurora says. "If I'm gone from this mortal form, then there will be nothing more for the lykins to fight over. No ring or person that will denote the power of a king."

"The lykin could return to packs," I offer optimistically, thinking of his ancestry in the woods. "Every lykin could live as they pleased, with those they pleased, governing themselves in their own way."

Evander slowly shakes his head. "The wolf king is a scar on the past of my people, but it is also our future. Our ways have been fundamentally changed from that time. The hearts of the lykin look to a king. I do not think it will be any different just because there is no longer a moon spirit to offer a single person power. They will find something different to squabble over."

The idea is too heartbreaking to bear. "You might be right in that the lykin have been forever changed. But there will be a time when a new precedent can be set. Maybe power is handed and gained peacefully and the leader is more of a spiritual guide—one connected with the old and the new—than a battle-ready warlord. Maybe they do lead all packs, but the leader is chosen from among them. There are many possibilities."

"I like your vision of the future better than mine." He gives me a tired smile.

"I believe that the lykin will fight for a brighter future, if given the chance. And that someone will step forward to lead them into that future." *You*, I want to say, *You should do it, Evander*. But I don't. If he is to lead, then it is a burden he must choose to bear of his own accord. It doesn't matter if I think he would be the most perfect choice. What matters is what he thinks.

But the idea of the fang crown of the wolf king landing on Evander's brow distracts me a moment.

I can see it so clearly—feel it, even. Evander's voice echoing throughout the main hall of Den, as he holds court with the alphas of the many packs of the lykin. People look to him for sage counsel on the history of their peoples. They do not make the journey to Den out of fear or force, but for guidance and to connect with an ancient past. And me…I walk among windswept grasses. The fresh scents of earth and water are my company as I, with the spirits' help, bring back trees and animals to the plains. I would help him rule, if there could be a place for me.

"Faelyn?" Evander's tone suggests that it might not be the first time he's called for me. I blink, returning to the present and abandoning the fantasy. Evander and Aurora have stood. He holds his hand out expectantly to me. I must've truly been lost in my thoughts to not notice. "We should head back."

"Right." I take his hand and he helps me up. Our grip lingers, but only for a second. Yet, as we walk back, side by side, our knuckles brush against each other in the cramped passageway. My fingers twitch as I fight the urge to lace them against his. Just one touch would be enough…one moment of him—of us.

But that is not to be had tonight. We head straight back to the king's chambers. The fire still crackles in the hearth.

"Good night," Aurora says, loud enough that Conri would hear if he's in the bedroom. The curtain is drawn and the shadows long on the floor, making it impossible to tell if he is or isn't there. "Thank you again, Faelyn, for your help. And for your escort and guard, Evander."

"It is my honor to serve the king," he says dutifully.

"Rest well, Aurora, Evander." My attention only briefly lands on Aurora, and sticks to Evander as she disappears behind her curtain. The flickering orange light of the fire highlights every dip and divot in his muscles. I shamelessly fantasize about how those biceps bulge when he grips my hips as I am atop him.

I love you, I mouth to him.

The shadows on his face seem to darken. His hand moves of its own accord, reaching for me, but he abandons the motion. Pain fills his moonlit gaze.

I love you. Always, he mouths back. Then he turns, striding out of the room with purpose, as though he had to gain momentum to ensure he would actually leave.

I linger, staring at the outline of where he just was. The caves are colder at night. But the winter in my heart only accentuates the chill. I have to move as well, in the opposite direction from him. But all I want is to run to him. To tell Evander to take me far, far from this place. Somewhere that we never have to think about any of it, ever again.

Soon, I reassure myself. My day was spent strengthening Aurora and plotting our escape. We will all be free within two mere weeks. They've endured this pain—worse—for years…I can hold out for a handful of days more.

With a bracing breath, I practically charge into the bedroom, past the point of no return that is the curtain. I slow the moment I'm plunged into near-total darkness. The only light is from the beam that is cast from the firelight underneath the curtain. It takes a second for my eyes to adjust and, not knowing the layout of the room, I don't move at all.

"I'm here, my queen. Come forward." Conri's tone is low, sultry, but that of a command. The shadows shift before me, accompanied by the sound of moving fabrics.

I do as he asks, my eyes slowly adjusting while I shuffle forward. The room comes into focus. It's all shades of black and gray, a hint of orange. There's barely enough light for me to make out the oversized bed that takes up most of the space. There's a table off to the side, against the wall, framed by two chairs. I can see the dark splotches of tapestries hung from the walls, but I cannot make out the patterns woven into them.

"Not far, now," Conri coaxes. I head toward the side of the bed he is not occupying, based on the sound. But he stops me with a *tsk*. "I'm not over there."

Bracing myself, I correct my course and walk around the foot of the bed, toward him, dragging my fingers to keep my bearing, they trail along the thick furs and quilted blankets piled to ward off the chill of the caves. As I near, he reaches out a hand. Conri is shirtless, blankets pooled around his waist. I can only hope he has something on beneath them.

"I have been waiting for you." He takes my hands in both of his and kisses their backs. It is a gentle and tender display. Which makes it all the more sinister, knowing his true nature.

Bardulf and Conri are men cut from the same cloth. But where Bardulf was overt and brash, Conri is cunning and methodical. He's a man who doesn't have a need for haste because he truly believes that the world will bend for him. It's merely a matter of time. And, if it doesn't, then he will break it by force.

"I am sorry to keep my king waiting."

"I will allow it, just this once. Is Aurora well?" Once I am in hand, always Aurora next. I doubt there has ever been a day in Conri's entire existence that he didn't spend worrying over the things that guarantee his control over the lykin.

"Yes." I rest a hand on his shoulder. "But I am tired from our time communing."

The silence that follows is unbearable. He takes far too long to formulate what should be a few words. I wonder what is going through his head. Fear fills my blood, weighing down my body at the absence of him saying something, anything.

"Then we should have you rest," he says finally. Without warning, Conri pulls me forward and I clumsily fall onto the bed. He expertly twists as I fall, arms shifting around my waist. I let out a soft *oof* sound almost identical to the plush mattress as it accepts my weight. "Comfortable, isn't it?"

I open my mouth to agree without thought, but pause, shifting, sinking in farther. It is easily one of the most comfortable beds I've ever lain in. The mattress itself doesn't feel as if it's made of hay, but rather—

"It's feathers," he answers my question without my needing to ask. "Only the best, for the king and his queen." Conri's arms tighten around my midsection, drawing me closer. We're chest to chest, noses nearly touching. His leg drapes over mine, foot wrapping around my calf like he's some kind of sea monster ensnaring me. "It will be a good life, you know."

"What?" I don't follow; the statement seems to come out nowhere.

"Witch Queen of the Lykin. Your new title even has a nice ring to it," he murmurs, looking down at me from the other side of the equally plush pillow with heavy lids. "You will be mighty. Feared. I will find any spirit you desire and none shall ever question your strength."

I smile, though I can feel it doesn't reach my eyes. Fortunately, he'll explain it away using my work with Aurora. He will see it as a tired smile, not pitying.

What a sad existence you have... To always be looking at the world in terms of might and conquest. To be looking at what can be taken as the measure of a leader, rather than what can be given. To value fear more than love.

"It will be like a dream," I say, hoping that it never becomes anything more than his dream.

"It can be, or it can be a nightmare." His heavy lids now look like narrowed eyes. Examining me. Studying. "You wield powers that exceed my own."

"I don't—"

"You can drop the pretense, Faelyn." Even though his tone has gone harsh, he frees a hand from my waist to caress my jaw. "We both know the strength you wield. If I'm not careful, you could get a mind to turn it against me."

"I'd never," I whisper.

"Good. Because you know what the other alphas murmur in my ears?" He dips his chin to better meet my eyes. "To kill you."

"What?" I feign surprise, thankful I know the truth—that it was Conri's inclination, no other alphas necessary. "But I—why?"

"They think I can take the power out of you that way. That instead of taking you before the great wolf spirit to wed you, I should do it to kill you. And ask that he help me draw the power from your blood into my own. That way, it will linger forever in my bloodline—the blood of kings."

He's really telling me everything. "But…there is another way to join our blood."

"Another fact I have delighted in reminding them. So, it's in your hands, Faelyn. Will you be my eager bride and carry my heirs?"

Old gods. I might be sick. My mind races with what I can say next and a wild plan strikes like lightning. "When we are wed, I will perform a spell that night to ensure my fertility."

"My alphas might need assurances before the wedding of your willingness."

"Then tomorrow, I shall gather the materials for my spell."

"Good. Then, when you are ripe for me tomorrow night, I will fill these caverns with your screams." He grins gleefully and leans forward to kiss me. I work to return the kiss, aware that he hasn't said they would be screams of passion.

Fortunately, the assurance seems to have satisfied him enough for the night. He leans away, releasing me, and rolls in the other direction. As if now that he knows he will have me when he wants, he no longer needs to pretend to woo me.

I shift onto my back, wiggling just enough that I can get some space between us without it being suspicious and I stare up at the ceiling.

Breathe, Faelyn, breathe, you'll be fine. There's a plan. You'll be fine. Yet my heart races as fast as the first time Conri chased me through the woods. I clutch my shirt over my chest, willing it to slow. It takes every shred of self-control not to get up and run to Evander right now.

But I stay.

I stare up at the ceiling and remind myself of every reason I have not to be afraid. Of the power Aurora has placed within me that has empowered me to commune with the spirits. Of the different magics my grandma taught me and wove into the cape at the foot of the bed, the plans I have to use all of them to thwart Conri. And Evander.

Evander…

The notions from earlier return. Of Evander being the king of the lykin and leading them to a glorious age. I play scenes in my mind of him being a just and fair ruler. And of us returning to this room at the end of a long day in service to his people.

I imagine what it might be like to sleep in this bed with Evander at my side. To be the bride of the wolf king when it is a wolf king of my choosing. That is the dream that finally relaxes me enough that I can fall into slumber. I need all the rest I can get, given what I've just done.

forty

When I wake, I'm alone. The moment I realize Conri isn't next to me, the blankets are lighter. The bed is warmer, cozier. But it doesn't make me want to stay in it. The idea of even remotely savoring his lingering warmth is too much for me.

I stand and the movement gets my blood moving. No, it's more than that. My heart is hammering. The night comes back to me in a dizzying rush. I'm out of the room in a blink, gathering my cape around me for whatever protection it can offer. Though not even it can protect me from what's coming—from what Conri expects of me.

The moment I step through the curtain and emerge into the common room, my eyes land on Evander, leaning by the archway that leads out into the hall. He turns, pushing away, drawn by the sound. It takes only a second for me to scan the room to ensure no one else is present.

"Fael—" He doesn't have a chance to finish, cut off by the soft *oof* as I crash into him, throwing my arms around his shoulders. The feeling of him against me. There. Holding me in an instant as tightly as he possibly can. *Safe*. It has the fear and panic I felt choking my throat looking for escape as relief floods me. He must hear the shuddering breath I try to hide in his shoulder. "What is it? What's wrong?"

I shake my head and pull away; the night still haunts me. "We have to leave."

"We will." He tightens his grip on my shoulders. "I swear to you."

"Now. Today. We must go today. We get Aurora, we take her and we leave. Together. No more fear, no more control, and no more Conri. The three of us, and then…just you and me. Forever."

A scowl nastier than the worst urges of the most foul furrows his brow. When Evander speaks, it's little more than a growl. "What did he do?"

"He—"

"What is it?" Aurora has emerged from her quarters, already looking alarmed. Her attention lands on me. "What's wrong?"

I wonder if she could somehow sense through our connection that things were amiss. Perhaps that's why she looks so alert despite just waking. Rather than answering, I step away from Evander. He slackens his grip, and just that small act reminds me how good it feels to be in the arms of a man who will just as easily hold me close as let me go. Taking him by the hand, I lead him to the edge of the sunken pit before the fire. Aurora follows suit and we both sit, Evander opting to stand at the edge, angled toward the entry—remaining our loyal defender and just far enough away should anyone enter.

"Last night…" I proceed to tell them everything that happened with Conri. It sounds so little as I say it all. How is it that such a small amount of time passed with such few words and yet everything changed? I finish with, :"…I don't know what else to do but leave. Unless one of you has a better idea?"

Aurora crosses her arms and leans back into the pillows, staring at the flames with a scowl as deep as Evander's. "The bastard," she mutters under her breath.

"We have to leave." It's little more than a whisper, and I can't tell if it's because Evander is making an attempt to be quiet. Or if it's because he has so much rage on my behalf that if he's not whispering, he's screaming.

"Aurora?" I ask.

She continues to stare into the flames. I can only imagine what's going through her mind. Lifetimes of subjugation. Of being controlled and passed around. Of watching her power being reduced to little more than a tool for mortals who fail to appreciate its might.

But, also…it has been lifetimes. For all the hatred and hurt she must have, this is all she's known for so long. Does she even remember what it feels like to be her complete self? Does she truly believe it could happen? The questions alone are heartbreaking.

"All right." The way she says those two words makes me wonder if she was going through the same thoughts as I was. Processing them each on her terms. She sits a little straighter, as if gathering herself and her composure for the first time in a long time. "We'll go tonight."

"Is it wise to wait that long?" I keep glancing toward the archway, feeling like at any moment Conri will come rushing through, demanding my life or my womb.

"My powers will be stronger at night," she says. "If we need to summon spirits and I need to offer you any extra energy, I'll have the most to give then."

"The day will offer you time to gather supplies." Evander's tone is still low and harsh. His biceps bulge as they tense, arms folded.

"I did say I would gather supplies for a fertility spell." I run my hands over my face, rubbing away the tortured emotions that keep trying to live there. "I was also thinking I could use that as a pretense to gather whatever we might need, or even as a shield to escape under."

"Yes, get the supplies and organize yourselves. While you do that, I can plan out a distraction to allow you two to slip away," Evander says.

I'm on my feet. "You're coming with us."

"I will." He holds out his hands, quickly reassuring me by rubbing my shoulders. "But you two are not going to be able to get out of here without some kind of excuse to take eyes off of you. You can't outrun him without a head start. Once Conri realizes you're gone—and I'll stall that as long as possible—I'll then ensure I'm the one sent after you. I'll join you. By the time he realizes we're not coming back, we'll be near the wall of the elves."

"And to safety," I finish softly. "But why would Conri send you if we escaped under your watch?"

"You won't be under my watch. I'll see to it that another knight is guarding you, emphasizing my competence in the process. You never escaped under my watch, but under someone else's you did. 'Send me,' is what I'll tell him." Evander smiles. It doesn't reach his eyes. It's forced. "I'll be all right."

"We can find another way; you need—*I need* you to be there with us." The idea of him staying behind is gutting me.

"He's right, Faelyn," Aurora says softly, still transfixed by the flames. "We're not going to get out of here without some kind of distraction to keep Conri busy. And you or I can't be the ones to make that distraction."

I keep focused on Evander. My face twists again with the pain that feels as though it's trying to rip apart every corner of my heart. His smile relaxes into something genuine. Evander reaches down and dares to cup my cheek, holding it and my heart at the same time.

"It'll be all right," he says softly.

"How can you be so sure?" I breathe, reaching up to cover his hand with my own, pressing it against my face. I need to know he's here.

"Because fate brought us together again, it won't tear us apart." He's confident and I try to make that confidence my own.

Evander's right hand reaches for my left. His thumb rubs over the yellow twine he tied around my finger. From the corners of my eyes, I can see Aurora shift, glancing at the motion. But she turns back to the fire, offering us privacy.

"This will guide you through the woods. It will guide my heart to yours."

"That's not the spell I wove." I shake my head. "It's not—"

"It's the spell I wove when I tied it to your finger and wished, with all my might, that someday you would be my bride." He leans forward to kiss me, daring the display of affection despite anyone being able to walk in. It's foolish, but I savor the brief second his mouth is on mine. My breath hitches. Evander releases me after, the risk too great for us to dare anything more than what we already have. And we have already dared greatly. "I will find you, Faelyn. Nothing will tear us apart, so long as you wish for us to be together."

I nod as his confidence makes room in my heart right alongside my love for him. He's right, we will find a way. There is no greater power than love.

"Right, then, what next?" I ask, refocusing the conversation away from my fears.

"I'm going to speak with Conri." Aurora stands. "Evander will escort us to him, and when we arrive, I'll inform Conri that I've sensed a threatening force coming from the western edge of Den."

"I'll insist that I be the one to go off and check," Evander says, picking up on the plan. "It'll also help reinforce that I am not too attached to either of you by being so willing to leave."

I'm seeing where this is all leading toward. "I'll wait till you're gone and then, when we're assigned another of his knights, go off to collect supplies for the ritual he's wanting."

Evander nods at me.

"I'll ensure I stay at your side," Aurora adds. "That way when the time comes, we'll be ready."

"We can claim that we want to stay together to maintain our strength. And I can say that Aurora will help me identify the best supplies for the spell work," I say, and they nod along. "But when do we slip away?"

A moment of pensive silence. Evander says, "I'll keep the patrol out until dusk."

"I don't think the return of the patrol will be enough of a distraction," I am reluctant to say.

"I agree..." Evander murmurs, rubbing his jawline and lips in thought.

"What about a bonfire night?" Aurora suggests. "If the king is thinking he will be taking his future wife to bed to sire an heir, it would be cause for celebration."

"He did say that he wanted the other alphas to know that I was willing—to reassure them. Why not make a display of it?" I add, somewhat eagerly. The circumstances still fill me with nausea. But the hope that we might have a path forward is winning out. I can see our path out of here. "Moreover, I could tell him that it would help empower the magic."

I'm already running through the lies I'll fabricate for Conri. I could say that the fire represents new life and that I must witness it build, my powers and fertility swelling with it. Or that I need to have a ritual of the elements combining—fire, water, earth, and air—the building blocks of existence—to help foster life within me.

Yes, I can come up with something.

"All right, then I'll distract him during the return and try to draw as much attention as I can onto setting up for this bonfire," Evander says. "And that's when you two will slip away."

We all nod and spend another moment of silence thinking through everything. It will be enough. It has to be.

"Then let's not waste any more time," I say with more confidence than I feel. No more falling apart. I have to be brave for both of them… and for myself. "We leave tonight."

forty-one

THE DAY IS A BLUR.

I'm a walking contradiction from the first moment we spoke with Conri to the late hours of the afternoon. On the outside, I am serene and wear a blissful expression. My voice is a level tone that verges on excited from time to time. I work to play it off as enthusiasm for what is to come for me in the night with Conri. This seems to please him, and he is all too eager to begin planning the bonfire as Aurora and I set out with a knight I barely recognized by face at first and now know as Farkolf.

Despite outward appearances, inside I'm all jitters and a stomach that is so tightly knotted that I have to force myself to eat for the sake of filling it as much as I can before we make our escape. My hands tremble from time to time as I gather things like thread and waterskins, all under the pretense of spell work for fertility. But everything I take is something that's going to make our journey easier.

We have the knight escort us back to the king's chambers as the sun begins to set. Conri is in the main hall, still arranging things for the bonfire. We pass by a mountainous stack of wood on the way in, arranged just outside the primary entrance to the great hall. It will no doubt be lit to coincide with the moon rising.

Farkolf takes his position where Evander would usually stand—right at the entrance to the king's chambers. But, unlike Evander, he keeps his back to us and remains at attention. He doesn't lean against the wall, arms folded. He doesn't angle himself inward, looking for me. The differences are a reminder that Evander isn't here with me.

Nasty thoughts drift through my mind of Conri having overheard us earlier. Of him knowing our plan and hunting Evander after he left. The images of the deep scars on Evander's back create strips of phantom pains between my shoulders. Evander could be dead on the ground, ripped apart by Conri, and I wouldn't know. I might never know. He—

Aurora's hand closes around mine. We're in the bedchamber, sorting through our meager items by candlelight and repacking only what's absolutely necessary. I shift my attention to her.

"He'll be fine." She squeezes my fingers. "And so will we."

"I know," I say. Even though I don't know. None of us do. "I wish he was here, with us, though." I'd feel better if I could see him.

"Soon. Just like soon you'll be able to touch him."

"Touch who?" Conri asks as he slips under the curtain drawn across the entrance.

Aurora releases me and we both straighten from our sorting. Luckily, I had been shoving most things into packs on the floor. The one in front of me I nudge with my toe, trying to subtly push it under the bed. Aurora does the same with the pack she'd been filling as I step around her, my movement distracting the wolf king.

"You, of course!" I say with all the delight I can muster, practically throwing myself into his arms and kissing him on the mouth.

Conri chuckles as I draw away. His hands settle on my hips, toward the back, where they can reach for the curve of my rear. "I do appreciate the enthusiasm. Is it this fertility ritual already taking shape?"

"Perhaps." I look up at him through my lashes. "I am most excited to touch all of you tonight."

"Who says we must wait for tonight?" Conri leans in, nipping at my earlobe. "What's to stop me from just taking you now?"

"My king, the ritual isn't ready yet." I force a coy giggle, as though this is all a mere playful game.

"I can take you without need of siring a child now, and then again later." He leans back, looking down at me with a smirk.

"Should I clear off the bed?" Aurora asks dryly, as if she's seen this play out a hundred times. She probably has.

"Perhaps you should. I think I have a few spare minutes."

Disgust at the idea of Conri pulling me onto the bed wars with pity and sorrow for all the past women he's slept with if he thinks "a few spare minutes" is sufficient. I run my hands up his chest with a sultry smile, as if I'm deeply tempted by the idea. Conri's eyes shine in the low candlelight of the room, like a predator about to feast.

I open my mouth, about to offer my next excuse to stall him a little bit longer. But Farkolf pulls aside the curtain, dipping his head in with a small nod.

"My king, the patrol group has returned. Evander is here to report."

My heart skips at the news.

"Good, send him back." Conri has yet to release me.

"There's been a bit of a complication." That has the wolf king's attention. And mine. Farkolf continues, "He has another warrior bound and gagged."

"Part of the original group sent?" Conri is now giving Farkolf his undivided attention and I'm free to step away. "Or someone else?"

"I'm not sure, my king." Farkolf looks deeply uncomfortable. No doubt because he lacks the information Conri is looking for. "Perhaps it'd be best if—"

Conri sighs before he can finish. The wolf king glances in my direction. "I never have a moment to indulge myself." He grabs my chin and holds my face in place as he brings his mouth to mine. "Keep that thought, my darling. Let it simmer until you're so hot you can't stand it. We will dance with magic tonight and I will make you mine."

"I am counting down the seconds," I whisper breathlessly.

Conri strides out of the room with a nod in Farkolf's direction; the knight follows. As the curtain falls back into place, my attention locks with Aurora's. We both stare at each other, holding our breath and straining our ears. The men's footsteps fade alongside their voices. Not much is said, and it's hard to make out anything past an initial "…yes, I'll go…" from Conri.

"What do you think?" I whisper to Aurora.

"Is Farkolf still there?" Aurora asks.

I shuffle to the curtain, pulling it aside ever so slightly. Farkolf is positioned back by the entry. I retreat into the room with a nod.

She curses under her breath. "I suppose Evander couldn't find an excuse to make him go, too."

What to do? I ask myself as I quickly round the bed and scoop my pack off the floor. There's no longer time to be judicious in determining what to bring and what not. Everything remaining gets shoved into the pack. Aurora follows my lead.

"We're going to head to the grove."

"All right." Aurora nods. Her implicit trust is apparent. It fills me with confidence as well as a deep sense of responsibility.

I grab her hand right before we leave through the curtain, stalling us one moment that we can't afford, but I need to take.

"I'm going to keep you safe," I vow. "And I'm going to take you to the sirens to have their old god restore your magic and free you of this halfway mortal coil. Nothing will stop me—not a wolf king, or spirit, or fate itself. I swear this to you."

Aurora squeezes my fingers and a surge of magic overtakes me, so much that the world briefly spins. Her brow relaxes and her head tilts slightly to the side. Her smile is one of relief.

"I believe you, Faelyn. You and Evander are the first mortals in a long time that I believed would look after me," she says softly. "Thank you."

"You have nothing to thank me for," I say. "This is long overdue."

"You have my gratitude anyway."

I release her and adjust the pack on my shoulder, hoping that it doesn't register as too suspicious to Farkolf. "Let's go."

We emerge into the central room and I try to set a leisurely pace. As though nothing is remotely out of the ordinary. Farkolf doesn't take notice of us until we're right at his side.

"Is everything all right?" I ask, curiously looking to the left and in the direction of the great cavern.

"Our king is handling it."

"Oh, good." I stop for a moment and clench my jaw to keep myself from asking about Evander. It'd be suspicious if I'm inquiring about him right before I go missing. "So there's no danger?"

"You're safe with me," he says dutifully.

"Exceptional." I turn to the right and start walking. Aurora follows. For a brief second, I don't think he's going to do or say anything at all. But Farkolf decides to be competent at the last second.

"Where do you think you're going?" Farkolf rushes after us, squeezing around our right and stopping in front of me.

"To the grove." I gesture ahead and furrow my brow. "Where else?"

"Are you supposed to be in the grove?" He steps in my way, again, as I try to pass.

I glare up at him.

Aurora answers before I can. "I am the spirit of the moon. Going to the grove to commune with my kin is essential. Especially before we perform any magic."

"Oh, right." He rubs the back of his neck. "Sorry, I'm not accustomed to this sort of thing. I'm usually relegated to menial tasks. But with Bardulf, well, gone…I thought it would be my chance to impress Conri. Maybe move up a bit in the pack."

Farkolf steps to the side and I start walking again. He falls into place at my side, where Conri usually is. I look at him for the first time and realize just how young he is. He can't be older than seventeen. The thick stubble on his chin disguises his youth at a glance. But the skin around his eyes is full. There are no sunken shadows. No lines that come with experience and time.

"I hope I've done all right by you both today. If I offended you just now, please let me know so I can properly make amends. I was probably a bit off-putting at first, wasn't I? Just nerves. I know you're probably more familiar with Evander, and Bardulf—though he's a poor example, I suppose. Given, well, you know… I promise I'm not like him." Farkolf had hardly said a word and now it seems he doesn't know the meaning of silence.

I come to a stop on the start of the path just outside of the caves. Columns arch around us, supporting the rock above. Moss climbs them and flowers and grasses hang from the ledge. Aurora slows to a stop two steps after, looking at me with a curious stare.

"Faelyn?" she asks.

Don't do this. I try and will myself to stop. *It's not your concern. He's not your concern. He doesn't matter so just keep focused on what does and get yourself out of here.*

But he's just a kid. An innocent bystander. And I am not Conri. I'm not heartless.

"Farkolf," I say sternly. The shift in my tone has him startling to attention. "I'm going to tell you something. I'll say it only once, and you only have a few seconds to make your choice."

"Faelyn," Aurora says more sternly, worry creeping around my name. I ignore it. *Trust me*, my heart wills her. Grandma always taught that I should trust my gut and use my powers to help this world.

Letting Farkolf get killed because of my plan helps nothing. I keep my eyes locked with his as I speak. My tone is as serious as the grave.

"If you make any motions to go back inside, I will summon a spirit and have the ground swallow you where you stand."

"Wh—What?" he stammers, taking a step back from me.

"I said don't move," I snap, holding out a hand. Farkolf ceases all movement. He has no idea that I cannot summon the spirits in this way. But none of them really comprehend how my relationship with the spirits does and does not work. So I keep the charade. "Here are your choices, Farkolf: You are either going to start running and leave Den as fast as you can. You won't look back and you won't be seen. You're going to leave the lands of the lykin for good—or at least until a new king wears the fang crown—and seek refuge with the elves, or fae, or even across the Fade, if you can make it.

"Or you're going to stand here and die," I finish simply, my gamble made. He's young, which means he's spent all his life under Conri's rule. But he's also young enough that he probably hasn't been a knight for very long. Perhaps he has yet to be fully brainwashed by Conri's efforts. Maybe he hasn't even taken the oaths yet that give him access to the charm, as I certainly haven't sensed any magic around him.

Farkolf opens and closes his mouth. His brow furrows, relaxes, and then furrows again. When Farkolf looks in Aurora's direction, she takes a step closer to me, as if to emphasize that this is her choice as well.

"Could I…simply stand here and say nothing?" he whispers meekly.

"We can't risk that." I glance over his shoulder, making sure there's no movement in the hall. "What's your choice?"

"I—I don't want to die." He really thinks me capable of killing him in cold blood like this. Ending Bardulf continues to yield unexpected benefits.

"Then you'd better get to running," I say, my hand almost trembling from the anxiousness I'm bottling. Farkolf goes to leave, but I stop him for one more remark. "No one can see you. No one can ever know."

"If anyone sees me again, I suspect I'm dead," he says softly. His gaze darts between us. "Though, I suspect if I stayed, I would've been anyway. One way or another."

I lower my hand and nod. Farkolf returns the gesture and then darts between the trees. He goes from man to wolf in an instant. Racing away. Consumed entirely by the thick, silvery trees of the grove.

"Was that wise?" Aurora asks uncertainly.

"I don't know," I admit. "But I know that it will be easier to live with myself—however much longer that is—knowing that I gave him a chance."

"How did you know he would listen?"

"I didn't. He seemed earnest, decent, and I hoped those traits would win out." I look at where Farkolf ran off. He headed north, into the cold and barren wastes past the edge of Den. Evander told me we couldn't go that way when we were making our plans in the grove because it was too harsh. But perhaps it'll be different for a lykin. I hope. But that's all the thoughts I can spare on Farkolf; the rest is up to him now. I turn to Aurora. "Are you ready?"

She looks once more into the dark hallway of Den, and then down to the grove.

"Aurora?" I probe gently. I can't rightly rush her when I also spent time on something for me.

"That was where Bewulf and I met," she whispers. There's a tiny smile on her face, but her eyes are filled with nearly overflowing sorrow. "It's where we wed and where I thought…" Aurora shakes her head and when she looks back to me, it's with a steely resolve. "I'm ready. Let's go."

I take her hand in mine and the two of us start between the trees. I set a swift but not careless pace as we run westward toward the great lake and the freedom and safety that lie far beyond.

forty-two

WE CANNOT OUTRUN THE LYKIN, SO WE MUST OUTSMART THEM. The moment Conri finds out we're gone, he's going to throw the entire might of the pack into finding us. So the first thing we must do is use the head start Evander is affording us to our advantage. We move quickly and stay out of sight—give them no reason to suspect us being out of place.

But our lead won't be enough alone. We have…half of an hour? An hour at most. Even without the time spent to save Farkolf, it wouldn't be enough. Conri will be able to make up for that gap in a third of the time. We have to do more.

I pull us behind a tree, both our chests heaving, and glance around. We're running in a wide arc around the camp of Den and haven't seen any sign of lykin coming out this far. But I know they're there. Conri's patrols around Den will only be waylaid by Evander for a short amount of time.

One hand holding Aurora, I grab with the other for a small embroidering of a tree on my cape. I close my eyes, squeezing both and sinking our magic deep into the earth. I hope she's had enough time to recover…

"Brundil, I beckon you. Come forth and lend us your aid," I say softly, curling my toes into the soles of my shoes as though they could sink into the soft soil underneath my boots.

The spirit of earth buds from the thick carpet of shining leaves. Tiny silver tendrils, like roots made of thread, grow in reverse—into the air, rather than the ground. Thousands of them weave and knot together. Thousands more stretch upward, looping and swirling. They take the shape of a living mass. A humanoid tree of silver and magic with wings like sapling boughs and horns of pure crystal.

"I was beginning to wonder if you would call again," Brundil says in her soft, rustling voice.

"I wanted you to save your strength for when the time was right," I say.

Brundil's head turns from me to Aurora. "My friend, are you certain of this path?"

"Only if you are the one to help lay it for me," Aurora says.

"We need to get to the great lake." I keep focused. It's too late now to go back. "If you can, clear the path ahead so we can move without any hindrances. And, when we are gone, churn the earth behind us to hide our scent."

"*If* I can," Brundil repeats with a scoff. "Remember to whom you speak." Brundil pauses, and contradicts herself slightly when she adds, "Though, to clear your scent from the air, you would need to speak with Zeeb."

"I was worried about that..." Aurora sighs. "He's so flighty."

I can only assume that this "Zeeb" is a spirit of air. "We can make do without him. Getting our scent off the ground will be enough. Scatter fresh leaves from the trees; that will help move the air."

"I will do this, but not for you, human."

"Thank you," Aurora whispers. "I merely want to be whole again."

"You will be." Brundil's optimism fills me with confidence. The spirit turns her attention west, in the direction we were running.

The ground ripples like water, tree roots and branches arching away to clear a path. The trees sway, as though a sudden wind has whipped through their branches. A rain of leaves cascades down, perfuming the air with earthy richness and providing an unexpected screen that will also help conceal our movements.

"Good luck." With the tired remark, Brundil sinks back into the earth.

"Thank you." Aurora and I both express our gratitude and we are off again.

I worry less about keeping our movements concealed with the cascade of leaves. I'm not staring at the ground, stumbling over root and snag. The forest moves around us—accommodating us. The path is laid and all we must do is take it.

As we run, I think of Aurora's first escape. She made it all the way past the Fade on her own. If she could make it so far with such little help, then surely the two of us together can make it to the land of the elves.

I glance her way. She's able to keep up with me without issue. We're both strong and powerful. *We're going to make it out of here.*

We don't slow as the lake comes into view. We race toward it, speeding into the water. My teeth chatter as I swim along the icy bank. The lake bed drops off precipitously from the shore, plunging into a yawning blackness so complete that it's impossible to see what might be lurking right beneath me.

Conri and Evander's stories of this lake fill my mind. Visions of ghosts and beasts plunged beneath its surface to a haunted, watery grave accompany the thoughts, prompting me to swim even faster. The pace keeps my blood moving and some sense of feeling in my limbs. Though my toes and fingers are almost completely numb.

Still, we swim on.

The magic of the lake makes the water heavy and potent. Our ripples don't reach much farther than ourselves. The splashes are muted. Both sound and sight are dulled from any lykin that could glance this way. I hope that whatever magic is in the water will also help hide our tracks and cover our scent when we finally emerge.

Aurora drags herself onto the distant shore. I drag my waterlogged boots up with heavy steps, turning back to see how far we've come. It's a far distance that we've swum around. We're nearly at the edge of Den. I can see where the silvery trees stop on the ridge high above. The sun has moved through the sky, dipping a bit lower.

"We need to keep going." I reach out a hand to Aurora.

"A moment." She pants, staring up at the sky. "I truly hate this place."

"Do you know what happened here?" I ask, continuing to scan the shores for any signs of lykin. I'll give her the answer before forcing her to move. "You've been around long enough that you would know those early times, right?" It's hard for me to speak, too. But I fight to get my breathing back under control.

"Vaguely. The world was very young then. And I didn't pay much attention to mortals." She stares up at the sky, as if remembering looking down upon the world in those early years. I step into Aurora's field of view and hold out my hand. She stares at it for another few breaths. "Should we stay here tonight? Use the water to our advantage? The banks get steep here…we could find a sheltered, out-of-the-way spot."

"No." I shake my head. The question is genuine enough that I know it's not just exhaustion talking. "It impacts our magic as much as the lykin's." I say "our" but I'm not completely sure if it has any effect on my magic. I do know, however, that it seems to have some impact on Aurora's. "We can't risk being caught at all, but especially not with diminished powers. Moreover, there's the town of Holfast not far from here. Conri will likely have them mobilize first on the roads—watching for us. We need to get across the main road and to the woods before they have a chance to establish proper patrols."

Aurora sits with a nod. She's lived with the lykin long enough to know their ways and all the places I'm mentioning. "Our best bet is through the forest," she says, repeating what we had all agreed upon in the grove.

"With luck, we'll make it before the moon is high." I hold my hand out to her again. It trembles as it hovers in the air.

She stares at it for a moment. "Are you scared?"

"Of course I am." I know what Conri can do—what he *will* do if we're caught. I am scared for Evander, who is back there with the wolf king, trying to buy us time, trying to navigate the first to be sent out for the woods since he is the one who "knows them best." He was the one who showed me the paths and could suspect where I might go. He'll have the rest of them go to the road and patrol the forest's edge while he escapes to meet us. "I'm also freezing."

"The water is never much warmer than that, winter or summer. But the farther we get from the northern tundra and scars of the ancient battles, the better we'll feel." Aurora takes my hand and I help her up.

"Once more into the water, then we run again."

Dripping wet, we scramble up the steep bank of the hills that lead to the Lykin Plains. We stay low until I have a chance to stand and scan the horizon for signs of movement. The breezes across the grasses trick my eyes three times, causing me to suck in my breath and drop to the ground. But when I dare to stand again, I don't see movement in the same place twice.

"All right, Mary." I kneel to meet the marigold that buds up, turning its petals toward me. "I need your help." I'm leveraging every spirit I have. And none are more loyal than Folost and Mary. "Track ahead of us—we're going to the forest. Warn us if there are any patrols or lykin ahead."

The flower folds back into the earth and then a single one appears beyond where the first was. I stand and approach it. The second flower collapses back under the soil and a third pops up.

"Just ahead, not behind?" Aurora asks.

"We know they're coming from behind. And if they catch up to us, no amount of warning will help us." Though I still have Folost and Devlan I could try and summon, if we had to fight… But my preference is to avoid combat. Not just because I know I am no trained fighter. But also because I still feel Grandma's teaching in my marrow.

The spirits are here to help us—to join our mortal souls with this world. They are stewards of the old gods, their first loyal subjects. Not tools or weapons.

"Right." Aurora nods and looks back toward Den. The silver trees still seem alarmingly close. "Lead on, then."

I follow the path that was seared into my memory, but also the path that Mary leads us on with every bud and bloom. We start off trying to jog at a steady pace, but are eventually forced to slow into a fast walk. Twilight is hazy in the fog of the plains when a line of marigolds stretches before us. I drop instantly, bringing Aurora down with me. Bellies against the grass, we don't move—we hardly breathe—and simply listen.

"…speak to the messenger?" an unfamiliar male voice asks.

"Of course not," a woman scoffs. "I'm not high enough in the pack for that."

"We're looking for a human though?"

"I guess his bride got cold feet." It is clear that the woman thinks my mental state is questionable for not eagerly jumping at the opportunity to marry Conri.

"What else can you expect from a fangless human?"

The voices draw near and swing past. Judging from the sound of boots on hard earth, we're right near the road Evander pointed out to me on our path to Den. I close my eyes and slowly suck in a breath, holding it until their footsteps and voices disappear completely.

Opening my eyes, I meet Aurora's waiting gaze. I give a slow nod. She knows to be even more careful now. Slow and steady. No sudden movements that could make noise. And no talking.

The line of marigolds sinks back into the earth. A single one appears ahead. Safe again…for now.

We move between patrols, crossing the hard-packed earth that's more of a glorified path than a road, and into the tall grasses beyond. I stay bent over and hunched, trying to crawl more than walk so that my head remains below the tips of the tall grasses. But as the land slopes down into the woods darkened with night, my feet begin to quicken their pace. I find energy I didn't know I still had, dredged by hope.

The moment we cross under the boughs of the trees, magic sizzles around my left ring finger. I pick up the invisible thread I laid previously in an instant and follow it like a tether deeper and deeper into the forest. The moon is still two weeks from full, but I don't need much light to see by. I'm drawn by my senses.

"Faelyn." Aurora's voice is distant. It isn't until she grabs my hand that I'm fully aware of her whisper. "Faelyn, we need to rest."

"No," I say restlessly, "We have to keep going until dawn."

"You're shaking. Your lips are blue." She tugs on my hand as if she's pulling my mind back into my body, making me aware of the chill that has soaked through my clothes and into my bones. "We need to get you warm."

"Being warm won't matter if Conri catches us." I shake my head. "And we can't risk a fire tonight. Not this close."

Aurora purses her lips then looks behind us. There's nothing there. There hasn't been for hours. "All right, we don't stop for the night, but we do rest for a little. And you call on Folost; if Conri is close enough to see him, then we've bigger problems."

"Deal. There's a shelter not far from here." I lead us deeper into the woods, angling away from Holfast and toward one of the first ruins Evander and I passed.

The collapsed house feels more like a wooden cave on the inside. It's little more than a nook for us to tuck into. But it gets us out of sight and will hide Folost's flame. I take the scrap of brick that is his anchor from my bag, calling him to us. I swear I can see worry in his golden eyes as I cradle him in my frozen fingers. Aurora leans against me, snuggling close. Between her and Folost, warmth gains purchase in me once more.

I let out a soft sigh. "What was it like?" I whisper. "When you did this on your own."

"Scarier," she readily admits. "I was alone for the first time in centuries. It was as freeing as it was terrifying."

"I'm glad I could be some comfort, then," I say sincerely.

"You and Evander…" She draws her knees to her chest and rests her chin on them. "The first people I could consider friends in years." Aurora laughs softly. "You make me remember why I fell in love with a mortal in the first place. You almost make it hard to leave this world."

Folost seems to lean toward her as his little flame hovers over the stone I still hold above my lap.

"Let's hope not." I stare at the small flame. If I look at Aurora, emotions might take me by the throat. "You're not made for this world—not as you are presently. We must put you back in your rightful place, Aurora. You deserve your power, all of it. To be whole and free."

"I know. But I'll come and visit you." That simple statement draws my attention to her. Aurora stares out into the dark forest.

"What?" I breathe.

She brings her eyes to me with a playful quirk of her lips. "You've interacted with spirits for months here in Midscape and yet you seem surprised? You're right, I wouldn't be as I am now, but I could visit you at first moonlight. I could stroll with you in Den, jumping from beam to beam that pierces the canopies."

"And if I'm back in the Natural World?"

"The moon also rises in the Natural World. It might be harder for my magic to sustain there, but it would not kill me to pay a visit now and again." She pauses. "Do you honestly think you will go back?"

"I don't know," I admit. So much depends on how gaining Aurora's freedom goes. "Would I be able to understand you, then?" I stare at Folost, thinking of how limited our communication was before Aurora's power. When I return the magic in me to her, I'll no longer speak the language of the spirits. Unless…somehow I've learned it after all this time?

Judging from her silence, I probably haven't.

"We will have to see," she admits. "But there are many ways to communicate and only one involves words. You have understood me from the moment we met. I doubt anything will change that."

A smile curves my lips. It's sincere and sad. "Once all this is over, I'd like to see you again. I don't want it to be goodbye between us."

"Then it will be so."

The declaration hangs in the air and we spend a moment sitting shoulder to shoulder, enjoying the comfortable silence and reassurance that the other will be there.

"So much of my life was spent with the love of my family—the love of a soulmate," I whisper. "I never realized how good it felt to have the love of a friend." It is a different balm to the loneliness I felt and feared. One I wish I'd had years sooner.

"That is a lesson we both learned." Aurora tilts her face to the sky. "As long as the moon shines, Faelyn, you will never be alone."

My chest squeezes and I hang my head a moment as the emotions weigh on me. I shift my grip on Folost. Everything I ever wanted is in my grasp. Now I have to make sure no one will take it from me. Ever.

"We should get going again. Thank you, Folost." I dismiss my fiery little friend, pocketing his scrap of brick. Aurora stands also and we begin moving through the woods.

There's no more running. We walk with determination and comfortable silence. But I'm constantly straining my hearing. Aurora's attention continues to dart around, looking for potential threats.

That's why we both glance behind us at the same time the moment we hear the rustle of trees and fallen branches. The heavy footfalls of a wolf's paws are noticeable in an instant. I step in front of Aurora and grab for the brick, ready to call Folost. To fight the only way I know how.

"If this isn't—"

"I'm not leaving you." Aurora knows what I'm going to say before I do. "We're doing this together, Faelyn. Until the very end."

Please, my heart begs, *Please be him.*

A dark wolf cuts through a beam of moonlight. A flash of its silver eyes, locking with mine. I inhale sharply and exhale a slight squeak of emotion.

Evander.

forty-three

UPON SEEING US, EVANDER RUNS EVEN FASTER. He's at us in an instant, leaping and changing his form midair. He lands heavily on two feet and takes three steps to close the remaining gap between us. I don't remember opening my arms for him, but clearly I did, because he crashes into me, pulling me up into his crushing embrace. I squeeze him just as tightly, bury my face in the crook of his neck, and inhale his scent.

"You made it," I breathe. Relief relaxes every muscle that was holding me upright. I lean into him for support, head spinning. "You're really here."

"I told you I would come." Evander pulls away, smoothing my hair away from my face. It's gone wild from the swim and the run. Sticks and mud probably cling to me as they do to him. Yet, I'm certain we've never looked more beautiful to one another. "Nothing will keep me from you ever again."

"Conri?" Aurora asks, bringing me back to reality. I ease away from Evander, waiting for his response. The severe expression that furrows his brow and fear that fills his eyes—that he tries to hide but I see with clarity anyway—doesn't give me much confidence.

"He's coming. I managed to convince him that you'd probably be heading back across the Fade since you learned the name of the spirit of the Fade when we came across."

"How did you do that while also managing to convince him to let you come here?" Aurora folds her arms. It could come off as skeptical of Evander, if I didn't know better. She's afraid.

"He couldn't be in two places at once. And he wants to be the one to find you." Evander doesn't have to expand on what it would mean if Conri did. The grit to his tone says enough. "So, that being the case, I encouraged him to go to the place you most likely were. But we also couldn't rule out this possibility."

"Send you as his right hand," I finish. Evander nods. "You're absolutely certain he went toward the Fade?"

"I broke away from the rest of the pack but waited just beneath the ridge for a while. No one followed."

"We should still move quickly," I say. I can't shake the feeling that Conri might be coming for us both. I realize I might carry that feeling forever. Even when Aurora is reunited with her power, he will always hunt me, as the woman who took her from him—who took his power. If he breathes, I'll probably never be truly safe. "The faster we get out of lykin territory, the better."

"Should we go into the mountains?" Aurora looks toward their frosty peaks, ghostly in the last dregs of moonlight against a lightening sky. "Conri wouldn't dare follow there. He wouldn't even think to look."

"He wouldn't think to look because he would, rightly, assume that we wouldn't dare go there." Evander shakes his head and frowns up at the mountains. I wonder if he's remembering the stories his father told him of the monstrous vampir they hunted. "The passes through the mountains are long lost, and who knows what vampir might still be lurking. It's safer to stay in the forest."

"Then let's keep going." I step away, beginning to walk.

"It'll be faster if you both ride," Evander says.

I pause. "Both of us?"

"Wouldn't we be too much of a burden for you?" Aurora is as skeptical as I am.

Evander chuckles and puts his hands on his hips, flexing the broad muscles of his shoulders and back. "You don't think all this is just for show, do you?"

Before we can object again, he transforms, trotting over and sinking to the ground. Aurora and I exchange a look and a shrug. I mount in front, Aurora behind me. It is tight with both of us astride. But there is enough room.

Evander stands. With two of us, he can't run at full pace. But he is right about moving faster than we would on foot.

I grip his fur and cast one more worried look over my shoulder, past Aurora. There's no sign of Conri or any other lykin. Which means I need to focus on what's ahead.

The sooner we see the great walls of the elves, the better.

Evander keeps his pace past the hours of dawn bleeding across the sky. I am blinking away fire from my eyes. My lids have never felt heavier.

Finally, he sags to the ground by another ruin of his former kin and Aurora and I dismount quite ungracefully. We three drag our feet into the structure. I think it's the last one before we'll be relying on my own huts. If we move too quickly to need them, then all the better.

The collapsed house has created a sort of lean-to against the tree, supported as much by the moss and tangling vines as the trunk itself. Evander hovers in the opening as Aurora and I collapse.

"Evander?"

"I'm going to keep watch." His eyes scan the woods for any signs of trouble.

"I'm sure it's all right. We haven't seen anyone all night." My exhaustion must be wearing down my better sense because I can't believe those words came out of my mouth after the fear that has gripped me for hours.

"I'll keep watch." He kneels next to me and presses his lips into my forehead. "Sleep, love."

"We should keep moving again soon." Aurora yawns, resting her shoulder and temple against the tree trunk. Even as she says that, her lids are going heavy.

"I'll sleep two hours, and then wake me. You can get two hours after," I say. Evander doesn't argue and simply nods.

The two hours pass in an instant. But the moment Evander shakes my shoulder, I am alert. After whispering that all is well, we trade places and I keep a vigilant watch over the woods.

In the daylight, they're as idyllic as I remember. Sunlight filters through the canopy, playing on ferns and dancing with butterflies. It's hard to imagine these woods as a place for violence or danger. But I know all too well how deceiving looks can be. How easily something sinister can hide beneath the veil of beauty.

After another two hours, Aurora and I are on Evander's back again. We keep moving.

I can feel the invisible thread that guides me through the woods. Through the trees, I can vaguely sense its origin. We're not that far from the last town of the lykin. Another day, another night of brief sleep and tired eyes watching out.

"We're almost to the forest's edge," I say optimistically.

It's late in the afternoon and I've otherwise lost track of the days and hours. All that I can focus on is getting out. Pushing through and escaping this nightmare.

"Truly?" Aurora shifts behind me, as if to get a better look.

"The final town of the lykin—the one shared with the vampir—will come into view soon," I tell her. "From there, we're out of the woods."

"And less protected."

"But out of lykin territory."

"Into a no-man's-land where no king rules that would stop Conri's pursuit of us." Her words are grave and exhaustion has me almost snapping at her for the pessimism. But I know she's right. And the worry comes from a good place.

"We aren't safe until we're behind the wall of the elves," I agree.

"*If* the elves agree to help us." She leans heavier against me.

"They will," I insist.

"How can you be so confident?"

I shift my grip on Evander, worried that my instinct on the matter will make me sound foolish. "Their queen, she's a witch like me—a human in a world that wasn't made for her. And the Elf King is from the line of first kings in this world, is he not?" I try to remember everything I've learned of Midscape over the past months.

"He is. His forefathers made both the Veil and, later, the Fade," Aurora admits.

"Then he'll know your importance. He won't turn his back on helping you." It's the same reasoning Evander gave me weeks ago when we were last in the woods. The logic our entire escape is pinned upon.

Aurora rests her cheek against my shoulder with a small sigh. "I am glad we met, Faelyn. I forgot what it was like to be so optimistic."

"No, you didn't." I categorically object to her sentiment. "You were the one to escape first. That meant you believed there could be a better future. You had hope. And what is hope if not the natural conclusion of optimism?"

She just hums, rather than wording a response.

A smile cracks my lips as the town comes into view through the trees. But the expression immediately drops as a shadow moves in front of the buildings. Then several more.

Evander stops and snarls.

The figures were wolflike, but some change into men and women. There are ten of them. But I suspect there are many, many more than that in the woods around us.

"Hope?" Conri's voice carries through the forest that suddenly seems to hold its breath. He steps forward, emerging from shadow and into a beam of sunlight that makes his usually softer features seem harsh. Angled. Dangerous. He holds out his arms. "Behold, your king, your hope. The best you can hope for is that he is merciful." Even though we're too far for me to see the details of his face, Conri angles his head slightly. I know he's looking down at me, his mouth twisted in disgust. I can feel it. "So, if I were you, I'd start begging. Now."

forty-four

THERE ARE TWO OPTIONS: PLEAD OR RUN.

Evander makes the choice.

He surges forward and the trees blur around us. I grip his fur as Aurora and I are nearly thrown off in the rush. Aurora's arms squeeze my waist, causing me to hold on even tighter. I'm sure I'm hurting him, but I can't ease my grip. If I do, we're liable to be thrown. He's already snarling and barking—practically roaring—as he charges toward the men and women in the town.

"Fine. The hard way, then." Conri rolls his shoulders and lunges, changing into his wolf form as well. The other lykin that never abandoned their beastly forms charge in.

"Evander!" I can't help but shout, though I don't know what I'm asking him to do. The opportunity to try and make excuses—to spin this in our favor—left the moment he decided to run for the edge of the lykin's territory. But what is he thinking we're going to do? We're not safe just because we're out of lykin territory. With no king or queen controlling it, Conri will still give chase. We're not safe until we're in the land of the elves, and that could be an entire day, perhaps two.

Horror descends upon me with a sickening chill. *This is futile.*

"Faelyn!" Aurora shouts as well. I feel her head move, looking at the wolves closing in all around in a panic.

I have to do something. I release Evander's fur to take Aurora's hand, asking without words, apologizing with a squeeze. I'm going to need her power once more. The spirit was summoned too recently.

"Brundil!" I have no command. No etiquette or specific desire. But the spirit of earth comes anyway, manifesting as action, rather than a humanoid form, no doubt saving her power. The ground cracks and rumbles around us, stretching open save for a bridge of stone that Evander runs along. A bridge that connects us to the town.

Conri scrambles along with his knights, trying to find purchase on the slipping moss and soil. Leaves and dead underbrush sink like a waterfall, carrying the lykin with the tide. Many don't make it out, falling into the yawning abyss that has opened wide enough to consume whole trees. But Conri is able to scramble up. The wolf king bounces off those falling trees to solid land, angling himself toward us as we plunge into the ruins of the town.

There's no water around. I try and fumble for my bag. I can get Folost and then—

Evander dodges. A wolf comes from the left, snarling and snapping. The movement has me reaching for his fur once more so I'm not thrown. At the cost of…

"Folost!" I scream, looking behind me at the brick shard that bounces among the grasses. It sparks, igniting a small fire, but does little more than that.

What else can I do? I close my eyes and rack my mind for spirits. I could try Brundil again, but she already expended so much energy.

But she's all we have.

I suck in a breath and it is forced out as Aurora and I are thrown off Evander's back. We tumble, cast apart. I dig my fingertips into the ground, trying to find purchase to slow my roll. Drawing my knees under me, I force myself to stand, ignoring the pain in my joints and the blood scattered across the ground from superficial wounds and scrapes.

Conri and Evander are a tumbleweed of fur and snarls. Just when one gets the upper hand, the other makes a snap. The flow changes. I notice other wolves—Conri's loyal knights—beginning to scramble out of the hole Brundil made. Aurora's hand closes around mine.

"Faelyn," she whispers, my name taut with pain and fear. There's a question in there, too. One I've been asking every second that's ticked on and don't have an answer for.

What are we going to do?

Evander is thrown. I almost let out a shout, grabbing for my chest, as if I could take my heart in my hands to protect it from what I'm seeing. From the images that flash before my mind at twice the speed of reality of Conri tearing out Evander's throat.

Evander twists midair, landing as a man on his hands and feet.

"Faelyn, run." He looks my way and I know what he's really saying. *Leave me; I'll buy you time.*

"No," I whisper.

"Run!" He changes back into his wolf form just in time to lock claws with Conri again.

"Faelyn?" Aurora says.

I can't. I can't leave him. I finally found him after all this time. My heart was just put back together and it's breaking again. There has to be a way for all three of us to make it out of here. Something I can do. A spirit? *Something!*

"Faelyn!" Aurora shouts, drawing close as the other wolves gather.

I let out a cry of pain, as if it's my flesh Conri's claws are sinking into. Squeezing Aurora's fingers with all my might, I turn.

I love him more than every spirit that walks the earth. I love him with all I am and all I could be. And it's because I love him that I will respect his wish, even if doing so inflicts a wound on my heart worse than any I have ever known before.

"Are you sure?" Aurora pants as we begin to sprint toward the center of town.

No. I'm not. I've never been less sure of anything in my life. I'm leaving my soulmate behind. How could I be sure about anything involving that?

"Stop." Conri's voice is chilling. He doesn't shout after us. It's not full of anger or rage. And that's why I skid to a halt.

The world blurs as I swing my head around, looking back. Everything comes into focus on Evander. I thought the other wolves would come after Aurora and me. But they didn't. They went for him. Two wolves have his arms. Conri has a fist of Evander's hair. His perfect, dark, silken hair that I ran my fingers through countless times…

Conri gives words to the threat that is already painfully clear. "Run and he dies."

Aurora's grip slackens on mine. In my periphery, I can see her looking between us.

"It's all right," she whispers, even though she's still slowly stepping backward, as if we might still run. "They were going to get us anyway." The words are an absolution. They're forgiveness for the pull of my heart despite my best efforts.

Conri chuckles, low and sinister. "I knew you'd stop. Just like I knew that if I let him go off on his own…he'd lead me right to you."

"What?" I breathe.

"You really take me for a fool, don't you?" Conri glares at me. "You think I didn't know? That I couldn't puzzle it out?" I open and close my mouth. He continues in the wake of my speechlessness. "A witch from that pathetic little corner of the Natural World I found him and his father rotting in. A place where witches have been for years. A woman that completely changed my knight's actions from the moment he laid eyes on her. Oh, I saw it from the start. And then when you smelled like nothing after being around him? Sweet Faelyn, no one smells like *nothing*."

My spell worked far, far too well. Here I thought I was clever, and all the while it was the proof Conri needed.

"Actions of a woman who had everything to hide."

"Let them go," Evander snarls.

Conri jerks his fist up, like Evander is nothing more than a puppet. He's going to rip Evander's hair out by the roots. "You are in no place to negotiate," Conri growls into Evander's face. "And you must think I've lost my mind if I would let my moon spirit go."

"Don't hurt him, please." My request brings Conri's attention back to me.

"And what makes you think that you have any leverage to ask me anything?" He snarls. "Moreover, why would I keep the man you love alive?"

"Because of leverage. Keep him alive, chained, and I'll do as you want. I won't run. I won't fight. I'll be your bride." The words are hard to say. But I force myself to say them anyway. *As long as we're breathing, there's a chance for us to be together*. That's what Evander told me in the grove as we sat, professing love in ways we'd only ever once dreamed of. He endured years of pain, for me. I will keep breathing, for him. We will both endure with our only sustenance being hope.

"As long as you have her power, I have you under my control." Conri shrugs.

"Faelyn and I made a pact," Aurora speaks up. Her hand is still wrapped around mine. "Death is better than coming back with you."

"You wouldn't." Conri's grip slackens some with horror.

"I have lived a long, *long* time," Aurora whispers. Her voice is as cold as a winter's gale. As lifeless as bleached bone. "I have watched kings rise and fall. I have fought for freedom and lost. Now, for the first time, I have the opportunity to end it." She grabs me. In one motion she digs into my bag and pulls out the small knife I use for my threads. Aurora yanks me to her and presses the blade to my throat. I gasp as its point draws a bead of blood. It's a small blade, but it doesn't take much when pressed against the bulging vein of the neck. "What makes you think I wouldn't take it? With or without her willingness?"

"Aurora?" I hide her name in a gasp. Not daring to ask another question.

She says nothing.

"All right. All right." Conri releases Evander with a shove. Aurora's grip slackens on me. "Then here's what's going to happen. We're all going back to Den. We're all going to pretend this never happened, and things will go back to the way they were." He locks eyes with me. "Tomorrow, come moonrise, you and I will be wed."

"But the full moon—" one of his knights begins to object.

"Damn the moon! Enough waiting and excuses—I will have my power!" Conri roars, stomping over to me. Aurora's grip slackens. She backs away as he grows near, releasing me so Conri can yank me into his grasp. The wolf king looks down at me with rage. Hunger. Hate. "And let it never be uttered that I am not merciful. I am far more than the likes of you ever deserved."

forty-five

DEN IS COLDER THAN I REMEMBER ON OUR RETURN.

I am deafened by the oppressive silence on the long ride back. Evander has been forced to ride in his human form. I don't know enough about the ways of the lykin to be sure, but it feels like a slight against him. He is on the back of an alpha to my left. They bound his hands with heavy rope that simmers with magic that I can only assume is intended to keep him from changing shape. Aurora rides on another alpha to my right. And I am in the middle, on Conri.

None of us talk. I try to catch each of their attentions once or twice, but Evander and Aurora both stare forward with dead gazes. Our thoughts overwhelm our hearts, and our mouths. There's no planning or attempting to flee. Conri has us confidently in hand.

Every plan has come to an end. Every hope we'd carried has concluded. There's nothing more…

When we arrive in Den, they waste no time descending on Evander again, overwhelming him in an instant. Evander puts up no fight, manhandled to the ground like a rag doll.

"Co—" I can't even finish formulating his name before the wolf king looms at my side.

"*What?*" he whispers. "Think long and hard about any objections you intend to levy. You have embarrassed me enough for a lifetime. Every single word out of your mouth tries my patience."

"This isn't necessary," I hiss back anyway. "He's doing as you wish."

"For now. I want to ensure it remains that way." The clank of heavy shackles underscores his words.

I am left with nothing to do but watch in horror as they bind Evander, hands and feet. A heavy collar goes around his throat. The weight of all the chains would have a lesser man puddled on the floor. But Evander rises to stand tall as the alphas step away. His stare holds all the defiance and hate in the world, directed solely at Conri.

"Take him to whatever forgotten corner you can find and leave him there to rot," Conri seethes. "Distorting the mind of my future queen against me is crime enough; kidnapping her is inexcusable."

So that's how he's going to try and play off what's happened. I doubt it will work, given what I overheard on the road. But no one is going to question Conri. Even if there's skepticism in their eyes, they keep their mouths shut. Yet again, what the wolf king says is reality. It doesn't matter how apparent the truth is.

"He can't escape. Must you—"

"Silence, bitch," Conri hisses at me. "You will go to the chambers and ready yourself for our union come moonrise. I'll entertain no other delays or objections. He's only alive because you are going to comply peacefully and quietly. If you fail to keep up your end of the bargain, I might fail to keep up mine."

I press my lips into a line and glare up at him. Then I force a smile as he slips his arm around my waist, guiding us back to his chambers. Aurora is behind, flanked by two knights.

"Ready yourselves," Conri says gruffly, practically throwing me into the room when we arrive. I stumble, but manage not to fall. "I'll return at twilight." With one more look of disgust, he leaves. To my surprise, the knights follow him. I wonder if he's trying to tempt us into fleeing. If the vicious side of him wants the opportunity to hunt us down once and for all.

My eyes swing from the entrance to Aurora. She stands at the edge of the divot before the hearth, staring into the flames, as still as a statue.

"Aurora…"

She moves rather than responding or even looking my way, stepping forward and down into the plush sitting area. Her attention remains fixed on the flames. Even as I slowly approach. Even as I sit next to her.

"Did you mean it?" I finally ask. The question is hard to word. Luckily, I don't have to elaborate, she knows what I'm referring to.

"I did." There's a lifelessness to the words. Never have I seen her look so heavy. So absent of any kind of spark. I want to take her hand, but I'm not sure if it would be welcome. "But, also, I didn't." She's the one to make a move for my fingers, grabbing them. "I couldn't hurt you, Faelyn. I wouldn't. You've done nothing wrong and have only tried to help me at every turn. But what I said about being ready to leave this form, one way or another…that was sincere."

"Aurora—"

She lifts her hand, stopping me with her open palm. "Don't try to placate me, or tell me it will be all right. I've walked several lifetimes. More than. I have seen this world and all its beauties; I have been subjected to its endless font of cruelties. Mortal life has become a sickness, one that I cannot free myself from, and can no longer bear… especially without hope of liberation. But I am not, and will not be, like the monsters that have kept me captive for centuries. I wouldn't hurt you just because it might benefit me."

I sigh and stare into the flames. The weight of her truth is crushing. And I don't wish to insult or minimize the trauma she's endured.

"I cannot imagine what you must feel," I whisper. "But I still have hope that we can free you." She scoffs softly. But a small smile curls her lips, optimistic even so. Or perhaps just amused by my foolishness. "However, if there comes a time where we feel that all options have been exhausted…that all hope for both of us to escape Conri is gone… then…I will help you be free."

Her brows shoot up, attention swinging in my direction. "Faelyn—"

"My turn to stop you." I grin slightly. "I don't say this lightly, nor would such a decision ever be. You might think my optimism and hope unyielding—and I want it to be—but I also live in the real world. There are things that I do not know if I can stomach, either." Things that I could face all too soon.

"Do you really think we'll get out of this, still?" She looks back to the fire, as if the answer lies somewhere within the flames.

"I'm going to try."

"How?"

"I don't know yet," I admit. "But I can do something none of them can: talk to spirits. And a great wolf spirit is going to be the one to perform the union. Perhaps I can barter with him?"

Aurora snorts. "He is a *brute*. As uncaring and vicious as any of the kings that rule on his behalf."

"Odd to see you speaking ill of a spirit."

"I do so rarely. But Ulfryk is a rare breed deserving of it."

"Could he have helped you?"

She sighs, shoulders sagging some. "Probably not…but I resent him anyway for not trying. He holds the lykin's magic in his hands. It is his doing that gives them their wolf shapes. Surely, he could've done something to coerce them."

The sentiment gives my thoughts surrounding the spirit new clarity. I'm going to have to be either as vicious as this wolf is or more cunning. But I cannot appeal to kindness.

"Would Evander know anything?" I ask.

"I don't know, we've never spoken of it together. Frankly, I never spoke much with him before he helped me. But he showed up that night of the first dark moon following the Blood Moon with the ring and told me to go… I never even knew he noticed my suffering." Her voice becomes soft, and sad. "It's clear you two are made of the same essence. Both of you are good to your cores."

I smile and nod. The mention of Evander has my chest squeezing my heart. I inhale slowly, trying to alleviate some of the pressure. It hardly works.

"Go to him," Aurora says.

I blink back to reality. "But…"

"Conri clearly doesn't care." She motions to the opening. "If he did, he wouldn't have left us without knights."

"I thought the same thing—wondered if he was almost daring us to leave again."

"To give him an excuse," Aurora adds bitterly.

"Just going to Evander won't be an excuse?"

"Does it matter if it is?" She shrugs. "How much further can we push him? How much do you care about what the cost might be?"

As long as Evander breathes, I care a little. And that's the only thought that keeps me from moving away. I don't want to be the cause of Conri deciding he's not worth being kept alive.

But…if we're all teetering at the edge of the abyss of death, does it really matter? What's one more risk? And it'd be worth it to see him again, one last time before Conri takes my hand…

"You truly don't mind?"

"I told you to." She grins slightly. "If Conri returns—which I doubt he will, but if he does—I'll make some kind of excuse. Or not."

"Don't bother. You're right, what does it matter now?" I stand and make my way out of the room, leaving Aurora to the fire and her thoughts.

In the passageway, I pause and start to the left. To the right is the grove; there are no other offshoots on the way there. I keep a slow pace, listening and looking. It's not quite sneaking, as I don't feel the need to stay perfectly hidden. But I also don't want to be unaware and caught off guard.

At least Bardulf is dead, this would be a nightmare if he were still around.

Farther down the passage, but not quite at the great hall, I come to a crossroads. Two other tunnels stretch in opposite directions. One has a sliver of pale light—sunlight. The other tunnel is lit dimly by some kind of flame I can't see, judging from the orange glow.

That's the direction I go in. Conri wouldn't leave Evander anywhere with sunlight, or fresh air. As the tunnel slopes down, I'm more and more sure of my decision until there's a fork in the path.

Right, or left? I fidget, debating. *Left.* I've never been surer of anything than that left is the right way. I'm so sure that I'm forced to pause and examine the instinct.

That's when I realize that I'm spinning the thread that Evander tied around my left ring finger. I rub the already familiar fibers. It's become so much a part of me in such a short time that I hardly notice it's there. I wonder if it's simply warm from my touch, or if by some kind of magic.

I bring my hand to my face, whispering into the back of my finger, my lips brushing over the threads, "Take me to him."

From then on, I walk without thought. I feel the tug of a power not of my weaving, but a thread stronger than any I've ever known. A pull that's both undeniable and fearsome, but gentle and welcome. Well-known. Familiar.

Rounding a final corner, I reach a small, rough-hewn room. There are no guards. Only Evander. One arm is chained to one wall, the other to the opposite. He hasn't been given enough slack to even sit and is slumped against the tension of the chains. The shackles around his legs remain, also pinned to the wall behind him.

"Evander."

"Faelyn," he says nearly in unison.

Our names are relief given sound. Sorrow and joy encapsulated on the other's tongue. The fragile threads that strung together my composure snap. I run to him. My hands are on his face, holding it to mine. His skin is marred with cuts and bruises. Crusted blood flakes to the ground like autumn leaves.

"What have they done to you?" I whisper and press my brow against his.

"I've endured worse."

"That doesn't make me feel better." I exhale a somewhat bitter and incredulous laugh. How could he be reassuring me at a time like this? When he's the one bleeding and chained to a wall?

I release him and go for the chains. The shackles are locked tight. Getting into them will be a problem. Perhaps I could go and see if I could find the key? But, knowing Conri, he would be keeping it on his person at all times right now. Maybe I could rip the shackles from the wall with Brundil's help? If she has the strength to come…which I doubt, after all I asked. Perhaps Folost could call upon his fiery companion and we could melt through them? If I can still call on Folost… Conri didn't give me an opportunity to collect his brick. But if there's any spirit I could summon by instinct alone…

"Faelyn," Evander says calmly.

"What?" I cease my inspection of his wrist to return my attention to his face. His expression is calm. Resigned. It elicits one word from me: "No."

Evander chuckles. "Yes."

"No," I insist. "I'm not letting you give up."

"It's not 'giving up,'" he says gently. "Even if you freed me, I wouldn't run."

"But…" I don't remember walking back to him, but I stand before him once more, my hands on his hips, stabilizing myself in this moment.

"I won't leave you ever again." Evander dips his head as best he can, chained as he is, to catch my gaze. "I swore it to you."

"What if I want you to go?"

"This might be one time that I dare to disregard that wish. Unless it's what you truly desire?"

My fingertips trail up his sides, palms pressing into his chest to glide up to his shoulders and grip them, massaging the thick muscle there. His eyes flutter closed with a sigh and I relish this small amount of comfort that I can offer him. It's not enough. Not nearly enough. But it's something, and all I want in this moment is to bring him comfort and assurance.

"It is what I desire. But also not what I desire," I admit to myself and him. "My heart is knotted."

"Then allow me to untie it." He opens his eyes again. "I do not wish to leave you. I will spend forever with you, whether forever is years, or one last night. If forever is free, or chained."

My hands return to cradling his cheeks and I draw his lips to my own quivering ones. I feel his mouth curl into a slight smile and I kiss him again. Frustration vines through me, tangling and rooting deep into desperation. It blooms into haste that manifests as ferocity, deepening the kiss.

"How can you be smiling?" I rasp against his lips, emotion making my voice thick and heavy.

"I am kissing you. How could I not smile?"

I choke out laughter. Smiling now myself. "You are ridiculous."

"Yet you love me all the same."

"And I always will." Another long, tender kiss. I would melt into this man if I could. Dissolve all space between us until we were one being—one soul, fused back as it should be.

"Stay with me a little bit longer?" It's the first time he's sounded desperate since I arrived. The first time I could feel the shroud of death moving through this room. *Hello, old friend, I know you,* my heart whispers as that specter looms over us.

"Of course." As if I could refuse.

"I wish I could hold you." His muscles flex as he strains against the chains. "Take you once more into my arms."

"Let me hold you, then." I wrap my arms around his waist, locking hands on elbows. He is so strong, yet, in this moment, feels as frail as a dove with a broken wing.

I press my cheek against his shoulder and he slumps into me as far as the chains allow. His face buries into the crook of my neck. Evander breathes deeply, exhaling warmth into my flesh.

"Tell me what you imagined all those years ago. If we were to have run away to marry, what it might have been like, looked like…"

I close my eyes and work to dredge up all those memories that I had drowned in the river of pain that had flowed through me following his loss and are now covered with the muck and haze of time. There is no reason for them to bring me agony anymore. All the fantasies I had lying up at night, heart fluttering after time spent with Evander, return in vivid detail. They come back to me like old friends, pleased to return after being shut out for so long.

My words weave images of flowers strung between trees. Of candles lining moss-carpeted grounds. Of a redwood that stretches high above us, connecting us with old gods and new, with spirits of old and with magics modern. How, in that moment, the world comes into focus. We see it all with perfect clarity—the great spinner's wheel that is time and all the threads that bind us together. Our single knot in a great tapestry.

The heaviness of my body slips away and I give in to the fantasy. That long-forgotten dream. Evander is there with me, existing in this place constructed by our hearts and shared wish. He inhales sharply as, in my mind, we come to a stop before the redwood.

His lips move soundlessly against my skin as he recites simple and pure vows to me. And I do the same. We exist beyond our mortal shells. Are more than flesh and bone.

"I love you," he breathes.

"And I love you." I barely have time to utter the words when footsteps sound in the hall, echoing like ominous thunder. I straighten, looking behind my shoulder in fear and panic. My arms are still tight around Evander's waist.

The nightmare that is Conri shatters our perfect dream. He appears, flanked by two knights and an alpha I vaguely recognize as the leader of the first pack.

"I am not surprised." Nor does he sound even mildly upset. A wicked smile curls his lips, as sharp as a sickle. I am the harvest. "Take her."

Fear and misbegotten desire have me clinging even tighter to Evander. It's not time yet, it can't be. Surely it's too early. How long have I been down here?

"A little bit longer." I wish my words were stronger, and without a slight quiver to them.

Evander barely has a chance to say my name—to make a sound—before the knights are upon me. They each take my arms, as they did to Evander earlier, prying me off of him. I try to fight, but I have little strength compared to them.

A heavy sigh has a bloodcurdling quality to it. Conri rounds the knights, positioning himself between me and Evander like the moon to the sun. An unnatural obfuscation—a violation of the laws of nature.

Wordlessly, he raises a hand and brings its back against my cheek with a swift and sharp crack. My head whips to the side and I see stars, supported only by the help of the knights for a moment. I blink, trying to bring the world back into focus.

"You bastard!" Evander roars. "Lay another hand on her and I will flay you where you stand and savor every minute of it!"

Conri looks over his shoulder, nose scrunched in disgust. But his eyes are lifeless. Two hollows void of any emotion. Any sense of mortality or feeling.

"Is this the real you?" He almost purrs the words. "The ferocity hidden behind the bowed head and lowered eyes all those years? I should have killed you from the start."

"Don't..." I say groggily, pulling myself together. Reality is rushing back. "Don't hurt him!"

Conri's hand is like a viper. It whips out and closes around my throat. I croak weakly. His eyes have found emotion again—a singular one, rage. "His life depends on you. On your compliance. And you are trying my patience."

Evander roars behind us. But I can't make out the words. The world has narrowed to Conri and I. To the fist around my throat, quivering with temptation. It would be so easy for him to squeeze and snuff out my whole existence.

As long as I breathe, there is hope.

I might not be able to see it with the tunnel vision closing around my eyes. But I can feel it. I can let it fill my lungs and rush through my blood. Hope will be my defiance.

"What will it be?" Conri growls, pulling my face close.

"Take me to the grove," I say, though the words are ash in my mouth. "And take me as your wife."

"Good." Conri releases me and starts to leave, pausing at the entrance. A wicked glint flashes in his eyes as he looks back to the alpha still waiting. "Take him, too."

"What?" I can't tell if it's Evander or me who says it. The rattling of his chains stops as he ceases to strain against them.

"I want him to watch as I take his woman in soul." Conri slowly walks back, stopping at my side. I resist every urge to step away, even though my muscles scream at me to run. I'm afraid even flinching might give him even more sinister ideas. But my-self control does little good. Conri has skewered us, and now he twists the blade. "Then, I'll force him to watch with the rest as I fill her belly with my seed, her screams a chorus to the great wolf spirit."

Conri's arm slips around my waist but I hardly feel it; my whole body is numb. I am hardly aware of him pulling me from the room, passing the knights and brushing by the alphas who stay behind to tend to Evander. All I hear are the sounds of Evander's shouts and the rattling—endless rattling—of the chains that keep him from me.

forty-six

CONRI TAKES ME BACK TO HIS CHAMBERS. He says nothing of what happened. Nothing at all.

Neither does Aurora. Upon seeing us, she stands from her place at the hearth, eyes darting between us. Her chin dips slightly, brow shading her gaze in an utterly sinister manner. She knows everything without my having to say a word.

She stands there, silent, as Conri calls in women. I can't tell if I don't actually recognize them, or if my mind is too far from the present to place their faces. Even as they touch me, stripping my clothes to expose my skin to the chill of the caves, I continue to stare into the distance—at a singular point that I vow to myself I will one day see:

Evander and me together, underneath a redwood, swearing our fealty to each other before gods old and new. Spirits known and forgotten.

That is the world I place my mind in. A world of light. Of hope. A truth that I know will come to pass because the moment I waver in that conviction, the nightmare begins to close around me, shuttering out my options and smothering my will.

When the women are finished with me, my hair is woven with ribbons, braids pulling half into a basketlike weave. The other half is loose, oiled, and teased into finger-curls. Perfume clouds the air around me with the delicate aroma of the wildflowers that dot the plains. An almost translucent, plain white shift covers my shoulders and arms, extending down to mid-thigh, just above my knees. It does little to fight against the cold, but I don't shiver, I'm far too numb.

But I return to the present in a rush the moment they try and take my cape from me. Take whatever they want, but not my family's legacy and my sole inheritance. Luckily, they don't fight me over my insistence on keeping it.

There's no time to.

I'm being ushered out of the back bedroom. Aurora is waiting with knights. But Conri is nowhere to be seen. We are escorted out and into the passageway. I imagine myself to be a soldier, marching off to war.

A year passes between Conri's room and the entrance to the grove. And yet, somehow it's over in a blink. The grove is lit by dozens of candles that line the pathway down to the grassy clearing.

The packs fill the spaces between the trees. Lykin look on with curious expressions. *Will it really happen? Will our wolf king marry a human?* they seem to ask with their eyes. Alphas have been given the most prime locations, on the lower ridge surrounding the clearing where Conri waits.

He wears a wrap of fur that looks distinctly wolfish. Are they the pelts of actual wolves, or of lykin? The latter thought makes my stomach churn. Such a thing would be akin to wearing a cape made of human skin. *Surely, he would not…* What am I thinking? This is Conri. He *absolutely* would wear the skin of his fallen foes.

The gap between us closes, though I don't have a recollection of walking to him. My feet betray every scream of my heart as they come to a stop at the edge of the large, flat stone he stands upon. Conri extends a hand to me.

I allow him to help me up, adjusting my stance on the boulder that feels more and more like a sacrificial altar than rock. He turns to Aurora next and she takes his hand. Somewhere between Aurora stepping up and her taking her place on Conri's other side, a soft clanking draws my attention.

Evander is here, and the sight of him returns fire to my flesh. Heat fighting against the numbing chill. Conri made good on his sinister design. Evander's chains are held by three knights. More surround him. He's been gagged, a wad of cloth shoved into his mouth and strapped there. Rage furrows his brow and desperation widens his eyes.

Even if we both knew what was about to happen…the moment is nearly unbearable. This is somehow worse than that empty cabin Evander left behind for me to find. Then, the unknown was what tortured me. All that space of nothing that my mind could fill with any explanation. Some worse. Some easier. But all could be banished in time. None of it solid with reality.

This…is happening. It will become a memory that will be forever seared onto our consciousness. There is no escaping what is about to happen. The point of no return for us both. I run my fingers along the edges of my cape, the familiar seaming offering comfort more than protection.

Conri turns to the large boulder—nearly a small cliff—that looms over the grove. As he outstretches both hands, a low wind howls through the trees. But the air is still… *No, not wind.* The lykin themselves howl. Whispers at first. But then louder as Conri raises his hands. When he thrusts his palms skyward, as if to hold the very moon itself aloft, Conri lets out a scream-like howl that the rest of them join with him in.

Then, a voice rises above the rest. It rattles the air in my lungs, leaving me gasping. Even Aurora shifts her stance, widening it, as if bracing herself. The greatest howl of all is the call of the wild itself.

Mist pours over the crest of the ridge, flowing down like a waterfall and pooling into the grove. It races through the trees, sending rivers out toward the Lykin Plains and leaving me to wonder if this is the actual source of the consistently mist-covered grasslands.

Two twilight-gray ears crest the ridge first, followed by eyes as white as the full moon, glowing with unnatural light. The muzzle of the wolf is white, as if the spirit ages with time. He moves slowly, as though every step causes him great pain. For a muscled beast as long as fifty paces, I would expect the ground to tremble under his mighty paws. But he moves without a whisper.

Ulfryk lowers himself to the top of the ridge, paws folding. The spirit manages to look somehow intrigued and yet exhausted at the same time. Even though his eyes lack any kind of irises or pupil, I can feel when his attention lands on me. Punctures me. He sees right through my flesh and bone to Aurora's magic within, and with that stare alone, he could set it to boiling. I am judged and exposed.

The great wolf spirit settles his muzzle on one of his massive paws as he lowers himself to the ground. The air around him seems to shift from intimidating to boredom, and somehow that is even more agitating. As if Aurora and I are not even significant enough for him to care.

"What have you brought before me, king of mortal wolves?" The words are a low grumble in the back of my mind. The great wolf spirit speaks without moving his giant maw.

"It is time for me to take a wife." Conri's answer confirms my suspicion—they can understand this spirit. Perhaps because Ulfryk's magic is within them.

"A human?" The spirit's ears twitch. Once more I sense his eyes on me.

"A human with the power of the moon spirit within her."

"An interesting conundrum."

The notion of begging this spirit for help briefly flashes through my mind. Surely, when presented with a need to help his kind, this spirit wouldn't turn his back, would he? I open my mouth, but close it promptly, remembering what Aurora said. She is still and silent. If she's not making any movements toward seeking help then neither will I. Aurora might be his kin, but the lykin are his children. Ulfryk's loyalties are clear.

"I will make her my bride—in spirit, body, and blood," Conri declares. "Here and now, as your descendant and spiritual heir, I ask you to preside over and bless our union and join our souls."

A low growl, almost like an amused hum, vibrates through the back of my mind. Ulfryk shifts just slightly, but it's enough that I get the sense his gaze is solely on Aurora. Especially when she stands a little taller.

"Is this your doing?" the great wolf asks.

"I might be powerful, brother—perhaps even more powerful than you." Aurora's jab is met with a flash of amusement in the wolf's eyes that could just as easily be read as a warning. "But you know as well as I that not even my powers can touch the work of the gods."

"I would prefer not to delay." Conri's agitation is as apparent as his obliviousness.

There's something amiss. Something that none of us had been calculating for or planning on. It's beginning to crystalize in my mind like the frosted edges of a lake, not quite fully connected. Not solid. *But almost…*

"Wolf king, if it were within my powers to bind your union, I would. But, alas, it is not." The wolf spirit doesn't seem to be particularly distraught about the subject. My perspective of the spirit is shifting, from a malicious image to that of an ancient being that has little care for much of anything. But ambivalence is its own malice.

"What?" The whispered word falls flat from Conri's lips. Heavy. I can almost imagine it toppling off the flattened stone on which we stand. Then, stronger, "What have you done?" He turns to Aurora.

"Did you not hear me? I have done nothing." She folds her arms and looks quite proud.

Conri whirls on me next, rage nearly bubbling over. It's only contained when he looks back to Ulfryk. "Oh, great wolf spirit, why is it not within your powers?" Each word is bitten out, terse and short.

"Because I cannot bind a soul that is already bound," Ulfryk answers plainly. "I cannot give you a mate that has already been claimed."

forty-seven

THE CONNECTION IS MADE IN MY MIND. What Aurora said about Conri's charm not being able to work on me once I accepted my soulmate because there was nothing for it to cling to any longer. About her being able to see our bond from the start.

One soul. Two halves.

I look to Evander and never have I felt so much joy and sorrow at the same time. He truly is everything. All my hopes, fears, wishes, and wants wrapped up into a single man. But for it…

Conri lets out a roar unlike any I have ever heard. Even the very trees of Den seem to tremble. He spins to Aurora, shoulders heaving with ragged breaths.

"You—"

"Did you not hear me? I couldn't do anything that would forge this bond," Aurora snaps back at him.

Conri looks back to me. But I don't have a chance to say anything before his gaze turns to Evander. My heart stops in my chest.

"Kill him," Conri commands to the knights.

"No," I gasp, shock softening the word but not the horror.

Yet no one moves. Evander stands a little taller, rolling back his shoulders. As though he is settling into the mantle of king. For a second, I have a glimpse of the fantasy again—of him ruling, of me at his side.

"I said *kill him*!" Conri's voice quivers slightly.

"He is bound with the power of the moon spirit," Weylyn,

one of the first alphas I met on this journey, says. "That means that, at present, his claim to the crown is as legitimate as yours."

"What?" Conri staggers, aghast.

"We have no king to follow until the matter of succession is handled." Drena's words are as begrudging as the nods of the other alphas, but she says them dutifully anyway. This is their custom and their way.

"She"—Conri thrusts a finger at Aurora—"has long been sworn to me. And she"—that accusing finger turns my way—"is an abomination, an affront to nature. Humans aren't meant to possess the magic of spirits. Their meager manipulations of nature are all they were destined for. You cannot honestly think that…that, *that thing* gives him any claim to our kingdom."

Me. I'm the "thing." It's oddly refreshing to hear him refer to me as he actually feels, rather than with the forced kindness and underhanded manipulation. I don't find myself wounded.

Evander, however, is angered enough on my behalf. He seethes, still silenced by the gag. But his breaths are ragged, as if he's barely keeping himself from screaming. If not for the chains holding him back, I think he'd be halfway to tearing Conri apart with his bare hands.

"There can be only one true king of the alphas. One pack, one king," Weylyn says.

The alphas lower Evander's chains, releasing them. Evander's muscles bulge as he lifts a hand, straining against the weight of the thick shackles, but finding movement where there previously was none.

"Fine. I'll do it myself." There's a murderous intent to Conri's movements. Everything seems to happen slowly. He steps away from me. I go to stop him. He's already out of reach.

"I should have slaughtered you like your father." Conri's words are forged of steel and dipped in the acid of disgust. His hands are balled into quivering fists. "You should never have been allowed to live this long. Once a traitor to the pack, always a traitor."

"It's not his fault!" I shout. Evander might be "free" of the alphas holding him back but he's not in any position to fight, not weighted as he is. Conri doesn't stop. But he does answer me.

"The fault no longer matters. The solution is simple. So simple. What I should have done from the start." Conri's usually composed demeanor is cracking, splintering into a thousand tiny pieces that will never be put back together. They see him now—the whole pack sees him for the desperate and hateful man he really is. Some look surprised, others disgusted, but some are impressed, even pleased.

"Stay away from him!" I sprint over, physically trying to hold Conri back as my mind whirls around the spirits I might call on to help. But every favor I had has been called. Every bit of power exhausted. And given the magic of the mist that crackles against my cape, I suspect this is the domain of the great wolf now. That no others would be able to intervene.

"Off me, traitorous wench!" Conri throws me from him with the care someone casts off a tattered cloak tangled around their body. I land against the ground, already scrambling up. "I will have you—in soul and body. No one, no one will take what is rightfully mine. I am the wolf king!"

"You sound like a petulant child!" Is this even about Aurora's power any longer? Or has it transformed into him massaging his ego? Evander has taken something that Conri sees as belonging to him and now Conri wishes to exert the same force as a toddler would following the loss of a favored toy.

Evander is trying to move, trying to match Conri's steps. But those chains are holding him back and preventing him from changing into his wolf form. There's no way he'll be able to fight as he is. The alphas might be letting the contestation play out, but it's only in show. They clearly do not see Evander as a worthy challenger. I doubt any even want him to be king…except for me.

Without another thought, I begin sprinting. Conri is a blur as I pass him, his shock barely registering. I dash to Weylyn and plow right into him, using the momentum to rattle him—stun him a moment. Lucky for me, lykin men seem to prefer only simple trousers. There are only two pockets and I have two hands shoved into both.

His eyes widen and he lets out a growl as my fingers close around the key that I suspected was there. It was a gamble, but I guessed right. On the way out of the dungeons, Conri brushed past Weylyn. He used that motion to give Weylyn the key to Evander's shackles. Passing on the responsibility of managing him to a trusted alpha.

Before Weylyn can fully react, I spin away and leave him to grab open air where I just was. I rush to Evander, fumbling with the key in my panic.

"Faelyn, get away!" Evander shouts at me.

Conri takes on his wolf shape at the same time as one shackle falls from Evander's wrists. The alphas might not appreciate my interference, but they're not stopping it, either. I move to the other wrist—Conri is bounding forward now on all fours. Behind him is a blur of white.

"Aurora?" I am startled a moment, midway through working on Evander's second chain.

The distraction costs me precious seconds. Conri is upon us. He leaps and Evander pushes me away, reaching up with his free hand to shove Conri aside by the throat as he dodges. Wildly off-balance, the three of us fall to the ground.

I crawl to Evander as Conri recovers.

"Faelyn—"

"You can't fight!" I jam the key in the lock and twist. His other wrist is free. Now for his ankles.

But Conri is already back upon us. It is a dizzying and chaotic mix of hands and arms, bites and snarls. Evander is clearly a better fighter because he manages to keep Conri at bay, even in his human form. But Conri has speed and full mobility.

I try to stay focused on getting Evander's legs free. One down. Evander lets out a scream, the knee of his freed leg bending as he tries to throw Conri.

The wolf king is atop him, claws digging deep into his shoulders. Conri strikes, and strikes, and strikes. There is so much blood. A rain of red splatters in the moss all around.

Leaping, I grab on to Conri's back, trying to pull him off by throwing my weight as Conri goes for another lunge. He has both claws up and I manage to pull him away. The blur of white I saw earlier drifts through my periphery. Conri's claws come down.

An explosion of blood is hot on my face and cheeks. A laugh cut short by a gurgle. A roar ends abruptly.

We land. I manage to twist myself out of the way at the last second so Conri's full weight isn't atop me. But I couldn't get an arm out in time. I'm pinned and so close to every horrifying, gruesome detail.

Shoved through Conri's throat is a familiar dagger. *My hunting knife*. The same one that I…

May I see it? Aurora had said. *I've never been able to hold a weapon before… May I keep it?* The way her eyes had gleamed, much like they are in this moment. The purpose with which she slipped it into the boot I'd gifted her. Was she seeing, then, what she intended now?

The knife is wielded by a trembling hand, coated in blood. Fingers so slick they're already sliding on the grip. Conri's massive paw falls from Aurora's shredded throat. Even as she gasps through blood and shock, she smiles.

"Die, bastard," Aurora rasps and then tumbles off to Conri's opposite side. As still as death.

forty-eight

CONRI'S EYES ARE WIDE. As if, for the first time, he was confronted with death itself—with his own fleeting mortality and the notion that he was not the god-king he so clearly thought he was. Even at the end, frozen forever in his wolfish form, he has never looked so human. For the first time, I see the man in the monster, and I cannot even manage pity. Not when he found that soul far too late.

Not when Aurora is bleeding next to him.

I wrest my arm from underneath Conri, feeling the bones stretch and tendons snap. It aches and my fingers are hard to move. But they do move. Which means I can help.

Do something, Faelyn! I scream at myself, vaulting over Conri in my scramble to get to Aurora. It barely registers that Evander is moving as well. Still slowed by the last chain I hadn't managed to free him of. But much faster than he was.

"Aurora, Aurora please. Hold on." My words are as frantic as my movements. Her throat has been savaged from one side down through her collar. I don't even know where best to apply pressure to try and staunch the bleeding but I press my palm into the loose and bloody flesh anyway. Her eyes flutter and she rasps out a weak breath. I curse in frustration, at the cruelty of fate and the fear of what her injuries might mean for us all.

This body cannot be killed by natural means…to kill me would take a magical act, intent by a mortal hand. Her words return to me as horror settles upon my shoulders.

I reach for my pouch of threads but grab only empty air.

That's right, they stripped me of everything. And I was too tired to fight it. Too weary from the world to protest when they took my strongest, and only, weapon from me.

"I can fix this." My attention darts to the wolves, all standing in shock and horror. "Get my bag of threads." No one moves. "She's dying. Do it now!" I shout with a rage and authority I didn't know myself capable of. One of the women darts away.

"Faelyn…" Aurora croaks.

"Don't try to talk," I command. Evander is at our side. "Hold her throat, stop the bleeding." He does as I ask. I reach for my cape, going for one embroidered shape out of a constellation of many—a heart done in crimson thread, vitality and luck. Bringing it to my teeth, I tear through the thread, frantically ripping at the stitching to pull it out.

She speaks anyway. "I'm sorry."

"Don't apologize. Please don't talk. I can fix you."

"I couldn't…earlier…I couldn't do it earlier. I had to leave the lykin's territory to be free of my vow. To break…to harm him."

"You…" I still as the connection is made in my mind. But then I resume my stitch-ripping with fervor. "You knew that we would probably be caught the night we fled, didn't you?"

"As long…as we made it out of…lykin territory." Her eyes open long enough to meet mine and she gives me a wry smile. "I truly hoped…we would leave. But if we didn't… It had to be me. I had to do it."

This whole time, she was going along with our plans, hoping they worked, that they were good enough to free her. But in the back of her mind, behind it all, she was secretly planning a backup. The hunting knife I gave her—that she kept even though it would be "useless" to her. The push for us to keep going and carry on even as Conri had Evander and she must have known I couldn't ever leave him. Those final moments before Conri took us, Aurora continuing to step backward through that ancient town, creeping to the border of lykin territory. So badly she wanted to be free, I knew that, and I explained her every action with that.

But she also wanted vengeance. And either would be good enough.

My eyes prickle. "You shouldn't have."

"Conri was mine to kill—all of the wolf kings were," she says, loud enough for all to hear, straining her voice against the wounds and against the pressure Evander is placing on her throat. "I started this vow. I had to end it."

The thread free, I carefully place it over her neck, over the wound in a zigzag patten as though I am planning how one might stitch the skin back together.

"Yes, and now that he's gone, we'll go to the home of the sirens." I touch one end of the thread, trying to draw out the power from within me.

Aurora lifts the less damaged of her two arms, gently gripping my fingers. Her touch is little more than a butterfly landing on my flesh. But it stills me.

"There is no time… No mending this."

"No."

"Faelyn, you don't have the power to fix this." The words are said as gently as possible. But oh, how they hurt. How inadequate I feel.

"I can—"

"Only if you draw from my power, and probably still not then."

The other alpha has returned with my sewing kit. She places it by my thigh and promptly backs away. None of the lykin seem to dare encroach on the sacred ground of the grove, still covered in the magic mist of the great wolf spirit.

The great wolf spirit! I look to his perch for help, but he's gone. I don't remember him leaving. *Damn him.* He probably couldn't have lent assistance; this is no doubt beyond his scope of skill. But blaming him deflects some of the pain from myself. The focus of this being my fault, and mine alone.

"Do not risk using my power. You need to take the rest," Aurora finishes.

"What?" I gasp softly. I hear a sharp inhale from Evander at my side. His brow is furrowed, eyes filled with all the sorrows of the world. In his own way, he, too, loved Aurora. If he didn't care for her, he never would've risked everything to free her months ago.

"Do what you did the first night we met. Take my power into you."

"I don't—I can't—that was an accident."

"You clearly have special talent, Faelyn." Aurora smiles weakly. "You can."

"But that was a ring shattering. It's not the same." I blink feverishly. Many times over. Tears are spilling over my lower lids.

"This body is merely a vessel for my power. It is no different than the ring was." Aurora's words are stronger, unfaltering. Which only makes the blood flow faster between Evander's fingers. "If it is destroyed, the power will be freed, it will seek itself out."

"Can I not give you the power in me instead?" I grasp for any idea that doesn't end with what she's suggesting.

"If you could, we would've done it before," she reminds me gently. "Faelyn, I am tired. I have lived a thousand years and do not wish to exist a thousand more in this form."

"What will happen to her if she takes all your power?" Evander's voice is thick and heavy with emotion. But there's a resignation underneath his words that I want to resent him for. I can't believe he would go along with this. In his worry for me, he is giving up on Aurora. "She cannot be a spirit, can she?"

"I do not know," Aurora admits. "But she has been fine with half. I believe she is strong enough to hold the rest." The optimism is heartwarming, though I can't help but think it's also misplaced. Her eyes open fully, gaze returning to me for what I can't help but feel is the last time. "Please, Faelyn…if it were to be anyone, I'd want it to be you. End this for me."

I blink many times, my vision blurring as the tears I can no longer hold back finally slip free. I grab her fingers with fervor, forgetting about the thread and her wound. I hold on to her like with this one touch alone I could keep her here, as she is. I could keep my friend.

Aurora smiles, her eyes fluttering closed once more. She is utterly at peace. Even the moonbeams that strike her seem to glow brighter.

The woman I have known, in this way, will be gone. But she will live on forever in another form. In me. In the moon that I will greet every night.

"It will be all right," I whisper for her and for me. "No more pain, you have suffered long enough."

Still holding her fingers with one hand, I turn and reach for the knife wedged in Conri's neck, freeing it with a grunt. I wipe the blade on my thigh. The linen shift is already stained in crimson. I wish I had a blade that was not used to kill Conri, a blade that could be for Aurora and Aurora alone. But this is all I have, and there can be no delays.

Setting the knife at my side, I select one of every thread. Loop them around the hilt and then cover them with my fingers. Every bit of essence from me, from my ancestors that wielded this hunting knife through the years as we used it as a tool for our magic—every bit of essence from the spirits we knew and those that are long forgotten. I wrap it all together.

A memory, long forgotten, returns to me. Of a rare time in the woods with my mother as a girl.

Faelyn, someday, there might come a time where you must use your strength to take the life of another. The words were so gentle for their darkness. For the metallic taste they put in my mouth even though I was not the one speaking them. *I know. I know, Grandma says that our strength is used only to help this world. But, someday, there could be a need for you to kill. Perhaps it is to save yourself. Perhaps for much needed sustenance to survive a long winter. Whenever this time comes, strike strong and true, my daughter. Do not hesitate. For worse than taking a life is causing suffering while doing so.*

"You will not hurt any longer," I vow softly to Aurora. The knife is in my right hand. My left reaches behind her head, cradling it. Evander slowly removes his bloodied palm, exposing the wound.

"Thank you, my friend," she whispers faintly, no longer having the strength to open her eyes.

"It is my honor." I place a gentle kiss on her forehead, positioning the blade over her breastbone. She has never felt so small, so frail. So much blood is soaking the ground around us that it will take little to end this. "Thank you, for all you've done for me."

"It was…my honor."

I thrust.

If I hadn't committed and thrown my weight into it, I might not have punctured through cleanly. But I didn't hesitate, and I feel the moment the last of her life slips from her weary form. I choke back a sob, kissing her forehead once more.

Then, light.

Magic explodes from within her. The blood and gore condenses into the brightest of moonbeams. A shockwave rips through the grove, flinging lykin like rag dolls. Scattering them back and between trees. Even Evander is pushed away. But I am unaffected.

I stay at the center of it, gasping as my friend disappears. As all the might she possessed is freed. Then, like a bowstring pulled taut, it snaps back.

The glow rushes back, not to Aurora, but to me. I feel her power surging through me. Filling me to the point that I throw my head back and lift my chest to the sky, gasping for air. There is no room in me for it. I can hardly breathe and yet I have never felt more alive.

The stars fill my eyes. The dark sky becomes my shadow. I catch a glimpse of the whole world spanning beneath me, as though I have levitated to the moon's vantage. I see flashes of islands, wrapped by clouds. Of cities deep beneath the sea and earth. Of snowy castles long forgotten and bustling towns teeming with life. The world feels small enough to be held in my palm and just as I reach out to touch it—

It ends.

I am falling. Wind fills my ears. The power sinks deeper and deeper within its new home—into me. The blinding light and visions fade away.

Two strong, familiar arms envelop me. I am encapsulated in Evander's warmth, like a chrysalis that I have yet to emerge from. He strokes my face, looking at me with eyes wide and tender. No longer fearful, but amazed.

"How… Did I?"

"I have you," he murmurs. "You're safe and—thank the old gods—with me."

Then my visions weren't real. Or perhaps they were, in a way. I blink the last of the haze away. The pale glow that covered my body, as if I was the source of moonlight itself, is beginning to fade as well.

The lykin on the upper edge of the grove stand. I'm vaguely aware of their movements as they begin to descend into the soft moss of the lower area. Toward Evander and me. He holds me tighter, pressing my cheek to his chest. It is still bloody, and mud covered, but it is him.

Evander lets out a low growl at those who are approaching. He still has the shackle on. He can't transform and I am in no position to fight, either. Despite the power surging through me, I've no idea how to use it. It is already overwhelming my mind, setting my head to spinning. My body feels as though it is laden with lead.

The alphas stop a few feet away, others in their packs behind them. Then, slowly, they drop to a knee, bringing their fists to the ground and hunching over, dropping their heads in what looks like reverence.

"Keeper of and bound to the moon spirit, we recognize you as our king."

forty-nine

THERE IS A CEREMONY TWO DAYS LATER ON THE NIGHT OF THE FULL MOON. The night that had originally been intended as my wedding night.

The pomp and circumstance are not for Conri's death. The former wolf king had been taken by some of his most loyal sycophants, who held on to him until the bitter, bitter end. We presume they buried him somewhere in Den and then fled. An unmarked grave for an unworthy king, shamed by dying at the hand of the one being who was supposed to—above all else—be loyal to him.

It was a better end than he deserved. If it had been solely up to me, he would've been left to rot as carrion scavengers picked the meat from his bones. His skeleton left as a reminder—a memorial to this grim era of the lykin's history so it would never be forgotten. But it hadn't been up to me. That had been Evander's decision, and it happened when I wasn't around. There was little point in fighting, after, so the matter was left at that.

The gathering today wasn't for Evander either. There are no great coronations among the lykin. The wolf kings are anointed in the blood of their predecessor. Their right to rule was ordained by the moon spirit's presence at their side—which I had now taken the role of. That is all the celebrations that are conducted. Nothing more is needed, as their validity is not questioned.

Though, a few things have changed with the ascension

of the new king… For one, I remained with him of my own volition, rather than being passed and traded along like a royal token. I'm still at Evander's side because of the vows that bound our hearts well before he wore the fang crown of the wolf king, and I carried the powers of the moon spirit within me.

So tonight's ceremony is not to mourn Conri, or coronate Evander… but to celebrate me.

We sit, sides touching and hands folded, his thumb tracing lazy circles over my knuckle. A pyre has been constructed on the flat stone in the center of the grove. The lykin dance with the flames, stoking them with their voices. Their songs weave stories of the moon's might. Of early lykin and great wolf spirits that could traverse the world in a few giant leaps.

It's a ceremony designed to honor the power of the moon spirit. They keep looking to where I sit, off to the side, with Evander. Bowing their heads in reverence from time to time. Seeking my approval, which I make an effort to give. But I struggle to keep my focus on them. Instead, I am drawn to the bright, full moon above. Wishing that the smoke curling up from the flames was a rope that I could use to tether the heavenly body and pull it to me. Or a ladder that I could climb to ascend once more to that distant, magical place of awareness. Somewhere maybe…just maybe…far enough from this world that I could find Aurora.

"I'm sorry the moment is not more somber," Evander murmurs in my ear.

"I'm not." I bring my attention back to the earth. "I have had enough quiet mourning for a lifetime. Aurora's soul was bright until the very end. I don't think she would want us to weep for her death, but celebrate her life—life that continues to live on, in its way, within me."

I mean the words, so they come out strong. But they're laced with a sweet sorrow that I know all too well. The shroud that has haunted me my whole life has returned. Death sits at my other side as I watch the dancing and listen to the music of the lykin.

Even though I wear a small smile on my lips, there is a part of me that's filled with doubt. That wonders if I should resent all these people who, mere days ago, allowed her to die. Who had for years allowed her to be subjugated as she was. Who would gladly force me into the same fate if not for Evander's kindness.

But perhaps I'm too quick to judge them. I know the power of Conri's charm. Of his mannerisms and how well he concealed the truth of Aurora's internal reality. Maybe Evander can really build something new here. The real question is what my place will be in all of it. Because I cannot imagine being anywhere but his side… But staying here, among them—among the mortals who allowed her to be hurt, especially when my body aches with the primordial power flowing through my veins—might be more than I can bear.

Evander holds court, just as I imagined he would. He allows the alpha to come to him in their own time, as they are ready—if they are ready. This confuses the lykin, as they have only known kings who demand loyalty or death. Perhaps it is this kindness that makes them bold…and resentful.

I sit quietly at his side as the alphas argue with him, debating how best the plains will be governed. How the packs will be overseen. Evander's fingers tighten around mine in the moment, allowing him to keep in all the words that he will unleash later.

Ruling frustrates him to no end. He sees the need for it and wants what's best for his people. He wants to do right by them. But, also, Evander doesn't relish being the one to do it. I think that is part of why the other alphas present such contestations, but I'd never say so outright… He needs my support right now, and, moreover, I think he knows.

Every night, I listen to his frustrations, allowing him to air them so his chest is lighter the next day. I try and kiss away the pain. And, shamelessly, indulge in my own pleasure as well.

As the weeks slip by, I notice a change in how the alphas look at me. Their eyes flick toward my stomach more often upon seeing me. I can feel their wonderings at best and unsaid expectations at the worst.

But it isn't brought up until an alpha asks outright about Evander's plan for succession. They all know what he sacrificed as one of Conri's knights.

"I'm sorry he asked that," Evander murmurs later as we sit in the pit before the fire. I knew what was weighing on his mind before he said anything. But it's still a relief to hear him tackle the topic.

"It's a natural thing for them to wonder, I wasn't upset."

The silence becomes awkward. He shifts uncomfortably.

"I don't… I don't know." Evander's face twists with pain. "There's no precedent for this." He shakes his head. "It's possible that my fertility returned. But—"

I stop him with a gentle touch on his knee. "It's all right."

Evander's eyes meet mine. "I know how important it was to you… All those nights we talked on the rooftop. You want a family."

"I did. I think I still do." I lock eyes with him, trying to pierce him so he doesn't look away and retreat from me. "But it's not only my decision any longer. And if we decide that is our future, then there are other ways to have a child."

"But…" His objection fades and Evander finally looks away, back to the flames. I reach out, guiding his face back to mine.

"No buts," I say gently but firmly. "A child need not be of blood to be your own. I do not need to carry one within me to feel a mother, if that's what I'm meant to be." I give him a reassuring smile. "Right now, I'm merely trying to survive this new role for us both."

"Survive," he echoes softly. It's part a question, part sorrow on my behalf.

I try not to shy away from the honest answers. "I'm still finding my place in this world, as you are."

"Right…"

The conversation trails off and neither of us reignites it. We stare into the flames listlessly. At some point, I shift into Evander's arms and he holds me tightly to him. The only way we will survive this is to cling to each other for dear life.

fifty

It only takes four months before the first attempt on his life is made.

We are alone, walking through the grove as we have done many afternoons, savoring comfortable silence and the hymn of the trees and birds around us. Sometimes, those dark halls of Den become too much for me, oppressive. I can still feel her ghost restlessly pacing in there. Hear the sound of Evander's chains echoing through the empty halls. Smell Conri in the bed no matter how hard it is scrubbed and the furs and blankets changed.

Sometimes, the council meetings are too much for me to bear. Their questioning stares. Unspoken expectations.

These little escapes are all that keeps me together. When I'm lucky, Evander joins me. We take in the company of trees, rather than other lykin.

The assassins come like shadows, darting through the silver trees of Den, striking for Evander—not for me. I am the one they need alive, and he is the one they need dead.

Evander reacts with breathtaking speed. They are a tumble of teeth and claws, growls and snarls. There are three of them—hulking and frothing for blood—and only one of Evander.

I am frozen with shock. My hand goes to my thigh, sliding up the long shirt I wear that hides the hunting knife that's strapped there. It is a different knife than the one I used on

Aurora's heart. That one is tucked away, safe and preserved. Using it now feels like it would dishonor her.

But that day taught me the need to fight—to have my own teeth among the company I now keep.

The lykin aren't expecting me to join the fray. I leap onto the back of one before it can lunge into Evander. My dagger sinks into his flesh between his shoulder blades. It slips through and the wolf lets out a horrible yelp in tandem with a crack.

I'm thrown a fair distance as the lykin whirls, trying to see the source of its attacker. His eyes meet mine. Wide with what looks like betrayal.

My own wide eyes meet it, holding its gaze for a long second as a question rips through my mind: *What have I done?*

The distraction is enough that Evander has been able to fell the other two. The third is so consumed by the betrayal of the woman he saw as the new moon spirit and all that came with the title—silent protector, uninvolved in mortal squabbles—literally stabbing him in the back that he doesn't see Evander lunge for his throat.

Evander's muzzle is stained with red, the corpses of his enemies around him. He slowly stalks toward me, the rise and fall of those massive, fur-covered shoulders reminding me of the ripples of a wave. But when he is nearly close enough to drip blood on my boots off his nose, he changes back. He still crawls, on hand and knee, to me. Blessedly bloodless.

"Faelyn..."

The sound of my name brings me back to my body. I realize every muscle is trembling.

"What... Why?" He knew the very question I had asked myself, because he is the one to truly know my heart.

"I—I knew it would come." The words quiver like my hands, dagger clattering to the ground. "I saw you be attacked once when there was nothing I could do and I voted it would never happen again."

"But a knife?" He kneels as I draw my legs to me. I don't know if it's intentional that he positions himself to block the carnage behind us.

"I knew I wouldn't be able to bring myself to summon a spirit for it. I won't seek their help for such grim tasks." Even though I already had once, and we both know it. This feels different. This would be choosing to use them as a weapon, not merely defending myself.

But Evander doesn't bring that up. Instead, he takes me into his arms, enveloping me in warmth. I am half pulled into his lap as though I am a child to be comforted. Yet I can't stop myself from leaning into him.

"Neither should you take on such grim tasks," he whispers.

"I won't be useless to you."

"Faelyn." Evander leans back, shocked I would even say such a thing. "I do not see you as a tool to use any more than you see spirits in that way. You are not measured in your 'usefulness.' Your value is inherent because you are my mate—the other half of my very soul. A half that I fear might be crushed under the weight of this place and its scarred history."

His thumb gently caresses my cheek as he looks deep into my eyes. This close, and I realize that it has been weeks now since we were last physically intimate. I reach up to touch his face as well and realize that…perhaps he's right.

"I see you and your restless pacing. That when you have tried to summon spirits to help the lykin, you are met with confusion and apprehension about your gifts." Evander shakes his head. "I won't allow these lands to destroy the heart that mine beats for. Your strength is your kindness, Faelyn. The good you see in this world. Do not trade that for the brutality that's watered this earth for far, far too long."

"What then?" I whisper.

"We leave." Two words, said so simply. Evander shifts his grip, helping me up, leading me away from the bodies of the dead. The way he says it makes me think that it's been something he's been considering for some time. "We leave these lands where power is earned with death."

"But you are their king."

"Faelyn, that is not the title that is important to me." His thumb brushes over mine as our fingers intertwine. "The title that I wish to honor and uphold is that of your mate. I would give up a thousand thrones for you."

"I couldn't ask you to."

"Good thing you're not asking and I am offering." He smiles slightly. The sun seems to shine brighter on his face than it has in weeks. The shadows under his eyes lift some, as if this realization is somehow easing the burden on him also.

"But these are your people."

Evander slows to a stop. He looks back in the direction of Den. No, past it. If his gaze were to take wing and fly straight, it would soar over the misty plains of the lykin, across a narrow sea, through a dark Fade, and straight to a home that is no longer there for either of us.

"No," he says softly, the wind tangling with his hair. "I thought the humans were my people, and spent my childhood among them. But I never really belonged. Never fit right." I know that feeling all too well. "My blood comes from these lands, but my true kin are long dead. The lykin that roam these plains are the ones who helped kill them. I can howl their hymns, but they are not my people, either." He turns back to me and the world narrows with his attention. The trees blur as my focus rests solely on him. The wind pauses, as if even it is holding its breath for his next words. "*You* are the only one I have ever felt like I belonged with."

The words resonate as truth, not just for him, but for me as well—for all the years I spent not quite human, not quite magic. Something between. I still exist in that space of both. Of not knowing quite where I should be. Perhaps I only ever thought it could be here because this was where he was.

My home is not a place, it is a person. When I look into his eyes, I am home. We are not kept by lands, or bloodlines, or any vow but the one we made to each other.

"When?" It's the only thing I can think to ask.

"Tomorrow."

"So soon?"

"Unless you have a reason to stay?" He smirks slightly, already knowing the answer. We both walk a little faster and readily leave the burdens we had assumed by default behind.

When I had fantasized about the mark we could leave on the lykin, I had thought of Evander ruling. Of me helping with the aid of the spirits to forest the plains once more and usher in a new age for a new people. I had thought of a king and a queen, united and equal.

But change is not made with commands. With new leadership that simply filled the same shoes as the old, walking the same paths. That was the cycle that had chained the lykin for centuries. It had disrupted the natural order of their packs and transformed them into something they were not. A never-ending struggle in which there could only be *one* victor, rather than the many that had roamed the plains as free as the wind that now pulls back my hair.

Evander is under me, running as fast as he can. Faster than we have ever run before. There is nothing holding us back now. No thread that binds us to the past. We leave it all behind, racing toward the breathtaking promise of the horizon, as a new dawn rises over the land of the lykin.

Those same rays will strike a shattered crown, fangs scattered among the silvery leaves of Den.

epilogue

Evander's kisses are frantic and breathy.

His mouth is as hot as our bodies—as our need. My lips part for him, as do my legs. He slides against my inner thighs, moving into a position we know all too well. We move like desperation, then relaxing into each other.

His eyes are no longer haunted. No…they are full of promise. Of intent. Of all the possibilities that we rise to meet each morning with.

I hold that gaze with my own as he pushes forward. Stretching. Filling all the way until there is no more for either of us to give. I feel him, not just in body, but mind and soul. It is everything, and yet somehow not enough. His lips move off mine, down my throat, biting my shoulder as he leans back and pulls me into his lap.

We move slower, like this. But every stroke is more accented. My flesh is aflame as his mouth encircles my breast. As he gives me teeth and claws at the same time as warmth and tenderness.

It should be forbidden to feel this good. The rogue thought is one I've had many, many times over the past few weeks as we have made our journey across Midscape. Every day of travel punctuated by nights, and sometimes mornings of passion.

I had never known it was possible to want so much, so freely and easily. To have completely, without fear of loss or rejection. The sweet serenity of a love that is as unflinching as steel, as eternal as the forces of nature.

This is where I belong. Right here. Right now, in these throes of breathless bliss. There is nowhere else for me. No past or future.

He reaches his climax before me, but ensures I am not long after. My mate has always made it a point to see that I never leave our bedroll unsatisfied.

I trail my hand through the hair that lines his chest, watching its rise and fall slow as Evander catches his breath. His arm drapes around me, pulling me closer, my head half on his shoulder as he presses his lips to my forehead.

"Are you ready?" he finally asks.

"I didn't come all this way to turn back at the last minute." I sit and begin to dress. The canvas of the tent is burnt orange with the sunset. Moonrise is soon.

Evander does the same, following me out of the tent and onto a sandy beach of pure white. Behind us is a maze of sandbars and islands. A barren and blinding land that was only easy to navigate because I had spirits to call upon for help. Though I tried to do it as little as possible. I still don't like troubling my primordial friends, whenever I can avoid it.

Ahead of us, on a distant shore, is a tree so massive that I have to crane my neck—even from here—to see the tops of its branches poking between the clouds. Evander told me of the myths of this place on our journey. The fantastical stories that shroud the very edge of siren territory in mysteries befitting of the edge of the world itself. Because, if the tales were to be believed, the Veil that separated our world from the Beyond is just over the edge of the sea. That proximity is what allows this distant, primal corner of the world to be the only place where one can hold court with the old gods.

The legends Evander told me spoke of pilgrimages to that distant tree across a sandbar, a temporary bridge to connect land with sea. But there is nothing but darkening blue barring our progress. Whitecaps dot the waves like quiet threats. *This is the land of the siren and the old gods*, they seem to say; *all others are unwelcome*.

"Are you sure the sirens won't resent us for this?" I ask as I walk to the water's edge, leaving our campsite behind and starting for where the land tapers to a natural point in the direction of the Lifetree. If there was to be a land bridge, I would bet it would be here.

"It's unclear if the tides sweeping away the land bridge were intentional or not," Evander says optimistically. I appreciate his confidence. "If they are upset, they can put it back when we're gone. But, as you said, we've come too far to turn back now."

I stare out at the distant tree as the stars bloom across the watercolor sky. The idea to travel here came to me on the first night after we left Den. I bring a hand to my chest, pressing it against my heart, where the weight of Aurora's magic still lives. I made her a promise that I would take her to the land of the siren. And while it might be too little, too late, I cannot think of any other way that I would rather have one final honoring of her memory.

Sucking in a breath, I reach into my magic, speaking with the ancient tongue of the spirits. "Gruvun of the tides, Volst of water, Brundil of earth, I call to you."

Gruvun is the churn of a vortex just offshore, two stationary white eyes in its center. Volst is a wave that lingers, rising to take a vaguely human shape. Brundil is a golem of sand that is perpetually rising and falling at my side.

"There was once a sandbar here that connected Midscape to the Lifetree. I ask for your help bringing it back to the surface."

None of them say anything, but I can feel their acquiescence. Even their approval. They disappear back into their elements, retreating. But their presence remains in the wild pulsing of magic.

The ocean churns. Whitecaps froth. Deep within the earth, there is groaning. The sand shifts, falling away as though it's melting into the waves. But Brundil is persistent. Gruvun pulls back the tides with Volst's help.

A ribbon of freshly made land stretches between us and the tree.

"Thank you," I say as I take my first steps upon it. I can still feel Gruvun and Volst expending great effort to keep the water from consuming the new sandbar. Just as I can feel Brundil continuing to shift the earth beneath, the forces of nature aligned but at inherent odds. As we walk, they begin to reach a stasis that will keep this land bridge long enough for us to return.

A reverent hush falls over Evander and me as we near the tree. Our suspicion from afar is proven right—it really does have the same silvery leaves as the trees of Den. Its roots are like a lady's hair, spilling over the beach and plunging deep, deep into the water, past the point where the fading light can reach. I see shadows moving as we near. Evander takes note of them as well. His muscles bulge, radiating tension. But the creatures beneath the waves don't surface. Not yet, at least.

A wall of the thick roots blocks our path when we reach the opposite side. I know better than to ask Brundil for help—not just because I already have. But also because I can feel the pure magic that flows through them in place of sap. It is an ancient and immense power.

Evander and I find an opening in the massive roots barely big enough for us to squeeze past. We contort and twist, navigating through. Right at the edge of irrational panic of being trapped within them forever, they end, exposing a sheltered beach.

Spears have been skewered into the sand, giving it a prickly appearance, almost like that of a porcupine. I weave through them, careful not to touch any, as they seem to be made of the same wood as the tree and I can only assume they signify some deep reverence I do not understand.

We make our way to the opposite end, where a man sits by a large blossom. He leans against one of the roots, snoring softly. I pause, staring. He has brown hair and a beard. Clothing I don't recognize but is distinctly…human. Everything about him screams, *human*. From his fashions, which are unseen in Midscape, to the curve of his ears. Yet, markings cover his skin, almost like the swirls of thread and delicately embroidered lines of my cape.

"Is he a siren?" Evander whispers hesitantly in my ear.

I shake my head. But I don't know what he is. My eyes tell me human. But my senses tell me…spirit? I don't know what to make of him. Perhaps he is some kind of witch like myself?

"Sir?" I ask softly. Not wanting to startle him. He continues to snore. "Sir?" A little louder.

"Kevhan is a heavy sleeper," a female voice says from behind us.

Evander and I both turn. Him a little faster. A little tenser, ready to strike. But I grab his wrist instantly the moment my eyes behold the figure sitting upon one of the petals of the massive flower. Neither of us even registered its bloom.

A faint sheen of gold coats her skin, swirling among an entire rainbow of color painted across her. Her eyes are the color of a sea on a stormy day, as if they hold all the water that surrounds this island.

Gossamer wings, six in total, are more iridescent outlines that catch the last dredges of sunlight extending from her back than anything solid. Honey-gold hair falls over her shoulders, tangling with the bark that she wears like clothing. It moves as though it is part of her skin. As if she is part of the tree itself.

No…she *is* the tree. The rawness of her, ancient and primordial. It strikes me a second later than I would've wanted that I am before the Old Goddess of Life.

"Lady Lellia?" I whisper in awe. Evander's eyes go wide and his whole body relaxes. I think he's about to fall over from shock.

"Not quite, but close. Common mistake, though. Lady Victoria, please." The corner of her mouth quirks into a wry smile. Then she clears her throat and loudly says, "Kevhan, we have guests."

The man finally jolts awake. Sputtering and mumbling. Eyes wide with surprise.

Lady Victoria lets out bright laughter. "Some Keeper of the Lifetree you are. The first time we have outside guests, you're caught sleeping."

I didn't expect an old god to have a sense of humor. A lightness to the air around her. Rather than unsettling me, I find the oddity of it vaguely…comforting. Even though she is clearly not human, there is a humanness to her. A sense of mortality that I don't even get from the spirits and certainly did not expect to find with an old god.

"Apologies!" Kevhan stands quickly, brushing sand from his trousers. "Welcome, to…the Lifetree?" He glances in her direction, rubbing the back of his neck. "We never really went over what I was supposed to say or do."

The goddess has an outright grin now. "I wanted to see what you'd come up with. You're usually so composed."

"This is all a bit new to me, too."

"You've had nearly three years to settle into your role."

"My 'role' usually involves lazing in the sun and enjoying the waves."

"Untrue," she counters, "I have seen you playing stones with Lucia."

"Only when you are not monopolizing her time."

Lady Victoria tosses her hair over her shoulder, shifting forward. "She can't be blamed for wanting a real challenge at stones."

Kevhan snorts and doesn't offer a rebuke.

"But I doubt you have come all this way, shifted land and sea, to play stones." Her eyes return to me, gaze settling expectantly. As if she's waiting for me to ask a question.

I am too stunned for a moment to say anything. I had imagined the interaction to be more like the ones I have had with the spirits. A sense of power—well, that's there, but also otherworldliness. I did not expect the Old Goddess of Life to banter.

"I… I made a promise." Once I start thinking about what to say, it sounds so small. "I promised someone I cared about that I would bring her here, to you. And I—" The words choke me for a second, but I force them out anyway. "—I couldn't. I failed. But I wanted to do this…as if…somehow it'd be enough."

The weight of that truth, of admitting it to this goddess as she watches me struggle through this mix of potent emotions with a patient, motherly smile, has my eyes prickling with tears.

Lady Victoria pushes away from the petal on which she sits. She seems to hover above the ground a moment before touching it. Her feet hardly move the sand.

"But you didn't fail," she says softly. "Your friend is here, isn't she?" The goddess rests her fingertips on the center of my chest.

"Only her power," I murmur, and shake my head. The spirits were the first offspring of the old gods. Primordial children, in their way. I expected this moment to be difficult, but I failed to consider the judgment I might face. Whatever it will be, though, I accept it. "I tried to keep her safe, I swear."

"We both did." Evander squeezes my fingers. "This wasn't just Faelyn's failure, but both of ours."

She hums, tilting her head. "I don't see any failure here… If anything, I think you did splendidly." Lady Victoria focuses intently on my chest. As though she is speaking directly to my heart. "It's time to come out now."

Without warning or explanation, the goddess pulls back her hand. I feel a familiar thread of magic pull from me. I see it. Moonbeams are drawn from my breastbone, curling around the goddess's fingers. She casts them off to the side, drawing a gasp as the magic spills out of me like a tipped-over bottle.

Everything goes bright, my vision blinded by light. Once more, I'm back far above the world. But this time, I'm falling. Aurora's power leaves me, and with it, so too does a greater understanding of time and space.

Glimpses of events rush past me, current, past, and future. There's a large hall, occupied by kings and queens. A celebration in a fae castle with a young child and her parents of two worlds. A festival in snowcapped mountains, overseen by a woman in a blacksmith's apron. A quiet cottage, on what side of the Fade, I cannot tell…but it feels like home. A pot simmers on the stove over Folost. Mary is in the windowsill. And in the window beyond…

I blink and it's gone.

But I saw Evander and three children playing in the tall grasses beyond. No child alike. None who have our jaws or our hair—none who came from my womb. But all undeniably ours.

As the light fades and reality crashes back into me, the last glowing strands of Aurora's magic leave my flesh. They form a familiar outline, and then light and power fill the shape. Lady Victoria twists her fingers through the air like Grandmother would twist wool into threads off her wheel. Organizing the raw essence of the world into a power that can be used and wielded.

I stagger, nearly falling. I would have, if not for Evander catching me. Kevhan murmurs a soft, "Wow," as if he has never beheld something like this either.

My eyes meet a familiar pair. Aurora is breathtaking. Her form shifts like moonlight through trees. Not quite solid. More akin to the mists of the lands Evander and I left behind.

She drifts to me, taking my cheeks in both of her hands. Her mouth opens and closes, as if to form words, but all that escapes is a melodic sound. Like faint chimes in the distance. A song, in a way, but like none I've ever heard before.

"I can't understand you." I laugh as tears spill over my cheeks. All her magic is gone from me, at long last. Returned to her as it should be. And now I can no longer speak the ancient tongue of the spirits. Aurora leans forward with a smile, placing a gentle kiss on my forehead like I kissed her in the grove when I thought it was goodbye. The sensation of her lips on my skin is little more than a cool whisper of a nighttime breeze. "But I think I know what you mean… All will be well now, won't it?"

Aurora locks eyes with me and blinks once. *Yes*.

She turns to Evander next, emitting the same incoherent melody, then kissing his forehead. She gives me one more look, wearing a smile I have never seen her have before. Brighter than any I could imagine her to make. As pure as the moon itself.

In a blink, she's gone. Returned home. Evander wraps an arm around my shoulder and kisses my temple, as we stare at the moon that seems to shine brighter than it ever has before.

"What now?" he whispers.

"I think…we should find a cottage of our own." My cheeks ache from the spread of my smile, and the future that is before us all.

Thank You for Reading

Readers like you mean the world to authors like me. From the bottom of my heart, **thank you for taking a chance on my work and being a part of my worlds**.

If you have a moment, **please remember to leave a review for this book on your retailer(s) of choice**, and/or Goodreads—along with any others you might have read but haven't reviewed yet. Reviews really are the lifeblood of authors.

Want to know what's next?

Turn the page to make sure you haven't missed a Married to Magic Novel and find out more about what's next...

Next from Elise Kova

ARCANA ACADEMY

Coming 2025

A woman who has devoted herself to learning forbidden tarot magic to thwart the crown. A prince who claims her as his bride to use her skills to seize a legendary power. Enter the mysterious halls of ARCANA ACADEMY, where strength is survival and your future is your tuition.

An adult, epic fantasy by bestselling author Elise Kova. Ideal for readers looking for dark academia, intricate magics, slow burn romance, enemies to lovers, found family, and twists you never saw coming.

Get ARCANA ACADEMY updates delivered right to your inbox:
http://elisekova.com/arcananews

Join the ARCANA ACADEMY reader group on Facebook to chat with Elise and other readers:
www.facebook.com/groups/arcana/

Subscribe to Elise Kova's general newsletter or text line to get updates on all her upcoming releases:
https://www.elisekova.com/subscribe/

Books in the Married to Magic World...

a DUET
with the
SIREN DUKE
a MARRIED TO MAGIC novel

Learn more at

https://www.elisekova.com/a-duet-with-the-siren-duke/

On the night of the Blood Moon, the Vampire Lord must die. But when it's up to a forge maiden to deal the killing blow, her strike misses the mark. Now, bloodsworn to the Vampire Lord, she must survive by helping end an ancient curse. Loyalties are tested and the line between truth and lie is blurred. When her dagger is at his chest, will she be able to take the heart of the man who has claimed hers?

a DUEL
with the
VAMPIRE LORD
a MARRIED TO MAGIC novel

Learn more at

https://elisekova.com/a-duel-with-the-vampire-lord/

ON THE NIGHT OF THE BLOOD MOON, THE VAMPIRE LORD MUST DIE. But when it's up to a forge maiden to deal the killing blow, her strike misses the mark. Now, bloodsworn to the Vampire Lord, she must survive by helping end an ancient curse. Loyalties are tested and the line between truth and lie is blurred. When her dagger is at his chest, will she be able to take the heart of the man who has claimed hers?

a DANCE with the FAE PRINCE
a MARRIED TO MAGIC novel

Learn more at

https://elisekova.com/a-dance-with-the-fae-prince/

Katria swore she'd never fall in love. When her hand in marriage is sold, her new, mysterious husband makes that resolution very difficult. But what's even harder is surviving after she learns he's the heir to the fae throne in hiding. After accidently stealing his magic, she's taken to Midscape where she learns the truth of the fae and her heart.

a DEAL with the ELF KING
a MARRIED TO MAGIC novel

Learn more at

https://elisekova.com/a-deal-with-the-elf-king/

Nineteen-year-old Luella had prepared all her life to be her town's healer. Becoming the Elf King's bride wasn't anywhere in her plans. Taken to a land filled with wild magic, Luella learns how to control powers she never expected to save a dying world. The magical land of Midscape pulls on one corner of her heart, her home and people tug on another... but what will truly break her is a passion she never wanted.

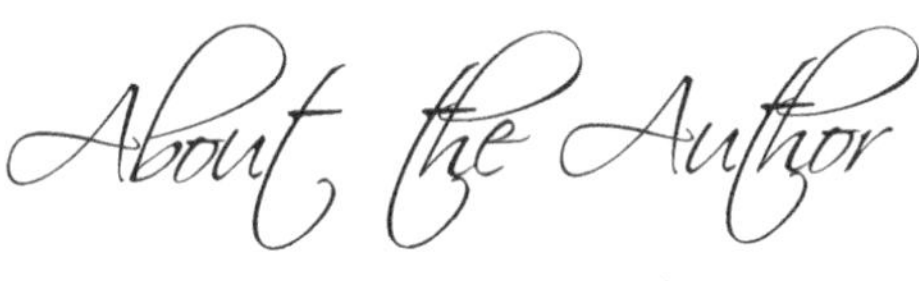

ELISE KOVA is a USA Today and internationally bestselling author. She enjoys telling stories of fantasy worlds filled with magic and deep emotions. She lives in Florida and, when not writing, can be found playing video games, drawing, chatting with readers on social media, or daydreaming about her next story.

She invites readers to get first looks, giveaways, and more by subscribing to her newsletter at:
http://elisekova.com/subscribe

Visit her on the web at:
http://elisekova.com/
https://www.tiktok.com/@elisekova
https://www.facebook.com/AuthorEliseKova/
https://www.instagram.com/elise.kova/

See all of Elise's titles on her Amazon page:
http://author.to/EliseKova

More books by Elise...

THE AIR AWAKENS SERIES

A young adult, high-fantasy filled with romance and elemental magic

A library apprentice, a sorcerer prince, and an unbreakable magic bond. . .

The Solaris Empire is one conquest away from uniting the continent, and the rare elemental magic sleeping in seventeen-year-old library apprentice Vhalla Yarl could shift the tides of war.

Vhalla has always been taught to fear the Tower of Sorcerers, a mysterious magic society, and has been happy in her quiet world of books. But after she unknowingly saves the life of one of the most powerful sorcerers of them all—the Crown Prince Aldrik--she finds herself enticed into his world. Now she must decide her future: Embrace her sorcery and leave the life she's known, or eradicate her magic and remain as she's always been. And with powerful forces lurking in the shadows, Vhalla's indecision could cost her more than she ever imagined.

Learn more at:

http://elisekova.com/air-awakens-book-one/

What started as a trial for the best sorcerers in the Solaris Empire, ends in a bloody upheavel where five kingdoms and one pirate queen all compete for power...

Ice is in her blood.

Eighteen-year-old Waterrunner Eira Landan lives her life in the shadows — the shadow of her older brother, of her magic's whispers, and of the person she accidentally killed. She's the most unwanted apprentice in the Tower of Sorcerers until the day she decides to step out and compete for a spot in the Tournament of Five Kingdoms.

Pitted against the best sorcerers in the Empire, Eira fights to be one of four champions. Excelling in the trials has its rewards. She's invited to the royal court with the "Prince of the Tower," discovers her rare talent for forbidden magic, and at midnight, Eira secretly meets with a handsome elfin ambassador.

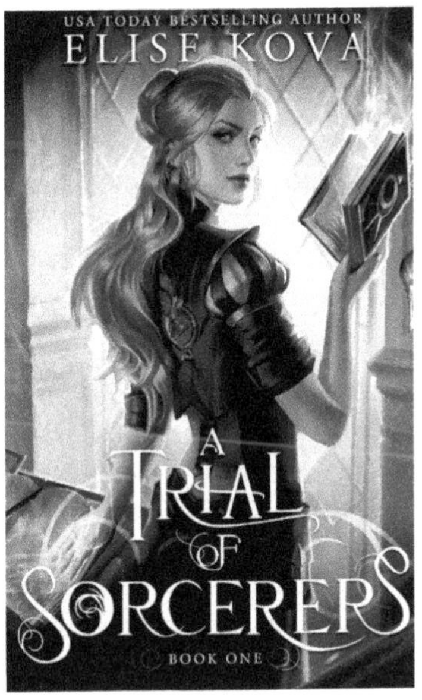

But, Eira soon learns, no reward is without risk. As she comes into the spotlight, so too do the skeletons of a past she hadn't even realized was haunting her.

Eira went into the trials ready for a fight. Ready to win. She wasn't ready for what it would cost her. No one expected the candidates might not make it out with their lives.

https://www.elisekova.com/a-trial-of-sorcerers/

In a world on the brink of destruction, Crown Princess Vi Solaris must choose between her magic and her throne.

With her empire faltering from political infighting and a deadly plague, Vi's rare and deadly power may be the key to saving her people.

To master her powers, she trains in secret with a mysterious sorcerer from a distant land. Despite her initial fear, Vi finds herself increasingly drawn to him, and their forbidden love threatens to unravel everything she knows. With her heart torn between duty and desire, Vi embarks on an epic journey of adventure, romance, family, and destiny.

But the ultimate triumph will require the ultimate sacrifice, and Vi must make the hardest choice of her life: to play by the rules and claim her throne, or break them for magic and a love that could change the fate of her world forever.

For fans of young adult, epic fantasy world filled with elemental magic, friendships as deep as blood, shocking twists, thrilling adventures, and slow-burn romance.

Learn more at:

http://elisekova.com/vortex-visions-air-awakens-vortex-chronicles-1/

All the Married to Magic Readers Around the World – These books exist because of you. Your passion and enthusiasm fed my own and kept me going whenever the process was rocky. If not for your love, this book wouldn't have existed. I've cherished all of your posts, stories, videos, and held dear every message and opportunity I've had to get to know you either in person, or online. While there are so many more that I might never meet, I still hold you in my heart. I hope you'll join me in my other worlds and adventures to come.

Erion Makuo – Thank you for bringing this final cover to life. Your compositions are so stunning and the details you embed into your work are breathtaking. You've been a joy to work with!

Robert – My muse…thank you for holding me together physically, mentally, and emotionally as this book came to be. And, above all else, for giving me all the love I'd ever dreamed of.

Rebecca – I loved talking this one through with you. I'm so grateful to have you both as a partner and peer in the creative process. Thank you for always being there to work through everything until the book is right.

Melissa – I know this book was a bit of a struggle, but we got through and I want you to know I will forever be grateful for the effort you put in to make it happen. Thank you so much for lending your expertise all the way through to the end!

Kate – Thank you for making sure that every last-minute thing was caught before this went to press!

Danielle – Dear friend, you are such a gem in my life. I am so grateful to have you through all the ups and downs of this publishing journey. Thanks for always being a resource, insight, and confidant.

Katie & Gideon – All the body-doubling, safe space, and cheering on helped make this book and so many others happen. I'm so grateful to have you both as such good friends. I hope you both know that you can't "escape" me.

NOFFA – Ladies, you are incredible. Thank you for all your help and feedback on covers, synopsis, marketing, and just general life support. With much going on personally and professionally I held our little corner of the publishing world to retreat to even closer. I appreciate all you've done for me.

Michelle – Long live happy hour!

The Tower Guard – You all remain a cornerstone of my career. Our little group is such a safe space for me where I can share things I don't share elsewhere, get feedback, and know you all are there for me when I need. Thank you for your help spreading the word about these books and making them happen with your love and support. Here's to many, many more!

Rhea and the Orion Team – Thank you for believing in and fighting for these books. I cannot wait to see what the future holds for us all!

Leo and the Urano Team – I still cannot believe how many readers around the world I've had the opportunity to meet because of you. No matter which Spanish-speaking country I go to, I know it'll feel like home thanks to all of you.

Marco and the Mondadori Team – Thank you so much for believing in my books and bringing them to the Italian market!

Hélène and the Bragelonne Team – Every stunning edition you've put out of the Married to Magic books has taken my breath away. I hope that we can continue to create more beautiful books together in the future! Thank you for believing in me and my work.

Jenny, Emma, and The Bent Agency Team – Thank you for helping see my books in territories around the world.

My Patrons – Lauren B., Winter M., Courtney, Maryalyce B., Nicole D., Dreamanne M., Allie Antolini, Karin, Amanda H., Jessica N., Christine P., Ayragon, Pippa S., Tiffany H., Zoegy, Brooke, Carolyn H., Nikki B., Courtney, Moa E., Kiera J., Aly N., Elizabeth H., Chloe F., Nelle M., Jade, Hannah M., Amanda C., Imzadi, Vixie, Caitlyn P., Rachael Leigh W., MasterR50, Rebecca R., Steffi aka. Lambert, Anne of Daze, Laura R., Missy A., Sarah T., Nancy S., Laura B., Mandi S., Melinda H., Kayla D., Taylour D., Stephanie H., Gemma, Rose G., Karolína N. B., Laura H., Dani W., Liz D., C Sharp, Kate R., Jennifer G., Marissa C., Claribel V., Sarah L., Nicole M., Lisa, Sorcha A., Tea Cup, Caitlin P., Bridget W., Sarah [faeryreads], Kristen M., Kelly M., Audrey C W., Amy M., Allison S., Ashton Morgan, Amanda T., Kayleigh K., Alisha L., Esther R., Kaylie, Heather F., Shelly D., Nichelle G., Giuliana T., Chelsea S., Alli H., Siera H., Matthea F., Catarina G., Elise G., Lindsay B., Sara E., Karin B., Ashley D., Stengelberry, Alexis P., Sheryl K B., Lindsay Shurtiff, NaiculS, Kira M., Charis, Kassie P., Angela G., Elly M., Asami, Amy B., Meagan R., Axel R., Ambermoon86, Bookish Connoisseur, Cassidy T., Kathleen M., Alexa A., Rhianne, Cassondra A., Emily R., Tamashi T., Nichole M., Dana A., Serenity87HUN, Alexa Z., Jamie B., Emmie S., Mani R-D., Christina, Dyani Sahr, Samantha C., Andra P., Justine B., Pauline Stv., Sarah M., Adrienne A., Stephanie T., Mary CSM., Eri W. – and all other Patrons who have joined and supported me along the way since this list was made, I am so grateful to you all.